I0635789

RIVER

OF

DEATH

RIVER

OF

DEATH

KIRBY JONAS

Cover design by Forrest Design Group

Howling Wolf Publishing
Pocatello, Idaho

Copyright © 2016 by Kirby F. Jonas. All rights reserved.

This is a work of fiction. The names, characters, places and incidents portrayed in this novel are fictional or were used fictitiously. Any apparent connection between characters used fictitiously and anything that they have done in real life is purely coincidental. No part of this book may be used without the express permission of the author. To request such permission, contact:

Howling Wolf Publishing
1611 City Creek Road
Pocatello ID 83204

For more information about Kirby's books, check out:

www.kirbyjonas.com
Facebook, at KirbyJonasauthor

Or email Kirby at: **kirby@kirbyjonas.com**

Manufactured in the United States of America—*One nation, under God*

Publication date for this edition: November 2017
Jonas, Kirby, 1965—
River of Death / by Kirby Jonas.

ISBN: 978-1-891423-29-1
Library of Congress Control Number: 2016918911

Dedicated to my amigo,
Bob Wilson,
who once was the real "Law of the Lemhi"

CHAPTER ONE

♦ *1972* ♦

Saturday, December 2

Big Coal Savage had buried his share of people, both loved ones and others not so loved. On an unseasonably warm winter's day, at nine in the morning, he stood in the hallway of his mother's house, preparing to bury one more: one-time hunting partner and fellow former Marine Hague Freeman—a man he had killed.

Tightening a black tie at his throat, he gazed at his hard, chiseled face in the mirror, still bruised from the big fight. He wondered if anyone else who looked at him these days could see in his eyes the sadness he felt inside.

KSRA was playing the old Tennessee Ernie Ford song, "River of No Return," and Coal couldn't help thinking of the last funeral he had attended before leaving Virginia. The burial of his Laura. She had loved that song, and the Robert Mitchum movie of the same name. He had had them play the song at her funeral.

Laura, the greatest love of Coal's life, was gone now too, swept on forever, as it were. It was hard to get her out of his mind.

He listened to the deep, melodic voice singing the song. Ford sounded nothing—nor looked anything—like Marilyn Monroe, but they both had made versions of the song that could never be forgotten.

Today's funeral, like Laura's, was one of mixed emotions. Hague Freeman had become a killer. First on the side of right. And then, in the end, for a darker side. But in their youth, he and Hague had had some good times. Coal could not forget those.

Neither could he forget that his own bullet had taken Hague's life.

Coal gazed in the mirror. What kind of a man had he become? Beyond the dark hair, the steel-blue eyes, the straight nose, hard jaw, and dark mustache, what was there of Coal Savage? A father. A son. A lawman. An ex-Marine and soldier. Did any of it tell the real story? Deep inside, Coal was a lost and broken man. And there were very few people who would ever guess. He was confident that he was hiding it well.

His mother, Connie, was dressing in her bedroom at the end of the hall. He could hear the faint sounds of her stirring, and it made him feel warm. His mother, his greatest friend—and still he could not talk to her of the man he had become.

On a whim, Coal walked to the bedroom door behind which his fifteen-year-old daughter was concealed. He hesitated there for but a moment, then knocked lightly. Katie Leigh's voice floated to him through the door. "Yes?" The sound made Coal's heart stop for a moment. Katie. His daughter. The only female in his life who could make or break him with a word, who only days before had not wanted to have one thing to do with him.

"Can I come in?"

Without an answer, the door flew open. Katie looked up at him, her long dark hair hanging lustrous and lovely over the shoulders of a peach-colored silk dress trimmed in cream lace. Her face had healed remarkably fast from their accident with the moose, leaving only the vestiges of bruises now. She was an incredibly beautiful young woman, as her mother had been. "Hi."

"Hi, honey." A feeling of joy burst over Coal. He wanted to throw his arms around his daughter. These last few days, he couldn't lay eyes on her without that urge overcoming him.

This time, Katie smiled at him, and it was she who stepped forward and enfolded him with her arms, resting her cheek against his chest. The big, tough Marine used every ounce of his strength keeping his eyes dry.

For half a minute, he just held her. It seemed like a dream. Katie loved him again. Ironically, he owed that to Hague Freeman, her kidnapper. If not for his crime, Coal did not know if Katie would ever have allowed him to hold her again.

"You don't have to do this," Coal said. "You know that, right?"

She spoke into his shirt. "I *do* have to, Daddy. I have to make sure he's really gone."

He smiled, though she couldn't see it. She was right. He could understand. Hague Freeman had held his little girl's life in the palm of his hand, and if Coal had not stopped him he would surely have taken it. Perhaps even more than the suicidal death of her mother, it was the worst nightmare of her young life, and something she would relive over and over, both awake and in her restless sleep. Seeing him go down into the ground would go a long way toward healing her.

"I'm proud of you, Katie," he said, striving to muster up the right words. He was not a man who talked that way—to anyone.

She hugged him tighter.

*   *   *

It was already forty degrees outside when they got into Connie's Chrysler Newport, and snow had even begun to melt along the feet of the mighty Beaverhead Mountains. While Coal drove, Katie sat beside him with a hand resting on his leg, and Connie sat against the passenger door and stared out at the sunshine. There was very little snow left to look at in the fields, and no ice shining along the banks of the Lemhi. Hard to believe Christmas was only twenty-three days away.

The memorial service for Hague Freeman was held at the Eagles Hall, where the Baptists had held church services since sixty-nine. Coal parked in the lot with a total of seven other vehicles, counting the hearse. In spite of all Hague had become, it made Coal sad to see his old hunting partner memorialized by such a small crowd. But he guessed Hague had pretty much burned his bridges. To the town, one funeral must have been enough—and the last one was the memorial service of a hero.

He saw the shock in the face of Don Freeman, Hague's father, when he looked over and spied Coal, Connie, and Katie sliding in through the door. Don nudged his wife, Nonie, and she also looked their way. Her eyes were puffy from crying.

It was the ultimate demonstration of the strength of a mother's love for her child for Nonie to be here today. After all, Hague had intended to blow her to pieces as well in the old trapper cabin where he had held her and Katie captive. Don was a strong man, too, for Hague had worked him over good and nearly broken one of his arms before Don was able to make his escape into the dark the night Hague kidnapped Katie. Coal was not sure he could have attended the funeral of a son who had hated him so fiercely.

Don came over and held out his hand to Coal. "I'm kind of surprised to see you, Coal," he said in his frail, high-pitched voice.

"Same here—surprised to be here, that is."

"Yeah. Nonie worked on me pretty hard. I guess we're burying our little boy from years ago—not the man he became. We didn't even know that man."

Suddenly, Coal understood why he too was here. "I'm sorry it had to happen like it did, Don."

"No! Coal Savage, don't you ever blame yourself," Nonie said as she came to stand beside her husband. "Young man, that Hague was not our boy. He was nobody any of us knew anymore. He had to be saved from himself." Her voice almost broke, and her chin started to quiver, but she pursed her lips for a moment and gathered her strength. "Just remember our boy like he used to be. That's all I want. You didn't do anything wrong." The old woman reached out and squeezed Coal's forearm. The strength of motherhood.

After the service, which was short and stiff, they stood at the cemetery and watched Hague Freeman's casket being lowered into the ground where before the monument of a hero had stood over nothing but a plot of grass, for the Freemans had told everyone Hague's body was buried in Arlington. Katie leaned close to her father and hugged him with one arm. She was shaking all over. He looked down to see her chin quivering, as Nonie's had, and her face streaked with tears. Connie reached out and rubbed her back.

Feeling someone watching him, Coal looked up. He scanned the few people at the service without catching one eye. Broadening his search, he noticed a beat-up red Buick Riviera, perhaps a sixty-three. It was parked fifty yards away downhill, toward the cemetery's entrance, and the driver and one passenger were staring his way through dark sunglasses. A strange feeling came over Coal as his eyes focused on the vehicle. He had never seen it before, at least not that he could recall. But he had a strange premonition that he would be seeing it again.

A study of the driver showed him a florid face and a mostly bald head with the vestiges of what appeared from this distance to be blond, almost whitish hair. There could be no doubt that the man and his female passenger were staring this way.

His eyes jerked away from the Riviera when he heard a sob come from Don Freeman. He looked across at the poor little old man, broken and alone but for his wife. The Freemans had never had any more children after Hague. How did a man say goodbye to an only son he had truly lost so long ago?

There was no twenty-one gun salute for this sullied one-time hero, as there had been at his first memorial service. There was no

American flag to be carried to his mother. A minister said some words of blessing over the grave, and then the few people who had come began to drift away. Other than Katie's, and now Don's, there were no tears on anyone's faces. This time they had buried Hague Freeman for real, but it was not a day of mourning, as it had been in sixty-nine.

Hague had been long overdue for the grave.

Katie was shaking again by the time they went to say goodbye to the Freemans, and Nonie came close and gave her a warm embrace. Now the old woman had started crying again too. Don could no longer meet Coal's gaze, or Connie's. He just shifted his weight back and forth from one foot to the other and chewed on the inside of his cheeks. His eyes grew red, and he stared off toward the mountains his boy had hunted so long ago, and where he had finally gone home. On the old man's conscience, Coal could feel not only the dead Vietnamese people Hague had unjustifiably shot down, but now a lot of people who had been Don's neighbors as well. And on top of that, he had to live with how he and Nonie had ostracized their son, shunned him when he needed them most.

Coal held the door open for Katie and Connie. Before getting in, Katie turned and threw her arms around him again, hugging him fiercely as she sobbed. He held her close and wished he could take away her pain, but at the same time, in truth, he was thankful for that pain. It was the thing that had brought his daughter home to his heart at last.

They finally climbed in the Chrysler and drove away, and it took thirty seconds for Coal to see the red Buick following them out of the cemetery. It tailed them all the way down Ninety-three, then onto Highway 28 to Savage Lane, and after Coal had turned off on the gravel and slowed to a crawl, he saw the strange car pause on the highway, then race on toward Leadore.

This would not be the last he saw of the red Riviera.

CHAPTER TWO

Monday, December 4

Coal performed a routine, meticulous rummaging through the drawers full of papers and other items in the home of his old friends K.T. and Jennifer Batterton. He was searching for financial records. Anything that could help Cynthia in any way.

The house seemed deathly still. An electric clock ticked loudly on the kitchen wall, and otherwise there was no sound but whatever Coal made opening drawers and shuffling papers. He studiously avoided looking over at the place on the living room floor where he had last seen Jennifer lying dead. So much of death lately. Death of good friends. Korea and Nam had been one thing. Death all around him. Commonplace. But this was not Korea. This was not Nam. These were people he had grown up with, living in a quiet valley that should have been filled with peace and happiness. It had left him feeling empty and cold inside—almost desperate in his hopelessness for the world around him.

He would never see the gentle smile of Jen Batterton again, or trade jokes with K.T., Larry, or Trent.

As if drawn there by thinking her name, his eyes lifted, and there from a frame on the wall Jennifer smiled back at him. The photo was years old, a hundred less wrinkles and thirty pounds ago. In the photo, Jennifer had aged significantly since high school, but she was still that pretty girl K.T. and Hague had fought over and K.T. had won. Her warm blue eyes looked right into him, and the dimple on one side of her playful smile seemed to be poked there by an invisible finger.

His eyes moved over, and in another frame was K.T. Older than high school. Less hair. More fat. But wiser. Full of more love and genuine brotherhood. And now it was all gone, and of these two good people only Cynthia remained.

He took the girl's photograph down. Hers was fairly new, probably within the last year. She was a beautiful girl, with expressive, impish eyes, but made more attractive by far because he knew the spirit inside her.

The file folder was nestled down in a drawer in a utilitarian gray metal desk buried in K.T.'s study. Coal had just opened the drawer, on the bottom left, and the file sat there, thick and yellow and scarred. An unexplainable chill came over him. Blinking, he reached for the folder and hoisted it out onto the top of the desk.

Slowly folding back the front cover, he saw K.T.'s letter of resignation—a mere formality, as anyone who knew the situation knew he had basically been fired, with the nicety of being able to say he had resigned. He turned that over and started looking back through notes and stapled sheets of paper, most of them meaningless to anyone but K.T.

Halfway through the packet, there was a big, thick sheath of papers, fresh and bright white, stapled together and sitting in a slick white folder of their own. On the front of the packet, a business card was stapled: Lenny Cross, New York Life. Coal's heart started to pound. He sat back in the chair with the packet of papers and pulled them out of their sleeve to lay them on the desk top. As he did so, a handwritten note on a torn-off sheet from a pocket-sized planner book fell out. Coal picked it up to see the words, in K.T.'s hand, "cancel Monday".

Cancel!

That was the last word he had hoped to see right now. He began to leaf through the papers, already fearing what he was going to find.

It was a life insurance policy, purchased just two years ago, in August of 1970, when K.T. would have been turning forty—that time when mature men start realizing they can't live forever and start wondering how their families would make it without them.

With a sick feeling inside, Coal saw the figure of 100,000 dollars, seeming to jump out of the page at him. One hundred thousand dollars—nearly a fortune to a young girl at that time. He reached his now trembling hand out and picked up the planner book page again, reading the date on it: October 18, 1972. It must have been about the date they had told K.T. he was going to be fired unless he turned in his resignation.

"Cancel Monday." The words almost spoke themselves out loud. K.T. had lost his job and was trying to come up with ways to cut his expenses until he could find another way of making a living. The first thing to go was his life insurance policy. After all, he must have been thinking, he wasn't anywhere near as likely to need this now, without the dangerous job of being sheriff.

Coal leaned back in the chair, and a long-held gust of air escaped through his nostrils. He had known this was a long shot, but he was so hopeful. So hopeful of discovering *something* that could tide Cynthia over, at least for a few years. Now his hope lay in sifting ashes.

Gritting his teeth, he reached into his shirt pocket and pulled out a dirty white piece of paper, as he had done dozens of times prior to that moment. Unfolding it on his knee, he stared at it. It was one of the pieces of paper he took from Roger Miley when he was arrested, the one with the names "Bud and Linda" written on it with a phone number. He closed his eyes, a feeling of near-resignation sweeping over him. He knew it was his responsibility to dial this number. This "Linda" might be the only blood relative he would ever find of Cynthia, and the way Jennifer Batterton had made it sound, she and Bud might be Sissy's mother and father. Yet even though it all seemed cut and dried, every time he thought about calling them, a feeling came into the pit of his stomach he could only describe as sickness. It was only a hunch, but something did not seem right. He was praying something would happen to save him from ever having to dial that number.

Taking a deep breath, he reached over and picked up the receiver of the telephone, mildly surprised to hear a dial tone. But then the power was still on, too, and who but he would have had either of them turned off? Cynthia was certainly in no state to think of it—as if that would *ever* cross the mind of a sixteen-year-old.

Ignoring the number for Bud and Linda, he dialed the one on the business card, a Missoula number. An older sounding secretary responded, in a humdrum voice. *New York Life, this is Martha, how may I direct your call?*

"Sheriff Savage, down here in Salmon. Martha, do you have a Lenny Cross employed as an agent there?"

Her answer shocked him. *We* did. *He took another job, just last month.*

"Oh. Okay. Another job... You mean other than with New York Life?"

No sir. Her voice sounded curt. *Or perhaps I should say 'yes, sir*—not *with New York Life. Something bigger, I guess.*

"Did he leave a number he could be reached at?"

Well, yes, he did. But he can't be.

"How's that?"

We've tried several times to contact him with no luck.

"Well, who would be in charge of his cases now that he's gone?"

Umm... Sir, I think I had better switch you to our owner. Hold please.

Irritated, Coal pulled the receiver away from his ear and glared at it. In another moment, he heard a man's voice.

This is Barton. How may I help you?

"Barton, this is Sheriff Savage, down here in Salmon."

Good morning, Sheriff.

"Say, I'm going through some records of a murder victim here in town, and it shows that he purchased a policy from your company two years ago. Lenny Cross was the agent?"

Oh. Yes. Cross. Well, he is no longer with us.

"I understand that. Can he be reached?"

Not so far. The man's voice sounded bored and condescending.

Coal's temper was starting to wear thin. "Listen, Barton... Is it Mister Barton, or just Barton?"

Barton Hudspeth, said the man, making the mistake of letting irritation creep in to mingle with his condescension.

"Fine... *Barton.* I'm cleaning up after a rash of murders here. There are things that need to be cleared up, and I have two little girls whose parents have just been taken away from them violently and left them with no money and no place to go. Now I've found this insurance policy that was bought two years ago from your company, and I really need to talk to someone who thinks they can help. Is there a number where I can contact the main office of New York Life?"

Now, hang on, Sheriff. Barton's voice seemed to have taken on a touch of humility. *There will be no need for you to do that. I apologize, but Lenny did not leave here under the best of circumstances, and we have been trying to clean up after him ever since he's been gone—which I assume is why he has been unreachable.*

"Well, just give me the contact number he left and I'll try to reach him there."

I will be glad to, but I'm not sure it will do you any good.

"The number. Please." Coal's patience had run out.

Barton read off an area code and phone number in Salt Lake City, Utah, and Coal then insisted he also give him the number for the head office—just in case. Barton must have realized Coal was going to get it one way or another, so he reluctantly gave it up, then tried to become suddenly overly polite and helpful.

Coal hung up on him.

*　　　*　　　*

That evening, Maura PlentyWounds and the girls ate at the Savage table. Fortunately, old Prince Savage had built it big, with the intention that his sons would one day bring their families back for Thanksgiving meals and such.

After supper, Coal put on his coat, and the dogs lunged up and ran for the front door. Coal stood there for a moment, and no one seemed to notice him. Finally, he said Maura's name, and she looked over.

"You wouldn't like to take a walk, would you?"

"I sure would," she said, jumping up. It was as if she had simply been waiting for an invitation.

Wyatt and Morgan dove out of their chairs. "Can we go too, Daddy?" shouted Wyatt.

Coal's first reaction was to tell them no, but then he realized that being boys, they weren't going to stay with him and Maura anyway, and since he hadn't been around much lately it would do them all good to have some kind of activity together.

"Sure, boys. That would be fantastic."

So the four of them and the dogs marched into the night, heading mountain-ward on Savage Lane until it merged with Lemhi Road, where they turned right.

By then, the boys were far ahead, tramping along the dusky lane in the shadows of the Beaverhead Mountains.

"Something's on your mind," said Maura.

"Yeah."

"Is it bad?"

"Yes and no. And maybe."

"Oh great. So I'm supposed to guess? You have brain cancer, but they found a cure for it, but when they got looking they realized the huge thing they thought was your brain was really the cancer, and the little spot on it was really your brain."

Coal couldn't help laughing. "Okay, you're funny. If you're ready to be serious for a second, I'll tell you."

Hands in pockets, she leaned closer and shoved her elbow against him playfully. "Sorry. It just seemed like a retarded answer."

He grunted his humor at her that time and saved a good laugh for another time. "So I was digging through the Battertons' stuff today—routine search—and I found a packet of insurance papers from New York Life."

"What? Really?"

He stopped, frowning at her. "No, I just made that up."

"Oh, jeez. Coal, grow up. I was just surprised."

He laughed. "Wow, you sure get riled up easy."

"I've had good training, believe me."

"Okay. Sorry. Anyway, here's this policy, and don't get all excited, but it says one hundred thousand dollars."

"That's the good part, I take it."

"Yeah. The bad part is there was a note in with it from about the time K.T. must have left his sheriff's job saying 'cancel Monday'."

"Oh." Her face fell. "So... I assume he did."

"That's what I don't know. That's the maybe part. I tried to call them to verify, and the agent, some idiot named Lenny, had quit and moved to Salt Lake. He left a number, but so far they can't get him to answer, and it sounds like maybe his cases are in limbo."

Maura let out a ragged sigh. "I suddenly feel sick. That is going to be tragic if he cancelled the policy less than a month before he died."

"Well, we didn't think he had a dime anyway, so I guess we'll be back where we started."

"Hey, Coal?"

"Yeah."

"Let me do something, will you?"

"I'm not about to answer you when you word it that way."

She grunted out a half laugh. "Stop it, you moron. I'm trying to help. Give me that number, okay? I'll get this guy to talk."

"I'm the sheriff. Why wouldn't he talk to me?"

"Because you can blow up and be a real butthead to people."

"What? And you're Miss Congeniality, right?" He almost brought up the night of their first meeting, but he decided that might change the whole mood of the evening.

She smiled at him and suddenly reached out with both hands to take him by the elbow, hugging his arm. "Come on. I can be nice if I have to."

He looked down at her and finally nodded. He was trying to put on the tough face, but he knew she didn't buy it.

"Yeah, I guess you can. Okay, I'll give you the number. See what you can do. Those girls have got to get into some counselling—especially Cynthia. It would be nice if there were some way to pay for it besides county taxes."

"So..." She leaned into him a little, and they walked in close step for a few seconds, the twins far out ahead of them, running with the dogs. "If I find anything out, what do I get?"

"Love and devotion forever—from Cynthia and Sissy."

"Oh!" Maura let go of Coal's arm and pushed him away, a playful frown on her face. "I keep forgetting—you're just a man, like all of them."

"No, not like all of them. I'm a Savage."

CHAPTER THREE

Thursday, December 7

Maura PlentyWounds could not stay off work forever and play mom to two children who weren't even hers. Eventually, she had to earn a living, so she hired on as a clerk at McPherson's clothing store, on the west end of town. McPherson's, owned and run by Florin Beller, was a true landmark of Salmon, and clerking there was the perfect job for Maura, Coal thought. He would never have admitted these thoughts to her, but she was the ideal woman if they wanted a model to show how nicely their blouses and jeans could fit an amazing figure. It was beside the point that most women didn't have anything close to Maura's build. Just like looking at a sculpted manikin, something about seeing a well-formed body inside nice-fitting clothes seemed to make people think that all they needed in order to look just that way was to own the same clothing. It was this fortunate trick of the mind that kept clothing designers the world over in business.

And in spite of the fact that he had no one to buy for, when Maura told him on Wednesday night that she was going to start work the following morning, Coal was suddenly afraid he was going to spend way too much time in the near future shopping for women's clothing at McPherson's.

Naturally, while Maura went to work, Cynthia and little Clarissa ended up at the Savage residence—another proof of what Coal always claimed, how all the strays ended up there.

It was lucky for them all that Sissy had taken a huge liking to Connie. How could she not? Coal's mother was a gem. She knew when to talk, when to listen, and she was always there with a warm shoulder and a hug. Not to mention a dozen varieties of the best cookies in the valley. Immediately, she had become Sissy's friend. It was taking Coal a lot longer, however. The frail little thing just could not seem to accept any other man in her life but Roger Miley, and her little mind still had trouble grasping that she would never see him again.

Coal wondered what terrors she must have gone through to turn her against men so.

Coal stopped by McPherson's at noon—just because it was on his way. On his way to where, he didn't know—maybe just on his way to trouble. He walked into the men's section, on the right side of the store, and passing the collection of sweat-stained, beat-up old hats from local ranchers that smiled, or sometimes frowned, down on the observer from a row high up near the ceiling, he found Maura. She was sitting on a tall stool midway through the store on the right, shaping a chocolate brown hat, with a moist cloud rolling out of the steamer in front of her. Her tapered, however work-stained, fingers seemed perfectly fitted to the work.

There were full-length mirrors there against the wall, but Maura was engrossed in her work and obviously had not seen him. Stopping for a moment behind a rack of shirts several feet away to enjoy the view, Coal took a deep breath. He had to chide himself. He had sworn not to get tangled up with any woman again for a long time—if ever. He had no time for such trivialities. To say nothing of the mystery of the dating game, and the emotion that was not always the good kind. And he doubted the kids would take a new relationship well anyway. But he couldn't help staring at a woman that God had put together the way He had Maura PlentyWounds.

Today, the woman's light golden hair was drawn back in a ponytail, and it etched a fat, wavy line about fifteen inches down the back of a turquoise blouse with curled fringe along the bottom of the yoke. Her Levi's were just snug enough to show every curve, and not a bulge out of place. Polished brown Lucchese boots proved that even a woman living on the verge of poverty was not going to scrimp on footwear.

Maura must finally have felt Coal staring, for suddenly she stopped what she was doing and looked up at the mirror. She pivoted around. He thought she might jump, but she didn't.

"Nice, Coal. How long have you been there?" she asked, standing up from her stool.

"Half a minute." It could have been five seconds, or it could have been five minutes. Coal hated knowing when he was ogling this woman time seemed to vanish.

"That's kind of creepy. Why didn't you say something?"

Coal laughed. "Because then you might talk."

She frowned. "Stuff it!"

Again, he laughed. "Besides, I was enjoying watching you work."

"Sure," said Maura, turning her head to the side suspiciously. "Or something."

"Okay, or something. So how's the new job?" Changing the subject seemed like the proper cowardly move.

"I like it. I really do. Good people. Great work. Wonderful smells."

Taking in a deep breath through his nostrils, Coal smiled. The smell of smoked leather goods that the Shoshones over in the Indian camp had beaded and brought here to sell mingled with the scent of new boots and belts. "I agree with that. Leather has a way of welcoming the nose. You wouldn't have liked it five years ago. It just smelled like cigarette smoke."

"Wanna buy a new hat?"

"You don't like my old one?"

"White?" She wrinkled her nose. "I don't know. I think you're more of a black hat kind of guy."

"Wow. I'm not sure how to take that."

She shrugged. "Just take it. What size do you wear?"

"Seven and a five eighths—long oval. But you're not likely to find a hat in here that I'll waste money on. My hats are custom made."

"Oh, I see! Yeah, I guess when you have a job like sheriff you can afford the finer things."

"Yeah, like spiced bologna instead of plain."

"Oh, hey!" Maura suddenly turned squarely to him. "I got a phone call this morning—about insurance."

"What?"

"Really."

"How'd you do that?"

"Ahh... Don't even think you're going to coerce a woman into giving away her secrets, Coal Savage. Just be happy."

He laughed. "Fine. So did you talk to Lenny Cross?"

"He was the first one."

"Oh?"

"Yeah. I guess he got mad at that Barton guy for something that happened at the office, so when he left he kind of sabotaged them. He took all of his files and turned them over to a friend of his in another New York Life office—in Idaho Falls."

"Ha! Wow, not very secure, are they? I would have thought they'd have ways to keep that from happening. So what else did he have to say?"

"He said Barton had been leaving him messages that someone from Salmon had been calling and really needed to talk to him, but he said he was making him sweat. And he apologized very nicely to me and said he didn't know it was causing us problems as well."

"Okay. So anyway..."

"Well, I got a hold of the Idaho Falls branch, and they were pretty hush-hush on the phone. But they want to meet with me as soon as possible. And they said it would be best to have you there as well, since you're the sheriff and there seems to be no next of kin."

A chill came over Coal. No company as important as New York Life was going to ask for a personal meeting if there wasn't something big in the wind. This brought Coal a new feeling of hope.

"Do you think they didn't get the policy cancelled for K.T.?"

Maura shrugged in reply, mostly by facial expression. "Who knows? But why else would they insist on meeting in person?"

"When?"

"I said, as soon as possible. I didn't feel I could set a time without talking to you first." She unsnapped a shirt pocket, drawing Coal's eye to places they should not be, and retrieved a slip of paper, handing it to him. "That's the number, and the extension. Talk to Jared. He's hoping to hear back from you today."

"What about your schedule?"

"Just set the time. Florin will work with me. He already said. Besides, you're the one who should really be there. You're the sheriff, and K.T. was your friend, not mine. So... does this sound promising to you?"

"It sure does," Coal said. "Keep your fingers crossed. I'll let you know." He paused then, not knowing quite how to say what had come into his mind.

Finally, Maura cocked her head cautiously. "What?"

"Well... Do you remember at Jennifer's that day she told us her sister might still be alive?"

Maura drew a sharp breath. "Not until now."

"Yeah. Sorry. And she said her sister's husband was the brother of Roger, so... Anyway, I have a piece of paper Roger Miley had on him when he was arrested, and it says Bud and Linda, with a phone number on it. Her name was Linda, right? Linda Miley?"

Maura's face fell, hard and fast. She caught herself and quickly brushed at a strand of hair, trying to avoid his eyes. "Yeah, I think so. Yeah, that's right. Linda."

Coal stared at her, finding no words. Finally, Maura spoke again. "Are you going to call it then?" She tried to act casual. She was anything but.

"I guess eventually I'm going to have to. Right?"

"How should I know? You're the sheriff." She paused and looked down again. "Yeah. I guess you will."

He nodded when she looked back up at him. He was far from happy about it himself. "Okay. Just keep that in mind, all right?"

"Why, what difference would it make to me?" She put on a stone face, but with Coal it wasn't working.

"Because you've gotten way too attached to that little girl. Both of them, for that matter."

Maura's hard veneer melted away, and a scared look came into her eyes. "Jennifer didn't make her sound like a very nice person, Coal. She couldn't just... No judge would just give the girls to a woman like that, right?"

"Maura, it sounds like Sissy's her daughter—*if* she really is still alive. And his, if she is still with the same man."

Maura cocked her head and repeated the one word: *"If?"*

"Yeah, if. Remember, Miley told me Sissy's parents died in a car crash."

A hopeful look came over Maura's face, and she took a calming breath. "Yeah. Maybe Jennifer just didn't get the word. She said there would be a good chance of that."

"She sure did."

"But there is still a chance he lied, right? And that they're alive?"

"I suppose so."

"But if they are, then they must have given Sissy to Roger for some reason. Given up their own daughter! Doesn't that mean anything?"

"We'll see. Try not to think about it." He stared at her. She stared back and forgot to breathe. Finally, he stepped closer and reached out to squeeze her arm. "Hey. Come on. If she isn't dead, the way Jennifer talked she's probably a million miles away from here by now. She probably wouldn't even know Roger's dead."

Maura drew a breath and gave him a quick nod. "Sure. Yeah. Nothing to worry about."

The woman smiled, and moisture filled her eyes.

Finally, she lifted her shoulders and then let them fall again. Another fake smile. "I sound pretty bad, I guess. I shouldn't be happy thinking someone died."

Coal smiled understandingly. "Maybe we both sound bad, Maura. But it's between just you and me."

"Okay." She reached out on a whim and squeezed his hand. But she was trying to reassure herself, not Coal.

*   *   *

Up at the jail, Coal sat down at his desk and ate a sandwich he had brought back from the Coffee Shop. He dialed the insurance company, an Idaho Falls number, and a pleasant-sounding secretary connected him with Jared.

Thanks for calling, Sheriff. I was hoping to talk to you. I feel more comfortable giving out information to you than to some stranger. So this Maura woman I talked to, clarify for me, would you: No blood relation, correct?

"That's right. Just a well-meaning friend. But the girls are both staying with her because there is no family that we know of."

Okay. By the way, I'm sorry to hear about all the troubles you've had over there. It's a rough way to start out a job.

Coal smiled to himself. Word sure got around. "Thanks. It's been a tough go. But it can only get better after a start like that."

Sure. So I would rather not go over any of this information on the phone, Sheriff. Is there any way you could meet me here at the office? Or if not, I could drive out there. But it might be a week or so. It just depends if you're in a hurry to get this figured out.

Coal thought about it. It didn't take long to see the benefit of going to Idaho Falls—especially if Maura were invited along. "Let me call you back in a few minutes. If I can come there, when would be a good time?"

Tomorrow would be great. Any day, really. A few minutes or even half an hour is fine—it's just a whole day out of the office that would be tough for me right now.

Coal made a call to Maura and dialed Jared back. "Tomorrow will work for us. We can be there around one."

Sounds good. Watch those roads. I hear they're pretty iced-over.

"Those high ones will be that way now for most of the winter. Welcome back to Idaho," said Coal.

CHAPTER FOUR

Friday, December 8

Cynthia still hadn't been back to school since the death of her mother. Coal wasn't sure how or when she was going to be able to make that leap. But it was he who chose to have her and Sissy come along on the road trip to Idaho Falls. He thought the drive might lift their spirits, and after all, the outcome of the meeting would affect them more than anyone else. Cynthia was the Battertons' direct descendant, and as far as Coal or anyone knew for certain, since Roger Miley's death, Sissy's only benefactors would have been the Battertons as well—unless it did indeed turn out that Bud and Linda Miley were alive and well.

When Coal asked Maura on the phone early that morning if she was okay with bringing the girls, Maura paused. Then she laughed. *And here I thought you were going to try and pull off the highway somewhere and attack me.*

Coal paused, momentarily speechless.

The silence quickly became unbearable. *I actually was kidding, you know. Coal?*

Coal still didn't have a response, at least not one he felt to be appropriate. "Um... So it's okay, right?"

Of course it's okay. He felt bad about the discomfort he could sense now on the other end of the line. *Should I pack a lunch, or do you want to grab a bite there?*

"Those girls could use a real date day, don't you think? Let's get something to eat at a sit-down place."

*   *   *

Later that day, seated in a plush chair at the life insurance office and facing Jared, a polished young man in a two-tone gray suit, Coal learned how important it was to be sitting down at certain times. This was one of those times.

"So not to let the numbers scare you," said Jared, after several minutes of letting the suspense build up for Coal and Maura, who had left Cynthia holding Sissy in a waiting room, "but I wonder if your friend Mr. Batterton didn't have some kind of a premonition or something. On the phone, we talked a little bit, and you had mentioned a hundred thousand dollar policy. That is no longer in place."

Coal stared, and beside him he felt Maura grab his leg. "Wait. It's not? But... Why did you feel like we needed to come all this way to talk then?"

"Because after Mr. Batterton called to try and cancel the policy, my friend Lenny convinced him to wait a couple of days. It was right after that when Lenny quit his job and moved all his clients over to me so they couldn't get the accounts in Missoula. I guess his boss there is a real piece of work—sorry to sound judgmental."

"Don't worry about that. I talked to his boss and kind of agree."

"Thanks. Okay, so by the time I talked to Mr. Batterton to see if he still wanted to cancel his policy he told me he had changed his mind. He didn't say why, but like I said before, it really was like he had some kind of premonition."

"But wait. I thought you said it *isn't* still in place."

"That's right. But instead of canceling, he raised the policy."

"Raised it? To what?" asked Coal.

"To two."

"To two... Two what?" Maura managed to get out.

"Two hundred thousand. The insurance policy K.T. Batterton was holding when he died, and which is still in place, is for two hundred thousand dollars."

CHAPTER FIVE

Coal personally could not believe any man in his right mind would buy an insurance policy for two hundred thousand dollars. A brand new house, a decent house, could be built for less than fifteen!

As Coal and Maura sat at Smitty's Pancake and Steak House in Idaho Falls and waited for their food order to arrive, with the girls sitting quietly, Cynthia against Coal and Sissy on Maura's lap, they contemplated the news. Coal had only to send the coroner's death certificate to Jared at New York Life, and he would send a check in the amount of two hundred thousand dollars back in Cynthia Batterton's name—to be countersigned by her legal guardian, whomever that was decided to be. It seemed like a fairy tale. Here Coal and Maura had been sick with worry over what was going to happen with the girls, and now suddenly they were set. That much money would pay off any debts the Battertons had left, pay enough for Cynthia and Sissy to live very comfortably for quite some time, and even provide enough for a good education for both of them. By the time they were in their twenties, the girls should be in for a great future, especially if Coal could get his friend Rick Cheatum, at the bank, to find a good investment broker for them.

At this point, of course, none of that meant a thing to Sissy. She was just happy living with Maura, the way things were. And Cynthia was, needless to say, still in shock over losing her parents. She could not emotionally even begin to think of what having that much money meant. The only salve for her would have been to have the two people she loved most back in her life.

Doctor Nancy Pearson, the psychiatrist who sometimes made trips to Salmon, lived in the Falls, so before leaving the restaurant, Coal dialed up her number from a phone booth in the foyer and was able to talk the receptionist into letting him speak with her. On the phone, Dr. Pearson's voice was not what Coal had expected. He had expected someone with a sense of their own sophistication, and perhaps a little haughtiness. Instead, he heard the voice of a woman who sounded like one of the "common people," as Coal referred to them. Like perhaps she had come from simpler roots and not come along through a line of doctors or other uppity folk. It was a good start—perhaps she was Coal's kind of people.

"Dr. Pearson, I really didn't want to bother you at your office without an appointment. I apologize for how our last appointment fell apart."

"Oh, please don't apologize, Sheriff! We were told all about what happened with the kidnapping. I am just thankful your daughter is okay."

"Well, 'okay' is sort of a relative term. Now it's not just the death of her mother, but the whole trauma of that kidnapping deal that's plaguing her."

"Of course! Of course. We will work through it, Sheriff."

"Well, like I said, I didn't want to bother you, but we happen to be here in town, and we have the other two girls I spoke to you about with us. Only my daughter Katie is not."

"Oh! Well, Sheriff, we had a cancellation today. I was just going to be working on some paperwork this afternoon. Could you come over now?"

"We sure could. Thank you."

Coal got directions to Dr. Pearson's office, and they drove over and met her in person. Like her homespun voice sounded, Nancy Pearson was one of the common people, her demeanor in person every bit as warm and personable as she had sounded on the phone. She spoke to Cynthia as one adult to another, then got on one knee to introduce herself to Sissy. Coal could see it was going to be the beginning of a good relationship. And he knew Katie would like her too.

Dr. Pearson took the girls in separately to talk to them. As Coal suspected, it was not going to be a rush job, simply trying to get the girls in and out of the office as fast as she could. To this doctor, talking to these young, vulnerable girls was not just something to make her money. She was gone with Cynthia for more than an hour.

In the meantime, Coal and Maura sat in the waiting room, with Sissy beside Maura, on the far side of the ogre that Coal must appear to be.

There were two wooden chair arms separating Coal from the full warmth of Maura PlentyWounds. But the emotional chasm he suddenly sensed was like Hell's Canyon of the Snake River. He had tried to speak to her a couple of times, but her response was anything but warm. Coal couldn't understand it, this sudden drawing inside herself. It was so without warning or apparent reason.

His first response was to get angry and stubborn and push her further away. He wanted to nonchalantly get up and go use the restroom, then come back and sit a chair away from her. He sat contemplating it for quite a while, and the only thing that kept him in his chair was not wanting to be conspicuous.

Then he took a deep breath and looked at Maura in the big mirror on the wall across from them. Coal didn't think of himself as a reader of minds by any stretch of the imagination. Especially female minds. In that way, he guessed he was a typical man. But he noticed something in Maura's eyes as she sat there fidgeting with her hands, looking around the room at every place but where Coal sat, and watching Sissy scribble pathetically in a coloring book she had obviously never been taught to use that pulled at Coal's heart. He couldn't place what that look was for a while, but then it came to him. It was the look of someone trying to hold herself together. Someone with painful thoughts on her mind who did not want anyone getting inside. Maybe Coal was making it up. But that was what a voice suddenly whispering in his head told him. Perhaps God really was not beyond talking to Coal after all, as he had so many times believed. It could be that he was warning Coal, or that he was trying to help him help Maura. And for the first time in recent memory, Coal actually felt fear of a woman.

By the obvious fact that Maura kept avoiding a glance at Coal, he could tell she knew she was being watched. She kept appearing

28   kirby@kirbyjonas.com

more and more agitated, and he kept feeling that way inside, because he knew he should make some move and didn't know how.
Finally, she turned hot eyes on him.

"What?"

"Nothing," he said too quickly.

"Then why are you staring at me?"

"Sorry. I didn't mean to."

She just turned her head away. He thought while looking at her
in the mirror that he saw a rush of emotion come into her eyes. But
just as suddenly as it appeared, she practically lunged up out of her
chair. "I have to use the restroom. Sissy, do you want to stay with
Coal or come with me?"

Of course Sissy leaped to her feet and held out her hand, glancing nervously at Coal. He smiled, but she was already looking
away and missed it.

Coal watched Maura walk away and cursed himself for looking. Maybe Maura was right when she claimed men were all pigs.
But she was just so... *watchable.* He sat there alone, glad that no
one else was scheduled to come in. He did not want to sit in that
close waiting room with another soul but whom he had come with.
Even having the receptionist not fifteen feet away at her desk was
annoying.

Maura was gone for a long time, giving Coal lots of time to
think about her. They had shared so much fun repartee lately. And
no kisses or hugs, but lots of light physical contact, like two pre-
teens, emotionally sparring, testing out an adolescent crush but not
knowing for sure what to do with it. And now this.

What had happened? He tried to think back to the last comfortable moment they had shared, the last exchange that had been light.
As far as he could remember, it was when they had first sat down
and ordered their food. Could this whole thing be so simple as
Maura having her stomach upset by something she ate? Maybe she
had gas. That could make *anyone* change their demeanor!

The thought made Coal laugh out loud, in spite of the moment. He blushed and looked over at the receptionist, who had glanced at him but quickly averted her eyes out of mutual embarrassment. Coal swore inside. He felt like the woman had read his mind, his stupid male thoughts that had no place in a tense situation like he was suddenly finding himself in, and which was going to get much more tense if he and Maura had to ride the entire way back to Salmon in this atmosphere.

After what seemed like at least twenty minutes or so, Maura and Sissy reappeared from down the hall. Looking at the girl, Coal saw a worried look in her face that startled him, and he looked up at Maura. Even with his man disease of not being able to read people, he could see she had been crying, and apparently quite a bit. Her eyes were puffed up and red.

Coal froze. He was way out of his realm of comfort. Maura set Sissy back on her chair with her crayons and book, but she didn't sit herself. She started walking around the room, pretending to study the couple of paintings on the walls. Both were actually very nice art, but both Coal and the woman had had plenty of time to look at them during their long wait. He didn't believe she was that interested in them now.

Maura glanced over toward Sissy once, but her eyes lingered on the chair next to her, the one on the other side from her, away from Coal. He could see the wheels of her mind churning, and a light in them made him believe she was going to walk over and sit down there, with two chairs between her and Coal. She was going to beat him to it, and then some.

Finally, she took a deep breath, which she tried to hide by taking it slowly, and then came over and sat in her original chair, turning her head away from Coal. After twenty seconds or so, she turned her head slightly but didn't look at Coal.

"I think I might go sit in the car. Can I have the keys?"

That was too much. "Sure. But... Maura, what's up? Did I say something wrong?"

"Coal, I'm just tired of you staring at me. Isn't there something else you could look at?"

"I wasn't staring at you. Holy cow. What in the world did I do?"

"Just stop, okay?"

Coal glanced over angrily at the receptionist, who had her head buried in paperwork, but whose ears were pricked every bit like a fox's in the direction of Coal and Maura. He raised his hands resignedly. "Let's just keep Sissy warm, okay? *I'll* sit in the car."

With that, he got up and reached in his pocket for the keys as he walked toward the outside door. Before he was halfway out, Maura was there behind him and caught his arm. "No, Coal, don't go out," she said as he was turning back to her. "I'm sorry."

He turned and looked at her, and their faces were only a foot apart. She wouldn't meet his eyes but instead stared at the third button down the front of his shirt.

"Maura, if I did something to make you mad, I sure didn't mean to."

Tears came into Maura's eyes. Her chin started to quiver, and she swore softly. "Just... Coal, I'm just being a woman, okay?" She looked up quickly, back and forth between his eyes, and as the moisture seeped into hers, she looked down again. "Just let me be a stupid woman for a while. I can't help it."

Coal had the stubborn urge to turn and continue on to his car. But he suddenly sensed that if he chose not to he might somehow salvage the long ride back to Salmon, which by now he could see was going to be a lonely road, mostly in the dark. He did not relish the thought of it being dark *and* cold.

A strange feeling came over Coal, who had too long been trying to be a man, in a man's world. And for once, he acted on the feeling. Without speaking, he encircled Maura with his arms, and she reacted with the ferocity of a Venus fly trap, throwing her own arms around him and squeezing with what seemed to Coal like all her strength.

CHAPTER SIX

By the time Dr. Pearson was done talking to the girls, it was already five-thirty, and as Coal had expected, they were going to make the drive home in the dark—both literally and figuratively. He was still in the dark as to what had upset Maura.

The good thing was he had gotten her to smile again, and although she asked him not to push her about what had gotten under her skin, she seemed almost back to normal.

When they got back in the car to leave, after discussing the girls for a few minutes with Dr. Pearson, Don McLean was singing his number one hit "American Pie" on the radio, and all of a sudden Coal felt very hungry—and very much in the mood to treat his girls to some fun. So they drove by McDonald's, where they went inside and waited for sixty cent quarter pounders, of which Coal got two for himself, twenty-six cent French fries, and twenty cent root beers all around (the only other choices were Coca Cola and Orangeade, both twenty cents as well). To top it all off, Coal bought apple pies for everyone, which were also up to twenty-six cents. But such extravagance seemed worth it, for the smiles on everyone's faces.

They drove to the banks of the wide, frosty Snake River and pulled over within the shadow of the sparkling LDS temple, then sat in the car eating their bounty, gazing, mesmerized at the wonderful sight that towered over them with much the same mystical, magical magnificence as the Emerald City—only shining white like alabaster. It was there, while little Sissy was munching on her apple pie, that for the very first time, she looked up at Coal and smiled.

The recollection of Sissy's smile warmed Coal to the core as they drove toward Salmon later, in the dark. Now Cynthia was snuggled up in the back seat with a soft blanket and her worn-out brown Teddy bear, Buddy, which her parents had given her years before. That bear never got far from her anymore. Sissy lay across his and Maura's laps, fast asleep. She was using Coal's leg for a pillow, a fact that left him feeling warm and not just a little stunned as well.

Now and then a pair of headlights passed from the other direction, but for the most part, after going through the settlement of Mud Lake, the high sagebrush desert was dark. The radio played softly, the signal crackling and going in and out, but no one in the car made a sound. Coal was almost uncomfortably aware of bits and pieces of the Sammi Smith song coming through the speakers—"Help Me Make It Through the Night." And finally, Lynn Anderson started crooning "You're My Man" as the radio signal began abruptly to fade, then finally died away.

Maura turned her head slightly, trying hard not to be conspicuous, and studied Coal's profile in the dim glow of the pathetic dash lights. The humming of the tires on the asphalt made an almost lonesome song that penetrated every corner of the closed space.

"Coal?"

The voice was so soft it failed to startle him. He turned to meet Maura's glance. "Yeah?"

"Do you ever wish you could go back in time?"

A nostalgic feeling came over him. "Sure. All the time."

"Where would you go?"

He stared at the twin beams of light on the highway, unconsciously scanning for wildlife or stock. For a long time, he was silent, and that silence finally got to Maura.

"You don't have to tell me. I was just wondering."

"I'd like to go back and see my daddy again, first."

Sensing the sadness she had brought to him, Maura reached out and squeezed his hand. "I didn't mean to bring sad memories."

"Hey, no you don't! They aren't sad. They're happy—honest. How about you? Where would you go?"

"Rapid City. I want to say I would have married a different man. Jerry Banks. He wasn't much for looks, but he was a real sweetheart. A gentleman. Then I realize I couldn't marry someone else. I would never have had my boys."

"Once there are kids, there's no going back, is there?" asked Coal. He expected no answer.

Maura had dropped her hand away from Coal's because both of his were on the wheel. He meant for them to remain there, too, safe from obligation. His heart was pounding. More than a hug or even a kiss, to Coal, holding hands seemed like a commitment. It wasn't something one did just out of happiness to see someone, like giving out a hug. And it wasn't something done out of sexual attraction, like a kiss. Taking a hand, other than to steady someone or maybe to help them up, was like signing an emotional contract. It held certain obligations that made Coal want to run and hide.

He breathed deeply of the warm air emanating from the heater. Closing his eyes for a moment, he took another breath. In spite of his strongest intentions, suddenly something inside him made him want to reach for Maura's hand. He almost let go of the steering wheel with his right hand. Her callused but feminine hand was resting on Sissy's tiny chest. It would have been so easy to reach out and hold.

But he couldn't sign that contract with Maura PlentyWounds. He couldn't, at least, until he knew what had upset her at Dr. Pearson's office. And that was something into which he had sworn he would not pry.

The miles fell behind them, and then, in time, the resting spot of Lone Pine, then the town of Leadore. Finally, around ten o'clock, they saw the lights of Baker. They were almost home.

Coal drove past Savage Lane and on to the front of Maura's house, where he pulled up and put the car in park. He looked over, and Maura smiled at him. It was a sad smile. That much he grasped. He didn't know why, but he could tell he had missed doing something that would have made Maura happy—perhaps taking her hand? But he was a man. That would always be his excuse for doing the wrong thing—or for not doing the right one.

He got out and came around to open Maura's door, and this time, unlike any other day, she allowed him to, because Sissy was sleeping on her legs. Together, they managed to get the tiny body up into Coal's arms, and he held onto her, feeling the heat of her against him as Maura slid out, and relishing in the emotional warmth of holding God's little angel to his breast, so much like his memory of Katie Leigh.

Cynthia was asleep in the back, clutching tightly to Buddy, so they went and unlocked the house first, taking Sissy in and laying her gently on the bed. The girl almost immediately began to stir, so Maura knelt down beside her and started caressing her hair and cooing to her.

"I'll go get Cynthia," Coal whispered, and slipped out without a word from the woman.

At the car, he opened the back door and leaned in, softly touching Cynthia's shoulder. The girl came awake with a start, crying out and striking out at him. Coal, lurching back and slammed the back of his head on the top of the door frame.

"Hey! Cynthia, it's me!"

Almost immediately crying, Cynthia came out of the car and grabbed Coal around the middle, Buddy still clutched by his arm. She was weeping with no sign that she could stop any time soon, and Coal held her, understanding.

After a while, he heard the front door open, but he couldn't turn. Maura's footsteps were soft on the porch, but it was a rickety affair, and she couldn't keep it from creaking. She came down the steps, and after a few moments he felt her hand on his back.

She gave his back a couple of soft pats. "You wanna come in where it's warm, Cynth?"

The girl, with her face buried in Coal's shirt, shook her head adamantly. Maura looked up in consternation at Coal. Finally, she looked back at the girl. "Hey, you're going to be all right, honey. Let's go in, okay? Coal's still here."

With that assurance, and after a body-wracking sob, Cynthia pulled away from Coal enough to allow him to walk with her up the stairs and into the house. Behind them, Coal heard the car door shut softly.

He took Cynthia to her bedroom, and Maura followed. In her room, they turned on the light, which was the only way she had been able to sleep since coming there. Cynthia turned again and pushed herself against Coal, squeezing him. It wasn't just an embrace, Coal could tell. She had no intention of letting go.

Behind Cynthia, Maura looked up at Coal, her eyes full of concern and questions. Finally, she came close and took the girl's shoulders gently. "Hey, sweetie. Let's let go of Coal so we can get you changed into your p.j.'s. Okay?"

Cynthia shook her head. Coal was starting to wonder if the doctor had helped her at all, or if the talk had brought her fears even closer to the surface. He rubbed her back compassionately. "Hey, sweetheart. I'll wait right outside the door. In fact, if you want, I won't even shut it. I'll just turn my back. Okay?"

Cynthia said nothing. Nor did she make a move, even to shake her head. She just clutched Coal tighter.

"Cynthia? I kind of have to go to the bathroom," Coal lied. "How about Maura stays with you while you change into your night clothes, and I'll go to the bathroom and be back as fast as I can?"

Those were the magic words. Cynthia looked up at him. "Please don't leave, okay? You promise not to go?"

"I promise."

Cynthia turned and looked at Maura, and Maura held out a comforting hand. As Cynthia let go of Coal, Maura put an arm around her shoulders and led her to her dresser. Coal heard her speaking softly as he left the room and sat down on the couch.

Suddenly, it struck him that he had indeed better use the bathroom, need it or not. He had no idea how this night was going to end.

After flushing the toilet, Coal looked in on Sissy, fast asleep on Maura's bed. It made his heart feel good thinking of her smile for him earlier. Maybe he was becoming one of her pack at last.

He stepped quietly back down the hall and stood listening outside Cynthia's door. He could only stand to wait for a few seconds, because the first words he heard were Maura saying, "Don't worry, sweetie. He promised he wouldn't leave, and that's one thing I can promise you about Coal. If he said he won't leave, he won't."

He knocked softly, and the door flew open. Cynthia, now in pajamas and still holding her bear, grabbed onto him again, and she was already sobbing uncontrollably before her arms could close all the way around his middle. Coal, his heart breaking, looked over her head at Maura. What was he supposed to do?

Maura watched him, and all of a sudden there were tears in her eyes too. She came close and encircled Cynthia in her arms from behind.

Softly, she said, "Cynthia, you just cry it out. Cry all you want, honey. We aren't going anywhere."

At Coal's feet, the dogs whined and cowered, not understanding what was happening in their home, but understanding that it meant a lot to these people. Like dogs do, they just wanted to help, and to have comfort of their own.

Coal didn't know how he was going to prove it to Cynthia, but somehow he would: She was going to be all right. And no one was going to hurt her, ever again.

Coal believed that with everything that was in him. He might not have been able to keep his own wife safe, or several of his friends, but he was not going to fail with Cynthia.

That was before the phone call came that turned their world upside down.

CHAPTER SEVEN

Coal tried once that night to leave. Each time, Cynthia awoke and clung to him tightly, like a little child waking from a nightmare. Even Buddy was forgotten now, lying on the bed, but only because something big and warm was there to replace him. Finally, he gave up and asked Maura to call Connie and let her know what was happening. He took Cynthia to the sofa with him, where he leaned against the back and let her snuggle up against him. Exhausted from her weeping, she was asleep within minutes, and Coal settled in for a long night.

Saturday, December 9

When daylight came once more, and Maura emerged from her room and began making pancakes, Cynthia slept on. She had obviously rested better than Coal, who felt stiff and sore all over. The smell of pancakes and bacon wafted all through the warm little house, and Coal's stomach started to complain. It wasn't the smell of a bodybuilder's diet, but nonetheless, it called to him.

The smells finally roused Cynthia, too, and little Sissy even came out of Maura's room to cling to her new surrogate mother as she moved about the kitchen. The little girl looked at Coal a few times, and one time she almost smiled, but she refused to come near him, and he didn't try to coax her. The one smile from the day before was going to have to be enough. She couldn't be rushed.

After breakfast, everyone was quiet while Maura did the dishes. Without being asked, Cynthia got up to help her dry them, and Coal shrugged into his coat.

He went and stood behind Maura and Cynthia for a while as Sissy held onto Maura's leg and shot furtive glances up at him now and then.

"I've got to get home," Coal finally said.

Maura looked over at Cynthia, who continued furiously toweling a ceramic plate as if bent on scouring the blue design right off of it. Then the woman looked at Coal. "We understand. Thank you for staying over."

"You're welcome." He waited for some kind of acknowledgment from Cynthia. None was forthcoming, simply the ongoing rush of the towel around the already-dry plate. "You'll be okay now, won't you, Cynthia?"

He saw the girl close her eyes, clenching her jaw. She nodded in reply, refusing to look at him.

Looking his frustration at Maura, Coal went to the door, the dogs following him. He let them out to perform their morning harassment of the horses, and he drove back to his mom's in silence.

*   *   *

Connie met Coal at the door and searched his eyes with deep concern. "Everything okay, Son?"

"I don't know, Mom. It seemed like Cynthia was doing pretty well, until she came out of the counselor's office. Last night, she just about fell apart."

"She's just lost the two most important people in her world. To a violent death. That will be with her forever."

"I know. But I can't stay over there every night. What happens tonight?"

"God will still be with her."

"God isn't enough for her right now, Mom. Neither is Maura."

"Unless they call, I wouldn't go over there or anywhere near them today," Connie said. "If she starts to get into the habit of having you there, it could be very hard to break. She's going to have to get back on her own feet."

"You didn't see her, Ma. She... I don't know what would have happened if I hadn't been there."

Connie sighed and touched Coal's forearm gently. "Honey, I don't want to hurt your feelings, but please listen to me. I know it might seem sometimes like you're the only human in the world who can make things better. But sometimes we give ourselves way too much credit. There are other people just important in her life as you."

Coal just nodded. His mother was usually right about this kind of thing, but this time he wasn't so sure.

"If you are truly concerned, there's another option I've been thinking about." Connie sniffed nonchalantly after she spoke.

"You probably think too much," Coal said, trying to smile.

She ignored the comment. "Son, what would happen if we asked them all to move in with us for a while? We have so much extra room, and anyone can see Katie could use a friend too."

Coal frowned suspiciously and narrowed his eyes as he watched Connie. Finally, he said, "What does 'all' mean?"

"All, Coal. The three of them."

Coal looked around. "Yeah, maybe we could set up cots in the living room."

"Don't be silly. I'm sure Maura wouldn't mind sleeping in the same king-size bed as me. I don't snore. And we could pull out that little bed we used to use for Katie and let Sissy sleep in it. Cynthia would just move into Katie's room with her."

"You *have* been thinking a lot, haven't you? But you didn't see Cynthia last night. I don't know if she could stay in there with Katie and actually sleep."

"That's exactly right—you *don't* know. So it's at least worth a try. Maybe she could slowly get back to normal if she had a lot of company around to make her feel safe. And maybe you wouldn't feel like the whole thing had to be on your shoulders alone."

"In all your thinking, did you ever stop to think how awkward that might be for me and Maura?"

"Awkward how?"

"Jeez, Mom. You must be getting old."

"I *am* getting old!" she retorted. "But not *that* old. I can see you like Maura. And she likes you... a lot."

"Stop it."

"Stop what?"

"I'm not saying I don't like her, but not like that."

"Okay, sure. Then you've got a big problem."

"When haven't I? I've got you for a mom."

Connie laughed, then pulled a serious face. "Coal, I'm not kidding. Maura likes you a lot. I think you're trying to cover up how you feel for her, but if I'm wrong, then you'd better start thinking how you're going to break it to her."

"There's nothing to break. She doesn't think about me that way. And even if she did, if I just never say anything, it will go away."

"Typical man. A woman's feelings don't just go away, Coal."

"Okay, whatever. The point is, if you ask her to stay here, you'll get one of two things. First, she will probably flat-out tell you no, because of her horses and dogs. And second, if by some weird miracle she does say yes, it's going to be so uncomfortable around here that you'll probably see me a lot less."

"Well, I don't know how we could see you much less than we already do. Maybe it would be nice to have another adult around that would actually be here for supper."

Coal ignored the hard dig. "Mom, you do what you want, all right? This is the first time I've had a chance to do anything for myself in a long time, so I'm going to go saddle up and go for a ride. You go ahead and make your phone call. Spin your little webs. She's going to tell you no, and all your hard web-spinning is going to be for nothing." At least he hoped it would be for nothing. He and Maura had fun bandying words with each other, but the honest truth he wouldn't tell *anyone* was that he was scared to death of her. Having her stay under the same roof with him was not an appealing thought—at least not on any sane level.

"Oh! Speaking of phone calls, I almost forgot. I got a strange one early this morning."

"From who?"

"They wouldn't say. But it started out as a woman's voice. She asked for you, and when I said you were out, a man came on and asked if we had two girls living with us."

"If *what?*"

"Yes. When I asked him to leave me his number so he could talk to you about it, he just hung up."

A cold feeling came over Coal. He pushed it down deep inside and hid it from his face, or at least hoped he did. "Mom, I'm going for that ride. If they call back again, you call Maura immediately, you understand? And I guess in that case only, you'd better tell her to pack up the girls and come over here. Just in case."

Coal went out and saddled up his dad's big gray, now perhaps twenty-four years old and gone almost completely white, at least from a distance. White, that is, if he hadn't been rolling in the mud, like he most generally had. The second horse whose lighter-colored dapples seemed actually to sit down in the darkness of a nest of almost-black bay hairs, especially when his winter coat was on, was his mother's horse, Bolt. He was a steady horse, but being only fifteen hands high and barely a thousand pounds, he couldn't pack Coal's weight for very far, and Coal would never have asked him to—even though in reality he had a much more genial temperament than Cody, his dad's big gray—who unfortunately was now pushing thirty years old and wasn't going to be ridable for much longer.

Before climbing up on Cody, Coal found his fingers in the pocket of his shirt, and there was the little slip of folded paper from Roger Miley. He almost pulled it out. But he didn't. He didn't want to see the names written on it.

Coal's intention had been to ride up into the foothills, but now something told him to go the other way, out toward the highway. He preferred the solitude of the hills, but suddenly he was thinking he should stay closer to home. He rode out to the main highway, and after only a moment's thought he turned toward town. It wasn't but five minutes before he wondered if he was discovering the subconscious reason he had made the choice, when he saw Maura PlentyWounds's ugly Travelette coming toward him down the highway.

The pickup slowed, he assumed just out of respect for a horseman, but as it came past him and Maura recognized him, it skidded to a halt. He stopped and cranked about in the saddle as he heard the pickup's gears grinding, and it came backing up the road toward him.

Maura backed the International up even with him, then sat there for a moment grinning. Both girls were watching him too. Just for a moment, whatever biting comment Maura was wrestling with was caught in her throat.

"So you really *can* sit a horse," she finally said.

"I really can. Where are you going?" He was immediately suspicious of his mother. Had she actually called Maura and asked her to stay with them?

"Where do you think?" Maura parried.

Coal stopped. "Oh. Yeah."

"Yeah, if you stayed around home more maybe it wouldn't be so easy to forget the girls stay with Connie until I'm off work."

He slouched over the saddle horn. "Okay, touché. So what I need to do is stop hanging around at McPherson's and stay home."

She giggled. "Like you're spending so much time at McPherson's. All one times, you mean?"

"Yeah, yeah." He saw another car coming down the highway toward her, a quarter-mile away. "You got somebody coming. When do you have to be to work today?"

"I'll have time to drop off the girls and have a cup of coffee with Connie," she said. "Then it's off to work. They would prefer ten o'clock."

"Well, if they would *pre*-fer it, I would say you'd better *de*-fer. They're the ones paying you, aren't they?"

"I suppose. Okay, I've gotta go." She ground the gears again and punched the gas, her ugly old rust bucket lumbering off before the other car, a gold Chrysler Cordova, had quite reached her.

Coal looked toward town, then back the way he had come. He grunted, dissatisfied with the short ride but feeling like he should return home. Turning, he put Cody into a long trot, in the style of what they called a "prowler" from an old-time roundup, the seasoned hand sent out after roundups to search for overlooked strays. Keeping the gray to that pace clear back to the mud lane, then putting him into a lope, he made it back to the corral in five minutes.

By the time he had unsaddled and curried Cody's curly, matted hair out, the coffee was hot, and its aroma filled the house. It mingled with the less aromatic Postum that Connie was so fond of.

Connie and Maura, cups in hand, turned as Coal shut the door. They just looked at him, and whatever conversation they had been involved in went dead.

He looked from one to the other. "I just heard a mosquito burp," he said. They both laughed. "Come on, what's up?"

Maura seemed suddenly uncomfortable, but Connie shrugged. "Coal, you told me to ask Maura if she and the girls wanted to stay with us, so I did."

Coal had already pushed the thought out of his mind. In truth, he didn't think his mother would really do it.

"You told me she would just say no, so I'm still waiting for her decision." With a spark in her eye, Connie turned, one eyebrow cocked, to catch Maura's reaction.

There was a change in the woman's demeanor as Connie's last words registered on her, and she looked straight at Coal. She frowned as if trying to decide how she should take his prediction, and suddenly she straightened up a little and turned her eyes back to Connie.

"You know what? I think that's a wonderful idea. But wait— are you serious?" Suddenly, she wasn't so cocksure.

"Completely serious, sweetheart. You have to be kidding! I'm not the kind to throw out an offer like that in jest. Coal thought it would be a terrific idea, too. And I'm sure it would be best for the girls."

Cynthia, sitting on the coach to Coal's left, was staring at him, and he could feel her eyes boring into his face.

Maura looked over at Cynthia, who now that Coal's attention turned that way he saw was holding Sissy on her lap. Cynthia's eyes were hopeful, while little Sissy hadn't even caught on yet to what was happening.

Coal returned his glance to Maura just in time to catch her dragging a fingertip quickly across the bottom lid of her right eye. She blinked and looked into his face, searching his eyes, searching his soul.

She was mining his being with her eyes when she spoke: "If Coal thinks it's okay, then we'd be glad to see how it works, Connie. I don't know how to thank you."

Coal felt his heart begin to thud radically. A sigh escaped his lips, but he kept it a silent sound so no one knew.

"But of course when my boys are here from their dad's, I'd have to go back home to be with them," Maura added.

"Oh, of course!" Connie agreed. "That's only right."

And then the phone rang, and for some reason everyone looked at Coal. And Coal stared the phone down.

Before the third ring, he was standing over it, and he picked it up. "Savage residence."

Is this Mr. Savage? The sheriff? A woman's harsh voice, abused by too many years of searing cigarettes and wracked with a sense of its own importance.

"Yes, on both counts. How can I help you?"

Mr. Savage, I have been led to believe that either you are holding my two girls, or you know who is. In either case, I am calling to inform you that you have taken them in illegally, and I want both of them back immediately.

CHAPTER EIGHT

Coal held the phone to his ear for several seconds, too stunned even to reply.

Hello? Are you still on the line?

"I'm here." Coal knew his voice had gone cold and hard.

How do I arrange to come and get the children?

"Who is this?"

My name is Linda Miley. Roger Miley was my husband's brother. Jenny Batterton was my sister. I understand you allowed her to be murdered.

"She was murdered, yes." Coal's mind was whirling, thinking of the now almost hated slip of paper in his shirt pocket. This was the sister of whom Jennifer had spoken, who had caused such heartache for her family. "How did you know about the girls?"

How did I know? I saw the death notices in the paper, of course. Besides reading the news of the murders and hearing it on the radio.

Coal gathered himself together, steeling his voice. "I talked to Jennifer not very long ago, and she told me about you. I don't see that you have any claim on these girls."

A pregnant pause, a caught breath. *So you do have them. Well, I think a judge will see it our way, not yours. Cyndi is my niece, and my relation to Clarissa is obvious. You can't break up family just because you feel like it.*

Before Coal could reply, a man's voice came on the phone. *Excuse me, sir. So my name is Bud Miley. I hope you understand that we are capable of giving the girls a good, loving home. They will be well cared for. So I'd just like to set you at ease there.*

Coal paused. Then, "I'm going to have to meet you, Mr. Miley. Both of you. And we're still going to have to ask for a ruling from Judge Sinclair."

Only a second went by. *Sure, I understand. Take your time. We can wait a day or two.*

"Or a week," Coal said.

The man chuckled. *Sure, whatever it takes. I'm a law-abiding man. I wouldn't want to rush things. But I* will *have those girls back.*

"It's my understanding that you gave Clarissa away, although we were told you had died in a car wreck. And Cynthia... Does she even know you? Have you even met her?"

A car wreck! I don't know what that's *about! Who told you that?*

"Your brother Roger."

After a moment, Miley began laughing. It was a grating sound, not much different from his hick-ish speaking voice. *He was talking about my brother, Thad! He and his wife did die in a car wreck, one year ago. They ran off into the river on the way back from the Owl Club. I'm not Clarissa's father—I'm her uncle!*

Coal stood and stared at the wall, his mind reeling. At last, the pieces all began to come together. So Linda Miley was *not* Sissy's mother, as Jennifer had seemed to believe. She was only her aunt. Then perhaps there was more hope for keeping the girls than Coal had allowed himself to believe.

Miley went on. *Anyway, that's enough questions, Sheriff. We'll be in touch. And I hope you will keep those girls safe. They mean a lot to us, and we'd sure take it bad if they were hurt.*

Coal grunted. "Yeah, I'm sure they mean the world to you." He was too angry to do anything but hang up.

Everyone in the kitchen and living room had their attention riveted on Coal as he started to curse, then abruptly stopped, looking up at his mother.

"Mr. Miley? Who is that?" Connie asked, as if he had never started to swear at all.

Coal took a deep breath, gritting his teeth. "Well, he claims Roger Miley was his brother. And his wife was the one on the line first—Linda Miley. That's Jennifer Batterton's sister. We thought Linda was Sissy's mother, but apparently there was another brother, Thad, and Sissy belonged to him and his wife, not to Linda. Either way, they want to take Cynthia and Sissy."

Maura took an involuntary step toward Coal. "They're taking the girls?"

"I didn't say that. I said they're going to *try.*"

Maura's eyes shot over to Cynthia and Sissy. "Yeah, right. *Try.* I know exactly what 'try' means." With that, she turned and walked briskly down the hall to the bathroom.

Coal turned and looked helplessly at Connie after they heard the bathroom door shut quietly. "I have no idea what she's talking about, Mom."

Connie shook her head, bewildered. "Can you... Do you want to try talking to her?"

"I think we can both guess about how that would go."

With a frown, Connie said, "You're not even giving her a chance, Son."

"I've given women chances before. Her in particular. What happened to the whole idea of learning from your mistakes?"

Connie walked close and put her hands on Coal's shoulders, looking up squarely into his eyes. "Buddy, there are some parts in life where it is worth making the same mistake a hundred times over—just on the off-chance that eventually you might do the exact same thing and it *won't* be a mistake."

"Did you and Maura go to school together? Jeez. You both talk about as cryptically as each other. I'm going for a ride," Coal growled.

"Coal!"

His mother's hard voice stopped him short. Turning back around to face her, he let his eyes pass over Sissy and Cynthia. Even the three-year-old knew something was wrong. And Cynthia, it was all she could do to keep her terror inside and hold still. Until now, he had avoided looking at her, because he had feared just what he now saw, before letting his gaze settle again on his mom.

"What, Mom?"

She came close to him again, and this time she reached out and took both of his hard hands in hers. "Son, you've got Cody all warmed up already. Why don't you ask Maura to go ride with you? You know Bolt could use some exercise too."

"Have you looked at the thermometer today? I don't think it's ten degrees out there. And there are some clouds moving in that look like they might put down a little snow. I can't imagine anybody but me would want to ride out in this. And besides, she has to go to work."

"Well, we're certainly not going to worry about that. Florin Beller will understand if she can't come to work after getting this news. I promise. So then how about a road trip? Drive up to the pass or something. Go out and show her the elk. Damnit, Coal, do *something*. That woman is crying out for help."

"Watch your language, Ma," said Coal. His attempt to lighten the mood didn't work.

"Coal. You listen to me. For once."

"You saw how well I was able to help Laura."

In sudden anger, Connie threw Coal's hands down away from her. "You have a chance to make that right! You've got to move on, Coal. I am going to get those two girls in here, and we are going to make cookies," she said through gritted teeth, lowering her voice. "So help me, if you don't talk to that woman before your kids get out of bed, I'll..."

"What?" said Coal softly.

"I'll be pretty disappointed in you. That's what."

Connie Savage knew exactly how to reach her boy, for he had spent most of his life trying to make sure he was not a disappointment in her eyes.

A long sigh came from Coal, and he turned and looked down the hall. It was a long walk to that bathroom. At least it was today.

Coal glanced at the girls, then quickly away. His pleading voice was quiet. "Then please get the girls in here now, okay? This is hard enough as it is."

Connie unhesitatingly went to the girls and coaxed them to follow her into the kitchen, where they started gathering the ingredients for chocolate chip cookies. Coal stood for half a minute longer and watched Cynthia, judging her movements as nothing but mechanical. The worst of fear filled her eyes.

Inside his mind, Coal cursed, looking one last time at his mother, and then started softly down the hall. When he reached the bathroom door, he paused, listening. He wouldn't just barge in. And even knocking could be a vast invasion of someone's privacy. After all, what if she had gone to the bathroom for... for what bathrooms were actually for? Coal felt his face get hot.

He started to knock, paused and put his ear closer to the door. What he heard was a sob. It was not a bathroom noise. With the knuckle of his middle finger, he tapped lightly. No reply. He tapped again. "Hey, Maura?"

Silence. "Maura?"

"What?" The word itself might have sounded harsh, but the voice in which it was spoken was soft. Even, perhaps, hopeful.

"Will you talk to me?"

The door cracked, then slowly swung open. Maura was looking down at his belt as she pulled the door open wider and stood out of the way, welcoming him in. He went in and shut the door very slowly, listening for what seemed an interminable time for that tell-tale click when the latch bolt slid into place in the strike. It was as if he could not begin to speak until that signal.

Maura had tried to dry her face, but she could not hide the red puffiness of her eyes. Coal stared at her. His big mouth was full of tongue and teeth and nothing to say.

His eyes flickered to one side, looking for a way out. But his mother had cut off all escape, much like she had done when she forced him as a ten-year-old to go admit to their neighbor that he had accidentally put a .22 bullet in the leg of one of their cows. Only as hard as that was, this felt worse.

An image went through Coal's mind of raising a hooked finger and lifting up Maura's chin so she was looking at him. He dismissed that instantly. That's what fathers or mothers did to their children. He thought of taking her hand—too much commitment. A hug? Too much chance of letting an emotional brahma bull out of the chute. Inside, Coal swore. He had been in the military and law enforcement long enough to know swearing solved everything.

He took a deep breath, wishing on one hand that Maura would at least look at him, and glad at the same time that she didn't. He was as big of a mess as she was. Who did he think he was kidding?

Maura's chin and lower lip began to quiver. She couldn't, or didn't, look up. The floor at Coal's feet seemed utterly fascinating.

"They took my baby girl."

Coal's eyes scrunched up in confusion. "What's that?"

"Coal... they took my baby."

Tears escaped her eyes and rolled down both cheeks, and she didn't even try to stop them. They landed on that floor that held so much interest for her.

Coal stood like a manikin. Helpless. Seemingly alone. He waited.

Maura lowered her head even farther, tucking her chin into her chest. She started to sway drunkenly, and Coal's hand darted out to catch her by the arm. "I told myself they couldn't do it, Coal, but they did it."

He sucked in a huge breath. He found no reply for her.

"Nobody helped me," she croaked. "I needed someone. A good judge. A counselor like Nancy Pearson. My mother and father. But nobody cared about me. They all left me alone. I didn't have a lawyer, and they did. And they took my baby away from me."

One second they were standing within two feet of each other, and the next thing Coal knew both of them were on their knees, and if Coal hadn't been there the woman would have fallen completely forward, as if praying to Allah. Instead, her hands fell to her thighs, bracing there, and the crown of her head rested on Coal's chest.

Coal could not stay a hard-hearted fool forever. Slowly, he put his arms out and encircled her, then cursed inside when she started crying again. He was not a man equipped to deal with the tears of a woman he cared about.

It was through a fountain of tears and a running nose that Maura managed to blubber: "I was fourteen. I had a baby. A tiny little baby girl from a man who— a man who—" The woman began to weep openly, and her hands came up from her thighs and found their way around Coal's back. His knees were hurting from the hard tile floor, but he would rather they be cut off than admit to Maura that he was in pain.

Again, he waited, gritting his teeth.

Finally, her tears slowed down, and they were close enough to the toilet that Coal could reach out and unwind a copious amount of pink Charmin from the gilded roller his mother was so proud of. He tried to dab at Maura's cheeks until she got herself together enough to untangle her arms from him, take the wad of tissue, and clean herself up, attempting to blow her nose daintily—as if any-one who had been bawling as long as she had could sound dainty when clearing their sinuses.

She kept the tissue in her fist as she slowly leaned in against Coal, her cheek against his chest, and quietly and simply breathed. "Her name was Emmie Lee. Like Katie, but spelled with two e's. She was so tiny—but strong. She could squeeze my fingers hard. Little monkey." A stray, belated sob escaped her lips. "My little monkey. Oh, Emmie Lee." A sobbing inhalation wracked her body, and for a few moments she was completely still, her ex-hausted frame holding loosely to a man incapable of giving any verbal comfort and wishing he was doing something more pleas-ant, like being dragged behind a truck through a lava field, or eat-ing mincemeat pie or thrice-gifted fruitcake.

"I was just a little girl, but I would have always loved my girl and taken care of her. I would always have kept her safe, no matter what it took. They told me nothing would happen, that I would always have her. And then they took her away from me and gave her to some white people that lived in Miles City, Montana. They told me I was too young to choose. And then that man..."

She started to shake again, and Coal could only wait it out. "That man..." Another bout of shaking, and more tears.

"He gave my parents... He gave them a real Navajo blanket and a thousand dollars to shut them up about what he did to me. And my dad drank all the money and sent me to live at a home in town. Back home, they told everybody I was a whore. That I got pregnant at a party. But when it happened, I was home. I was home. I was home..." She cried once more, and once more Coal waited, and he was starting to wonder how much saline one person could contain.

At last, his knees couldn't take the pain anymore—pain that was by now mixed in with a lot of numbness as well. "Hey, lady. Up off the floor now. Come on." He managed to stand up, his own legs wobbly now, and got her to her feet. "Come with me."

Opening the door into the hallway, he left it wide open so any-one who came seeking would know it was vacant, and he led her down the hall to his mom's room. He took her in and quietly shut the door behind them, and once he got her to sit down on the edge of the bed, he pulled off her boots and threw them on the floor.

As gently as a man with zero knowledge of women could, he eased her back onto Connie's pillow, then spread an afghan over the top of her. Last of all, he pulled off his own boots and put them beside hers, and then Coal stretched out onto the bed, his torso across Maura's, but partly supported by his elbows. His cheek touched hers, and as it did he felt one last, lonesome tear roll down and crush itself out in the valley where their skin was touching.

"Close your eyes, Maura."

"Don't go away, Coal," she whispered. "Promise me you'll stay."

He nodded, his face pressing against hers. "I'm not going any-where. I'll be here when you wake up." His voice, like hers, was a whisper. Somehow, whispering made the words seem like they came from someone else's mouth, and somehow it made him feel brave.

CHAPTER NINE

Connie Savage waited as long as she could stand. In fact, the cook-ies were already in the oven, and Sissy was sitting on Cynthia's lap at the table waiting for the timer to buzz before Connie's impa-tience got the better of her and she crept down the hall, followed by both of the dogs, who were always ready for a little intrigue.

Connie found the bathroom door standing open, with no visible proof of the emotional drama that had recently occurred inside. She saw that her bedroom door was firmly shut, and she was pretty sure she had left it ajar.

Shooing the dogs back toward the living room, she stepped quietly to her bedroom. She took a deep breath and listened to the utter stillness on the other side of the door. Raising her hand to tap on the door, she suddenly stopped. She put her ear to the wood and listened once more.

At last, she eased the door open slightly, just enough to poke her head in. She was confident enough in her own son, and in Maura as well, to know there was no hanky panky going on between them, under her own roof and especially in her own bedroom. What she saw was both of them, lying on the bed, shoes off, and to all appearances both of them fast asleep. Neither stirred at the whisper of the bottom of the door on the shag carpet.

The lower part of Coal's body was a-slant on the bed, and his torso lay across Maura, who was straight dead-center down the middle of the king-size bed. Their faces were touching, she could tell, but there was no movement.

Struck with wonder, Connie gently pulled the door shut and returned to the kitchen, wondering what had happened with her son and Maura to bring them together in what appeared to be such an intimate way. It was obviously more than simply physical attraction. They were both fully clothed and unmoving, and if physical attraction had suddenly overcome them, they probably would have left and gone back to Maura's house.

In time, Coal might tell Connie what had happened. If he didn't, then perhaps Maura would. If neither volunteered, then Connie would never know. One thing she had always prided herself on was her strength of character and her ability to mind her own business.

*   *   *

In Connie's bedroom, Maura had fallen into exhausted sleep. Emotional breakdowns, Coal knew, could bring on sleep faster than hard physical labor. And the emotional trauma of Maura's memories, held in for who-knew-how-long, was huge. Even though the release had washed out her soul, a feeling Coal remembered well from the day he had finally been able to cry over Laura, it was a draining experience. If she slept for two hours it would not have surprised him.

Coal moved a little farther away from her, so he would be in contact with her, his arm draped over her, but not his whole torso, which position had been making his arms and shoulders go to sleep. He wiggled his face in on the same pillow she was using, which put his nose in direct contact with her soft golden hair. It smelled of shampoo and remotely of the women's cologne, *Chamade,* which Coal was embarrassed to admit he recognized, since he wasn't exactly anyone's first image as a connoisseur of women's perfume. But in a last-ditch effort at romance with Laura, he had bought her a bottle of that scent back in sixty-nine, and it might likely stay with him forever—mostly because in one of her fits of anger she had shattered the entire bottle against their bedroom wall.

The two scents kept Coal from smelling the normal lilac odor of the room, coupled with the smells of horses—not all of them good. It was cool in the room, since the stove was what heated the bedrooms, and the door had been shut for quite some time.

Coal felt his arm rise slightly each time Maura took in a deep breath, but she didn't move. Her slumber seemed to be deep and all-encompassing. He lay there thinking of the road ahead. He had no idea who Bud and Linda Miley truly were. What kind of people. What kind of power they could wield. How determined they might be. All he knew was that Maura had become extremely attached to the two girls she had chosen as her protegées, and now Coal thought he finally understood why. Ever since the age of fourteen, this woman had carried with her the emotional burden of having a child, a daughter, she had carried to full-term "stolen" from her— at least stolen in her eyes. She seemed to be doing a good job raising two sons, but losing her first child that way had affected her more deeply than even Coal probably realized. Now she must feel she had a chance to start over. She must have started setting her mind on somehow adopting the two girls, or at least Sissy. That was Coal's guess, anyway, even if that was all it was.

Having the Mileys show up and swear to take those girls away was a blow to the woman that she was not prepared to handle. And Coal, because he cared about Maura, and because he also had a bad feeling about the Mileys, had to do everything in his legal power to keep them from winning.

It was under Coal's watch that four of his best friends had been killed. If he lost a legal battle with the Mileys now too, he was going to feel pretty worthless as the so-called protector of the citizens of Lemhi County.

Coal had promised Maura that he would be with her when she awoke. He had things he wanted and needed to get done today, but right now he did not care. He had broken too many promises in his life. This was one he must keep.

*   *   *

Maura PlentyWounds dreamed of being in a dark room. It was damp and cold, and everywhere she turned she encountered a wall. Suddenly, a light appeared, apparently a candle, and she walked toward it. It glowed in the direction of one of the walls she had touched, but now that wall was not there, and the candle seemed to float along down an extremely long, winding corridor. She kept trying to reach out toward it, but when she did it would flicker and almost die, and the flame would bend away from her. It was as if it was beckoning her to follow.

Maura walked after the candle, afraid to run and frighten it away. She began to hear a voice. So distant. At first it almost sounded like wind whistling around a door frame. Then it took on the voice of a girl—perhaps a young woman. She could not make out any words at first, but then as it grew louder and louder there was one word. It sounded familiar, but strangely, she could not place it.

She realized the candle was moving faster and faster and getting farther away from her, and she began to run. Suddenly, the candle dropped from in front of her as if it had been let go, and instinctively she came to a stop. As she looked down, she could see the candle, tumbling away below her into an abyss.

Then she heard another voice, the voice of a woman. She tried to shake herself out of a mental and emotional fog. She recognized a name, and then she heard words.

Her eyes snapped awake, and looking up she saw Coal Savage sitting up on the bed beside her, and Connie was speaking to him. The woman looked past Coal's head and saw Maura as she struggled to sit up in the soft bed.

"I'm so sorry I woke you up, Maura. Please forgive me. You seemed to be having a bad dream."

Maura shook her head groggily, looking over at Coal. She seemed confused to see him there, and she blinked her eyes forcefully. "It's okay," she managed to say. "I'm fine."

Coal turned his head and looked at Maura, giving her a small smile. Then he turned back to his mother.

"What did she say exactly?"

"Just that she needed to see you as soon as you could come. She sounded pretty upset."

"All right." Coal stood up from the bed. His mother had just informed him that Kathy MacAtee had called. He hadn't seen Kathy in a week or more, it seemed, and he had sworn to check in on her and the girls more often. Now he silently cursed himself for neglecting that vow.

He turned and looked at Maura, stiffly conscious that his mother was still standing behind him. He put one knee on the bed and reached out to rub Maura's shoulder. "You okay?"

She smiled sleepily without showing her teeth. "I am."

"Good. Well, I've got to run out to the MacAtees' for a while, okay? Mom has some cookies she and the girls made. I'll try not to be too long."

Maura smiled again, and Coal thought he saw her eyes get misty. "Thanks. I'll be fine."

He turned to go, and her voice stopped him. "Coal?"

"Yeah?"

"Thank you for staying with me."

He paused, then nodded. "Hey, that's what friends are for, right?"

She just nodded, and he left the room, leaving the two women alone. He could hear his mother telling Maura that she had called McPherson's for her and had a talk with her boss, Florin Beller, about why she was late.

In the kitchen, Coal took a deep breath of the homey aroma and grabbed a couple of warm cookies, winking and smiling at Sissy, who sat at the table with cookies and a glass of milk. Caught in the room with no other adults, she stared at him, too startled to offer even the slightest facial expression in return.

Coal walked to Cynthia, who was standing at the oven.

"Hey, you doing okay?"

"Yes," she said and smiled.

"We're going to make sure everything is taken care of, all right? You try not to worry."

"Okay. I'll try."

On a whim, he reached out and stroked her hair. "I'll be back soon. Just have to go check on a friend."

Connie came into the kitchen and walked over to Coal, reaching up to rub his arm. "Hey, honey, before you go, could you go back to Maura for a little bit. She wants to tell you something."

"Hey, Mom, what about Kathy? Isn't she waiting?"

"I think Maura might be a little more important right now. Just give her a minute, okay?"

"All right." He nodded, and turning, he went back to Connie's room. The door was ajar, but he tapped on it anyway.

"I'm good." He smiled and stepped inside, shutting the door behind him and standing at it for a moment.

"Yes, you are," he finally said.

Maura smiled at him, lying on the bed propped up by three pillows. She raised her hands out to him, and looking at her curiously he went to her and sat on the bed. "What's up?"

"I have to tell you something before you go."

"Okay?"

"I feel stupid, Coal, but I just don't know if I'll ever find a way to tell you this if I don't do it now."

"I'm all ears then." He felt himself start to get warm, a result of discomfort rather than peace.

Maura slid her hand across the bed spread until her fingers closed over his. Now he *knew* this was going to be uncomfortable: He hadn't made that move of commitment, but the woman had.

"Coal, you know how I acted at the counselor's office?"

"Yeah, sure. It's okay, I—"

"Please. This is hard enough."

This time, he just nodded.

"I still feel stupid about that, but I at least have to explain, and then just hope you won't think I'm crazy."

Well, you are *a woman,* he thought.

"I wanted those girls to get help. I wanted it really bad. And Katie, too. But then I started thinking about when I got hurt, when I was... when I got pregnant and had my baby girl, and then they took her from me and sent me away." Apparently, Maura had cried herself out, for now there were no tears.

"I never got any help. From anyone. It was just the opposite, in fact. No one cared about me, even my own parents. In fact, maybe they were the worst. Coal, I've never told a soul about this. I've been trying to hold it all inside. But the other day, it just hit me how unfair it all was for me, a little girl, barely old enough to have a child, and left alone like that, with no one to defend me. No one to counsel me. I started feeling like I was jealous of Cynthia and Sissy for getting the help no one ever cared about trying to get for me. And now I know how bad it sounds of me."

"It doesn't sound bad. It sounds human. And it never made you think less of those girls."

Maura took in a deep breath. "There is some bad stuff coming, isn't there, Coal?"

"I hope not."

She grunted quietly. "Hope or not, it's coming. I have been there before. And I don't know if I can face this kind of thing again."

"You're a strong woman." Coal could think of nothing more comforting to say.

"I am sick of being strong. I just want to be a little girl again— a little girl that somebody actually cares about."

* * *

The low-hanging sky was starting to spit snow as Coal drove out to the MacAtees' with Dobe and Shadow in the back seat, panting. It wasn't that it was hot in the car, but the excitement of getting to go for a drive always made them pant anyway.

As he turned into the MacAtee place, Coal couldn't help his eyes being drawn to the straw stack, and he thought of Larry lying there. The rust-spotted white truck was still parked in exactly the same place, a little dim in the low light and among the ever-thick-ening snowflakes. Gritting his teeth, he pulled his eyes away and drove up to the house, throwing the car in park and piling out with a departing command to the dogs to stay.

Kathy MacAtee opened the front door and came out onto the porch, still wearing house slippers, and a robe over her clothes. Her eyes were full of worry.

Oblivious to the snow that began sticking in her hair, she stepped off the porch and met him before he made it far from the car, giving him a fierce bear hug. "I'm so sorry to bother you, Coal. I really need you, though. Something is wrong with Rowdy."

His feeling of curiosity turned immediately to concern. "What? Where is he?"

"He's in here." She turned and led the way.

The black and white Border collie was stretched out on the couch, with the MacAtee girls, Milo, Sara, and Jen, gathered around him. Poor little eleven-year-old Jen's eyes were puffy from crying.

Rowdy lay still on the couch, raising only his head and thumping his tail a few times to greet his master's friend. Coal immediately crouched down, patting Jen on the shoulder and giving it a squeeze. "Hi, girls. What's our little buddy doing?" He could feel Kathy beside him.

The girls all looked up at their mother, and dark-haired sixteen-year-old Milo took charge of replying. "We couldn't get him to eat for two days, and now he's just lying here and doesn't seem like he can get up."

Coal rested his hand gently on the dog's ribs. "Can't, or doesn't want to?"

Milo shrugged, and Kathy put her hand on Coal's back and crouched down beside him. "We haven't tried to force him up yet. I wanted to see what you thought first and if he would react different to you than to us."

Coal wiggled a finger up inside the dog's mouth and felt his upper gum. It was sticky. "When's the last time he drank anything?"

"Maybe yesterday morning," Milo replied.

Coal nodded. "He's pretty dehydrated." One glance at the animal's nose told him the same thing, and when he felt it it was warmer than it should have been. The same was true for the skin behind his ears. "He's got a bit of a fever, too. Let's see what happens if we try to stand him up, okay? Give us some room."

He stood up and then sat down at Rowdy's head, stroking him down the length of his body. "Hey, old buddy. Not feeling good, huh?" Rowdy's reply was a couple of wags of the tail.

Coal reached down under his head to his shoulder and started hefting him, telling Kathy to get his bottom end. Together, they got him off the couch and knelt beside him, steadying him as they set him on his feet. He stayed standing, but he was shaking badly and started to sway. He just looked up at Coal, a helpless light in his eyes.

"Well, girls, I think we had probably better see if the vet's open today."

Kathy looked up at Coal with concern. "Coal, with the funeral and everything, I'm not sure how much I have left right now. How much do you think it will be?"

"We're not going to worry about that right now, sweetie. If you can't pay it, just remember I'm a rich sheriff now."

Kathy stopped herself just shy of crying. "Thank you, Coal. Okay. But I'll pay you back for anything you spend."

"That's not really fair." He reached out and squeezed her arm. "I mean, he's my buddy too."

That time the tears made it into Kathy's eyes as she smiled at him. The girls seemed to have taken on a huge feeling of hope, now that Coal was here.

He leaned over and got the dog under his body, standing up with him. "I'll get him in your car, okay? And then I'll follow you in. I'd take him, but I have Dobe and Shadow with me."

Of course, the girls all insisted on going to the vet's too, so after they got Rowdy loaded up, Coal sat with him and waited while the four of them got dressed. Rowdy just kept looking up at him with those dark, expressive eyes. There was no pleading, however. The look was one of resignation.

As the snowflakes fell around them, Coal looked again at the straw stack and thought of Larry's funeral, and the tragedy of it all. He looked back down at Rowdy, his old friend. He didn't want to know it and would have given anything not to, but his gut instinct told him what was happening here.

Rowdy had lost his buddy, and he had held out as long as he could, waiting for him to come home.

Rowdy was giving up.

CHAPTER TEN

The veterinarian, Scott Darger, had not been hopeful for Rowdy. They had taken the dog directly to his house, because he wasn't open on the weekend, but Dr. Darger was a kind man, with a genuine love for animals, so he did not turn them away.

He had checked him over and said that yes, he had a slightly elevated temperature, but nothing dangerous. He was simply dehydrated and lethargic, weak and unsteady on his feet, the latter three things all a product of his dehydration and lack of nutrition.

"I'm not really sure what to tell you to do," Dr. Darger had said. "Just give him a lot of love and try to see if he won't drink something, maybe some warm chicken broth with a lot of extra water in it. I'll come out to your house and put him on a line and get some fluids in him if nothing changes pretty soon. I'd do it now, but I don't have everything I need here with me."

Now Coal sat holding Rowdy on the sofa in the MacAtees' living room, with Milo and Jen on his left, Sara on his right, and Kathy kneeling at his feet. Jen and Sara were both teary-eyed.

Coal looked up and met Kathy's gaze just as she looked up from the dog. "We all miss him, Kathy. I guess Rowdy just feels it deeper."

The tears swam in Kathy's eyes once more. "Yeah. We all miss him."

Thinking of his old friend Larry, Coal could almost hear him chiding the lot of them, saying to *Just give Rowdy some burger and he'll be all right.* Larry might even be surprised to know his dog was so attached to him that he would stop eating and drinking because he was gone.

Coal kept stroking the dog's soft fur, and where Kathy's right hand was on the dog's neck, he reached up and took her fingers, squeezing them. "Just keep trying to get some water in him. Maybe warm up some chicken or beef broth—lukewarm. Get something in him. He's just in a funk. Depressed. He could still come out of it if you can start getting a little into him. Just don't overdo it until he starts getting his energy back. Chances are by tomorrow afternoon he'll be eating you out of house and home again."

Kathy smiled through her tears. "Okay, Coal. We'll try."

When Coal had gotten up a while later and settled Rowdy back down on the laps of the three girls, he crouched in front of them and ruffled the dog's head. He finally leaned forward and put his forehead against Rowdy's, and this elicited a quiet whine from the dog. "Yeah, buddy, we miss him too." He patted the intelligent old head and stood up. Kathy stood with him.

Outside, the snow had stopped, with less than half an inch on the ground. Coal opened the inner door and stood looking out. It was still dark and gloomy, in spite of the fact that it was noon, and the mountains to the north were once again blanketed in dingy white under the low-hung blanket of clouds.

Kathy leaned sideways against Coal, and he encircled her with his arm, putting the side of his face down on top of her head. "Don't give up on him, Kathy. Just show him a lot of love like Doctor Darger said. That might be all you can do."

She managed a nod, no more.

"I want Larry back, Coal," she said quietly, after twenty seconds of silence. "We had so much more life left to live together."

"Larry will never leave you, Kathy. No one who is loved as much as you girls loved him ever truly goes away."

*   *   *

Bud Miley was short, nearly bald, overweight, red-faced, and homely. To those who knew him very well, he was downright ugly. What hair he did have was so thin and pale blond that it looked white, and it only showed up as well as it did on the back of his head and over his ears because of the ruddy complexion of his skin.

He sat on a hard bed in a room at the new Stagecoach Inn, twirling a yo-yo around on the end of a tangled string and staring at his equally unattractive wife, Linda. "Don't start getting any ideas about keeping those girls, dummy. I can see the wheels turning in your head."

Linda, a woman of perhaps forty-five years of age who looked somewhat younger because she was caked with makeup and had great big, fluffy, honey blond hair, stood at the television set across the room from her husband, fiddling with a bent antenna to try and get better reception. It would have been nearly impossible for Bud or anyone else to see even a sliver of the television screen with her standing there, because the size of her butt, in far too tight-fitting jeans, rivalled the rump of a horse, and fat sprawled over the top of her jeans like the protruding sides of a muffin.

She turned to her husband and extended her middle finger, which made him call her a bad name, only slightly in jest. "I'm not thinking about keeping them. Not for very long, anyway. You obviously don't know me very well. But on second thought, they might be better company than you!"

Bud chuckled. Even a laugh on his face didn't do his looks any favors. As the old saying went, "beauty is only skin deep—but ugly goes clear to the bone."

"Just so you remember," he said, staring through her face.

"I'll remember. Just shut up."

"So you wanna go get something to eat?"

"Yeah, I'm hungry."

"Sheesh. You're *always* hungry. Look at you. Turning into the Goodyear Blimp."

Linda stuck her tongue out at him, replying in a whiny but cigarette-roughened voice. "Look who's talkin'!"

"Yeah, right!" He poked his generous belly with a finger, and it hardly sank in at all. "It might stick out, but it's hard as a rock. You're not!"

"Right. Women keep their fat on the outside, and men keep it inside, and if you ever bothered to read *Cosmopolitan* you'd know that!"

"Oh, Judas Priest, woman. Right, like I'm going to sit and read about what positions one woman thinks some other woman should enjoy and why. Besides, ever since they had that buck naked centerfold of Burt Reynolds in there I'm sick to think of what I would find next."

"Yeah, I guess that would intimidate you, wouldn't it?"

"Not me, Dumpy."

"Call me Dumpy!" She turned and launched the *TV Guide* at him, and he dodged it. She shook her chest at him. "If I wasn't dumpy, I wouldn't have these."

"Not to mention a great plastic surgeon! And you'd also be kicking turds down the road if you didn't have those. Come on." He suddenly lunged up off the bed. "Grab the phone book and let's go find some place to sit down and eat. We've gotta start locating some lawyers before Monday so we can get this ball rolling."

Going outside, they climbed into their red Buick Riviera. After ordering Linda to get a beer out of the back seat and pop the cap for him, Bud Miley shoved half the long neck in his mouth to take a few swallows, then thrust it back at Linda, threw the car in reverse and backed up, then spun his tires out of the parking lot and back out onto Ninety-three.

Monday, December 11

Coal got up Monday morning still feeling uneasy to know Maura and the two girls were living under the same roof with him. They had even gone so far the day before as to move Maura's four horses into Connie's expansive pasture, and her official horse-harassers, Chewy and Dart, the heelers, were living out in the barn.

Coal had warned Maura about the dangers of that last move, since Cody, the big gray, was not tolerant of dogs and had a lightning-fast right rear leg. But Maura seemed ready to deal with the consequences, so the one-time Savage ranch became the Savage Zoo.

Connie had already been outside taking care of the horses, a three times bigger job now but one he knew she was up to, and her red cheeks and nose attested to the bitter cold that had settled over the Lemhi Valley.

With Dobe and Shadow in the lead, Coal came down the stairs still barefooted, carrying his boots, with his shirt hanging open. It was a morning to get to the front of the Franklin stove as fast as humanly possible before frost started forming on his mustache.

Maura, busy in the kitchen frying bacon and tending to a huge pot of cornmeal mush, saw him from the corner of her eye and laughed when she looked over to see his shirt hanging open to reveal the valley of muscular striations in the center of his chest. "Trying to look like Burt Reynolds this morning? If you are, you're wearing too much."

Coal grunted. "Hardly. I'm just trying to get down here where it's warm. I think I'm going to start sleeping on the couch if the whole winter's going to be like this."

"Me too!" Maura replied with a wicked grin.

Coal stood there with a mock reproving look on his face as he buttoned up his green plaid shirt. "Well, at least you have a bed partner to keep you warm."

"Well, there *is* only one couch," said Maura with a wink.

Connie looked over, all grins, while she was pulling off her coat in preparation for jumping into the chore of helping with breakfast. "It's much better than one of the dogs crawling into bed, Coal."

As he finished buttoning the shirt, he suddenly snapped his fingers! "Hey, that's it! New rule: No dogs sleeping by the stove. From now on, they're in my bed."

Maura giggled. "I see how it is. You prefer dogs. Okay, fine. Well, then you should bring Chewy and Dart in out of the barn and you can let them in bed with you too. Four-dog nights!"

As the aroma of breakfast floated through the house, Coal threw two more logs into the stove, then glanced at his watch. "What time does the bus come, Mom?"

Connie looked at him and frowned. "You're joking, right?"

"What? Is it a holiday?"

"No, it's not a holiday. I just can't believe you don't know when the bus comes yet."

Coal shrugged her off, tucking his shirt into his tan Dickies. Then he sat on his favorite chair to tug his boots on his feet. Without another word about bus times, because he had already had enough criticism for one day, he went upstairs and opened Virgil's door. "Hey, Virg. Time to get up."

Never one to let a pillow hold him down, Virgil sat up instantly, making his father smile. Coal went to the twins' room and looked in at them, walking in to shake them awake. Unlike their brother, it wasn't with springs that they came out of bed.

When Coal came back downstairs, he went into the kitchen and commandeered a strip of bacon, biting off half of it as he looked approvingly around at the spread his two cooks were preparing.

"Looks like this living arrangement might work out okay after all," he said, grinning when Maura looked over at him. "As long as you don't make the cornmeal too thin, of course. Then I'd have to send you back for re-training."

"Ha! I'll tell *you* who needs some re-training!" She playfully slapped his arm.

Coal walked over to lean against the countertop. "I left the girls for one of you to wake up. And I also wanted to ask what your thoughts are about Cynthia."

"What about her?" asked Connie.

"Well, she can't stay out of school for the rest of her life. When do we decide if she's ready?"

"Don't be a typical man, Son," replied Connie reprovingly. "What has it been, something like nine days? She's a teenage girl. Both of her parents were killed violently. Nine days isn't much time for an emotional recovery after something like that."

He pondered that and tried to ignore the hurtful comment about typical men. "So what is too much and what is not enough? You can't baby somebody for the rest of her life."

"I think I want to go back to school today."

No one had seen Cynthia Batterton walk in from down the hall.

CHAPTER ELEVEN

Coal, Connie, and Maura stood in the kitchen, stunned. Coal was undoubtedly the most stunned of all, since it was his big mouth from which the poor girl had heard that last pronouncement come. What did a man say now? In all his years of stumbling over his lips and tongue, Coal couldn't remember many times being caught more flat-footed than this. To run to the girl and apologize would look fake, and it would make him look stupid in front of Maura and his mother. But to stand there would make him look like an ogre. So to try to play it off as something smaller seemed his only choice.

Coal took a deep breath. "I guess we need to talk, Cynthia."

"It's okay. I don't really want to right now."

When she spoke, she looked directly at him, her expression stoic. If she had cried and run back down the hall he would have felt better. In the face of this kind of reaction, he was lost.

"No, we need to talk." His voice was firm. He was playing his last card, while heat raged through the house and all of it was aimed right at him.

"Okay." Even though the word was one of agreement, Cynthia just stared at him, her face blank, noncommittal. To say Coal felt two inches high was to make him seem gigantic. He felt more like the egg of an ant—and wished right now that he was buried under a similar rock.

Machine-like, he walked to the girl and took her by the upper arm. She didn't fight that. He turned his face halfway and said, "Mom, we'll be in your room for a while."

And then down the hall they went.

Coal eased the girl inside his mom's room, his heart galloping. He had no idea what he was going to say, so his mind was spinning like a tornado. He was just going to have to play it by ear.

"Let's sit down." He motioned at the bed. When she sat on its edge, he drew up a chair backwards in front of her and eased into it, holding onto the back as if it were a shield between them.

"Are you ready to go back to school?" He didn't know what to say but something direct.

"Yes."

Dead space. An expressionless face, a face hiding hurt Coal knew was inside and understood and felt suddenly incapable of ever healing. It was like the man she trusted most had thrown her into a lion's den.

"I'm at a loss what to say here. You heard me say something in the kitchen just now that must have sounded terrible to you. It wasn't meant that way. I have to go to work today, and I can't go through the day thinking you believe I'm somehow angry with you, or disappointed. I'm not. Not one bit."

"You think I'm being babied."

There. She had said it. The words were out, and he could not deny them. But now, instead of dread, he felt relief.

"Nobody is babying you, Cynthia. Not me, not anyone. I was speaking of things in the future. There isn't a soul in this house who is old enough to understand life who would think you have been babied."

Her face remained stone-cold. Her voice did too. "I'm sorry I made you feel like you had to stay at Maura's with me Friday night."

Coal stared at her. He was hoping she wouldn't bring that up, but of course it would be her first reaction to the "babying" comment. Coal's mind whirled. Was there anything he had learned in his past to fix this? What did this girl need this very moment? What kind of medicine would make her feel better? Or did he just wait? Could he buy her some flowers later, or send her a note? Maybe this would just go away.

But it wouldn't go away. It was here to stay, because suddenly Coal knew he could not fix it. He had opened his mouth at exactly the wrong time and said exactly the wrong thing. It was there between them again, and Cynthia Batterton would never feel about him or look at him the same again.

"I will always cherish the closeness I felt with you that night, Cynthia. Please don't feel like you ever have to apologize for that."

She tried to stare him down until finally her eyes filled up with the tears she had been trying to delay. Then she dropped her eyes to the hands folded up in her lap. "Okay, if you say so."

Emasculated and sad, he stood up. "Well, if you're going to try and go to school, I guess you'd better get ready, huh? Let's get some breakfast."

"I'm not hungry. I'll go get dressed."

She got up off the bed, opened the bedroom door and shut it partway behind her. Coal was left standing there alone, wishing he was under fire in some friendly jungle in Vietnam.

*   *   *

Coal dialed up Kathy MacAtee before leaving the house, although now he had the Cynthia incident on his mind.

"Hey, Kathy. Sorry to call so early. How's our boy doing?"

Good morning, Coal. Well, he drank a tiny little bit yesterday, but only because we poured it in his mouth. I don't think he even got an eighth of a cup.

"Okay. Well, that's something, right? Just keep trying today, and don't forget to try the broth. If I get a chance, I'll come over later. I don't know how my day's going to go."

If you can it would be nice. Please don't make a special trip, though.

"Hey," Coal chided. "Rowdy's my buddy too, you know."

All right then. We'd love to see you, Coal. You know that.

After hanging up, Coal went straight to the jail, where he greeted big Jordan Peterson as he was getting ready to head home.

"You're kind of late getting out of here."

"Yeah." The night jailer tried to meet his eyes, but he couldn't seem to.

"What's up, Jordan?"

"Um... Well... Oh, it's nothing."

"You're not a man to hem and haw around. I just left a bad situation at home that involved a teenage girl, big guy. I have no idea how to talk to one of them, but I sure do know how to talk to you. And I can see something's on your mind. I'm going to make a wild guess and ask if you've hung around just to talk to me."

Jordan forced a grin. "Yeah, okay. You guess pretty good. Well, I'm thinking I might have to leave here and find some other work."

"What?" Coal was stunned—and instantly unhappy.

"Sheriff, I can barely pay my rent and my car payment. I'm scraping by at the end of every month. I've had to start shooting jackrabbits just to get meat in my diet."

Coal sighed. "Damnit. All right. I knew you jailers weren't making enough. I've been meaning to go talk to the county clerk, but you know how busy I've been."

"Oh, yeah, of course! I wouldn't ever think—"

"Buddy, don't even try to make excuses for me," Coal cut him off. "You can't eat dirt. I know it, and I've just gotten preoccupied and left you with few choices. How bad is it? How much do you need?"

"No! Nothin', Sheriff! I won't take anything from you, and I sure won't let you get anything out of petty cash, not after what happened to K.T."

"Damnit, Jordan, how much?" Coal pressed. "I'll go talk to my friend Rick Cheatum today. Promise. But in the meantime, I can't have a starving jailer, and there's a lot of you to feed."

Jordan laughed, blushing. "Yeah, I'm kind of a big ox."

"You're a good big ox, Jordan. I don't want to take a chance on losing you." Coal pulled out his wallet and slipped a twenty dollar bill out of it, handing it to the deputy.

"Wait! Sheriff, no. That's way too much—and it's your own money."

"Jordan, if you call me 'sheriff' one more time, you're fired, got it?"

Embarrassed again, Jordan laughed. "Okay, right. Coal. But that's too much. You're not John D. Rockefeller."

"No, and you're not a sparrow. You've got to eat, buddy. That's final. Take the damn money or I'll cram it down your throat. And I guarantee you a good burger downtown will taste a lot better than government paper."

Jordan reached out slowly and took the twenty from Coal's fingers. "I'll pay you back every dime, Coal. I promise you that."

"You'll pay me back by not quitting on me. That's just your Christmas bonus. When I'm on my next day off I'll drive the family to Idaho Falls in the county car and use their gas. It'll be a fair trade." He stopped suddenly and looked quickly around the office. "I guess I shouldn't make comments like that, huh? I might end up without a job myself!" he said, half in fun, half seriously.

Jordan laughed. "Ned Harpy had his release this morning. His time was up. So I'm the only one here."

"Oh, good. Yeah, speaking of being alone, where's Todd?"

"I think you signed him up to come in at noon, right?"

Coal grinned. "Oh, yeah, probably. Keep me on track. That's another reason I need you around."

"Well, I'm going to go get a bite before I go home to bed," Jordan said. "Thanks again, Coal. This means an awful lot to me."

"Good jailers are hard to come by. Get out of here."

After Jordan had gone, Coal sat at his desk cleaning his Smith and Wesson. It didn't need cleaning, but he liked the smell of Hoppe's 9 and gun oil, and the mechanical movements helped him to think.

"First things first..." He was startled to realize he had spoken the words out loud, and it made him chuckle. He had to go talk to Rick Cheatum as he had promised. He had to try and get something moving for both of his night jailers. He couldn't expect them to stay around for the wages the county had been paying. Then he had to go see Judge Wiley Sinclair and talk to him about the phone call from the Mileys. He couldn't take the chance that those girls might be stolen from him, legally or otherwise. And really, they would not be stolen from *him* anyway. Somehow, he knew Maura had gotten it into her mind that those girls would end up with her. And in her emotionally wounded mind she thought they could make up for the little baby she had lost so long ago.

But of course there was something even more immediate, and perhaps more important. Both of those girls had suffered some kind of emotional trauma. Cynthia's was obvious. Sissy's, no one seemed yet to understand. But unless perhaps she was simply shy by nature, something had happened to her, too, something to make her fear people, especially men. The chances for her recovering from whatever had happened to her before were going to plummet, Coal feared, if two total strangers came and took her away. And especially strangers, Coal sensed, that had some kind of ulterior motive he did not yet grasp.

There was a fourth problem Coal had to deal with, but one he had no tools for in his toolbox. He had to somehow reach Cynthia and let her know how he truly felt and that what she had heard was not what it had sounded like. That was a puzzle he might as well have tried walking on water as to try and solve.

Getting up, Coal went and looked into the jail, out of habit. It was empty. That made him feel happy. He wished it would stay that way forever. He wanted to think Salmon was a law-abiding place.

Going back to the desk, he wiped his revolver down with a rag and reloaded it, then thrust it into the holster and snapped it in. He made a quick phone call to Doctor Nancy Pearson, in Idaho Falls, to set up another appointment for the girls. Then he went out and got into the LTD, driving down the hill to the bank. His friend Rick Cheatum was in his office shuffling through some paperwork, with a half-eaten chocolate donut near his hand. Sight of it instantly made Coal's mouth water.

"Hey, amigo!" said Cheatum, looking up. "Jeez, did you lose your house or something? What brings you in this dingy place?"

Coal laughed. The office, and in fact the entire building, were anything but dingy. Furnished tastefully and beautifully, with immaculate woodwork and carpet, it was the kind of place Coal wished he could come to every day—providing it was still a sheriff's office and not a bank.

"Just came in to rattle your chain—and see if you have another one of those donuts!"

Now it was Rick's turn to laugh. His smile and laugh were contagious, and doubtlessly one of the reasons that he had so many friends in the valley. "Well, Janet brought them in." He motioned toward one of the tellers. "Want me to see if there are any left?"

"No!" Coal said quickly, holding up his hands. "You don't actually think that's on the bodybuilding diet, do you?"

"No, but I thought maybe you grew out of that phase," said Cheatum with a giggle, poking playfully at Coal's midsection. "Huh. Guess not!"

Coal laughed, but then his face went serious. "Say, Rick, there actually is a reason I'm here. A kind of big one. But take off your banker hat and put on your county commissioner hat for a minute. I'm going to lose one of my jailers if I don't figure out how to get him a raise. Don't you think the county could swing for even fifty bucks more a month?"

"Fifty a month? I don't know, Coal. There's always talk of cutting things out of the budget. The whole financial world is starting to talk about the oil thing, and Lemhi is reacting to it about like everyone else. But of course I'll talk to Nate Hanson if you want."

"Man, Rick, seriously, if I could even get some kind of a stipend, a check that could be written out in my name once or twice a month, I'll go to the store with him if I have to, just to make sure he isn't squandering it. You've got to help me out. There's no way I can run that office without a good jailer. You know that."

"Okay, Coal. Okay." Cheatum reached out and squeezed his arm. "I'll do what I can, all right? Jeez. It's like you're begging for yourself."

"No, I wouldn't be here if it was for me. I'd just starve."

Cheatum laughed. "Yeah, that's probably true. Or you'd be out picking up road kill."

"Which isn't a bad idea at that!" agreed Coal with a laugh.

After the bank, Coal returned to the courthouse on his next mission. Unlike the bank and Rick Cheatum, he was not going to leave Judge Wiley Sinclair with a hopeful smile on his face.

The answer became pretty plain in a very short few minutes: It did not matter one whit whether Bud and Linda Miley were Sissy's parents or not. Blood relation was blood relation. With a little re-search, a few bucks for certificates of birth, and a form of photo identification, if Linda and Bud Miley really were who they claimed to be, they would be able to walk right up to the front door of the Savage house and walk away with two helpless girls, whether the girls wanted to go or not.

There was not one thing Coal could do legally to stop them.

CHAPTER TWELVE

Coal went home early that afternoon. A day that had started out in the pre-dawn darkness at fifteen below zero had skyrocketed all the way to seven above by three o'clock, but the sun was well on its way behind the mountains now, and although it didn't feel like it was going to be as bitterly cold as the night before, it was not going to be horse riding weather either.

The house was empty and cold. Everyone, including the dogs, was gone, and Coal found the Franklin stove banked with firewood but consuming it fast. He wiggled two more logs in on top, breath-ing in the homey fragrance of the escaping smoke-demons, then sat down for a minute on the couch and stared into the abyss of the blackened wood and the orange tendrils of flame that began to lick back and forth over the new lodgepole pine.

Judging by the clock on the wall, school would be letting out in another fifteen minutes or so, and then the house was going to get noisy again. Coal sighed. He loved his children deeply, but mo-ments of peace like this did not come often enough.

On a whim, he got up and shrugged back into his heavy blue and black buffalo plaid coat, rocking his hat onto his head. He shook his pocket to make sure that was where he had dropped the keys, then went back out and got into the LTD.

Firing it up, he drove back to town, but to the high school, on Daisy, instead of back to the courthouse. Slipping into the empty hall in the last five minutes before the bell, he asked the secretary to page Cynthia Batterton, then waited anxiously for her to come, hoping she would arrive before the school erupted in noise-makers.

To his good fortune, Cynthia was the first person he saw coming around the corner. He was disappointed to see a slight pause in her step as she recognized him standing there, but he smiled to pretend he hadn't seen.

"Hi, Cynthia. How did your day go?"

"Okay." She stopped in front of him, her folded arms snuggling a couple of books up close to her body.

"I'd like to take you for a drive." He had to state his intention fast. Otherwise, he was afraid he would think of some other excuse, tell her hello, and then just leave.

Looking slightly bewildered, she glanced around. Before she could reply, the end-of-school bell rang, signaling a general rush of students from behind every opening door.

The flood of children seemed psychologically to propel her closer to him, but it also distracted her from whatever answer she had been about to give.

"Would that be okay with you?" he pressed.

"Um... Sure."

He smiled. "Want me to pack those books? That's quite a load." His attempt at humor was lost on her.

"No, I can hold them." Her face was as straight as a ruler.

"Okay. Come on before we get trampled in the stampede."

They went out, and the buses were starting to line up already. Coal opened the car door for her and then shut it after she climbed in. He went to the other side and revved it up, then started to drive slowly through the mass migration of escaping students.

As they were passing the last bus, he saw Cynthia wave at someone and glanced over out of pure reflex. There, staring at his passing car and its passengers, were Katie and Virgil. The looks on their faces could only be described as surprise.

Coal didn't even have a chance to wave, because the kids' bus hid them from view as he passed it. Thinking of their expressions, he found himself feeling a little guilty. He probably should have at least told them where he and Cynthia were going. But the crowd was too heavy, and it was too late to turn back.

Coal kept the Ford cruising on down the street, turned at the next block, and then went west for a block before they could turn again and finally make the last turn that put them back onto Main Street. He made a mental note of Wally's Cafe, on their left, as they passed. He had been meaning to visit Wally and Beulah ever since returning to the valley, but no time had ever seemed right for that kind of reunion. If his visit with Cynthia went as he hoped, perhaps they would stop there on the way back home.

The car, other than the hum of the tires on the pavement and the crackle of scattered gravel, was quiet. Cynthia stared out her window, very studiously keeping her eyes in that direction.

Coal turned onto Highway 93, and they drove toward Carmen, still in silence. After leaving behind the town limits, he turned and looked at the girl.

"Hey, can we talk?"

She turned her head. "Sure." She tried to look perky. It didn't work. There was something dead behind the look in her eyes. Something lost, and perhaps betrayed.

"Cynthia, you know I'm just an ignorant man, right? Sometimes men say things that might sound pretty harsh."

She just stared. Deer in headlights appeared to be deeper in thought.

Coal drew in another breath and sighed it out and wished he were still sitting on the sofa back home. He decided to try another tack.

"I know you miss your dad and mom. I do too. They were some of the best friends I ever had." He knew the inherent dangers of the turf onto which he had just wandered, but right now no matter where his talk took him it was going to be full of hazards, so he bulled on. "I miss them a lot too, Cynthia."

Hurriedly she turned her head to look back out the other window again. Coal's instincts told him to keep on. "It's okay to cry, sweetheart. I've done it too. And it's okay to keep missing them. You're always going to."

In a moment, the girl was shaking violently as she tried to keep her emotions silent. Coal pulled east onto Carmen Creek Road and drove for a hundred yards or so, then pulled over. The ice chips along the road crackled like .22 fire as he came to a stop.

"Don't hold it in," Coal said. "Let it come out."

And so she did, and it was a flood of epic proportions. With high hopes, Coal reached out and patted the girl's back, and she whirled and fell against him, crying so loud he thought it would make any coyotes in the neighborhood take up their lonesome song. This was the reaction Coal had been shooting for, in his desperation—not to make the girl cry, but just to get her emotions out and to make her rely on him while doing so. It could have gone either way, but something had begged him continue.

When the girl had cried herself out, Coal was still holding her, stroking her hair. "You can cry on me any time, sweetie. I hope you know that."

Sniffling, she just nodded.

"I need you to know something else, Cynthia, and I mean this with all my heart. When you heard me yesterday, what I said sounded hard. But it wasn't meant to be. I really don't believe anyone has been babying you. You are a teenage girl who has lost a couple of people who meant more to you than anything. *No one* would recover from that fast. Not me, not Connie—nobody. I was talking like that because I was worried about you."

Again, she sniffed, but she didn't let go of him. Her cheek kept resting against his shoulder. When she replied, her voice was muffled against the cloth of his coat. "It's okay. I understand. I love you, Coal."

The words stunned him. He had no time to think of a way to respond, and he felt trapped into replying in kind: "I love you too, sweetheart." And then he realized that he really did love this girl. In a very short time, he had come to feel responsible for her and to love her as if she were one of his own.

*   *   *

Going back over the river bridge, Coal pulled the car over on the south side of the street just past the Owl Club and parked at the curb. Cynthia shot a question at him, and he said, "Now you just hold tight. A lady always waits for a gentleman to open her door."

He got out and hustled around to let her out, taking her hand and helping her stand up. She giggled at him, and a warm feeling rushed through his heart. They were going to be okay.

Now he held out his elbow to her, and when she just looked at him, puzzled, he told her, "You're supposed to take it in your hands. The gallant knight is escorting his lady to Wally's Cafe for a hot chocolate."

Again, she laughed, then took his elbow, and they walked to Wally's, where he held open the door to let her in. The inside of the cafe felt like it was on fire compared to the ice in the air outside. It smelled of fresh coffee, burgers and fries, slightly over-powered by the cigarette smoke that hovered toward the ceiling in a faint kind of mist, left over from the noontime crowd.

They seated themselves on stools at the long, wide counter at the right side of the room, and in a moment the owner's daughter, Karen, walked in from the back room, to their left. "Hi, Cynthia," she greeted with a big smile. She gave Coal a glance, and a flicker of recognition came to her eyes, but he was sad to perceive she was not sure who he was. She had not been around the last two or three times he had been in over the years.

"Hi, Karen." Cynthia smiled back. Her smile looked genuine and easy, and Coal took great hope from this.

Karen was a pretty girl, about fifteen years of age and nearly five and a half feet tall, with long brown hair tied back in a pony-tail. She wore a white apron over her clothes, and Coal could see she wore it with pride.

"Hey, Karen. I'm sure you don't remember me, but I'm a friend of your dad and mom's. Coal Savage. I don't suppose they're around, are they?"

Karen smiled at him. "They are. Dad's back cutting up meat, and I think Mom's downstairs working on the books. Want me to get them?"

"That would be great, if it's okay."

"Sure," Karen said. "It's slow anyway."

She left, and after a moment Coal heard faint pieces of conversation beyond the door into the kitchen area. A man's voice exclaimed something he couldn't make out, and in another half a minute a man with black hair smoothed straight back on his head and just barely starting to turn to silver came rushing in drying his hands on a towel.

"Coal! Oh, man. How in the heck have you been? I've been hoping to see you since you got back to town."

Coal had stood up, and he met a hearty handshake from cafe owner Wally Richardson, who at about five-foot-ten or eleven stood several inches shorter than Coal but had plenty of upper body muscle from years of throwing sides of beef around.

"Sorry about that, my friend. I've been meaning to come in. I think about you and Beulah all the time. But you know how things have been since I got back."

Wally looked over and seemed suddenly to recognize Cynthia. A sad look washed over his face, and for just a moment he was uncharacteristically silent. His eyes searched for something to say. But with Wally Richardson that never took too long. "Hi, young lady. Hey, I sure was sorry to hear about your folks. They were mighty good people. Mighty fine. Best folks I ever knew."

Cynthia's eyes misted over, but Coal swelled with pride to see her hold it in and give Wally a smile. "Thank you, sir."

Wally suddenly whirled on his daughter Karen. "Hey, run downstairs and get Mom, will you, honey? Don't tell her who's here, just that I need her."

"Okay, Daddy," was the girl's reply, and she hurried off.

Wally then turned back to Coal and Cynthia, seeming just then to notice the big countertop between them. "Say! That's enough of this nonsense!" He hurried around the end of the counter and came out to stand a few feet from Coal and the girl.

"So where's the family, Coal?"

"Not here. Just me and Cynthia."

"Wow! You're dating them a little young now, aren't you?" Wally laughed and gave Cynthia a wink. He jabbed a finger at Coal. "You watch out for this guy, now. He might be wearing a badge, but I can tell you he's a little sneaky. You just be careful."

Wally's comments drew a giggle from Cynthia, and silently he thanked his old friend for his warm and timely sense of humor. Wally had always loved people from all walks of life, and he had a strength for making tense situations seem light.

"Seriously, though, did you two come in just to visit, or do you want to eat something?" He suddenly stopped. "Say! Have you seen my new oven?"

Coal looked behind the counter to the gigantic microwave oven toward which Wally jerked a thumb.

"Huh? Huh? What do you think? Cost me a mint! It's a G.E. A genuine microwave oven! First one in the whole valley, you know.

That puppy can heat up a sweet roll in fifteen seconds flat. Serious! You remember how we used to have to set the rolls on a piece of lettuce and put 'em on the grill to heat 'em up? Well, not anymore! You two got a minute? I'll prove it to you." He looked back and forth between them, and the gleam in his eye let Coal know he would not take no for an answer.

Coal grinned. "Well, I'm guessing you're bound and determined as usual to ruin my appetite, buddy. Sure, show me how that thing works."

Coal was thinking about all the microwave ovens he had seen in Washington, D.C. The novelty had long since worn off. But he wasn't about to ruin the fun for Wally.

"And before you get too far, Wally, don't let me forget that the real reason Cynthia and I came in—besides seeing you and Beulah, of course—is to get two steaming hot cups of chocolate."

"Oh, sure!" said Wally as he hustled back around the counter. "I'll let Karen do that. That little gal loves her cocoa machine, I'll tell you. I think she could make cocoa all day long as a living and never get tired of it."

Wally was still chuckling to himself as he took a spatula and scooped two cinnamon rolls up from a tray inside a glass case and set them on saucers, pulling open the big door of the microwave oven. Before inserting them, he slapped big slabs of butter on each one.

Even as Coal saw Wally twisting a big dial on top of the oven, he heard an exclamation of surprise off to his left and turned to see red-haired Beulah Richardson standing behind the checkout counter with her hands over her mouth.

"Coal! Coal Savage! Oh, my stars!"

Beulah almost ran around the end of the counter and greeted Coal with an enormous bear hug. She stood only about five-foot-four, so Coal had to lean far over to return the hug properly, but a hug from lovable Beulah Richardson was worth any effort.

After squeezing half of the life out of Coal, Beulah stood back from him, gripping his arms. She looked him up and down. "I declare, Coal. You get more handsome every time I lay eyes on you. If Wally ever leaves me, I swear on my grave I'm going to come a-courting, and I won't take no for an answer."

Coal felt himself blush, but everyone laughed. He took his turn looking lively Beulah Richardson up and down. As always, every tiny strand of her shiny red hair was in its place, piled high on her head. She took great pride in that hair being perfect, and because of that she often cursed the wind. She was dressed in a blue, flowered dress, most likely one she had made herself. That was another of the things Beulah most prided herself in—her ability with a sewing machine.

While Coal and Beulah were still smiling at each other, and she was going on about how good it was to see him, Coal heard Wally tell Karen to make up two cups of rich hot chocolate.

"And make sure you put an extra spoonful of raw cocoa in Coal's, okay? I remember he likes it strong and bitter."

Even though he tried to keep his attention on Beulah, Coal couldn't help smiling at his old friend Wally. The man never forgot a thing, it seemed. He could listen to ten orders at a table and get them all perfect down to the last detail. Wally's Cafe was highly successful because no one did personal touches better.

"Mom, look what you went and did now," Coal heard Wally say after a while, and he and Beulah turned in surprise. "I was trying to show Coal how the microwave oven worked, and he missed the whole thing."

"Well, then I guess he's just going to have to come back again, honey."

Coal laughed. "Yes, ma'am, I sure am."

A somber feeling once again fell over the room as Beulah seemed to notice for the first time that Cynthia was with Coal, not merely some stray customer. She looked beyond him, and in a moment she recognized her.

"Oh, you sweet girl. Cynthia! How are you?" She came close, not waiting for a reply, and enfolded her in her arms, patting her back.

Cynthia finally stepped away. Knowing all eyes were on her, she showed her first signs of discomfort. But Beulah wrapped an arm around her and led her back to a stool. "Now you just sit down here and enjoy this roll, sweetheart. Get it while it's hot. You too, you big lummox," she told Coal, reaching out to ruffle the back of his hair.

Coal and the girl seated themselves, and while Beulah stood with an affectionate hand on Coal's shoulder, Wally leaned back against a big ice cream cooler that sat behind the counter, and he pulled a pack of Camels out of his shirt pocket, tapped one out of the pack and put it in the corner of his mouth. He squinted as the match he lit made bitter smoke curl out the end of it and into his eyes, and he shook out the match and set it behind him on the ice cream cooler to get cold.

Coal and Cynthia sat sipping their chocolate and making appreciative faces as they munched on Wally's rolls, which were far better than they had any right to be. Wally took it upon himself to regale them with jokes and stories, managing to keep Cynthia smiling and laughing, and all without a single drop of her drink coming out her nose. It made Coal feel good to see these smiles on her face. It was like she had returned from the dead. He suddenly realized he should have brought her to Wally's much sooner. For that matter, Wally and Beulah's kind of medicine was pretty good for him as well.

When the evening crowd began to arrive, and they finally, regretfully, had to leave Wally's, Coal shook his friend's hand, hugged Beulah, and Wally and Beulah both embraced Cynthia.

Coal looked at Karen and smiled. "Karen, I'll try to come around more often so you don't forget me next time." She only giggled in reply.

Coal drove home slowly, and Cynthia told him about her dad and the plans he had been talking about for their future. He had been entertaining the idea of moving the family to the Falls, for a better chance of finding work, and he told her he would help her get through college and get a degree at Idaho State University, in Pocatello, if she chose that route. She managed to get all the way through the conversation about her dad and mom, and only once did tears dim her eyes.

They pulled up at the house, and it was now long toward evening. The last of the sunlight was gone, and the bitter cold had returned, although it wasn't yet below zero. Maura's truck wasn't in the yard, so she must still have been down at McPherson's, but her heelers, Chewy and Dart, came running out to greet them. Coal noticed that Dart had a limp, and he grimaced as he crouched down to stroke his head. "Dang it, Dart, I told you that old horse would kick you, buddy."

The dog gave a little whine, in sharp contrast to the silly grin on his face, and his tongue flopped out one side of his mouth. Apparently, outside of the limp, the kick had not affected him too much. Cynthia was petting Chewy, cooing to him in baby talk that should have made the little guy feel foolish but instead seemed to make him overjoyed to see her, and he squirmed around like a two-month old pup, all but peeing himself.

"All right, guys." Coal stood up. "You better run back to the barn. We're freezing! Come on, Cynthia." They went inside, assaulted on the instant by Dobe, Shadow, and a seventy-five degree wall of heat from the Franklin stove.

Sissy was sitting on the couch with the twins, watching TV. When she saw Cynthia, she hurried over, skirting far around Coal, and threw her arms around her. They had become almost like the sisters that neither had.

Wyatt and Morgan ran over and jumped all over their dad, much like the dogs were doing, and Coal felt loved. Looking around, he didn't see Virgil anywhere, but that was no surprise, as he was likely in his room reading. But Katie was sitting on his chair, and she got up. Coal thought for sure she was coming to greet them too, and he gave her a big smile. "Hi, Katie!"

She looked at him, her face bland, and said, "Hi," then turned and went down the hall. A few moments later, Coal heard her door click shut.

Wondering what that was about, Coal glanced at Cynthia, who was kneeling down now to continue her long greeting with Sissy, then looked around for his mom. "Boys, where's Grandma?"

"Feeding the horses!" they replied in unison.

"Should have known. How come you boys aren't helping?"

"It's too cold," Morgan said.

"Well, you're going to have to get over that if you want to grow up to be strong men. Grandma can't do that alone, you know."

"She's not alone!" corrected Wyatt. "Virgil's with her."

When the words registered on him, a big smile came over Coal's face. "Well, I'll be danged. Good for him. Wait—did Grandma have to go get him out of his room?"

"Nope," said Wyatt, cocking his head proudly. "He came down and asked her if they should go out and do it."

"Well, there you boys go. That's the kind of thing I'd like to see you learn to do too."

The sound of stomping boots beyond the kitchen signaled the entrance of Connie and his oldest boy. Feeling proud of himself for being able to do it, Coal went and clapped Virgil on the shoulder. "I'm proud of you, Son. Good job stepping up to help your grandmother."

Virgil gave him a shy smile. "Thanks."

Coal then turned to Connie, after glancing across the room to see Cynthia and Sissy snuggled up together on the couch. Cynthia was already holding Buddy, the Teddy bear that she must have been missing all day, from the looks of how she clung to it now. The twins were crammed together on their father's chair, unwilling to miss today's episode of *Daniel Boone* even if they had to crowd up to do it.

"Hey, Mom, did anything happen with Katie at school today?"

"Not that she said anything about. Why?"

"Well, we just got in and I said hi to her, and she said it back, but then it seemed like she couldn't get down the hall to her room fast enough. It was almost like I wasn't even here. And she didn't say one word to Cynthia."

"I don't know. She's been acting a little strange since they got home. Virgil, do you know anything?" queried Connie.

Coal knew that would be about like talking to the dogs. Only so many words were likely to come out of that boy. True to form, he just shrugged.

Coal looked at Connie, and he shrugged, too. At that moment, he caught Connie motioning him over with an inclination of her head. He left Virgil rummaging in the fridge, and he and his mom went over by the back door. "What's up, Ma?"

"I hardly even know how to say it. Some lawyer called today, Son. Lawson, maybe? Peter Lawson?"

"Doesn't mean anything to me," said Coal, feeling apprehensive.

"It's going to, I'm afraid. Coal, I'm broken-hearted. I don't even want to be here when Maura gets home. According to this Lawson clown, we have just one or two days to say goodbye to the girls."

CHAPTER THIRTEEN

It seemed that Coal Savage had felt helpless more times since he had come back home to Salmon than he had ever felt in the whole rest of his life put together. His first reaction to Connie's words was a monumental surge of anger, and the determination that no-body was going to take those girls away even if he had to barricade himself and the girls in the house with his guns.

But almost immediately the lawman side came out in him, and he knew that in reality his only recourse here was not violence, but the law. There were other lawyers in this town besides whatever sleaze bag the Mileys had found.

He thought about that. He thought about the fact that those two girls had just barely moved in with him, and had not lived with Maura for very long before that. And he thought about the fact that they were both related to the Mileys by blood—basically every-thing the judge had already told him.

He looked over at Cynthia, holding her little shadow on the couch, the worn-out Teddy bear in her other arm.

And the helplessness swooped down over him like a hawk.

Almost numbly, Coal walked to the living room and picked up the green phone, twisting its cord to untangle it. He dialed in retired sheriff Jim Lockwood's number, then waited during the endless sound of each ring.

Hello? It was the voice of Betty Lockwood, not Jim.

After a moment's hesitation, for more than one reason, Coal said, "Hi, Betty. It's Coal."

Coal Savage! Well, I don't believe it. Why have you not come to see me?

"I'm sorry. I've been meaning to."

Betty's voice got quieter. *I know, sweetie. I'm sorry. I didn't mean to come across like that. I saw you at the funerals. I should have said something then, but honestly, I didn't know what to say, and at the time you seemed pretty tied up. I know how close you and those boys were. And Jennifer too. You'd think when you get to be an old woman you'd have the right words to say at times like that. But God never gave me a silver tongue.*

Coal chuckled. "Don't worry, Betty. It's totally all right. I knew we would see each other when times got a little calmer. Hey, I don't suppose Jim's in, is he?"

Oh, you know him, she said. *Out tinkering with his guns. I think he's bluing some barrels.*

Coal knew enough about that process to know better than to have her call him to the phone. "I need to see him."

Well then you just come on over here, Coal. That will give me a chance to get my hug too.

"I'll be over in a while, Betty. First I have to stop and see someone else."

Coal hung up and looked at Connie, who had followed him from the kitchen. She was already watching him.

"You want some company, Son?"

Coal felt helpless. "I do, Mom, but I'm afraid to leave the kids here alone."

She started to say something, then sighed her resignation. "Yes, you're right. That wouldn't be good. Will you be long?"

He cocked his head sideways at her, frowning.

"Right again. No way to know. Okay, Son, I will keep supper warm for you and Maura."

Coal drove in and pulled up the wrong way in front of McPherson's. As he got out and breathed in too deeply, he thought his nostrils were going to stick together, and he let out a cough. He couldn't get out of this miserable cold quickly enough.

Pushing the glass door open, he heard the friendly tinkle of the doorbells and smelled that warm mix of aromas that belonged exclusively to a Western wear store. It smelled like there was still a pot of coffee brewing, and someone recently had blown out a lung or two full of cigarette smoke, but both smells were faint, and they blended pleasantly with the odor of smoked buckskin and newly died leather, boots on the shelf, and new clothing on the rack.

As Coal undid the snaps on his coat, he searched the store with his eyes, finally seeing movement in a far corner, beyond the checkout counter. He went there only to find a young, dark-haired girl with her hair in a ponytail.

She turned when she sensed Coal coming up to her. "Hi!"

"Hi, Miss. I'm Coal Savage."

"Oh, yes, everybody knows who *you* are, Sheriff." The girl smiled broadly, pronouncing deep dimples show on both sides of her mouth. She was as cute as a Border collie pup. The girl thrust her hand straight out in front of her. "I'm Nellie."

Coal took her hand. "Nellie? Good to meet you. Say, you look like one of those Ferguson girls."

"Yes, I sure am. The youngest."

"How're your folks, Nellie?"

Jade and Sadie Ferguson both worked for Lemhi Lumber and raised Limousin cattle on the side—as far as Coal knew the only herd of them in the entire area. They were as good as any people he knew and had raised a whole string of children who mostly left home on coming of age, headed out to more civilized parts where work was easier to find.

"Oh, they're doing fine," replied the girl. "Just working with lumber and cows, like always."

Coal laughed. "Say, is Maura around?"

Nellie's face became serious. "Um, sure. She doesn't seem to be very happy today, though," she said, leaning closer conspiratorially. "She's over in the women's section unpacking a new shipment. Maybe you can cheer her up."

Taking a deep breath, Coal said, "I hope I can. Thanks."

Coal turned and crossed through the breezeway into the area where they sold women's clothing. He found Maura at the back of the store, taking clothes out of big wooden crates and putting them on hangers. He paused for half a minute, this time not to admire her, but to prepare himself.

He started toward her, and the dark old wooden floor creaked beneath his feet. Maura turned slowly. She tried to smile when she realized it was not one of her co-workers. If it had been a test on smiles, she would have gotten a D, with no chance for extra credit.

"Oh, hi, Coal."

"Hi. You doing okay?"

"Sure." She set aside a shirt that was too wrinkly for the hanger. "I'll have to iron that one," she mumbled.

"When do you get off work?"

She looked up at him again, her mind elsewhere. "Uh... Six, I think. Why?"

"Oh, okay. Well, I was thinking of taking you with me to see Jim Lockwood."

"Why?"

"Well, something's come up. I need his advice. *We* need it."

The look of dread that came up in her eyes was only thinly disguised, but it was obvious that she thought she hid it well.

She stood up, forgetting her work. "So what's it about?" She tried to sound casual, but she had a hard time meeting his eyes.

Coal was at a loss as to what to do or what to say. "Well..."

"That's a deep subject," she jumped in, trying to lighten the mood.

He couldn't laugh. "Maura, a lawyer called and spoke with my mom."

She just stared at him. Her blue eyes were suddenly wet, her lips parted.

Now that he had said that much, he didn't know how to finish.

"Okay," Maura said at last. "I get it. I knew it couldn't last." With those words, she turned back to her work, kneeling down at the crate, her back to him once more.

Coal watched her as long as he could bear, waiting to see if she would turn back around, then said, "Come home as soon as you can. They told Mom we have just two days to say our goodbyes." When there was no obvious reaction, he turned away with an even heavier heart than he had come inside with and weaved his way through the racks of women's clothing and out the front door.

*   *   *

Betty Lockwood opened her door at Coal's knock. She was already looking right into his eyes, her own adjusted to the perfect height, because she had been looking at this man as long as any other person had besides Connie. Her eyes jumped back and forth between his, and she stepped forward and hugged him fiercely. "Oh, Coal. You look so good."

Betty stepped back from him, and they looked each other over. Betty was a couple of years younger than Jim, which put her in her early sixties, and except for her hair, a lustrous, beautiful silver, she hardly looked a day over fifty. Her eyes, a deep chocolate brown, turned slightly down at the outside edges, where they met a faint field of crow's feet. Her nose, long and elegant, stood at just the right distance above expressive, deep pink lips that always gave off the right emotion at the right time, and were framed at the sides by two long, vertical wrinkles. Even the wrinkles on Betty Lockwood were elegant.

"It sure is good to see you, Betty. You never age."

Her laughter was a tinkling sound, like rattling china. "You are such a flatterer." She leaned close and hugged him again. "Ah, Coal, it's so nice to have you back home."

He didn't reply except with a smile. So far, he wasn't sure it was good to *be* back.

"Well, Jim's out back, but I'll warn ya. He's pretty scroungy."

Coal laughed. "Well, he's always scroungy."

He went around back and found Jim bent over a couple of big, steaming tubs of liquid, adjusting a propane heater that was running burners beneath them. He turned when Coal spoke his name.

"What's up, son?"

"I need some advice. And maybe some help."

Jim wiped his hands on his pants. "I'd shake, but you don't want this on you. So how can I help you?"

"Who's the best lawyer in town, Jim?"

"Well, that depends. You prosecuting or defending?"

Coal laughed. "If I was prosecuting I wouldn't have a choice, would I? But how about a third choice: civil."

"Ah, civil. Then Keith Perkins."

"Don't know that one."

"You probably wouldn't, off gallivatin' around the world like you were. He moved up here from Mesa, Arizona. It's been quite a few years now. Lives out on the river toward Challis."

"He square?"

"Son, you know how I joke about lawyers. Hell, we all do. You know, how ninety-nine percent of 'em give the other one percent a bad name? But Perkins is about the most honest man you'd ever want to meet—not to mention one of the friendliest. If he believes in your cause he'll get behind it and do you more good than a whole herd of shysters. He's a good man all the way around."

"Then I need him. Connie got a call from some guy named Peter Lawson." Coal didn't miss the sour look that came to Jim's face. "I haven't told you much about what's been going on lately, so I guess I need to catch you up."

He went on to tell Jim about the insurance policy and about how Bud and Linda Miley had shown up out of the blue claiming rights to the children. But as far as anyone knew, they had no way of knowing about the insurance money.

Jim's face was grave. "What did that damn Lawson say? And by the way, his name is Phillip, not Peter."

"Oh. Okay. He said we can expect to hand over Cynthia and Sissy in two days."

Jim nodded. "You have any idea what these folks are like? The Mileys?"

Coal told him all he knew.

"Then maybe you've got a shot. Judge Sinclair won't just let those girls go away with these people without knowing they can provide for 'em. Sounds like they're drifters to me."

A frightening thought suddenly hit Coal. "Jim, what do you suppose happens to the Battertons' house now that they're both gone?"

"It'll be in probate, I reckon. Rightfully, it will go to Cynthia, I would suspect."

"Is there any way the judge might let the Mileys move in there with the girls?"

Jim thought for a moment. "Damnit, Coal, I wish I knew, but I don't. I have no idea how that kind of stuff usually goes, honestly. But it's sure something to ask Keith Perkins about. I'm going to give you his home phone number. I think he'll see you tonight, if you want. Or at least talk to you on the phone."

They went inside, and when Jim had given Coal the number to Keith Perkins's house, he left so Coal could talk in private and so he could check the progress of his bluing job in the back yard.

As soon as he was gone, Coal dialed up Connie. "Mom, listen to me. I've got a bad feeling about something—*real* bad. I might still be tied up for a little bit, but I need you to do something for me."

"What is it?"

"Drive over to Saveway and get five or six big apple boxes. Then go to the Battertons—with Cynthia's key. Take all the kids with you and start going through all the desk and dresser drawers in the house. Anything in folders or envelopes, start throwing it in boxes, all right? Take all the family photos and stuff off the walls, too. Anything that looks like it would mean nothing to a stranger moving in there. In fact, think of it like the place is going to be rented out as a furnished apartment. Everything else goes."

"I thought you did that, Coal."

"Mom, I started going through things, but I didn't pack even one piece of paper. When I found that insurance policy I got distracted and never got back to it. Everything goes, understand? I have to talk to a lawyer really quick, and then if I can I'll meet you over there. And Mom?

"Watch for a red Buick Riviera—the one we saw after the funeral. You remember. I've got a big feeling that was them. If you see that car around there, you call me at Jim's, okay? Or call dispatch and have them get me on the radio."

"What's going on, Coal?"

"I've got a bad hunch, Mom. We've got to protect any paperwork that's in that house—before the Mileys can get to it."

CHAPTER FOURTEEN

It is never easy to judge someone by talking to them once on the phone. But Coal had found himself going on gut instincts a lot throughout his life, and his conversation with Keith Perkins, coupled with those gut instincts, told him Perkins and he were going to become good friends. Hard to imagine, being friends with an attorney.

Perkins hadn't been able to meet with Coal that night because, as he told him, he always set aside Monday nights to be with his family and read the Scriptures, among other family-oriented things. That made Coal like him all the better, although simultaneously making him feel guiltier than he already had about not being home with his family.

After making an appointment to meet with Perkins the following day, Coal went out and jumped in his car, driving back to McPherson's. He entered into the men's section, which was his habit, and glanced about the store. As soon as he spotted pretty Nellie Ferguson coming toward him through racks of clothing, she saw and recognized him as well. She pointed. "Still at the back on the other side," she said quietly. "And she's worse." The last was spoken almost in a whisper.

Coal nodded understanding and went through the breezeway, nodding at a clerk who was cashing out some woman's purchases at the square counter that sat mid-store. This time, Coal made plenty of warning noise on his way through the clothing. The shipping crate at the back of the room was sitting abandoned on the floor, and Maura was nowhere to be seen. He walked around the dim-lit room, seeing no movement anywhere but a black and white cat that looked at him and then wandered away on whatever errand it had been performing.

The clerk walked back and found him. She was an older lady with a kind face. Coal knew he should remember her name, but he didn't, and at the moment there was no great reason to care. "Well, hello, Coal. It's nice to see you. Can I help you with something?"

"Thank you. I'm actually looking for Maura."

"Okay. I think she might be in the restroom."

Coal went back to the cross-over between the men's and women's sections, where the restroom was in the wall that faced out toward the front of the store. The door was closed, and he listened for movement inside—a deadly business for a man to do when he suspected a woman was on the other side of a restroom door. But some things could not wait.

At last, he knocked lightly. He heard a sniffle. No one replied for five seconds. He rapped three more times.

Another sniffle. "Yes?"

"Hey, sorry, Maura. It's me again."

Long silence. Finally the sound of a toilet flushing. Silence again. No rustling of clothing, no clinking of a metal belt buckle. The toilet flush was only a stalling tactic, as he had suspected. After a moment, the faucet turned on, and he keened his ears closer. It turned off only ten seconds later, and in that time the stream had not been disturbed by hands being washed. He heard the towel roller working, but by then he was already walking away. He had decided Maura was only pretending to use the restroom. If she needed her privacy that badly, he was not stupid enough still to be standing outside the door when she emerged.

Coal walked to the front of the building and stood looking out at the street. The few people who moved around in the glow of the street lamps were bundled up tightly. One man wore a huge fur cap with the sides sticking straight out like airplane wings.

He had purposely left a clear line of sight from the breezeway to where he stood, so that there was no possibility of Maura coming out and not seeing him—unless she went over to the men's section. But he never heard the door open. He kept standing there, and still it never opened.

What was he supposed to do now? He had about used up all of his knowledge, what little there was, of how to deal with women. Did he have to wait here until she came out? Did he warn her he was leaving and then go, so she wouldn't have to face him when she came out, in her sorrow, her embarrassment at hiding from him, or whatever other emotion she had to deal with? Or did he just go, not saying anything at all?

What he suspected was the wrong choice, as far as Maura was going to be concerned, was the choice he made, for by now a little of his own stubborn pride was creeping back in. He was sorry Maura was hurting. But if she wanted to play the game of ignoring him and just expected him to wait around on her every emotional whim, she had not learned much about Coal Savage.

He had been at the window for no less than seven minutes, he guessed, when he turned and saw Nellie, looking at him hopefully. He tried to give her a smile, but he shook his head. "I guess she's stuck in the bathroom, Nellie. Thanks anyway."

Nellie said goodbye, and the jingling doorbells announced his exit to the frigid outdoors. A glance at a sign on the door proclaimed that the store would be closing in twenty minutes, and then Maura had some choices to make. At this point, there wasn't one choice at which he would have hazarded a guess.

*   *   *

Coal drove south to the 500 block of Hope Street and parked across from the Battertons', seeing Connie's Chrysler right in front, and the lights on in the house. He went in without knocking to find everyone but Sissy busy piling about everything that wasn't nailed down into boxes set haphazardly around the room.

Taking a chance when he didn't see Cynthia, Coal went down a hallway with four doors facing it. The door on the right at hall's end was open just a crack, and a light came from inside. "Cynthia?" He spoke to the crack.

He was about tired of listening to female sniffles, but that was the response he got at first. "Yes?"

"Can I come in?"

"Sure."

He pushed open the door, and there sat Cynthia on a queen-size bed. It was just a mattress now, for Cynthia had taken her parents' bedding and pillows home to be near her. She looked up at him, her face stained with tears, and he saw she was holding a framed eight-by-ten photograph. Maybe this sixteen-year-old was one female Coal could still help. He walked to her and sat down, putting his arm around her. She lay her head over on his chest, and a sob wracked her body—the kind of sob that said she had shed many tears and they were in the drying-up stage.

Reaching down, Coal took the left side of the picture frame Cynthia was looking at in his thumb and two fingers and tilted it up so the light wasn't glaring off it. It was a portrait of the three of them together, Cynthia seated in the middle, with K.T. and Jennifer standing on either side of her with their hands on her shoulders. By the looks of all of them, it had to have been taken three or four years earlier.

"I look so terrible," said Cynthia. "I was a real ugly duckling."

Cynthia was wrong, and Coal didn't even have to lie about it. "I beg to differ with you. You were a doll, Cynthia. I'll bet you never had an awkward stage."

She laughed. "Well, you're nice. That sure isn't what the boys all told me."

"You have to be kidding. I never saw a cuter girl."

"I used to have freckles," she said. "I think that's what it was, anyway."

"I like freckles."

She sniffled. "Daddy said he did too."

"There you go. Your dad would never have lied."

She smiled. He could see it in the mirror on the wall in front of them. For a long moment, they looked at each other in the mirror.

At last, Cynthia's lips began to move, but it was a couple of seconds before any words emerged. "I would like you to be my daddy, Coal. Do you think that will mean anything to the judge and lawyer?"

Coal squeezed her more tightly. "I sure hope so, honey. I sure do."

*   *   *

Maura did not come home that night.

Coal was sitting on the sofa instead of his big chair, so Cynthia could crush herself up next to him while they watched Nick Barkley beating sense into some hapless troublemaker on *The Big Valley*. Everyone else was gathered around as well, because no one was willing to miss that week's episode of one of their favorite programs. Connie was seated in Coal's chair, and the boys were stretched out on the floor. There was only one person missing: Katie. She had claimed she had homework and gone to her room right after supper—a supper Coal had miraculously made it home in time for. But the jolt of seeing Katie be willing to miss watching her heartthrob, Heath Barkley, was almost too much for Coal.

There was something wrong with Katie. Katie and Maura both. Coal knew what Maura's problem was, and as he felt Cynthia's warm body pressed up against his and looked down to see how tightly she clung to him he was starting to suspect what Katie's was as well.

Desperation. And jealousy. How much more could a dad without the benefit of a female partner be asked to endure?

When the credits rolled, Maura still was not home. The store had been closed now for two hours. Coal looked over at his mother. "What now, Mom?"

She had been waiting for him. "She's a big girl, Coal. You won't find her if she doesn't want to be found, and right now I don't think she wants to be found."

Coal nodded. He felt like she was right, but he couldn't help but wonder if things would have been different if he could have swallowed his pride and waited for her at McPherson's just a little while longer.

He didn't have much more time to think about it, because at that moment the phone rang. It was Kathy MacAtee on the other end.

I know it's late, Coal. I'm so sorry. Could you come over to-night? The girls and I really need you. And Rowdy... Coal, can you please just come?

CHAPTER FIFTEEN

As Coal drove through the night, he thought about the attorney Keith Perkins and how he had told him he always set aside Monday evenings for his wife and children. Why was Coal incapable of doing something like that? Every time he thought he had a free night, something happened, and he got called away. At least he had been able to spend an hour with them watching *The Big Valley* re-run, but it wasn't enough. He had had to tell them all good night before leaving, go out and scrape the early frost off his windshield and get the car warming up, and then load up Shadow and head out. He wanted some company, but under the circumstances there was no one he wanted to see the sadness he was expecting tonight. And Dobie would not have tolerated the cold car as well as old Shadow, his buddy. It was down around four degrees tonight.

Coal pulled up in front of the MacAtees' house, but this time Kathy did not come out to greet him. After peeking through the window and seeing Kathy and the girls gathered around the couch, he pushed on inside, tapping on the door glass as it came open enough to allow him entry. Kathy got up and came to him, giving him a hug. "I'm afraid he's almost gone."

Coal, with his arm around Kathy, walked to the couch, where the dog was lying on a pile of old blankets. This time the girls had all been crying. He looked down at old Rowdy. The dog really wasn't even all that old, he knew. But age doesn't matter to a broken heart.

The dog's eyes were shut, and his mouth partway open. His lips were dry. Coal reached down and stroked his soft head and ear. After a moment, he lifted Rowdy's upper lip and looked at his gums. They were gray, and when he touched them they were very sticky, almost no longer even wet.

Coal looked over at Kathy, and she just nodded. "I know. Doctor Darger came over earlier and told us he is so dehydrated he probably isn't going to make it. He said he'd take him to the hospital and give him fluids, but he thinks it would just cost us a lot of money for nothing. He says he thinks Rowdy just gave up."

Coal had to nod. "I think so too, Kathy. I'm sorry. I had no idea he was so attached."

"Mom, it's not fair," wailed little Jen.

"I know, honey. It isn't." Kathy reached out and squeezed her daughter's arm. She turned and looked at Coal again. "How long do you think?"

"I don't know. I really don't. I wouldn't be surprised to see his heart still beating in the morning."

Milo, Sara, and Jen looked up at him quickly, their eyes full of sudden hope. He didn't want to take that away, but he didn't want to feed it falsely either.

"Hey, girls. I know how much you love this guy. But I think he misses your dad way too much, you know? He wants to go see him."

Jen started crying. Her tears made Coal ache inside. "I don't want him to die," she cried. Kathy reached out and hugged her close with one arm.

"Nobody does, sweetie. There are just sometimes we have to let go."

Coal had set his hand softly on Rowdy's ribcage, behind his leg, when he felt him draw in a deep breath. For a moment, he held it, and then it gusted out slowly. He looked over at Kathy, whose eyes had gotten big. She was watching him. He frowned sadly. It was another two or three seconds before another breath came, and that one was weaker. When it went out, none came back to replace it for another five seconds.

Coal took a deep breath. "Hey, girls, you need to give Rowdy a hug, okay? I think he's saying goodbye."

The tears started rolling down all of their faces now, and that made them pour out of Kathy as well. With all that feminine sadness, even Coal was filled with sorrow as he looked down at his and Larry's buddy and felt the last of his life's breath leave his lungs.

The four girls were crying out loud and stroking their pet almost fiercely. Coal had to get up and walk away. He stood at the back door staring out into the darkness. He wished he were almost anywhere else.

*   *   *

Coal drove home in the darkness, his heart heavy. Now and then he saw the flicker of eyes out in the darkness, some deer or moose gaging its chances of making it across the road safely.

Coal had stayed as long as he could with the MacAtee girls, trying his best to comfort them. But how does one comfort someone who has just lost a beloved family pet? He hugged them all, Kathy last, and he gave her a kiss on the forehead. He told her he would try to find a way to thaw the ground out behind the garage so they could lay Rowdy to rest there, close to the house.

Now he was coming up on Savage Lane, and suddenly he could barely see the sign through the moisture in his eyes. He reached over and ruffled Shadow's ears, glancing at her old eyes when she looked over at him. There is no love in the world like the love in the eyes of a faithful dog.

Shadow's time was coming too, he knew. He could see it in her eyes. It was something he would never be ready for. He hated to think of the sorrow in the MacAtee home tonight.

Coal turned into the lane, but then he came to a stop. He sat there for a moment, then finally backed out onto the road again and continued on toward town. It was hard to see anything now, for it was nine-thirty, and most homes were dark. But he knew when he was close to Maura's, and he slowed down and turned into her driveway. The house was completely dark. Dark and still. No Chewy and Dart came out to bark at his car, and no horse eyes came to shine over the top pole of the corral at him. There was no International Travelette in the yard, and Coal needed nothing more than that. He sat there for a few more minutes, stroking old Shadow's head until she lay down on the seat and put her chin on his leg.

On a whim, Coal drove the rest of the way into town, cruising Main Street and looking for the ugly white pickup. It was nowhere to be found. He drove around back of McPherson's, and the alley was empty. She must have gone home at last, and he wondered how she had gotten past him. He drove back out on Main Street and headed east.

He should have driven one more mile.

*   *   *

In a quiet room in the newly built Stagecoach Inn, Maura PlentyWounds sat on a hard bed, staring at the black screen of the television she had yet to turn on. No one could find her here. They would never think to look in this place, even if they did come looking for her, which she doubted. She knew they would just assume she went home. And hopefully Coal would know her well enough not to come looking anyway.

Maura thought about Coal, and her jaw clenched. For a long time, she had felt herself getting closer to him—too close. She remembered their first meeting, and a grim smile almost came to her lips except that she forced it back. He had seemed so arrogant. So much like a typical man. And, in spite of herself, so good-looking, and built like a Greek statue of a god in his blue Wranglers and plaid cowboy shirt and boots. And for all of that, she hated him instantly.

But then that irritating feeling began inside her that she was actually starting to like him. First irritating, then aggravating... then irresistible. She had fought it as long as she could. She kept making verbal jabs at him, but she could tell he didn't take them seriously, and on top of that he was a master at throwing them back her way. Inside, she wanted to be infuriated. And then it became a game—something she looked forward to. And then the night in his car, on the way home from Idaho Falls, she found herself wondering what it would be like to kiss Coal Savage.

Yet after her long-awaited—and long-needed—divorce from Nyle TrueBear, she had sworn she would never let her head be turned by another man. She hated them all, and she always would. And there were times she hated Coal Savage most of all. And why? Because she wanted to hate him so badly, even while her pathetic little girl heart wanted to love him.

She thought back to that late afternoon at McPherson's. After Coal had left her the first time, she could not stop the tears. After losing her little girl, so many years ago, she had never dreamed she could heal. And then, as if God had decided finally to show her some mercy, little Sissy and Cynthia had come into her life. She had fallen in love with them, and somehow she had stupidly convinced herself of the likelihood that they might be awarded to her, if she was able to demonstrate herself fit to care for them. And then along came the Mileys. She had tried to hold onto hope as long as she could, but his first visit that afternoon was just too much. It was the moment she had expected but could not prepare for.

When Coal returned, it took her completely off-guard. She was hiding in the restroom. She couldn't deny it. But she knew Nellie wouldn't come bothering her. She had thought she was safe. And then Coal was there, like a nightmare coming to revisit her. She tried to tidy up so she could go out and face him. It took a little time. But how much? Five minutes? Seven minutes, tops.

She finally came out, ready to face him. She looked all over the upstairs. Then she ventured down. Coal was gone. He had abandoned her. He had abandoned her, just like every other man had abandoned her her entire life, from her own father on. Well, all except Nyle TrueBear, whom she had prayed so many times *would* abandon her. The alternative—and the reality—was much uglier than simple abandonment.

Maura had gotten in her truck after work and driven out of town. She drove out Highway 93, most of the way to Challis, where she had decided she was going to spend the night in a hotel she couldn't afford. But she finally got the sense to drive back to town, knowing she could not afford simply not to show up at work again in the morning. She still had two boys to provide for, and animals to feed, besides herself. She had to keep her job.

So she drove to the Stagecoach Inn, swore Julie, the manager, to secrecy, and took her room overlooking the nearly frozen Salmon River. Here she sat, and here she would stay the night. Tomorrow she would have to decide what she was going to do—

probably return to her own home, then ignore any attempts by Coal to contact her. She was through with him. Through with a man who would walk away from her so easily when she needed him most.

Maura could hear a man and woman talking in the room next to hers. She had seen them come in earlier, not packing any bags, so they must be longer term guests.

Suddenly, she heard him yell, in a nasally, irritating voice. Something struck the wall hard. She pulled herself up onto the bedspread, yanked a pillow out from under it, and lay back, smashing the pillow over her head in an attempt to block any more noise from the strangers. She instantly didn't like them, and she didn't even know why. She didn't care, either.

She could never have guessed that it was these two people who had come to steal her girls.

CHAPTER SIXTEEN

"Stop messin' around and get in bed," growled Bud Miley. "We've got to start figuring some stuff out here. Get some paper and a pen."

Playfully, Linda Miley stuck her tongue out at Bud, glancing down at the can of Oly beer he had just thrown at her, leaving a little dent in the drywall. "Why don't you get your own paper and pen?"

"Listen, dummy, do you want to get rich, or don't you? Will you just get me some paper and a pen and get in bed? Otherwise, I'm going to sleep."

"Fine," said Linda, frowning. Obviously, the fun for the night was over.

She rummaged into a backpack and came up with a spiral notebook and a number two pencil. "Pencil okay?" she said, crawling into bed beside him.

"I don't care. You're the one writin'. So what's our next move? Lawson's got the legal crap in the bag as far as grabbin' the girls. That's not even a question to worry about anymore."

"Okay. You want me to write that?"

"Cut it out. No, I don't need you to write that. Judas priest."

"Wow," she said, raising her eyebrows.

"I don't know what to write. Just not that. So how about the house? Write that down. We've got to talk to Lawson about the Battertons' house. Legally, it's pretty much gotta go to that girl. So he said we're going to need to be stable for the judge to side with us. How much more stable can we be? We move into a ready-made house—on a street with a name like Hope, no less. Oh—that's another thing. You gotta get a job."

"Me? Why me? What about you?"

"Well, of course me too. But I think if we had double the income it would look better."

"I'm not sure about that. He could say one of us should be home with the girls for a stable environment."

Bud thought for a moment, pursing his lips. He looked over at her shrewdly. "Fine. Maybe you're right. So I get a job. Write that down. That's the first thing I've got to do, tomorrow."

"You're just going to waltz out and get one? Half this valley's looking for a job."

"They don't have my skills."

"Ha! Your skills at fleecing people are the best. You should get on with a real estate company. Right up your alley!"

Bud sat there staring at her for a long moment. Finally, a light came into his eyes. "I wonder what that would take. You know what? You're right. The perfect job for a guy like me. Look up realtors in this valley and write down the numbers."

Bud Miley sat brooding while Linda did his job for him. Now and then, as a thought hit him, he would nod his head, plying the inside of his bottom lip with his tongue.

"Okay," he said when she finished. "We talk to Lawson tomorrow. Find out about the house. Go out and get me a job. And then... we sit back and start waiting for the money to come rolling in."

Linda looked at him, her lips pursed to one side as she pondered something. Finally, she said, "You're not just going to waltz in and start selling real estate, I bet. Don't you have to take some tests or something?"

"You sure like ta talk about waltzin', don't ya?"

"What?"

"You said waltzing a minute ago."

"Oh, brother. Sorry! But you didn't answer my question about taking tests."

"How should I know? I'll tell them I sold real estate back east. They won't know the difference."

"Yeah, until you try to produce a license or something."

"Why don't you just stop being negative? This is gonna work. I guarantee it."

"Okay, I'll wait and see."

He laughed. "Luckfully, little girl, you married the brains of this outfit. You'll see."

"Luckfully, you married the body of this outfit," she replied teasingly.

"Uh-huh. And now I got twice what I bargained for!"

"Yeah, but you still got the best part."

"The best that money can buy," he agreed with a laugh. "We're gonna be rich, Linda Miley."

*   *   *

Coal was driving east on 28, headed home, when he saw a car up ahead, stopped in the middle of the eastbound lane with its hazard lights on.

He swore. It was after ten o'clock now, and he was still hoping to get home before Connie went to bed, at least to prove he wasn't an absolute workaholic. But he couldn't just leave a stranded traveler out here alone.

He pulled up behind the car, and reaching onto his dash, he grabbed his blue light and put it out on top of the car, flicking it on.

Checking his mirror, he got out of the car, and putting his hand on his gun butt, he sidled toward the disabled car, a sky-blue Buick LeSabre convertible with the top buttoned tightly down.

"Hey! Coal?"

The female voice coming not from the car but from the right side of the road just about made him jump out of his skin and start to jerk his gun from the holster. Coal looked into the darkness.

"Who's that?"

"Me, Annie Price. Wow! I'm sure glad you're here."

"Did you break down?" he asked, wondering why she had left the car.

"No! You're not going to believe this." She came over to him, all bundled up in a mid-thigh length coat of fake brown suede leather with three buckled straps on the front and a white collar. She had only her hair to keep her ears warm, however.

"What am I not going to believe? That you're out here at ten o'clock at night on a lonely highway? That you have been left here by aliens that abducted you earlier but decided to throw you back?"

"Very funny."

He laughed. "You're not drunk, are you?"

"No, silly. No, I was driving down the road, and I saw what I thought was a deer coming toward me down the middle of the road, so I stopped." She motioned for him to follow her over to her driver's door and pointed down. "Can you see that?"

Coal peered in. "See what?"

"There's a big dog in there, Coal. Seriously! When I stopped, he ran right up to my door, and I got out and saw he had a rope around his neck and was pulling that little red wagon." She pointed off to the side of the road. "As soon as I got the rope off, he jumped into my car, down there on my pedals. Now I'm a little nervous. What should I do with him? I don't want to get bit."

Coal started laughing. "Wow. This is even almost as believable as the alien story. I've heard it all now. Hey, go around on the passenger side and open the door, would you? I want to see if your light will come on so I can see this guy better."

Annie hurried around to the other side and opened the door, and the dome light popped on. Coal looked in to see what appeared to be a golden retriever staring up at him, panting nervously. Scared to death.

He told her what kind of dog it was. "I've only ever seen one mean one," he said. "And even he wasn't mean. I think I just surprised him, and luckily he hit the end of a chain before he hit me. Now I'm wondering if there's some little kid lying out here somewhere that got dumped off this wagon."

She turned worried eyes on him. "In the dark? I hadn't even thought of anything like that."

"Well, let's get this guy loaded in my— Oh, man. Annie, I just thought of something. I have Shadow in my car with me!" Her glance threw the obvious question at him. "Oh! Sorry—Shadow's my German shepherd."

Annie looked back down into the shadows in front of her seat, then back at Coal. "So what am I going to do?"

"Well, I'd take him with me, but it's probably not a good idea to try and get two dogs this big acquainted with each other for the first time in the back seat of a car. So we could do one of two things. If you're brave, I can help you get that guy moved into the back seat and you can drive him back to town—except I'm not sure where he's going to go once he gets there. Or I could put Shadow in your car and I'll put this guy in mine. I'd hate to have this one freak out on you while you're driving, and I'm a hundred percent confident Shadow won't."

Annie looked back toward Coal's car. "Or I can drive your car, and you can drive mine."

He started to reply, then clamped his jaw shut. "Smarty pants," he finally said.

With a laugh, she said, "Can we do that? I'm not real good with dogs."

"Sure. Hang on a second." He went back and popped open the trunk of his car, rummaging around until he came up with a leash he kept for occasions just like this. Taking it back to the Buick, he eased open the driver's door, talking soothingly to the retriever. It would have been a beautiful dog, but now, closer up, he could see it had big clumps of burrs tangled in its coat, especially around its ears.

The reassuring sound of the dog's tail thumping the floor gave Coal the courage to move a little closer, and he held the back of his hand out to the dog. It made a couple of test sniffs, then looked up at him and whined. "Hey, buddy, you're going to be all right." Moving slowly, he let the dog sniff the collar he had brought, then slowly unbuckled it, let the animal sniff it one more time, and eased it around the burr-covered neck, buckling it on.

"Come on. Come." His voice was soft, and the dog responded perfectly, standing up as high as he could with the steering wheel pressing down on him and stepping down out of the car. Coal let the dog walk around outside the car for a few moments, then invited it to jump back in, this time into the back seat, where he attached the other end of the leash to the seatbelt.

Then he turned to Annie. "All right. I guess we're ready. My engine's still running."

The second vehicle Coal had seen so far tonight came pulling up from the area of town and stopped alongside Coal and Annie. A passenger rolled down the window of this dark-colored pickup and leaned out. "Hey, Sheriff. Everything okay?"

"You bet. Thanks for stopping."

"That's what folks do," said the stranger, and then he pulled on past and continued east.

"So I'm going to follow you, right? Where to?" Annie asked.

"I'm not sure. I may have to just tie him up outside the court-house."

"Oh, no-o," she said worriedly, looking down at the dog. "But it's so cold tonight."

Coal smiled. "I thought you weren't a dog person."

"I only said I'm not very good with them. That doesn't mean I want him to freeze to death."

"Look at all that hair, Annie. He's not going to freeze. To be honest with you, I've got a feeling he's spent more than one night outside already."

"Really?"

"Well, it's just a guess. He looks kind of skinny. And that's a lot of burrs in his hair for just one day out."

"So he's been dragging that wagon around for a long time?"

"I'm kind of afraid so."

"The poor thing." Reaching down, she petted his head. "Hey, Coal maybe I can just keep him at my house tonight."

"Oh, great. First you're not very good with dogs, and now you're going to take in the first wayward stray. Are you always like that?"

"What, taking in strays?" She laughed. "Not really, but I can see when someone has had a bad day."

"All right, the choice is yours. Where do you live?"

"Oh-ho! You think I just tell perfect strangers where I live?"

Coal laughed. "I never said I was perfect."

Her laugh matched his. "Well, all right, in that case. I'm just about half a mile up the road."

"Really! For some reason I would have thought you'd live in town."

"Well, I don't know how to take that. Hey, I'm a country girl, Coal. I would hate to be stuck in town. Working there is bad enough."

Coal raised an eyebrow. He was taken aback, but in a good way. Somehow, he just had not taken Annie for a country girl. But then, his first hint should have been the fact that she was living in a remote place like Salmon. It wasn't exactly the hometown of choice for those who needed the comforts of a city.

"Then I guess I'll eat my hat," he replied. "All right, then, why don't you lead the way home?"

CHAPTER SEVENTEEN

Coal let Annie pass him in the LTD, and then he followed her east for just under a half mile. She pulled up to a double wide trailer house with straw bales all around the bottom of it, hiding any skirting that might otherwise have shown.

They got out, and Coal looked around at what he could see of the place in the dark.

"I'm sorry it's not much," Annie said as they came together. "It's all a nurse can afford in a place like this. I plan on building a real house here someday."

"Don't worry about it, Annie. Almost any place in this valley is a good place to live."

He went around and opened the back door, coaxing the retriever out. He reached down and ruffled his ears, feeling the burrs gouge his fingers. "Wow! Boy, you really *are* a mess. You sure you want him in your house?"

"Well, if I don't then he might as well have gone back to town with you."

"I guess that's true."

Annie led the way up onto a redwood deck. Coal handed her her keys, and they jingled as she opened the door, then turned and looked at the dog. "Okay, buddy, come on. Maybe we should come up with a name for you, huh? Covered all with burrs like that, I think I'll call you 'Burr-oh'." She laughed at her own humor.

"Burro! That's a terrible name for a dog."

Again, Annie laughed. "Well, it isn't like I can keep him anyway. Come on, Burro." She motioned for him to precede her into the house, and somehow the dog seemed to understand.

Coal was still standing at the front door, and Annie turned in surprise. "Do you want to come in for a while? Sorry about the cold. I'm going to make a fire."

Her invitation took him by surprise—such surprise that he just stepped on in and shut the door.

The inside of the house was cute, his mom would say. The floor of the living area, to his right, was covered in soft blue carpet, and the walls were cream, with a tasteful chair rail about three and a half feet up the wall. There were three framed paintings on the wall, one of them of a green meadow and a red barn, one of a softly sunlit beach with seagulls flying above it, and the third a portrait of Jesus walking with two young children.

To the left was a kitchen and a dining nook, and both were spotless, with almost nothing on the countertop, and only a small vase of plastic flowers on the table. A hallway ran down to the left and vanished in the dark.

The golden retriever—Burro—walked over and lay down on the floor in front of a cream-colored couch with peach and blue flowers on it. Annie went and sat on the couch, looking down. "So he's a boy," she affirmed. "I just had a feeling."

"Why?"

"I don't know. How many girls would be wandering around in the dark on a lonely country road?"

Coal chuckled. "Well, you got me there. No girl but you, probably! So where's your wood pile?" he asked as he saw Annie start picking at burrs on the dog's chest. "I can get you a fire going before I go."

"I already have some wood right there in that box," she said, pointing. "Kindling and everything, too."

He went over and knelt down by her little stove, and in five minutes he had a good blaze crackling inside. He added a few larger branches to it, then one split log crosswise over it all. Gently, he closed the door and latched it.

When he turned around, Annie was looking at him, and even when she realized she was caught, she didn't look away. "Would you like some chocolate or something? Maybe herb tea?"

"You don't have anything stronger?"

"Oh. I guess— Are you not on duty?"

"No, ma'am. I was just headed home."

"Okay, so I keep some beer here, for guests. I think it's Schlitz."

"You think?"

"Well, I don't drink beer. It's just the first thing I saw at the store that day, and I thought I'd buy it in case I ever had company who drinks. It might be kind of old."

"So... what you're telling me is either that your guests don't drink beer, or else... that you don't have many guests."

"Pretty much the last part."

Coal didn't say anything about it, but that surprised him. With Annie's beauty and sweet nature he would have thought male callers would be rampant at her house.

"So do you want one? A beer?"

"Can't stand the smell of the stuff," Coal said with a grin.

"I have a bottle of whisky—a bourbon. That one I do know—it's Wild Turkey."

"Well, you talked me into it. It's been a long time since I had a drink. In fact, I think it'll be the first since I came home."

"Okay, then it's time to celebrate."

Annie went to a cupboard and pulled down a fifth of Wild Turkey 101 in an unopened bottle. Coal stayed on the couch, scratching the dog's head between the burrs.

When Annie came back, she was bearing two mugs and the entire bottle of Wild Turkey. "101," said Coal. "Must be a special occasion."

"Must be. I almost never touch alcohol."

She poured the cups half full and then sat back on the sofa, looking down at the dog. "Well, Burro, what are we going to do with you?"

"You're not planning on trying to keep him now, are you?" Coal asked.

"Heavens, no! I'm at work a lot. I don't have time for a dog."

Contemplating the dog's future if Annie didn't take it, Coal sipped the bourbon. It felt smooth and warm going down his throat. He leaned back and felt himself sink into the luxury of the sofa, which felt new. There were only five or six inches between his arm and Annie's.

"So what have you been up to?" Annie asked.

"Keeping my head above water, mostly. Dealing with Cynthia Batterton and little Sissy."

"How are they doing?"

"I don't know. I'm just a man, Annie. It's hard to know what goes on in the minds of young women and little girls."

"I'd like to try and talk to them sometime. Maybe I could help."

Coal thought instantly of Maura. Both of the girls had connected with her. And now he wasn't sure it would do any of them any good. He hesitated for a moment with Annie. But the whisky was warm, and the house itself was getting warm, too, and it felt good just to sit here and talk.

"I don't think we have long with them. Some relatives showed up that nobody knew were even alive. They're talking about coming to get the girls."

"Oh! Well, that's good, right?"

"I don't know. My guts tell me maybe not."

"Oh. So... what do you know about them?"

"Not a lot. Jennifer told me some stuff about this lost sister of hers that had run away from home and she never saw again. Sounded like she kept in touch with a cousin, who kept in touch with Jennifer, so she had a good idea of what had become of her. Honestly? It sounds like a pretty radical life. I can't imagine she's amounted to much."

"But the judge won't see it that way?" Annie asked.

"I don't know yet. I'm going to fight it. Cynthia told me tonight she wanted me to be her dad."

"Oh-h. Coal, I'm sorry." Annie put her hand on his arm. "That would be a burden on you, wouldn't it?"

"Not really. She's a great little lady. And she's already sixteen anyway. It's not like she'd be around forever."

"What about the little one?"

Coal smiled, thinking about little Sissy. "Now *that* one is a challenge. She's only smiled at me once the whole time I've been around her."

"You'll win her over. I have faith in you."

Coal laughed. "Well, it honestly looks like I might not get that chance. That's the heck of it all."

"You know what, Coal?"

"What?"

"I like how you won't swear around me. My— I mean, a lot of men when they get comfortable around a woman don't care."

He laughed again. "My mom would have beaten me with an ax if I swore in front of a girl."

Annie giggled, squeezing his arm as if to remind him her hand was still there. "I doubt it would matter. You're just a good man."

Without warning, she scooted closer and put her arm up over his shoulders and squeezed. He didn't think about responding. He just did. His right arm was trapped between them, but with his left one he twisted around and gave her a gentle hug. She turned part-way on the sofa so that her right arm could encircle him as well, and he buried his face in the side of her neck. The smell of her hair, the same as the perfume on her skin, was intoxicating, perhaps even more so than the whisky.

"So now you've got two strays in your house," Coal said, his voice muffled against her skin.

Annie laughed, her breath warm on his neck as she continued to hold him, not seeming to have any intentions of letting go. "I guess so. But like I said, I can kind of tell when someone's had a bad day. And it seems like you and Burro have both had one."

When Annie began to pull away from Coal, he dropped his hand, expecting her to sit back against the couch again. But she didn't pull away very far. She stopped with twelve inches between their faces, and her beautiful eyes searched his. He found himself lost in them. Her lips were pink and expressive, and moist, too, he suddenly noticed.

Without speaking, Annie sat up a little straighter and leaned forward, and her lips touched Coal's. It was a gentle, tender kiss, at the same time both the best and the worst thing that had happened to Coal Savage in a long, long time.

CHAPTER EIGHTEEN

In that moment when Annie's lips touched his, Coal felt warmth flow all through his body. He had found Annie sweet, attractive, and a gentle lady, from the very first time they had talked—which was far more than he could say for Maura PlentyWounds. He was still very much attracted to her, in spite of telling himself over and over again that he was not going to become romantically involved with another woman—at least not for years.

So when their lips met, Coal responded, feeling the heat rise up inside him. He worked both arms around her and pulled her body in closer to his, pressing their chests together as she scooted around to face him more fully. He heard Burro whine, and he didn't care. There was no one else in the entire world right now, and no one knew where he was. He might have been lost on a deserted island.

Even as turned on as Coal was by this woman's softness and beauty, and the smell of her, it was quickly plain to him that she, not he, was the aggressor here. As she continued kissing him, she moved around, coming up farther onto the couch until she was kneeling, and her body was pressing down over his, forcing him deeper into the cushion. Coal thought of himself as a passionate man, when the time was right. But Annie's onslaught was that of a woman who cherished physical closeness and intimacy, had felt it in her life, and now had missed it for too long. She kissed him almost hungrily, in a way that, even while it set his blood to raging inside him, began to actually scare him a little. The moment the tip of her very warm tongue came out and darted across his lips, he knew he had to stop her. He knew that, at least for tonight, this unforeseen passion had already gone too far.

Pulling his lips away from Annie's, Coal drew her deeper into his embrace, hugging her fiercely to him, his face over her left shoulder. He was hoping he could hug her tight enough that she couldn't just pull free, that she couldn't work her face back around again, to make her lips connect with his. He was a man, and he only had so much fortitude in reserve. He could only quench so much fire.

For just a moment, Annie seemed to struggle with him, to try and ease his hold on her to be able to turn her face back to his. She kissed and sucked briefly at the side of his neck, and he heard her say passionately, "Oh, Coal." But then, several seconds later, he felt her body give in to what she must suddenly have realized was the inevitable. The taut strength of her body relaxed, and without warning she settled her arms and torso into a hug that, although remaining firm, was no longer one of passion. It was the embrace of someone who had suddenly resigned herself to the knowledge that nothing further was going to happen tonight.

Annie's breaths slowed down gradually, and several times she sighed against Coal's neck. That alone was nearly enough to set his body raging again, but for tonight, he was a man who had faced an absolutely certain fall, then had conquered it, in the face of all odds. There would be no defeating his willpower now. And, for Annie Price, perhaps never again.

For a long time, no less than ten minutes, Coal and Annie held onto each other, struggling with their inner selves until slowly the desire died away, leaving two lonely people folded in each other's embrace, and soaking in the feeling of being cherished.

"I guess I'd better get going," Coal said finally.

Annie whispered "Okay" against his skin. She pulled away after a couple of seconds and looked into his eyes. "You really are a good man. I hope things work out you way you need them to."

"Thanks. Me too."

Before letting go of him, she fixed her gaze to his. "I don't know what's on your mind, Coal Savage. I won't even pretend to. Okay? But I can't let go of you tonight without saying something."

"Okay. I'm listening." She had his full attention.

"Coal, I was not always bold with men. Ha! Really, never. But with you I can't not say this, okay? I want you to know that you could have... stayed the night with me tonight." She spoke delicately, as if afraid to make him bolt and run. "There is nothing you could have asked from me that I would have denied."

How could a man reply to words like that? He replied by holding completely still. He couldn't even breathe.

"I am letting you go home tonight but hoping someday you will want to come back here. Okay? If you never come back to my house, that has to be only your choice. For you, this door will never be locked."

Coal nodded. His throat, for a moment, was just too tight to speak. He reached out with three fingers and gently touched them to her wet lips. He gazed into her eyes, so loving, so mystical... so haunted. "I have some hard thinking to do, Annie. Please don't think I'm leaving tonight because I want to."

And then he was gone. He had to be, or risk staying with Annie Price forever.

Tuesday, December 12

Coal awoke even before Connie and got dressed. In the deadly crisp dark, he went out to greet a waning crescent moon, just a golden sickle in a sky of ebony. It was a moon that would soon be conquered, he guessed, for the southwestern sky was cloudy to the point of starlessness, and tiny balls of hard snow dribbled down to tap on the frosty ground.

Chewy and Dart came out of the barn on stiff legs, their backs rounded, and greeted him briefly before running out in front of him to harass the horses with their barking and false charges.

Most of the horses had learned to ignore them, but big gray Cody was still looking for a good opportunity to plant them in a permanent place in the corral. He pretended to watch Coal forking hay into the enclosure, while most of his attention, and his backward-thrust ears, were attuned to the movement of the dogs.

Coal left the horses, and the dogs, knowing they couldn't go in the house, ran back to their sanctuary in the lower hay pile in the barn. With his heart in his throat, Coal walked to the front yard and looked around. The one new thing he hoped he would see was Maura's truck. It wasn't there. Well, if something he had done had set her off, then so be it. He had never been able to figure out a woman in his life. Obviously, he wasn't going to start now. And it wasn't as if there was anything between them anyway.

He let Shadow and Dobe out, and as they walked up the dark lane and merged onto Lemhi Road, the crescent moon finally vanished, and the snow began in earnest, but still just little, hard balls.

Coal couldn't stop thinking about Maura, and about Annie Price, until their faces seemed almost to meld together.

Going back to the house, he changed into shorts and a tank top and did a hard forty-five minute workout in the basement, then came up and caught Connie in time to keep her from feeding the horses again. He showered, then drove out to the MacAtees' place before the kids' bus had even arrived.

The lights were on inside, so Coal knocked. Kathy let him in and gave him a big hug. Her hair looked like the worst of Nagasaki, and her eyes were swollen. She didn't seem to care, and he didn't either. The girls emerged, one by one, and he hugged them all tight.

He sat to breakfast, since he was there, and talk was small. The girls mostly just moved their eggs and toast around on their plates, and Coal downed his four fried eggs and one piece of wheat toast without much taste for it.

After the bus came and took the girls off to school, Coal and Kathy went out behind the garage and dug up some old pieces of lumber. There was enough to make a box out of, a box about six by two by three high, with the bottom open. Afterward, Kathy fetched a space heater and an extension cord, and they plugged it in and left it running inside the box. Then Coal got Larry's truck and filled it with straw, which he brought back over and used to surround the box.

Telling Kathy he would return when the kids were out of school, he gave her a long hug, then drove into town.

His first stop, and one he had meant to make for quite some time, was at Ken Parks's auto shop. Ken already had his hands covered in grease, and he rolled out from under an old Dodge pickup, and looked up when Coal greeted him good morning.

"Sorry to bother you, buddy."

"Sorry! Don't be. Anything to get me out from under one of these stinkin' Dodges for a minute. What's up?" Ken came to his knees, then grabbing the wheel well of the truck pulled himself up, looking around for a rag.

"I see you still have that GMC."

"Yeah! No thanks to you." Coal shrugged sheepishly, and Ken grinned. "Just kidding. Why? You want to buy it?"

"Actually, I do."

"No kiddin'! You finally got smart, huh?"

"Well, since I was the one that busted it up, I figured it was the least I could do."

"No biggie. The county paid for every dime on the busted window. If you didn't know better, you'd think you'd gone back in time."

"Well, I'll pay cash for it, so have a bill of sale and the title ready for me this afternoon, would you?"

"Sure thing. Anything else?"

Coal laughed. "Nope. Looks like your reprieve from the Dodge is pretty short-lived."

"Yeah, thanks!" said Ken with sarcastic humor. "See you later."

*   *   *

Coal's next stop, around nine, was at the law office of Keith Perkins. They sat down together and went over every detail of the case Coal could make for keeping the girls, and then over every detail of the case it sounded like the Mileys had already worked up. When they were finished, Perkins laid down his yellow note-pad, then clicked his pen down on top of it. It made a sound that, to Coal, sounded altogether too final.

"I sure would like to tell you, Sheriff, that we have a strong case. I don't want to lead you one way or the other right now, but I'm not going to say it looks real good for us. The blood relative thing is huge, and the fact that they're a married couple—even bigger. The question is do they have a house, a job—are they going to be stable for those girls? I'm going to try and set up a meeting with Phillip Lawson sometime today and see what he can present. Until then, I really don't have any idea where we stand."

"Do I need to be there?" asked Coal.

"Listen, Sheriff. I'm going to tell you something flat-out. I instantly liked you the moment we first talked on the phone. And after talking to you today, I like you even more. I don't want to sugar coat anything, so I'm going to tell you this: If I like you, then Phillip Lawson is going to hate you. And honestly, you're probably going to hate him too. I think it's best if I handle this one myself. I'd better keep you and Lawson separated as long as I can. I think it's still illegal to kill attorneys—even in Lemhi County."

CHAPTER NINETEEN

Maura PlentyWounds didn't have to be to work until ten that day. And she didn't particularly care what she looked like when she got there. When the alarm clock in her room went off, she slammed her fist down on it repeatedly. When it didn't turn off, she finally jerked the cord out of the wall in frustration. Then she pulled the pillow over her head and lay still, thinking of Coal.

It was her fault he left McPherson's. Of course it was. If she had at least said *something,* he would have stayed. She didn't mean to ignore him completely. She just didn't want him to see her until she was a little more cleaned up. She didn't want him to hear her voice and know she had been crying.

Why did all this matter anyway? Cynthia wasn't her daughter. Neither was Sissy. And she couldn't afford to feed two more mouths. So why did it matter if someone else took them? That someone was family, after all. The girls were going to the right place. Who could love them and care for them more than family? Maura didn't need any new problems, and she knew from her own childhood that girls brought problems. There were those obvious emotional problems that came with a girl's physical changes. She had dealt with plenty of those herself. But it was the everyday problems of being in a young woman's body, with a young woman's new hormones inside that she didn't understand—that was the kind of problems she could live without. She liked the quiet of her little house anyway. And if she wanted noise, she could get it from Chewy and Dart, or she would get it when the boys came home—which, unfortunately, was less and less often.

Anyway, she had to find a way to at least try to apologize to Coal, she guessed. It wasn't his fault, really. He must have thought when she didn't answer him that she was hoping he would leave, so he did. It was her own fault. One hundred percent.

But that didn't make the thought of going to him with an apology any easier.

Finally, she sat up on the bed. She didn't have a watch, so she no longer had any idea what time it was. Since she had unplugged it, the clock still said eight.

As she was rubbing her eyes and getting up to get in the shower, she heard voices outside, and then her neighbors' door slammed. Not them again! She had had her fill of them the night before and was hoping they had left for good. Now it sounded like they must have just gone out for breakfast.

The man growled something at the woman, but he spoke in a lower voice she had a hard time making out. The woman barked, "Jeez, turn it on yourself."

Another mumble from the man. The woman came back with a bunch of unintelligible words, and then something about "those girls." There came the typical rejoinder from the man, hard to make sense of, and then the woman said something, much more loudly and in a much clearer voice that Maura could not help but hear: "Maybe we ought to just call the whole thing off. They'd probably be better off with Coal Savage."

Maura, just heading to the bathroom to escape the endless garble, whirled around. Goose bumps suddenly appeared on her arms as she looked around and spotted a plastic-covered glass beside the sink. Almost running, she grabbed it up, then rushed to the common wall between her and her bickering neighbors. Carefully, she set the closed end of the glass against the wall, then put her ear to the open mouth. She could hear the woman a little more clearly, but the man was still muffled. Frustrated, she tore off the plastic, then set the glass back in place, this time with the open mouth on the wall. She put her ear on the bottom.

"... don't give a crap if they both fall in the river," she heard the man's voice saying, "as long as we find out about the insurance first."

"So tell me again how you can be so sure about the money? I'm getting so tired of this whole game. And by the time that lawyer gets finished with us we're going to be broke if you're wrong about insurance."

"Oh, come on, Linda!" The man's voice was highly condescending. "Don't be an imbecile. He was a sheriff. You think some lawman that high up the ladder, with a wife and daughter to look after, isn't going to have some kind of nest egg for them in case something happens to him? And especially at his age? I've said that before."

"I know." The woman's voice was whining. "But it just seems like such a long shot. I have maybe one hundred dollars left, and then we're eating peanut butter and jelly."

"There's always other stores."

"No, honey! I don't want to do that again. It's too scary."

"Jeez. Not a thing to it."

Maura stood there, nailed to the floor, her ear frozen to the glass. She hadn't even noticed, but tears of pure fear had filled her eyes. She couldn't believe what she was hearing. *Other stores? What was he saying?*

"Well, let's just hope there's some money," the woman said. "Then the quicker we can dump those girls off somewhere the better. I know what teenage girls are like. I don't need their crap."

"They're little witches—that's what I remember," he replied. "And I'll bet you were the worst!"

Suddenly, Maura heard a knock on the hallway door to the couples' room, and she jumped back in fear. The glass tumbled from her hand and slammed on the top of a little round table that sat against the wall.

There was a moment of silence, and then Maura heard the door open. The man spoke in a muffled voice, and then the door shut once more. A few moments later, the same rhythm of knock came at her own door, and she jumped again and turned to stare at it. Was it the maid? Or was it the man from next door? Had he heard the glass fall? He couldn't possibly know she had been...

Maura's eyes darted around the room. She felt panic slip over her. But then the knock sounded again, and a woman's voice: "Housekeeping."

She nearly ran to the door and opened it. A blond girl in her late teens was staring at her with a strange look. "Is everything okay?"

"Yes, why?"

"Oh, nothing. Are you checking out today?"

"Um, yes, I think so. I can be out in fifteen minutes, after I shower."

"Okay, take your time. I'll come back."

Maura thanked the girl, then hurriedly shut the door and slipped the chain lock in its little slot. Turning, she put her hands against the door and leaned back against them. Her heart was pounding.

She had to get to Coal. It was the Mileys next door to her. They were after the money. And... what had they said about a store? It made it sound like they had gotten money perhaps from robbing a store. She tried to think back over all the words, but they were already starting to seem jumbled in her head.

Taking a peek out the peep hole, she saw that the parking lot was quiet. She tiptoed back over to the wall, although she didn't need to, because the floor was solid. The sounds she heard were no longer of speaking. They sounded like... Blushing, she stumbled away from the wall and almost ran to the bathroom.

Maura's only thought upon entering the bathroom was of showering and then getting to Coal as fast as possible. But in front of the mirror, she stopped and stared. No matter what, she couldn't let him see her this way.

Her hair was sticking out everywhere, and her makeup was smeared. Last night, she had been so out of it that she hadn't even taken it off. She hadn't taken off her clothing, either. She had slept in it, all except for her boots, in the same clothing she was going to have to wear back to work today. She took a deep breath, trying to calm herself. Continuing to look in the mirror, she slowly peeled off her pale pink, plaid blouse. As she set it on the top of the toilet tank, she looked back up at herself, in a flesh tone-colored bra— all the rage now. But the three-inch scar going down her chest, from where it started three inches below her collarbone, to where it ended, down inside her bra, certainly wasn't in vogue.

Raising her hand, she ran her fingers gently the length of the scar, staring. Her fingers stopped at the reinforced upper edge of the bra, yet the scar did not stop there. Her image in the mirror dimmed, just for a moment. Her chin quivered. She tried to think back to an innocent time before that scar. She could hardly remember innocence. But since the scar, she would never be the same.

Slowly, she continued to undress, transfixed. She didn't look horrible, in spite of the scar. Did she? What would someone else think? Perhaps a stranger? Why should she care? No one else would ever be made to suffer seeing her scar. Again, her eyes dimmed.

Turning away from the mirror, she slid her jeans down over her shapely legs, finished undressing, and stepped into the shower. The water was warm, and, falling against her bare skin, it should have been relaxing. But all she could think of once the water started running was Alfred Hitchcock, Norman Bates, and *Psycho.* Her "relaxing" shower lasted all of three minutes.

Maura kept a towel wrapped tightly around her while she dried her hair. She couldn't help looking toward the door, what seemed like every few seconds.

She wondered what time it was. She had to be to work at ten. But she had to find Coal first. She didn't have any makeup with her, nor time to put it on if she had. Looking at the door, wishing she had her revolver with her, she started across the room.

*   *   *

Coal left Keith Perkins's office and went to sit in the car, starting it up so the heater could begin its magic. Midmorning traffic on Main was typical—logging trucks, lumber trucks, now and then a semi hauling ore from the mines, and then a bunch of pickups, going on this errand or that. The land of the pickup, Salmon, Idaho. Coal smiled.

He watched the vehicles pass, and the few pedestrians, bundled up tight, rushing to and fro between businesses and their sheltering cars. It was still under ten degrees, and now and then spitting snow, so nobody wanted to be out very badly.

Coal wondered if Annie Price had an early or a late shift today, or if she was going to work at all. He had left her so abruptly the night before, it seemed, and every time he woke up in the night he was thinking about her. He wondered if he had left her feeling bad. Of course, she couldn't have felt much worse than he had.

On a whim, he threw the car in drive and pulled down the street, turning at the hospital. He drove slowly through the packed parking lot, and to his surprise he felt his heart jump when he saw the light blue LeSabre. He paused a moment with his foot on the brake, then drove on around the lot and out the other side. He was just being silly.

But something drew him back again. He drove all the way around the block, feeling his heart pound inexplicably, and ended up parking at the curb in front. For a couple of minutes, he sat at the curb, trying to calm his breathing down. What had gotten hold of him? He was a Marine. A soldier. How had this woman affected him this way? For that matter, *any* woman.

He stepped out, and this time he left the car running. Taking another deep breath, he walked to the door and went in. A glance around showed the place to be pretty quiet. He started down the hall, looking into rooms that were mostly dark.

Toward the end of the hall, he heard a surprised, "Hey!"

Turning, he saw Annie standing there, holding a clipboard. She was fetching in her nurse outfit, the little white cap and all. Couldn't have been any cuter. He couldn't help but meet her smile with a big grin. Not that he was any judge, but he could detect no sign in her face that she was upset with him.

He walked ten feet as she came toward him, and they met in the middle. "How are you doing?" he asked before she could speak.

"Fine." She cocked her head to one side, studying him for any sign of why he was here. "How are you?"

"Good."

"Can I help you?"

He smiled. "Wow. That's a loaded question."

That got a laugh out of her. "Know what? It's quiet in here. I can take a quick break if you want to grab a cup of coffee or something."

"Sure." They walked down the hall to the break room. There was a younger, heavyset woman in there when they opened the door, but she quickly excused herself and left, looking very preoccupied.

Coal poured two cups of coffee and sniffed at one. "Hmm. Smells like some of that nasty stuff."

She laughed. "Finicky about your coffee, huh?"

"I don't know why. Honestly, I don't know if I even like it that much if it's the so-called good stuff."

"About like bourbon, huh? You didn't even finish what I poured you last night."

"Sorry. No, that was the good stuff. I hope you saved it for me."

"You'd have to come back to my house to finish it."

"Would that be all right with you?"

Her face went serious, marked by those parted lips and that strangely haunted look she seemed usually to wear. "I told you, Coal. Any time."

"Why?" he asked point-blank.

She looked down at her hands, warming around the blue ceramic cup. Finally, she looked back up and gave a little shrug, with her shoulders and with her face. "Coal, I honestly don't know. Can I ask you something?"

"Sure."

"Are you all right? I mean, are you okay with what happened last night?" Before he could form a reply, she added, "I promise you that isn't something I normally do. I just... Well, I can't explain it, I guess. But I'm just a little worried about you."

"Why? Nothing happened, right?"

"Well, no. But I guess... Well, I mean I kind of made it pretty plain I was hoping it would. I didn't mean to be forward. I'm just... Okay. I'm kind of lonely, Coal, and I'm really attracted to you."

She had said it. Instead of something great like, "Sorry about that, it will never happen again," she had to drop a stick of dynamite down his well. The problem was that at the moment, he felt the same. But there was that other side of him that felt strangely connected... not to Annie, but to Maura. He couldn't really explain it. They had never shared a romantic moment. They had never even spoken to each other of any kind of obligation toward each other. But for some reason he felt attached to her—even obligated.

Coal nodded. His male mind was swimming in the mire, trying to find something smart to say.

Finally, staring into his face, Annie shook her head, raising her eyebrows a little. "Nothing to say to that? I just threw my heart at your feet, you know."

Coal was at least able to give her a little laugh. "I'm attracted to you too, Annie. I was the first night I saw you. I've just... I've got a lot of skeletons that are pretty fresh in my closet."

"You came here just to tell me that?"

He stared at her.

"Well, we all have those skeletons, Coal. Believe me. Yours can't be any worse than mine are. Is there any way I can help? I mean really, if you just want to come over and have a listening ear, I can do that too. I promise I won't take advantage of you." She winked. Coal grunted out a little chuckle.

They heard Annie's name being paged, and Coal's heart fell. He didn't know what he was doing here or what to say, but he just felt the need to stay with her a little longer. He had to know he hadn't made her feel terrible about last night.

"I have to go. Sorry," she said. "I'm home tonight, if you need me. All by myself."

The door opened, and a man in a suit walked in, greeting Annie and going straight to the coffee pot. Embarrassed, Coal motioned toward the door, and they went out. They stood in the hallway, Coal holding his hat in his hands, sort of a shield between them.

He started to turn toward the exit door, but Annie pointed the other direction. "I have to go this way."

"Oh. All right."

"Hey, Coal, don't feel bad about last night, okay? I knew I was taking a chance."

He smiled, and perhaps that was the permission she had been seeking. Without warning, she came close, put her arms around him lightly, and planted a tender kiss on his lips. Then she turned and walked down the hall.

Looking down at his hat to make sure she hadn't crushed it, and knowing his face was red, Coal turned to leave.

There stood Maura, not twenty feet away, staring right at him.

CHAPTER TWENTY

Coal had no chance to recover from the red face Annie Price had given him. With his mouth ajar, staring back at Maura, he sort of wished he was sitting at the bottom of the Mississippi, buried in river ooze, with a two-ton boulder resting on top of him as a blanket. He swore out loud, something he very seldom did.

Maura all of a sudden took a deep breath, tucked her chin down as if protecting it in a boxing match, and came on down the hall, her strides long and purposeful.

She stopped six feet away and folded her arms tightly across her pink button-front shirt. Coal noticed that she wasn't wearing makeup, or at least not very much. Other times, she would still have looked attractive. Right now, she didn't.

"I just overheard a conversation between the people who are coming to take Cynthia and Sissy. I came to tell you about it."

"Uh... Okay," he stammered. Someone may as well have run a wood screw through his tongue down into his jaw. He could barely speak.

"They flat-out said they don't care about the girls. They are expecting there to be insurance money involved, and that's all they want."

Coal's heart jumped. This was something his guts had told him, but only a guess. His elation passed when he realized it was not as if Maura could have recorded the words.

"All right. We figured that."

"And you might want to start checking your records for any recent store robberies involving a man and a woman. They said something to each other that made it sound pretty suspicious."

"What was that?"

"I don't remember right now. I'll have to think about it."

"Is that all?"

"It's all I have time for right now. See ya."

And then she turned and walked down the hall toward the exit door. Coal stared at her all the way out, but the last thing on his mind was her shapely figure.

Coal drove around town for a while, listening to the hard bits of snow patter against the roof of the car. A logging truck came in and turned toward Challis. He thought of grabbing lunch, but he didn't know where to go where he wouldn't take a chance on meeting someone he knew, and right now he didn't feel awfully sociable.

Taking a chance, he stopped on Main at Saveway and bought some fresh maple doughnuts. Then, finally, he drove home beneath the lowering gray sky. The head and shoulders of the Beaverhead range were lost up in the heavy clouds.

Connie's Chrysler was in the yard, and Coal went inside to find her sitting on the couch, snuggled up with Sissy, watching *Family Affair*. He had to look at Connie twice to make sure, but it was plain from her puffy eyes that she had been crying. Without a word, which was not normal for his mother, she smiled at him sadly and lifted a hand out to him.

He walked over and took her hand, squeezing it and holding on. "Things okay, Mom?"

"Sure," she said in a soft voice. "I'm always okay. Just thinking about what's coming with the girls."

He nodded sadly, then held up the white paper sack "I bought some doughnuts."

She brightened with amazement. "You? Doughnuts? Coal, are you giving up?"

He laughed. "Very funny. I remember you buying these for us when we were boys. Guess I just had a nostalgic moment."

She tugged at his hand. "Sit down, Son. Watch a show with us. Little Buffy's about to get herself spanked if she keeps up her antics," she said with a little laugh. "At least you boys would have."

Coal found himself lost for a moment in the show, the tiny little blond girl, Buffy, and her adorable voice. As hard as things got on *Family Affair,* they were never as hard as life in the Lemhi Valley.

He looked down at Sissy. Her face was turned upward, and her brown eyes were watching him. He smiled, and for only the second time she smiled back. It started tiny, just a faint upturning of her lips. And then it melted into a full-fledged smile, and stole his heart.

Letting go of his mom's hand, Coal reached into the doughnut sack and pulled one out. He tore off a piece and held it out to Sissy. She stared at it, her eyes large. Then she stared at him. Finally, her hand reached, tentative and shy, and she took it from his fingers. She put it up to her nose and sniffed it, and then, seeming satisfied, she opened her little mouth and slid it inside. After a couple of seconds, the big smile returned to her face. She looked up at him as if he had just given her a whole zoo.

"Did you like that?" He didn't expect an answer.

"I did like it."

Stunned tears came into Coal's eyes, and they jumped up to see his mom watching him. The tears had returned to her own eyes as well. Blinking his emotion away, Coal said, "You can have as much as you want." He held out more of the doughnut, and the girl took it eagerly.

While she was eating, Coal reached into the bag again, feeling for a doughnut. When his fingers latched onto one, he looked at Connie. "Mom?"

"Oh, sure. I'm not quite fat enough."

Without arguing, he pulled one out and handed it to her.

"No argument, I see," she chided him.

"Right. We both know better. You're tough as wang leather."

Connie laughed and took the doughnut. Halfway through, she said, "Wow! Those are sticky. Let me get some moist napkins." Getting up, she went into the kitchen.

When she was gone, Sissy looked over at Coal's hand. Her face was turned down, but he could see she was studying his hand intently. All of a sudden, with no warning, she reached over and touched it. Her little fingers felt cool, and they sent a shiver up his arm. Oddly, it was a shiver of warmth.

As he continued to watch her, she scooted forward on the couch, a movement he guessed she had been planning out in her head for several minutes, making sure in her mind that it would actually work—analyzing. Then she reached behind her with one hand and started pushing his hand over to the left. When she judged that it was at the right distance, she wiggled her little rump backward, to Coal's amazement, until she was leaned back into the crook of his arm. As if it would break a spell, he held perfectly still, staring at her as if she were some foreign creature.

Connie returned with napkins and three glasses of milk, and with a startled look on her face she stopped just before passing between Coal, Sissy and the television. She opened her mouth to say something, then thought better of it, raising an eyebrow at Coal as she stepped in front of him.

Coal fully expected Sissy to move back over to Connie when she sat down, but instead, she pushed ever farther into his embrace.

With a feeling of real trepidation, he gently brought his hand back in until his palm was against the side of her left leg, and then he hugged her to him.

When she laid her head over against his middle, he could not help the tears that came to his eyes. As he got older, he was turning into a little girl himself.

But right then, he didn't care. Little Sissy Miley had decided to trust him at last.

*   *   *

Not until Sissy had faded to sleep, snuggled into Coal's embrace, did Connie turn to him, her smile warm. "I wondered if I would ever get to see that, Coal. It sure reminds me of someone else about eleven years ago."

Coal nodded. Yes, Katie Leigh had once been this shy little girl, around Connie. Perhaps that explained the emotion, in part.

He decided to tell Connie what he had come home to tell her, about what had been going on with Maura, how she had suddenly turned cold and distant, how Annie had kissed him at her house— although he kept to himself the level of their passion—and then how she had kissed him again in the hallway of the hospital, only for him to find out that Maura had walked in on them.

"You're a woman, Mom."

Connie raised an eyebrow. "Yes, that's pretty certain, Son," she said with a smile.

"Yeah, sorry. Okay, so you've got to help me out. What am I supposed to do about that woman? She's never let on that I mean anything to her other than being a friend. But now she's turned cold on me, and especially after seeing Annie kiss me. And what about Annie? I never saw that coming in a million years either."

Connie just sat there motionless for a second, her mouth open with dismay, then finally tilted her chin down and gave her son a direct look as if she were looking over the top of a pair of glasses. "Wow."

Coal waited a second for some great revelation. Then he shrugged. "What?"

"Wow. Coal, I have to apologize, but I'm a little speechless here." He started to reply, and she jerked a flat hand up in front of him. "Just hush for a second, okay? Allow me to sit here gaping at about the biggest dope I've ever seen." In reply to his frown, she again held up her hand, stilling any words out of him. "It's as certain to me that you're a man now as it is that I'm a woman to you, buddy. But even for a man, you take the cake. If you can sit there with a straight face and tell me that you honestly don't think Maura has ever given you any clue that she is head over heels in love with you, then you are just about hopeless. For one thing, I already tried to warn you."

"Yeah, but Mom, she's never said a word!"

"Son, a woman doesn't need to speak about things like that in words. Every time she looks at you she is saying a million things in one glance. If she touches your hand, or your sleeve, or maybe taps your leg with her fingertips, she is telling you volumes. If she does her hair when she's not even going anywhere, or puts on a spritz of perfume, or even slides your eggs onto your plate a certain way, or laughs at your jokes, no matter how stupid you and everyone else knows they really are, she is stating plain and certain facts. She is telling you that her heart is putty in your hands. That woman has been screaming her love for you for so long I can't stand to think of it."

"What about Annie?"

Connie gave him a sad smile. "Well, Son, you must be putting two and two together. Unlike Maura, who is obviously shyer that way, Annie decided not to leave anything to chance. I could see how she looked at you the night she first laid eyes on you, the night you got home."

"What? What did I do?"

"Oh, Coal. Do you think since you were in junior high I have told you how hard it was going to be keeping the women off you just because I'm your mom? Yes, I am your mom, and yes, I love you. But Coal, you have a kind of charisma and looks that are always going to draw women to you. I promise you even when you were just going along being a typical boy, and then a typical man, women were dropping at your feet all around you. You were just lucky enough for the most part to be blind to it. I was the one who had to sit back and watch the aching, breaking hearts. I thought we were all saved from it when Laura came along. Now she's gone, you've blossomed into the man you are today, and it's only going to get worse."

"Worse? How could it get worse?"

"Because, Coal. Those girls who went head over heels for you in school were immature. Their hearts could change in a second and let them move on. But when a woman gets to be the age of Annie or Maura, she sets her cap for a man, and that's that. Come hell or high water, she is going to do anything short of murder to win him."

"But I think Maura and Annie are friends."

Connie scoffed. "Sorry, Coal. I don't think they're *that* close of friends. And besides, friendship has nothing to do with this. A woman who's gotten to their age, and who knows that all her happiness rests upon winning the man she loves is going to go blind to friendship—at least during the heat of battle."

"What if the man wants nothing to do with the whole thing? What if he doesn't want anything to do with either one of them?"

Connie gave her son a direct gaze. "Well then, Coal, I'll tell you what—that man is lying to his own mother, and to himself."

CHAPTER TWENTY-ONE

Connie had given her son a lot of things to think about. And that was exactly what he did that day: think. However, the first order of business was to call Kathy MacAtee and tell her he would try and be at her house after school let out, so not only could her daughters all be there to say goodbye to Rowdy, but he might also bring Sissy and Cynthia. He felt the burial of the wonderful dog could be made into an important life experience for them.

He went up and checked in at the courthouse, glad for the long reprieve from having anyone in jail to take care of. Todd Mitchell was just coming in, and he sat at Coal's desk looking through the latest bulletins from around the state and the nation.

"Hi, Coal. How are things?"

"Slow, Todd. You?"

"Same. Hey, Jordan told me something about maybe you'd try to get him a raise. That's great of you to do that. He's a good hand."

"The same goes for you, Todd." Coal was glad to be able to say this honestly to a man he had recently almost decided to help put in prison for his bad judgment.

Todd nodded. He seemed at a loss for words.

"I mean that not only about your being a good hand," Coal went on. "I'm also going to try and swing a raise for you. This county's bringing in plenty of money from the logging and mines, not to mention all the ranches. We can afford to pay to keep good help here."

"Thank you." Todd seemed too emotional to say anything more, and he started absently swirling the coffee around in his cup, then swore when some of it sloshed over on the desk. "Sorry!"

"Don't worry about it. That desk needed a little antiquing anyway."

Coal sensed from the way Todd was acting that he was trying to say something, so he kept watching him out the corner of his eye. But nothing was forthcoming. He sipped at the black coffee, which was hot enough to make him happy but tasted like bad tea. Making a face, he set the cup back down. He glanced back over at Todd, catching him looking at him.

Todd hurriedly looked away, standing up from the desk.

"You're looking at a man who likes to hold everything inside until half the time it's too late," Coal said conversationally.

"What's that?"

"I think you're doing what I do, Todd. I have a feeling there's something on your mind."

Todd gave a little chuckle, swishing his coffee again, putting it to his lips for a taste, then making the same face Coal did and setting it down on the desk top. "I need to have Cindy show me how to make coffee, too, I guess. Seems like you and Jordan are the only ones who can do it right now."

Coal smiled patiently. "That's not what you've been wanting to say."

Todd took a deep breath. "Yeah. Right. Hey, I don't—"

The ringing phone cut off the rest of his sentence. Todd almost dived at it, as if it were a lifeline for him. "Hello. Uh, yeah, he sure is, Chief. Hang on." He held out the receiver to Coal. "Chief George."

Chief Dan George. As it often did, the name brought a little smile to Coal's lips. He found humor in the strangest things, and wondered if anyone ten or twenty years from then would even remember the old Indian actor from the movie *Little Big Man*.

"Hello, Chief."

Hi, Sheriff. Listen, I've got a bit of an awkward situation on my hands. Are you going to be around today? At your house, that is?

"Maybe around four-thirty."

I know it's out of my jurisdiction, but I need to come pay you a visit. Plan on me between four-thirty and five. Still Savage Lane, right?

"No reason to move," replied Coal.

He hung up, and no sooner had the receiver touched the base than it rang again. With a disgruntled sigh, he picked it up. "Sheriff's office."

Yeah, Coal. Ken. Hey, I've got to run out toward Leadore and trailer a car in. You going to come get that pickup, or what?

"Um, yeah, I planned on it. Do I have a minute?"

As long as it's only a minute. Billy Frieze is broke down halfway on the road, about thirty miles out. Sounds like his transmission just froze up on him.

"All right, dang it. Okay, I'll be right down." Hanging up the phone, Coal looked an apology at Todd. "Hey, can you hang on?"

Todd waved him off. "Yeah, sure. No big deal anyway. Go get done what you need to do."

Coal headed down off the Bar and pulled in at Ken's just four minutes later. Ken was just setting the safety chains under the hitch on his tow trailer, now hooked up behind his pickup. Coal already had a check written, and he handed it to him.

"I thought you were paying cash? How do I know this is good?" Ken grinned and tossed him the keys. "Hey, we'll deal with the rest later, all right? Have fun with it. I gotta go."

With that, Ken jumped in his pickup and pulled out of the lot onto Main. Coal turned back to look at his new pickup. It was a real beauty, known as "light green," by the GMC company, but to Coal more of a greenish teal. Other than a small ding here or there, it was pretty much in mint condition and had only a little over thirty thousand miles on it.

On a whim, Coal parked the Ford in the back lot, stopped into Andy's Body Shop to say hi to his friend Andy Holmes for just a minute, and then took the pickup and headed back up to Courthouse Drive to finish his conversation with Todd Mitchell. The deputy had already departed. He looked around for a note of explanation, but there was nothing.

He left and patrolled up to the Montana border, enjoying watching the herds of elk that had come down from the high country to winter out and now resided often quite close to houses, sometimes eating in the same pastures with horses and cattle.

On the way back, he stopped in at Gibbonsville—often called Gibbtown by the locals—to say hi to a few old friends and show off his new vehicle, then hit North Fork and turned right on the river road. It was pretty messy there, however, and he didn't want to take a chance on getting stuck or sliding off into the river. There were a few bad stretches, and the river, where it wasn't clogged with ice, was running pretty deep. Even the places where it was almost all the way frozen over weren't going to hold this two thousand pound-plus bullet if it went over the side.

With that unsettling thought in mind, Coal turned the pickup around, after quite a bit of careful maneuvering, and headed back to town. It was pushing time for the kids to be out of school.

Coal swung by the courthouse to see if Todd had come back yet. When he didn't see his car, he headed back down, and he got to the house just as the big yellow bus was pulling away. Virgil and Cynthia were marching toward the house side by side, but he noticed Katie Leigh seemed to be distancing herself from them. He frowned. Something was up with her the last couple of days that he was going to have to get to the bottom of while their relationship was still good. But he had a more pressing priority than that right now.

Parking the truck, Coal went in and hugged the kids—all except Katie, who had already disappeared into her room. He kissed Connie on the cheek when she came in from the kitchen with biscuit dough on her hands.

"Already on supper?" Coal asked.

"No, just an afternoon snack. Biscuits and jam."

Coal had not been hungry, but the thought of his mother's wheat biscuits and homemade strawberry preserves set his juices flowing instantly.

"Well, I hope they're just out of the oven when I get back."

"Get back? You just came in. Where are you off to now?" Connie couldn't hide her disappointment.

"I've got a spot thawing behind the garage at the MacAtees', Ma. I told them I'd help bury Rowdy this afternoon."

"Oh, okay. I understand. Sorry you have to do that."

"No reason to be sorry. That dog meant a lot to me. And I guess he's kind of my last big hold on old Larry."

Connie nodded her understanding and reached up to pat his cheek—then quickly had to brush away the flour she left there.

Coal laughed, and then he looked over at Cynthia, who was in his big chair holding Sissy. The little one had crawled up on her lap the moment she had the chance. "I was thinking of bringing Cynthia—Sissy, too, if she'll go. If there's a chance we might get to hang onto them—and I'm pretty hopeful of it with Keith Perkins on our side—I'd like to start sharing some life lessons with them."

"You'd really like to keep them, wouldn't you, Son?"

"Yeah, Mom. I would. I think we can make a huge difference in their lives." He thought of Cynthia's statement that she wanted him to be her dad. It brought a lump to his throat.

"Well, I'm going to hold onto this biscuit dough until you call me from Kathy's and tell me you're on your way," Connie said suddenly. "Please don't be long."

Coal smiled. "I'll try." He started to turn from her, then suddenly came back around. "Hey, Mom—did Katie say anything to you when she came in?"

Connie glanced down the hall. "No, she didn't. She went straight to her room. She's been very quiet."

"Something's wrong," Coal said.

"That's another reason you need to get back soon. I think that girl needs some of Daddy's attention."

Coal nodded. As he was turning away again, Connie caught his arm. "Do you think maybe it would be a good idea to ask *all* the children if they'd like to go with you?"

Coal studied her face, and then he looked down the hall. "Are you thinking Katie's getting jealous?"

Connie shrugged. "I don't know, buddy, but she seemed great until Cynthia and Sissy moved in. It's something to think about."

"Well, shoot, Mom. Uh... I just bought a pickup from Ken Parks. And I left the car at his shop."

"Then take the Chrysler."

"Mom..."

He glanced over at Cynthia and the little girl.

Suddenly, it seemed like it was Connie's turn to understand. "Okay, Son. I'll keep the kids busy. See you soon."

Connie always seemed to grasp the important things. This time, she knew he was afraid of the chance of losing those girls, in spite of his most valiant fight. He just needed a little "just in case" time with them alone—provided that Sissy would agree to go.

He walked over to the girls and knelt down. The boys were already on the couch watching Dick VanDyke, to wind down from their day.

Coal put his hand on Cynthia's arm. Out of habit, when Sissy looked over and saw him, she shied away, but then she gave him a little smile. Half of her face was hidden behind Cynthia's arm, but the crinkling of her eyes gave the smile away.

"Hey, Cynthia. I'm going to go over to the MacAtees' and help them bury their dog, Rowdy. I was wondering if you and Sissy would like to go for a drive."

"Sure. I'd love to. Are you sure it will be okay with them?"

"Sure I'm sure."

Cynthia looked down at Sissy. "Do you want to ride somewhere with me and Coal?"

The little girl looked at Coal, her big eyes melting his heart. She gave one firm nod.

"All right," said Coal, patting the arm of the chair. "Then let's get going so we can be back here for some of Grandma's biscuits and jam. Bundle up."

Leaving the dogs shivering at the door, in excitement that quickly began to melt away to disappointment as they watched their hopes for an afternoon ride quickly vanish, Coal opened the door for Cynthia, who was holding Sissy—she wasn't quite ready for Coal to hold her, it seemed. Then, in the achingly cold afternoon, they piled in the GMC.

Coal's mind was jumbled with thoughts and questions all the way to the MacAtees': How was he going to survive the anguish if the law let someone steal these helpless girls from him? He had not intended to get so attached so fast, but somehow he had. More immediately, once at the MacAtees, how was he going to handle the sadness of laying one of his biggest reminders of his best friend Larry in the ground? What was eating at Katie Leigh, making her withdraw back into herself when they had come so far? And would he and Maura ever be friends again?

There was one other question that he had not even addressed yet. That was the question Maura had brought up about the possibility that the Mileys were wanted somewhere for some kind of robbery. He wanted that so bad that he was afraid to research it for fear he would find nothing.

He could not stop all the questions from swimming around in his brain, but he had no answers for any of them.

And the sadness of it all washed through the cab of the pickup like the gloomy sky that obliterated the Beaverhead Mountains.

Coal wondered if his life, now that he was the head county lawman, would ever again be anything but daily worry and stress. He thought about the life his mother and father had led when he was a child, and he dreamed of a peaceful existence like theirs.

CHAPTER TWENTY-TWO

Kathy had kept Rowdy wrapped in an old blanket by the back door because neither she nor the girls could bear to see him frozen out in the cold. Coal agreed with them, even though he knew it was strange, because Rowdy would soon be buried under two feet of frozen ground.

The first thing Coal did was to go out with a pick and a shovel, and after moving the box he had made, and the heater, he dug a hole in the ground, about four by three feet by three feet deep. Then he went back in and pulled off his coat, joining the others in the warm living room.

He had not realized that Kathy planned to make such a big production out of their sad chore. It was, as it turned out, more of a funeral than a burying.

Kathy had let her girls pick out a couple of hymns to sing. She had also pulled out an old record by Elton Britt, and from it she started out their little funeral program with the song, "There's a Star-Spangled Banner Waving Somewhere." Coal could normally sing along with it, as it was one of the songs he played with his guitar, and he knew it by heart. But it was a song his father had loved as well, and between that and all the tears of the girls, and the thought of Rowdy being gone, Coal wasn't sure he trusted his voice.

Kathy seated everyone on the couch and some of her kitchen chairs, and after they sang, "Abide With Me, 'Tis Eventide," she showed them a slide show on a white sheet that got Kathy and all the girls crying. It was all Coal could do to stay dry-eyed himself.

The slides showed Rowdy when he was just a pup, and photos of Larry when he was a much younger man. One of them was a portrait-style shot of him walking away across an open field with Rowdy by his side, a hunting vest and cap on, and a shotgun in the crook of his arm. It was a shot of Larry and Coal standing laughing, side by side, with Rowdy at their feet, that almost broke him down. Kathy came over and put an arm around him and gave him a big squeeze, and he felt her tears even through his shirt as she leaned her head over.

Sometimes Coal wasn't quite sure about this ritual of funerals, with people purposely trying to make everyone cry one last time before putting their loved one down in the frozen earth, to sleep their last sleep until the resurrection. And he had had a gut-load of them in the last month—more of them than he had ever been to in his life in that short amount of time.

Finally, they sang "Amazing Grace," and then Kathy told everyone to get their coats on, and they went outside. Sixteen-year-old Milo insisted on being pall bearer, and she bore their little buddy proudly to the side of his open grave, where Coal knelt down and helped her lower the still form to the earth. Rowdy seemed so small inside the blanket, not like the lively black and white powerhouse who for so long had chased cattle and sheep all over that property, and guarded it from coyotes, foxes, one wily bobcat, and so many skunks they could not keep track. Coal remembered a time both he and Larry had gotten sprayed over the dog's proclivity to take on that entertaining chore. He smiled now, through the tears that were starting to dim his eyes. He sure hadn't smiled then.

Kathy looked around at the other girls through her own tears. She sniffled and asked bravely, "Girls, do any of you want to touch Rowdy's fur? This will be your last chance."

Sara and Jen immediately started crying harder. Little Jen, through her wall of tears, said, "I do, Mom."

And so they knelt together, and Kathy unwrapped a corner of the blanket so they could see Rowdy's floppy black ear and the back of his head. Weeping, Jen caressed the fur, and Sara got down and joined her. That was too much, and finally Coal could not hold back the couple of tears that ran down his cheeks.

It was strange to think how a good friend died, and then every time something you remembered him for was lost, it was as if he died all over again. Coal had the sudden urge to get down with the girls and pet Rowdy's head one more time, but he held himself back. He was trying to be strong for Kathy and the girls, and it was hard enough already.

At last, while everyone sobbed except little Sissy, who didn't understand what was going on, Coal slowly covered the body over. Everyone's tears and wailing increased as the last of the blanket disappeared beneath a shovelful of dirt.

*   *   *

On the drive home, Sissy seemed to sense that Coal needed someone soft and warm, and she scooted all the way over beside him and put one hand on his right leg. Then she nestled her little face against his side, and Coal could hardly see the road. Big, tough Coal. A darn Marine. But apparently what they said was true: When boys grow up into men and have children of their own, they become babies again.

He reached an arm around the little one and pulled her closer, and Cynthia watched them happily and scooted over against them until they were just a big sandwich.

Finally, they turned off at the exit to Savage Lane, and Coal took his arm off of Sissy to shift gears. They drove up the long road, and Coal, whose mind was elsewhere, had almost reached the yard before he realized something was wrong.

There were police cars everywhere.

His heart leaped. He counted two of the baby blue Salmon city police cars, and one that was a vehicle of the Idaho State Police.

He whipped into the driveway and killed the motor with a lurch, forgetting to turn it off before jerking his foot off the clutch. He was lucky even to remember to set the brake.

Leaving the girls to fend for themselves and ordering them to stay put, Coal almost fell from the cab, looking around for sign of life. He heard Dart and Chewy barking, as they came toward him from the direction of the barn, but he completely ignored them, pulling his .357 from the holster on his hip.

Hearing voices inside the house, he threw open the door.

There at the kitchen table sat Chief Dan George, patrolman Bob Wilson, and some state bull Coal didn't know. Connie was leaning up against the kitchen counter with her arms folded, and the moment she saw Coal she came hurrying to him. She had been crying.

Confused, Coal looked around. The state bull had started to stand, his hand going for his gun, but Bob Wilson reached out and touched his forearm to stop him, saying something that didn't register on Coal.

Smith and Wesson still in his hand, Coal growled, "What the hell's going on?"

Chief Dan George and Bob Wilson slowly came to their feet.

"Easy, Sheriff," spoke the chief. "I called to tell you I'd be coming over, remember?"

Coal stared at him blankly. Finally, the memory came back to him. After a few more seconds, he eased his gun back into the holster. It wasn't until then that the state officer relaxed.

"Okay, I remember, Chief. But you never said anything about a big crowd. I thought you just needed to talk to me."

"Somebody was worried that this might escalate."

"What? What might escalate?" Confused, Coal looked around, his eyes landing last on the state officer.

"Chief, can I talk to Coal?" Bob Wilson cut in.

Chief George looked over at his underling, seeming to suddenly realize he was in the room. "Sure, of course."

Bob came around the table and clapped a hand on Coal's arm. "Hey, buddy, why don't you come in the front room with me."

Coal nodded, and they walked off. Bob turned Coal with a hand on his shoulder until their backs were to the others. "I told them they wouldn't need the big show, Coal. But I guess the lawyer had some reason to feel worried."

"The lawyer? What's this about?"

"You don't know?"

"How the hell could I?"

"Coal, they have a court order. We came to serve the papers at Judge Sinclair's request. I know it's a county job, but with you being the sheriff... You understand."

"No, I don't." Coal looked back at the others, his mind flying over a hundred different scenarios, right past the one that should have been most obvious. All he could think of was the incident with K.T. Batterton being fired over the theft of petty cash. "I haven't done anything wrong, Bob."

"No, Coal, nobody's saying you have. But the judge issued an order that this couple named Bud and Linda Miley can take the girls, as the only living relatives."

Bob Wilson may as well have kneed Coal in the groin. Instantly sick, he looked over at the other officers. "I thought we had another day."

"I don't know, Coal. I guess Judge Sinclair didn't see any reason to prolong it."

"Bob! Have you met those people?"

"I have. They're actually out in the back of my car. Have *you* met them?"

Coal stopped short. "Well, not in person. But I talked to them on the phone. And I don't trust them."

Bob shrugged. "Hey. I understand. But the chief has a court order there, so there's not really anything we can do about it now."

Coal turned and looked over his shoulder at the others. Suddenly, his whole body seemed to slump. Absently, half blind, he gave Bob's shoulder a couple of pats, then turned and went to the table, where Connie, Chief George and the state patrolman were standing.

"Do we know where they're taking them?"

The chief nodded. "Yes. The judge decided that since Cynthia Batterton is the sole heir of K.T. and Jennifer that the house belongs to her. That was one of the Mileys' petitions—to take over the house on Hope Street."

Numb, Coal nodded. It made him sick to think of driving by Hope and knowing that not only did K.T. and Jennifer no longer live there, but the Mileys did. Ironically, it seemed to Coal that there *was* no Hope.

"Where are the girls, Sheriff?" asked the chief.

"In my truck."

"Why don't we get their things together?"

"Chief, does it have to be right now?" Connie cut in. "Can't we even have one evening to say goodbye?"

"I'm sorry, ma'am. I'm afraid not. The order says we're to see that the girls are placed with their new guardians tonight."

"Can we at least ask the Mileys?" she pressed, almost begging.

"Well, I guess you could ask," he said with a shrug. "Listen, ma'am, I didn't want any part of this whole thing. I hope you know that. You're good folks, and I'm sure those girls would have been more than happy here."

"Will you go with me to ask them?" she asked the chief hopefully.

"Sure, Mrs. Savage. I'd be happy to."

By now, Coal had let his mother take over. His shock had gone away, and too much anger had replaced it for him even to dare do any more talking. Still, when the three officers and Connie stepped outside, leaving all of the boys and Katie standing inside with scared eyes, Coal followed them. He kept his distance from Bob Wilson's car, but he wanted to get a look at the Mileys, and he wanted to see how they reacted to his mom's request.

Bob went and opened up his back door, asking the Mileys to climb out, which they did. Coal couldn't help staring at them. His mother had always told him not to judge a book by its cover, but fortunately his father had a little more sense, and after those lessons of his mother's, old Prince would often take him aside with a wink and remind him that he often judged people by their appearances, and more often than not he ended up right.

Coal instantly did not like the Mileys. He already hadn't liked the sound of their voices. Now the instinct bore over into their slovenly, arrogant appearance. It only went downhill from there.

He heard the chief introducing Connie, and then she began to speak. "Hi. I would just really like to ask you for one more night with the girls. It would mean a lot to all of us if we could bring them to you in the morning."

Connie's words were muffled, because her back was to Coal. But Linda Miley, who instantly elected herself the spokesperson of the two, was facing toward Coal, thus very easy to hear.

"No, I don't think that will work out for us."

"Just one more night? How could that hurt anything? You kind of took us by surprise."

"Sorry about that. But we'd like to start getting on with our lives and letting the girls settle in. This has been an emotional time for us, with losing so much of our family."

Coal surged forward. "Your family? Hell, you haven't even seen Jennifer Batterton since before she was in high school!" he growled.

The chief moved in, putting an arm straight out to block Coal's advance. "And this is why they asked us to have more than one officer here," he said firmly. "Sheriff, you need to back up."

"I'll thank you not to insult my wife," said Bud Miley.

"I haven't even begun to get insulting," Coal retorted.

"Coal!" It was Connie speaking now. "Honey, come on. There's no talking to people like this. Come on." She came and put her hands on his chest and gently eased him backward a few steps. "Come on, calm down." These were the words of a woman who had seen her son when he lost his cool. It was not pretty. And judging by the fact that three officers were here on the property, Judge Sinclair had heard about this temper as well.

All of a sudden, Coal realized there was another vehicle coming up the road, and in a moment it flew into the yard and came to a stop with a spray of gravel. It was a white Travelette.

Maura threw open the door and leaped out, looking around as if disconcerted. "What's happening? Coal?" Her voice was barely controlled. "Where are the girls?"

Forgetting his near confrontation with the Mileys, Coal hurried over toward Maura, Connie almost running to keep up.

Coal tried to take Maura's shoulder and turn her away from the scene with the Mileys. She angrily threw off his hand. "Where are the girls?" Her voice was like a tiger's now.

Coal heard his pickup door slam shut, and Cynthia and Sissy came rushing over and threw themselves against Maura. She dropped to her knees, hugging them fiercely to her.

Instinctively, Sissy must have sensed that something was wrong, for she was starting to cry. "It's okay now, Sissy," soothed Maura. "I'm home now. Don't cry."

Cynthia looked up and glanced all around until her eyes fell on Coal. "What's wrong? Why are all the police cars here? Did something happen?"

Mouth open, Coal just stared at the girl. Connie stared too. Neither could speak. They both looked at Maura, who now, because of their lack of response, was also staring at them.

The woman looked back and forth between them. In her eyes was a waiting. A hoping. A plea.

Coal looked at Maura, at her big, pleading blue eyes. He looked at Cynthia. He looked at little Sissy, with the tears in her eyes.

In the yard, Chewy and Dart were barking ferociously, but Coal could not even hear that.

CHAPTER TWENTY-THREE

Coal took a deep breath. He stood before Maura and the girls. He stood before the whole world right then, it seemed. But at that moment, only three people really mattered.

Coal tried to speak. Cynthia was staring at him. Cynthia, to whom he had sworn his protection. He had promised her that no one would take her away. And now there was no recourse. At least not on this night. The police were here, they had a signed court order with them, and that was that. No legal means was going to stop the Mileys from driving away with his girls tonight.

After twenty seconds, Maura stood up. She looked around at all the police cars, and Coal saw her shoulders slump. Biting her lower lip, she stooped down and scooped Sissy's little body up into her arms, hugging her tight. At the same time, Coal walked to Cynthia and put his hand on her shoulder. The silence was more powerful than the first atom bomb.

Coal Savage was the big, tough lawman who had come home to take over the simple job as sheriff of Lemhi County, and to live out his life in peace, and yet at the moment he was helpless. In the end, it was Connie who finally broke the tension.

"Girls? This is not the end, okay? You all have to listen to me. We are going to do everything we can, Coal, Maura, and I. I promise you that with all I have in me. Right now, tonight, there is nothing we can do about what's happening. Cynthia, your aunt and uncle have come to take you to live with them." She tried pretending not to see the horror in the teenager's eyes. "We need you to help Sissy understand what's happening. We need you to be strong for her, okay? They are going to take you both with them tonight, but we understand that they are taking you to your old house. So you will be safe."

"No! I don't want to go back there!" Cynthia cried. She whirled on Coal, making his hand fall away from her shoulder. "You promised me you wouldn't let me go! Please don't let them take me!"

Coal knew every eye was on him now, probably including the police and the Mileys. Cynthia's outburst had been that loud. He saw Linda Miley start forward, but Chief George reached out and took her shoulder, turning her back around. He heard him tell her something, but it was quiet enough that he could make out no words.

"We're going to get you back," said Coal, trying to sound confident. "But tonight there is nothing we can do. The judge signed an order saying they have the right to take you because you're related to them. They have our hands completely tied."

Tears rushed into Cynthia's eyes, and she opened her mouth. Coal stepped close to her and took her arms. He spoke softly, guarding the words from reaching the police or the Mileys. "Honey, you have to listen to me. I need you to be strong. I know it's hard. I know that's the last thing you want to do. But if you fall apart now, Sissy is going to be terrified. No matter what happens, you have to stay strong."

Cynthia's lip quivered, but to her credit, the tears that trailed down her cheeks ran in silent rivers. She nodded and tried to look in his eyes, but Coal knew she could not see him, at least no better than had she been looking through a kaleidoscope. Slowly, he folded his arms around her and pressed his face down into her hair.

"You listen to me, sweetie. Listen close. I have friends too. I have a great lawyer I found to help us. I'm going to get you back here with us. But you are going to have to make the best of this and do everything you can to keep Sissy safe."

The girl tried again to speak. At last, in broken words, she said, "I want you to be my dad. How will I know how everything is? And how everyone is?"

"I can see you at school," he said quietly. "We'll work it out. And tonight, I'm going to park across the street from your house, all right? I'll sleep in my car there, and if I have to leave I'll find someone else to stay there. If you need to know I'm close, just peek out the window."

"Promise?" she asked through her tears.

"That is a promise I know I can keep," he replied. "Yes, I promise."

Linda Miley was finally allowed to come forward, and she stood smugly in front of Coal and looked down at Sissy. After a moment, she smiled at her. "Okay, honey, I'm going to be your new mom now. Come with me." With no more ceremony than that, she took her by the hand and started walking toward the state police car.

Sissy whirled around, her eyes full of terror. She stretched out her hand toward Maura and started screaming. There wasn't one intelligible word. Only screams and tears, and that one hand, reaching back to be saved. And finally, when the police car door opened and no one had come to save her, she collapsed in defeat. Linda picked her up without gentleness and stooped down into the back seat of the police car.

Unlike Sissy, Cynthia went quietly, but with no lesser appearance of defeat. She could not even look back at the people she loved.

The state police car, now honored by the presence of the Mileys and both girls, pulled out of the yard and onto Savage Lane five minutes later, with all of the girls' meager belongings in the trunk. They were headed for the little house on Hope Street.

Chief Dan George came over to Coal, Connie, and Maura. It was so cold that they had sent the boys back into the house, and they all stood at the front window, staring out. Katie had never come out at all.

"I'm sorry that had to happen that way, Sheriff."

"You and me both."

"You do understand, right?" There was genuine worry in George's eyes.

"Sure. It was just a shock to see all the cars here. I know how it is to get called to do a dirty job."

The chief nodded. "Thank you. That makes it a little easier on me. Listen, if there's anything I can help with... I don't know what it would be, but please call, all right?"

"Sure." Coal took the chief's proffered hand and shook.

They all bade the lawman good night, including Bob Wilson, who told him he would be coming along shortly. Bob then stood before the others, the look on his face sorrowful. "I'm sure sorry about that, folks. That isn't a scene I'd ever choose to be part of again."

Connie reached out and squeezed Bob's arm. "Don't you worry now. Things will all work out. God still answers prayers."

Coal stood there wondering, but he sure wasn't going to contradict a woman of such powerful faith.

"Coal, we're still on your side," Bob said. "I've never seen my boss struggle so hard with anything."

"That's good to know. Just keep an eye on that house, all right?"

"I will. If I get out and about tonight, I'll cruise by."

"Don't worry about tonight. I promised Cynthia I'd be in my car across the street."

"Are you serious? It's supposed to get below freezing tonight."

"It doesn't matter. I already had to break one promise to that girl. I'm sure not going to break this one."

"Well, in that case I'll come around and bring you some hot coffee. Man, that's gonna be a long night, buddy."

When Bob was gone, Coal, Connie, and Maura stood alone in the yard with Chewy and Dart. The dogs just stood around shivering, unwilling to go far away when they could sense how upset these people were.

The boys were still staring out the window, probably unsure of all that had happened and why. Maura hugged her body with one arm, the other hand pressed to her mouth. She stared blankly at the open door of her pickup.

Finally, as if a dam had broken, she began to sob. Coal was unsure how she felt about him right then, so fortunately his mother was ready with a warm hug. As she stood there patting Maura's back, Coal stared down the lane at the darkness, his mind a blank. There was nothing about which he wanted to think.

At last, Connie reached up and took Maura by the back of the neck, pulling her closer and giving her a gentle kiss on the forehead. "Let's go on in the house, hon. We're going to freeze out here. I'll get some cocoa, and we can sit by the stove for a while."

Maura glanced toward the door of her truck, but before she could move, Coal went over and slammed it shut. It made the sound of a cannon in the ice-chip night.

When he turned back, Maura was walking toward the house with his mother's arm around her. He followed them into the house, where he immediately started looking for the warmest blanket he could find, along with a fur-lined leather cap his father used to wear ice fishing.

The boys came over and stood before him, even Virgil. Wyatt was their spokesman. "Daddy, what happened? Did Cynthia and Sissy get arrested?"

Coal couldn't help a little laugh. He knelt down. "No, buddy. Nothing like that. Those people that were out there were the aunt and uncle to Sissy and Cynthia. They took them home with them. That's all." He put his hand on the outside shoulders of his twins, moving them together, and looked from them up to Virgil. "You understand? They had a court order from the judge, so there was nothing we could do."

"Will they come back?" asked Morgan, after looking over at Wyatt and trying to gage his reaction.

"I sure hope so. We'll do all we can."

"Okay, Daddy. I really like them," Wyatt put in. "I hope they can come back home."

Coal hugged the twins, then stood up with his hands on their heads. He looked at Virgil. "You have any questions, Virg?"

"No, sir."

"Did that whole thing kind of scare you?"

He knew the answer to such a foolish question, because the answer would have been the same for him, at fifteen years old.

"No! I'm not scared."

"All right." He wanted to tell Virgil, and the little boys too, that it was fine to be scared. But he didn't know if he was ready for his boys to know how terrified their father was tonight as well.

Katie still had made no appearance by the time the hot chocolate was ready, so Coal went down the hall and tapped on her door. When she answered it, he looked in. She was sitting on her bed with a text book open in front of her and a notebook and pen lying to one side. She came close to smiling at him, but it didn't seem genuine.

"You okay?"

"Yeah, just doing some homework."

"You know the girls are gone, I guess."

Katie looked quickly down at her book, absently turning a page. "Yeah, I thought so."

"So, um..." After a moment, realizing he had nothing wise to say, he simply said, "Okay, we're going to have some chocolate if you want any."

She replied "okay," but she never did come out of her room.

Coal and Connie went out and fed the horses, and then for the next several hours, they took turns watching television, piecing on macaroni salad and grilled cheese sandwiches Connie made, and then snacking on the cookies that came out of the oven as if by magic every time Connie sensed something amiss in her house. She had simply put the biscuit dough in the fridge for morning. No one was in the mood for biscuits anymore.

The dogs traipsed from person to person at any whimsy, looking for a new hand to scratch behind their ears. Maura was curled up in Coal's chair. She had eaten nothing, and she had hardly moved all evening.

Around nine-thirty, after Coal had gotten the boys off to their beds, he looked in on Katie. Her room was dark, and the mound under her blankets told him he was too late to tuck her in. Leaving the door open, for the light, he went closer. The blankets were drawn right up to her mouth, and her eyes were closed, but a little too tightly. She was feigning sleep.

He sat down on the side of her bed and rested his hand on her shoulder. *Little Katie.* He longed for the right words to say to her. He was scared to death to think of losing her again, after they had come so far. What had happened to cause the sudden change in her demeanor? Something at school? Boy trouble? He wished for a crystal ball, but in the end he simply bent and kissed her cheek and left, closing her door softly.

In the living room, Coal sipped the cup of chocolate Connie handed him. Connie stood before him, her arms folded tightly. "It's so cold out there, Son. I don't think you can do any good by staying over there."

Surprised, between sips, he looked down at her. "I don't have any choice, Mom. I promised her I'd do it. It's the only thing I have left to offer her."

"Well, I might come by and check on you in a few hours then."

Coal reached down to stroke the head of Dobe, who had come over and leaned against his leg for comfort from whatever bad vibration had filled his domain. "No, Ma, you need to be here in case the kids wake up. I'll be fine."

A door suddenly squeaked, down the hall, and Coal and Connie looked that way. In the dim light, they saw a shadow moving their way. It was Katie, wrapped in a blanket. When she came into the light, Coal could see her eyes were swollen.

"What are you doing up?"

"I can't sleep."

"Well, you'd better figure out how, okay?"

"I heard you talking."

"Oh, sorry. We'll keep it down."

Katie just stood there, momentarily stymied. "Daddy, I want to come with you."

"Come with me? Where?"

"To spend the night in your car at Cynthia's."

"Oh, sweetie, you can't," Connie cut in. "You have school in the morning. Don't worry—Cynthia will be there, I'm sure."

Katie got a pained expression on her face and looked at Connie, then shifted her eyes back to Coal. "But please, Daddy. *Please.*"

"Katie, your grandma's right. It's late already, and it's going to be too cold anyway."

The girl suddenly bit her lip, fighting back tears. Coal looked over at his mother for rescue. "Hey, what's wrong?" Connie asked, stepping closer. She reached out a finger and tried to raise the girl's chin, but she was too strong and kept her head down.

"I want to go," she said to the floor.

"Hey, honey, it makes me really glad to hear you want to be with me," said Coal. "But it's just not going to work out. Maybe if it was the weekend I'd think about it. You want me to tuck you in?" he asked on a whim, not realizing she was well beyond that stage.

Looking down, Katie just nodded. That response gave Coal his biggest alarm bell yet. He looked his surprise over at Connie, who shrugged and motioned with her head down the hall. Taking his cue, Coal put his arm around his girl and took her back down to her room. This time, he helped her crawl into bed. He couldn't see much now, in the dim light, but he could see one thing: Katie had never fought so hard against tears. Just for a moment, he thought about staying. But he had promised Cynthia. Leaning down, he kissed his girl. Her only response was to hug the covers tighter around herself.

CHAPTER TWENTY-FOUR

Coal walked back out to the front room and picked up the fur-lined hat, snugging it down over his ears. It felt strange not to have a cowboy hat on, but on a sub-zero night like this, he would have regretted that. He pulled a wool sweater down over his head, then shrugged into his heavy old wool coat, which he had always left here in Salmon because he knew he would never need it in Washington, D.C.

Then he turned to Connie. To his surprise, Maura had gotten up and was standing beside her. His eyes only touched Maura, then flickered away. "Mom, can you do me a favor and check on Katie in a while? There's something really wrong with her."

"Did you ask what it is?"

"Of course not. It's bad timing, and she obviously didn't want to tell me anyway."

"Obviously? Coal, sometimes our children are *begging* for us to care enough to pry. And testing us. If we don't pry, they feel justified in claiming we don't care."

"I don't have time for games. Just check on her, okay?"

Connie frowned. She glanced over at Maura and hesitated for a second before speaking again. "You made a mature enough decision to bring four children into the world, Son. You'd better figure out what they need from you before very long or you'll be lucky not to lose them all."

Mothers. Coal blew out a derisive breath. Sometimes you couldn't even talk to them.

Coal turned around, walking to the door with Dobe beside him, hopeful. Shadow lunged up from her place by his chair and ran over to be part of the farewell committee. "Check on her if you want, Mom. I don't have time to talk about it."

As his hand touched the door, Coal heard fabric rustling, and he turned to see Maura getting into her coat. He looked at her blankly for a second. "You're not leaving, are you?"

"I'm going with you."

Coal's glance darted past her to his mother, then back. "What? It's too cold out."

"Wait and I'll get a blanket."

"And I'll be gone by the time you get it."

"Fine. I have a truck I can sleep in too."

Coal looked at Connie again, feeling cornered. His eyes returned to Maura. "Why are you doing this?"

"Why are you?"

"Because she's— I'm—" He stopped in mid-sentence. "All right, get your blanket. You'd better make it two or three. But I'm not going to be able to bring you back here if you get uncomfortable or cold."

"I have the blood in me of a Sioux Indian, Coal. If anyone gets cold and gives up, it won't be me."

He shook his head. "Judas priest."

"Coal!" Connie said sharply.

He looked at his mom and huffed. "I'll go warm up the truck."

On the way to town, it reminded Coal of the first date he had ever been on. He was in the driver's seat, and his date was smashed so tightly against the passenger door that she seemed in danger of pushing it open and falling out.

And there she stayed, through the long, cold night. It was his side that faced the Batterton house, but Maura kept as good a watch on the house as she could, considering the bulk of man that was in her way. One time, around two in the morning, Coal looked over and saw the front room curtains part, just slightly. After twenty or thirty seconds, they slowly closed again. He sighed with relief. Cynthia had come to check on him. And he had been here for her.

He looked over at Maura, and she was snuggled into her blankets, asleep. He wished she were awake, because he suddenly wanted to quiz her more on what she had heard the Mileys saying in their room, and what had led her to believe they might have been involved in some kind of robbery. But she didn't wake up until an ugly green and white Nash pulled up and stopped in the middle of the street. The door opened, and big Jordan Peterson unfolded himself out of the front seat and sauntered over holding a thermos.

Coal rolled down the window, the steam of his breath instantly rushing out into the cold night to meld with Jordan's. With his left hand, the big jailer held out the heavy green thermos, and Coal took it.

"Bob Wilson came by the jail earlier," Jordan said in response to the question in Coal's eyes. "He said you might be needing some warmth later."

Coal laughed as he heard Maura coming awake beside him. "Well, buddy, I'd invite you in to snuggle but as you can see I'm on a date."

Jordan laughed. "Okay, maybe next time." He bent down and looked in at Maura. "Hi."

"Hi," she replied. She couldn't introduce herself. She was supposed to be cool and aloof at the moment with Coal there so close.

"That's Maura," said Coal. Instantly, his use of the word "that," instead of "this," made the introduction seem impersonal. But he couldn't take it back. "This is my jailer, Jordan Peterson," he said over his shoulder.

Jordan nodded and smiled, but by the uncomfortable way he looked back at Coal, Coal could guess at the reception the woman had given him without having to see it. "Well, you're tougher than

I am, Coal. I'm gonna get back up the hill before somebody tries to break out of jail."

Coal laughed. "No one's in it, right?"

"No, I was just kidding."

"Go home, buddy. Get yourself an early sleep."

"Serious?"

"I'll show you getting off work at eight. If I need you I can call you back."

"Okay, Coal, if you're sure."

"In this quiet town, what can happen?" asked Coal.

Jordan looked at him askance.

Wednesday, December 13

When the day began to break, Coal shook himself out of a doze and backed the pickup down the street another forty feet. Around sun-up, the front door of the house opened, although Coal had never seen any lights come on, and Cynthia stepped out onto the concrete stoop with a couple of books in one hand. She turned and quietly shut the door just as a big yellow bus rounded the corner down the street.

Hurriedly, she looked along the street, and her head stopped turning when she saw the green pickup. She sent a little wave of her hand Coal's way, and he waved back as she hurried down the sidewalk, waving the bus down. The driver, seeming caught by surprise, slammed on the brakes, and Coal heard the door open. Cynthia got in, and after half a minute the vehicle lumbered on past him. Coal picked Cynthia out, with her face almost pressed against a window. They waved at each other one more time as she went past.

Now little Sissy was trapped alone in the Batterton house, a place she did not know, with two people she had never seen in her life. Beside Coal, Maura tried to hold back tears.

Coal just sat there for a long time, feeling punch drunk. He refused to look at Maura, who could have stayed in a nice, warm bed all night had she chosen to.

Still without looking over, finally he said, "Do you have to work today?"

"I was supposed to. I'll call Florin and see if he can get a replacement, or else I'll just have to go."

"He's a good man," Coal said of Florin Beller. "I'm sure he'll understand. Did you get any sleep?"

"I think so."

"Well, let's at least go have some breakfast, if we can keep our eyes open long enough. I'd like to talk to you more about what you overheard the Mileys saying in their hotel room."

"Where are you going to eat? You mean back home?"

"The Coffee Shop. Or Wally's. Sound okay?"

"I'd rather not."

"Not hungry?"

"Not enough to eat in public. I don't want to see anybody."

Coal thought about that for a moment. Did she just not want to be seen with him, a two-timer? After a moment, without replying, he put the pickup in gear and pulled out, going down to St. Charles, then back to Main. He turned right and drove right past the business district without looking left or right. Maybe home would be the best place to eat after all.

*   *   *

Coal slept for only two hours before getting up and getting in a half-hour pull-up, pushup and sit-up workout, showering, and dressing in a smoky-blue wool shirt and Wranglers. The kids were all gone to school, so he had only to contend with Dobe and Shadow while eating cold fried eggs and bacon. He left hashed browns in a pan on the stove. He wasn't getting enough working out to be able to afford many carbohydrates.

The house seemed deathly still. Looking out the front window, he saw Connie's Chrysler parked in its place and frosted over, and he looked out the back door glass to see her out riding around the pasture on Bolt, her dappled bay. Steam gushed from both of their faces every time they released a breath, and even Bolt's body was steaming now. Crazy woman.

Coal scrubbed at his face, realized it was whiskered, and walked back into the bathroom. He was startled to see the silver whiskers beginning to show low down on his chin. His beard had always been black, even darker than his hair, which still hardly had a gray hair in it. Old age was creeping up. A quick shave brought back his youth, and Coal smiled at the irony of that thought. Old age was coming, and a shave could only disguise the fact.

Without saying goodbye to Connie, Coal went out to see that Maura's pickup was gone. She must not have gone to sleep at all. He drove down to the Coffee Shop, where he sat in a stupor at the counter and drank coffee while Tammy Hawley tried unsuccessfully to carry on a friendly conversation with him.

Finally, he drove on over to Keith Perkins's law office. Perkins was in, and they sat and talked for quite a while about what had taken place the night before.

When the conversational part of the visit was over, Perkins leaned forward in his chair, his elbows on his shiny red desk. "I wish I could give you something promising, Coal, but it's going to be an uphill battle. Now that they have that house, and the judge has okayed them living there, *and* they can prove blood relationship to the children... I've seen cases turned around, but at this point unless those people do something wrong, I have to say our chances are pretty slim."

"What about the insurance money?"

"Well, I'd love to tell you it's safe, that it can only be spent by Cynthia. But I would be lying. They're working on legislation to cover this kind of case, but who knows when it will ever make it through the system? In the meantime, Cynthia will get her check, and once it's hers, it's hers—in theory. But we all know how that goes. There are zero safeguards at this point. Those people could force her to cash her check, and then they could spend every last dime—supposedly in her name."

"So there's nothing we can do legally to keep them from the money? Put some of it in bonds or something?"

"Not unless you can talk the Mileys into it."

"Fat chance of that. So, legally speaking, if they spend all that money, are you going to tell me there is no way to charge them with theft, withholding—nothing?"

"They're her guardians—as the term goes."

"And probably no way to force them to keep the girls once the money's gone, either."

Perkins gave him an odd look. "As if you would want to, right? Having that money gone is probably the best way to get those girls back, I'm guessing."

"Why do you suppose they took both girls? They have to know Sissy couldn't have a penny coming to her in insurance."

Perkins shrugged. "To look magnanimous? I don't know. It's all speculation at this point. They're certainly not going to want anyone to think they only took the girls in for insurance money, though. So what better way to prove that than to take them both?"

Coal nodded. "So here's a question for you: What happens if they go to jail?"

"To jail? Have they done something wrong?"

"Not that I'm positive of—yet."

"Well, if they do then it will go back to the judge. That's when we would have a good chance at overturning his original decision."

"But not until."

"We can try to find something. We could hire someone—a private investigator. Or you could try to do it yourself. Dig up anything on them that might help. Anything's worth a shot."

"You say 'we,' but you mean me. I'm only making sheriff's wages, in a small county in Idaho. No offense, but I can't afford lawyer's fees on the off-chance we *might* find something."

"I sure understand that. No offense taken. I'd love to say I'd take this one on for free, and maybe if I weren't in such a busy place I would, but right now it wouldn't be possible."

"All right. Thanks for your candor. If you think of anything else, just call me."

Coal stood up and shook hands with Perkins, then left. His lack of sleep, and lack of answers, was making him feel a hundred years old.

Thinking of little Sissy, alone and afraid, he drove slowly back past the house on Hope Street, thinking how little hope they truly had anymore, and then drove out toward Leadore. He might as well be patrolling the outer reaches of the county as be stuck in a town where he was useless.

On the way out of town, and then once again after dealing with a minor wreck around noon, fifteen miles out along the Lemhi River, Coal watched Annie Price's house as he passed. Her Buick wasn't there, so even though he had thought about stopping, he drove on. He drove by the hospital when he got there, and her car was in the lot, so he went in and parked.

For a long time, he sat in the pickup, wondering why he was here. Finally, he thought about the golden retriever. The excuse he had been searching for.

Inside, Annie was cleaning up a bad cut on a man who apparently should have been watching television or reading instead of paring potatoes. He watched them from the hallway for a while before going to the receptionist's desk, saying hi to her, and pouring himself a cup of scalding black coffee.

After a while, the male patient, his hand now bandaged, walked past, and Annie came down the hall massaging lotion into her hands.

"Well, hi!" A huge smile broke over her face. "Checking on my first aid?"

Coal laughed. "If it was me I'd have put that guy out of his misery. He'd better stick to TV dinners."

She returned the laugh. "What's up?"

"Not much. Just came by to check on the dog."

"Really? Okay, fine. I thought you came to check on me."

Again, he laughed, this time embarrassed. "Well, okay, that too."

"I for one am okay. Burro, on the other hand, is a star in the Recorder-Herald today."

"Huh?"

"I put his picture in the paper and advertised for his owner to come get him."

"What if they don't? You have a new dog?"

"No, I'm afraid not. I'll just give him to a new home, I guess."

Coal frowned. "Too bad. Seemed like a nice dog."

"He is! He's a great dog. I just don't want him to be cooped up at my house all day with nothing to do. Why don't *you* take him?"

"Right. My zoo is already full."

"Darn! No room to take in a tiger?"

"What?"

Annie laughed again, waving him off. "Sorry, bad humor."

Suddenly realizing what she had meant, Coal felt himself blush. He wasn't used to that. He wanted to make a comment about Annie being a tiger, but the joke caught up in his throat.

He found himself staring at her. Her haunted, and perhaps more so *haunting,* eyes were too sparkly today. Her hair too perfect. Her lips too soft and alluring. She *smelled* too alluring, too much like...

"What is that perfume you're wearing?"

"Why?"

"It's... Wow. It's nice."

Her face reddened a little. "Actually, it's called Tigress."

Again, Coal laughed. "You're joking, right?"

"Nope."

"So you really *are* a tiger!"

Looking around, Annie suddenly reached up and put both of her hands on the back of Coal's neck, drawing his face down to hers. It was almost no challenge at all. Her lips touched his, a gentle caress. She pulled away, just far enough to search into his eyes.

"I really am a tiger."

Coal felt breathless. He was conscious of the receptionist having to put her attention elsewhere. Helpless to find anything appropriate to say, he just stood there. Annie brought her hands down and took both of his. "There's a new movie at the Roxy tonight at nine."

"Oh?"

"Yes. *The Poseidon Adventure.* Just released today."

"Really? And already at the Roxy?"

"I know, strange, huh? I don't know how they swung that one, but it must be a sign I'm supposed to go to it, since I do happen to have the evening off. You don't happen to know any handsome, kind, single man who might be willing to take me, do you?"

Coal hated not feeling able to breathe. What was he, fifteen years old? But looking at Annie's hauntingly perfect face, perfectly framed by all that perfect golden-brown hair, was drawing away from him all the ability to control his faculties. And even as *imperfect* as he was, Coal felt like a perfect fool.

An image of Maura PlentyWounds was hammering at the back of his brain, trying to hang onto some piece of him, but at that moment, somehow he found he couldn't let her back in.

CHAPTER TWENTY-FIVE

Coal sat in his office with a stack of papers in front of him. In a half-daze, he read one after the other of the notices and reports, a few of them recent, but most of them old and tattered.

Nothing seemed to fit at all except for one report of a late-night robbery of a Circle K in Missoula. In that case, a shorter, heavy-set man had come into the store around eleven at night, pulled a revolver, and demanded all the money in the cash register. He had backed out of the store with a sack full of cash and coins, and when the clerk ran to the door he thought he saw a light brown or rust-colored sedan race away from the parking lot. He couldn't tell if there was anyone else in it.

The part that really drew his attention was the report of a second possible witness who had been in a near-collision with a car that he claimed was red, racing down the street several blocks away. The second witness was pretty adamant that the driver had larger hair and possibly had one passenger, but he didn't try to run it down, and the car vanished into the night. Both incidents were reported within minutes of the same time.

If it was indeed the same vehicle, which at eleven o'clock at night in a town only the size of Missoula, and coming from the same direction to which the robbery car had fled, seemed pretty likely, then it was very possible the store clerk simply hadn't been able to judge the paint color because of the darkness. And although Coal hadn't seen it since Hague Freeman's funeral, his guts told him the Mileys drove the red Buick.

He shuffled through the other reports, eliminated them all, one by one, and pushed them aside. Then he went back through the one robbery report again, several times, looking for some clue he could cling to. Short, stocky man. Large caliber revolver—although to someone with a gun in his face an air rifle might look like a cannon. Possible brown or rust-colored sedan, but possible red. Possibly only a driver, but possibly a driver and passenger. And if it was the same car, the second witness's report seemed to indicate that the robber, the man in the stocking cap, had not been driving. So either a man with "bigger hair," or a woman, might have been waiting in the car as a getaway driver.

He had all this, and he had whatever he might get from Maura, if she could remember any of it at all, as upset as she had been. It certainly was nowhere near enough to convict someone in court.

Coal closed his eyes, and bending forward, he laid his forehead on the desk.

*   *   *

Far back in his consciousness, Coal heard a noise. For several seconds, it did not register on him. Finally, there was the sound of a woman's voice. "Hey, Coal. It's me. Should I come back later?"

Startled awake, Coal looked up, hardly able to focus on the face and shape before him. "Wow! You're really gone."

He heard himself laughing and was surprised by it. "Hi, Annie. Yeah. Sheesh. I must be bushed." He told her what had happened the night before and about how he had stayed up all night watching the Batterton house.

Unexpectedly, Annie's eyes filled up with tears, and she brought her hands up to her face. "Oh, Coal! You really did that? You stayed up the whole night just so she might look out and know you were there?"

"Yeah, I already know—I'm an idiot."

"No! No, you're not an idiot." She hurriedly wiped at both of her eyes and came around the desk, putting her arm around his shoulders and squeezing. "Are you kidding? Any girl or woman's fantasy would be to have a man do something so gallant and caring." The tears suddenly rushed back to her eyes. "Jeez. I'm sorry. Can I use your restroom?"

He jumped up. "Sure. Right in there. You okay?"

"Uh-huh. Just give me a minute."

Like an expecting father, Coal found himself waiting near the bathroom door, wondering what had happened. He was about positive he was never going to figure out how women thought.

Finally, Annie came out, and very carefully she closed the door behind her. Turning back to him, she eased up against him without the slightest warning and folded her arms around him, resting there, quiet. It wasn't a powerful squeeze, like a happy greeting. It was more just like she was soaking his presence in. He held her and waited. But by now, with the experience he had with Laura, Maura, and Katie, he no longer expected that he was ever going to find out what had really brought this on. He did not have the energy to dig that deep into a woman's mind.

*   *   *

Perhaps it was not good fortune in this case, at least for her, but because the Batterton house was so close to the high school, Cynthia was home not long after three. Holding two books, and thinking about the little Teddy bear her mother and father had given her, she took a deep breath and started toward the front door.

As she opened it, she saw Linda Miley sitting at the table, facing her way, like a spider waiting for a fly. "School's pretty early, huh?"

"Yeah," she said, shutting the door.

"I'd appreciate it if you'd show some upbringing. You can say, 'Yes, ma'am'."

"Sorry. Yes, ma'am."

"Good. Okay. That's a start. Listen to me. I kind of have a problem with you just getting up and leaving like you did this morning. How was I supposed to know where you went?"

Cynthia was startled. "Oh! I, uh... I didn't think you would like me to wake you up, since you stayed up so late."

Linda raised her eyebrows. "How late we stay up isn't any of your business, Cynthia. How you leave here is. And mine, too."

"Sorry."

"I wish you would stop saying that."

Cynthia stared at her. She tried to think of something she could say that would not be offensive. Finally, she uttered, "Yes, ma'am."

Linda Miley stood up. "Okay, I'm glad that's out of the way. So how was your school day? Did you learn anything? When I was in school, I always thought it was a pretty big waste of time. In fact, I didn't like any of my teachers. I didn't like any of the students, for that matter! Ha!" She stood there for a moment, one chubby hand clenched on the rim of her obese hip. "Well?"

Cynthia had almost forgotten that she had asked her anything. She panicked, trying to think back. "It was fine," she said at last.

"Good. I'm glad you're doing better than I did. Well, Bud went to the store with Sissy."

Cynthia's heart leaped, and Linda must have read the emotion in her face. "What? Is something wrong with that?"

"No, but I... Sissy is usually really scared of men she doesn't know."

"Well listen here, missy. We're your parents now, so she knows him. And don't ever forget that."

"Yes, ma'am."

"Oh, for the love of pete. Will you stop repeating everything? Have you ever learned to cook at all?"

"Uh-huh."

"Yes, ma'am?" said Linda, putting her other chubby hand on her other obese hip.

"But I thought—"

"It's not your job to think. Come over here and start peeling these potatoes. Bud likes to eat at a certain time. Or 'dad,' I guess you can start calling him. I think he'll like that."

Her heart racing, Cynthia walked over and set her books on the table, moving nervously toward a bowl of potatoes that sat near the sink.

"Whoa, whoa, whoa. Wow, it looks like we've got a lot of re-training to do, girl. You're not just going to start off putting your garbage everywhere in the house like that. Go put your books away in your room. And they better be stacked neat."

Cynthia whirled around. For a moment, a flash of anger had come to her eyes, and she tried to set it aside.

The first truly mean look Cynthia had seen on the woman's face bloomed there like a jack-o-lantern. "Listen, missy. If I *ever* catch that look in your eyes again, your dad's going to hear about it. And I guarantee you won't like what happens then."

"Yes, ma'am." As Linda glared at her through eyes that were sheltered under eyelashes with far too much mascara on them, Cynthia picked up her books and went to her room.

She needed to touch Buddy the Teddy bear. It was silly, she knew, but right now it was the only comfort she had. As she put the books down on her dresser top, she started to turn away. Then she hurriedly turned back and took great care to push the books up on one corner of the dresser, their spines and top lined up perfectly with one side of the desk and the wall. She was taking no chances.

She reached down and pulled open the bottom drawer, then froze. Her clothes were neatly arranged there, but to their left was only an empty hole. Buddy was gone!

In a panic, Cynthia yanked the drawer open farther. No longer thinking, she started throwing the clothes around the drawer in her frantic search, and some fell onto the floor.

"What are you looking for?"

Cynthia froze. She turned slowly to see Linda Miley standing in her doorway, one shoulder leaned against the frame. She had a hand behind her back.

"I have a... I think I lost..." She stopped and stared at the woman, afraid to go on.

"What's the matter, cat got your tongue?" The smirk on Linda's face filled Cynthia with revulsion. She wanted to run at her and shove her backward into the hall.

"I have a stuffed bear my mom and dad gave me."

"What did you say?"

"A stuffed bear?" Cynthia's heart was filling with terror.

"No, the other part."

"About my mom and dad?"

"Yes, that. Listen, little girl, you might as well start understanding that Bud and I are your mom and dad now. Can you get that through your thick skull?"

"I know, but—"

"There isn't any but!" Linda said sharply. "You will not speak of them in this house again. Get it?"

Cynthia had the sudden feeling that she was going to pass out, but fortunately it vanished. When it was gone, she simply stood, her chest filled with an icy dread.

With a fake half-smile on her lips, Linda Miley pulled her arm out from behind her to reveal Buddy. "Is this what you're looking for?"

Cynthia jolted upright and froze. Carefully, she said, "Uh-huh. I mean, 'yes, ma'am'."

Linda looked at the bear disdainfully and twisted it around so it faced her. Her face displayed a haughty, sniffing expression. After a moment, she huffed and turned back to look at Cynthia. "Don't you think you're a little old to be playing with stuffed animals?"

"Well, I'm not really playing with it—ma'am. I'm just... It's just... It makes me feel better to—"

"To what?" Linda growled.

"I need it," said Cynthia, her heart filled with pleading. She took a step toward Linda.

"Listen, girl. We're going to have to get some things straight around here. You're too old to play with toys. You will *not* mention those two people you used to call your mom and dad. And you're going to learn real fast to keep your stuff picked up in this house, or your dad is going to be very upset. And you know what? I'm kind of looking forward to when he is. You really need to learn a lesson. And as for this disgusting bear, it's going straight in the trash. You need to grow up, sister. In fact, you can just stay in your room the rest of the night and think about what I've said. I think your dad and me are going to go out and eat."

"But... what about Sissy?"

"What about her?" Linda squared herself against Cynthia.

"Are you going to take her?"

"Why? She has a room too. She can just stay in it. Maybe if you decide to start getting smart with me again you'll think about her first, if you both go a night without any food."

"No, please!" Cynthia cried. "I'll do whatever you want. Please at least let her be in here with me."

"You're about on my last nerve, sister."

The look on Linda's face was the closest thing to deadly. Cynthia had been about to make a reply, but she clamped her mouth shut. She suddenly realized that there would never be any talking with Linda Miley. The woman was insane. Flat crazy. Nothing

Cynthia could ever think to say would appease her. She and Sissy were going to be lucky to get out of this house alive.

CHAPTER TWENTY-SIX

Linda Miley stomped away from Cynthia's bedroom door, throwing open the garbage can lid. She had raised the stuffed bear up above her head, intent on throwing it full-force into the can, when something stopped her. Turning her head, she looked up at the ugly little bear while slowly bringing it down almost to her face.

What was she doing? There might be a good use for this bear yet. Just how much did Cynthia Batterton care about this hideous thing? It was, after all, a gift from Jennifer and her idiotic husband—perhaps the only thing Cynthia now had with any meaning that was connected to those people she wanted to call her mom and dad. Holding the bear eighteen inches straight out from her face, she glared at it until a crafty little grin began to appear on her smug face. Yes. This bear would serve a great purpose if it was as powerful as the emotion she had read in Cynthia's eyes.

Turning about, she walked back across the room and down the hall again, this time softly. She paused for a moment at the door, listening. It gave her heart great satisfaction to hear Cynthia Batterton sniffling. Taking a deep breath, Linda threw open the door, making it bang against the wall.

"What are you whimpering about? Just how old are you?"

Cynthia looked over at her but didn't reply. Her eyes dropped to the bear, his belly clamped so tight in Linda's fist.

"Well?"

"Why are you doing this?" Cynthia sobbed. "Why didn't you leave us with Coal?"

"Ha! We're family, Cynthia. I couldn't leave you with some stranger." She smiled, tilting her head. "Don't you understand family?"

Cynthia didn't bother to respond.

"Cat's got your tongue again, huh? Nasty old cat. So, sis, how much does this disgusting little rat mean to you, anyway?"

A glimmer of hope flickered in Cynthia's eyes. "A lot."

"Really. Huh. Well, maybe if you're good, and you act nice around people we see, and you always do just what we say, I might actually let you keep it. I just hope it doesn't get fleas in the house."

Cynthia turned more toward her, an involuntary sob escaping her.

"Here, ya big baby. Take it." Linda disdainfully threw the bear underhanded at Cynthia's face and left the room. A second later, she peeked back in. "But you're still not going to eat tonight."

"What about Sissy?"

"What about her?"

"Can I make her something to eat? If I promise not to have any?"

"Right! Like I would believe your promises. I was a girl just like you, dummy. It hasn't been all that long ago, you know. I know the whole routine—and the lies. I wouldn't trust you with a ten foot pole."

"Then can Sissy stay in my room?"

"Listen, Cynthia. I told you Sissy is staying in her own room. You have both got to start growing up sometime."

"But she's only a baby!"

"Right. I wasn't much older than that when I started trying to figure out how I was going to get out from under my mom's thumb. You just sit here and think about how you want to act from now on."

With that, Linda slammed the door. She went to a drawer she had found during the day while scrounging around for important papers or other things she and Bud might be able to use and jerked it open. From it, she extracted a black-handled hammer. She dug around and couldn't find a nail, so finally she settled for a screw.

Going back to Cynthia's door, with a little smile on her face she raised the screw and set it against the door trim, then gave it a sharp rap to get it started. The second rap was on her thumb, and she swore. Sucking on her thumb only for a moment, she angrily raised the hammer once more, striking the screw again and again and driving it into the wood, effectively locking Cynthia's door from outside.

"So I hope the house doesn't catch on fire or anything while we're out!" she said through the door.

Then she walked back into the other room, chuckling, to pull up a chair and watch out the front window for Bud and Sissy to come home.

*   *   *

Coal could hear a horrible, grating noise. Then all was silent, and he could feel hot air blowing in his face. The noise came again, and this time the sound of his radio registered on him.

Over an hour ago, Coal had picked up the Ford from Ken's and left the pickup with him because it didn't have a radio in it yet and he had been out of radio contact too much already since picking up the truck. Then he had driven out to the MacAtees' and pulled out beyond the straw stack where no one could see him, and there he put the car in park, cranked the heater all the way up, and leaned back to close his eyes.

Salmon dispatch calling Sheriff Savage. Do you copy?

Coal groaned. He could barely open his eyes. Wondering what time it was, he fumbled for the radio mic. Finally, he got it loose and replied.

Sheriff Savage, I was asked to deliver a message to you from a young lady. Are you any place where you can landline?

"Roger. Can you hold on for a couple of minutes?"

Coal threw the car in drive and went back around the straw stack, blinking his eyes to clear them. He pulled up to the front of the house and got out. He almost looked around to see Rowdy come running up to greet him, and a feeling of sadness swept over him.

There was no car in the yard, but he knocked anyway. When no one came to the door, he tried the knob, and as always it opened. He leaned his head in. "Hello? Anyone home?"

No answer. Glancing around outside, he stepped in and went to the black phone Kathy kept on her kitchen counter, picking it up to call the operator. "Hi, Lucy. This is Coal Savage."

Well, hello! How can I help you?

"I just need you to put me through to my dispatcher. Six-five-three-one-six."

Okay, Sheriff. It'll be just a moment. Good to hear your voice.

"Same here, Lucy. Take care."

The phone started ringing, and after two rings Flo the dispatcher picked up. "Hi, Flo. What's up?"

A young lady asked me to have you call her. Annie Price?

"Sure. Do you have a number?"

Flo gave him the number, and he thanked her. Annie picked up her phone after one ring.

Hello?

"Wow! Waiting by the phone, huh?"

Well, of course! I did ask you to call, didn't I?

"You did at that."

Hey, Coal, I was just thinking when I left earlier I wasn't very thoughtful. You haven't slept much, and I'm pretty sure that movie's going to put you to sleep. Want a rain check?

"That's thoughtful of you, Annie. Thanks. You know, that might not be a bad idea."

A long pause on the other end. *So... instead maybe you could come sleep with me like you did Maura.*

Coal's heart leaped. *What?* "Wait—what did you say?"

The musical sound of the woman's laughter floated over the line. *I'm just teasing you, silly. I was referring to you spending the night with her in the truck.*

Coal sighed. "Jeez! Don't scare me. I was hoping I wouldn't have forgotten sleeping with her that fast. I'm not even forty-five years old yet. And for the record, I was asleep the whole time."

You're terrible! Annie scolded. *But funny. Hey, but Coal, seriously, Burro needs some attention, and I'm not much for walking alone at night, and... If you came and took a walk with us down by the river I promise I'd let you go as soon as you needed to. I bet you'd sleep a lot better after a nice walk in the cold air.*

Coal paused. The woman sounded so hopeful he just couldn't turn her down. "Okay, okay. What time?"

Six sharp?

"You want me to bring anything?"

How about just that sexy, handsome sheriff?

Taken aback, Coal paused too long, and a nervous laugh came over the line. *Sorry! Boy, you really* are *sleepy! So make it at six, and I'll be ready and waiting—we'll be ready and waiting.*

It wasn't until Coal hung up that he thought of Connie and the kids, and he swore out loud. He had to find some time to talk to Katie. And he really hadn't taken a chance to really talk to the boys about what was happening. It seemed like no matter what he planned, something was always getting in the way. And he still hadn't forgotten that Todd Mitchell had wanted to tell him something.

There were not enough hours in a day.

*   *   *

Annie had told him to bring nothing but himself, but Coal, on a whim again, brought doughnuts at Walt's IGA. He had stopped eating sweets for the most part many years ago when he got serious into bodybuilding. But fond memories of childhood die hard, and the memory of the doughnuts from the other day was still calling to him. He almost regretted doing it, however, because with that smell in his nostrils, all the way to Annie's from town all he could think about was little Sissy. On the moment, he hated the Mileys more than he remembered hating anyone in a long time—maybe even Hague Freeman.

Wearing a thick white sweater and a royal blue down coat, Annie was waiting near her door, as she had said, with a leash on Burro, attached to a brand-new blue collar. Coal laughed. "Hey, you two match! Wait. I thought you said you weren't going to keep him."

Coal felt almost guilty when Annie stood up on her tiptoes and kissed him. He forgot on the instant what he had even said to her, because instead he was thinking he needed to talk to her about all this kissing.

"I'm not keeping him! That's right. But I had to have some way to keep him from running off until his owner comes. That rope around his neck sure wasn't any good."

"You're a nice lady," Coal said with a smile.

"What's wrong?"

"Huh?"

"What's wrong? Just tired?"

"What are you talking about?"

Annie shrugged as they stood in front of the door with Burro prancing around to get out. "I don't know. That just didn't seem like the smile I'm used to."

A feeling of discomfort rose up in Coal's chest. She was probably right. He hadn't really felt like smiling that much. In all honesty, Annie was starting to make him pretty nervous. She was moving way too fast, and he wasn't sure he was ready. She had started kissing him like they were a serious item, and he did not feel that way, at least not yet. He truthfully couldn't get Maura out of his mind every time Annie kissed him, and whenever Maura showed up a strange feeling of guilt came with her. That was foolish, too, because there was no understanding between them—was there?

But Annie had given Coal an easy out, and he took it. "Yeah, just tired. Sorry."

"It's okay. If we walk for a half hour out in this arctic air, you're going to be wide-awake."

* * *

Annie was correct. With bright red cheeks and noses, they stomped off their boots at the front door forty minutes later, and Coal was just about as awake as he could be. *No one* could have been sleepy now!

But it didn't last long. In fact, not ten minutes after finding their way to the sofa, he felt sleepier than he had in the first place. Annie got up and poured them some more of the Wild Turkey bourbon, and when he had sipped half of it down he felt himself slipping even deeper, heading quickly for a coma.

He heard Annie laugh after a while, and he remembered saying something about her drugging him, at which she laughed again. She said something about building up a fire, and he felt her get off the couch, and then he was gone.

* * *

With her heart pounding, Annie held the receiver of her ancient phone and stared at Coal. It had gotten to be late—almost time for the movie, had they still planned on going. Coal had been asleep for two hours, and he showed no sign of waking any time soon.

She had promised to let him sleep. But... should she wake him up and send him home? She sighed. He looked so peaceful, in one way, yet in another so full of care. He had sure had a rough go of it since coming back to his hometown. It seemed like he could never get a break. He loved those girls, Cynthia and Sissy, and they must be on his mind constantly. When she had heard what he did for them, and how he cared for them, it had made her like him that much more.

She longed suddenly to reach out and stroke his cheeks. To run her fingers through his dark, full hair. Even in his sleep, to take his hand and just hold it. Or maybe she could just sit back down next to him and lay her head on his chest, and they could sleep together. Then she really *could* tease him. That amused her, and she let out with a little laugh. Then she sighed.

Well, she had to at least tell Connie what was up. She owed that to everyone involved.

Dialing the operator, she asked her to put her through to Connie's line, then waited. After four rings, she heard the clicking of the phone being picked up, and then she heard a woman's voice say, *Hello.*

For a moment, she was silenced. It did not sound like Connie.

And then she realized it wasn't. It was Maura PlentyWounds.

CHAPTER TWENTY-SEVEN

When Bud Miley got back from the store and pulled his red Buick Riviera up in front, his face was red to match the car. With a cigarette clamped firmly between his lips, and smoke swirling all around the interior of the car, he reached across the seat and grabbed Sissy by the wrist, jerking her across to him. The look in the little girl's eyes was one of terror.

Suddenly, the short, fat man stopped and scanned the area around his car. The fat around his eyes crunched them smaller, made them look something like the eyes of a lab rat. There was no one on the sidewalks, and as far as he could tell no one was looking out of any windows. But still, he had to calm himself, just in case.

Taking a deep breath, he leaned down close to Sissy's face, the loose ash on the tip of the cigarette almost touching her nose. His lips parted as his teeth took over the job of holding onto the cigarette. Smoke curled out into Sissy's face, and she gave out with a little cough.

"Now you listen to me, you stupid little piece of garbage. I'm going to reach down and pick you up, you hear me? And then we're going to walk around to the trunk and get the groceries out. And if you make one little cry, when we get in that house I'm going to stick you with a knife. You understand me? And if you ever make a scene like you did back in that store again, I'm going to put you in a bag full of rocks and drop you in the river, where nobody will ever find you. Now shut your stupid mouth and stop crying."

The girl was shaking like an aspen leaf, and tears streaming down her cheeks, as he reached under her legs and hoisted her up. He struggled out of the car as she settled against his ample belly, and again he scanned the neighborhood, willing himself to calm down, allowing some of the red to fade from his face.

They walked around to the trunk, and he opened it and pulled out two bags of groceries, carrying them, and Sissy, up onto the stoop, where the door opened for them and they went inside.

The second the door shut, Bud walked over to the couch and threw the little girl down onto the cushion, then turned and shoved the groceries at his wife. "Put those away!"

"Jeez! What the hell's the matter with you?"

"What's the matter? She's the matter!" He jabbed his finger at Sissy's face. "I will *never* take this sniveling brat out into the public again. I'd just as soon beat her with a ball bat."

Sissy stared up at him, sitting on both of her hands and shivering all over. Her face was whiter than ever.

"You hear me, girl?" he roared in her face. "A ball bat. You know what that is?"

Sissy could only stare up at him. She was too scared to respond.

Linda was standing near her husband, and suddenly she said, "Oh, great. Look, you made her pee herself. Stop yelling, Bud. Before you get the neighbors calling the cops on us."

Suddenly, they could hear pounding down the hall, and Bud whirled. "What's that?"

"Oh, hang on." She marched down the hall. "Stop pounding on the door! If I have to come in there you're going to think all hell broke loose." Silence returned to the house.

As Linda walked back over, Bud leaned a little ways to one side, trying to see the door. Then he laughed. "What the hell'd you do, nail her in there?"

"Ha! No, I screwed her in there. There weren't any nails."

Bud chuckled. "Leave it to you. What about this one? Wanna put her in there too?"

"No way! I told Cynthia she had to stay in there alone and Sissy's going to her own room—without supper."

"Why?"

"That girl is mouthy, Bud. I've about had my fill of her."

"Well, don't get your fill yet. We don't have a check. And you're going to have to figure out a way to keep both of these pieces of garbage healthy until we do, and until we're a long ways out of this state. Don't forget that."

Linda turned her head and stared at Sissy. "Oh, what are you looking at?"

Sissy whipped her eyes down to the floor.

"Jeez, Bud, get her off the couch. It's gonna stink forever now."

Without replying, he reached down, grabbed the girl by the leg, and pulled her off on the floor. Then he jabbed a finger down the hall. "Go get on your bed!"

Sissy turned over on her hands and knees and went scrambling across the living room floor, then jumped up and ran down the hall as fast as she could. When she got into her room and quietly shut the door, they almost instantly could hear her start crying.

Bud looked at Linda. "Tell me why we had to have that one again? She isn't worth a thing! I guarantee my brothers didn't have one dime between 'em. And for sure no insurance policy."

"So? We talked about it before, smart guy. How would it have looked for us to go apply for custody of one niece but not the other? You don't think that would have looked suspicious? Besides, I didn't want any other folks raising kids that are my own flesh and blood. Who knows what might have happened to 'em."

Bud stared at her for a moment. "Don't backtalk me, woman. I can still take a paddle to you, too."

Linda laughed. "Yeah, and let's see how long you go without gettin' any then."

"So?" Suddenly, Bud looked over toward the kitchen. "What's for supper?"

"We're going out to eat."

"Oh, great idea. I just spent five bucks at the store. You think we're made of money?"

"We will be pretty soon. Come on, Bud, I'm not going to stay here with those brats. It's time you treated me."

"Or?"

"Or I'll go turn you in for a robber!" she said and giggled.

"Yeah, Mario! When they find out you drove the car, you'll be in the pen right along with me. Besides—" he lowered his voice "—you need to watch your stupid mouth. What if that girl heard you?"

"Whatever. Let's go eat."

"What about the girls?"

"I told Cynthia she's staying in her room, and Sissy's doing the same. Maybe she'll think twice about back talking next time."

Bud laughed. "Well, maybe I should screw you in your room, too!" When he thought about what he had said, his own words made him laugh even harder.

Linda made a face at him. "Wow, you didn't think that one out, did you?"

"I don't know. Maybe I did! So you seriously gonna nail the little one in her room too? What if there's a fire or something?"

"Well, then I guess we won't have no insurance money. But we also won't have those two big headaches."

"Okay, then, get it done and let's go eat. I'm starvin'."

*   *   *

Annie Price froze when she recognized Maura's voice on the other end of the line. She and Maura had known each other ever since Maura came to town, although they weren't best of friends, by any means. In fact, they had never gone out together to do one single thing. They both had their own lives to lead, and other than living out the same direction from town and both being involved in the medical community, they really didn't know what they had in common. But they were certainly friendly acquaintances, and they had spent plenty of time at the hospital in idle, friendly chatter, mostly telling stories about patients Annie had cared for, or calls Maura had taken, either here or back in her former life.

Maura had never said a word to Annie about Coal or how she felt about him. She, like Annie, was pretty close-mouthed when it came to her personal relationships. Maybe that was because, also like Annie, she didn't have any. But Annie had sensed early on that Maura had an attraction for Coal, that perhaps she had developed feelings for him. As far as the attraction, well, what woman wouldn't? But feelings, that was something different. That could be dangerous ground, and Annie knew it. But short of hanging up, the idea of which just for a moment she actually entertained, there wasn't a whole lot she could do but finish the task she had started. And then, perhaps this was for the best. Perhaps if Maura had started thinking *anything* about Coal, she would find out now that it was futile.

"Hi... Is this the Savage residence?" The coward's way out.

Yes, it is. Maura's voice was brimming with curiosity.

"Oh, thank you. May I speak with Connie?" If it worked, she was home free. She would get her message across, stake her claim on Coal, and avoid talking directly to Maura, all at the same time.

She's tied up right now. Can I give her a message?

Annie hated to swear. Annie swore.

"Um, yes, please. I just wanted to let her and the kids know that Coal is fine. I guess he had a pretty hard night, and he fell asleep on my couch, and... Well, that's it."

Long silence. There may as well have been crickets on the line. *Ohh... kay. And who am I to tell her... Who is this?*

Deadly silence. She knew who it was, didn't she? Annie almost panicked and gave a fake name. *Get it over with, you idiot!* she thought.

"Uhh... This is Annie, from the hospital."

Fatal, eternal silence.

"Are... you still there?"

Yes, thank you. Um, okay. Thanks for the call. Goodbye.

The line went dead, and a little bit of Annie Price died too. She turned her head and looked down at her sleeping knight. She felt sick to the pit of her stomach.

There was so much in the sound of a voice, and tonight Annie had heard it all. Maura was not simply attracted to Coal. She did not merely have feelings for him.

Maura PlentyWounds was in love with Coal Savage.

Annie pulled up a plastic chair from the kitchen and sat and watched Coal sleep as Burro came over and she absently stroked his sleek head. What was she going to do? Did she have any right to break Maura's heart? Did she have any right to even stake a claim on any man, when at any minute being in her life could mean disaster?

Coal was a handsome man. Smart. Strong. Charming. Yet vulnerable, too. He had said something about skeletons in his closet. She wondered what they could be. Were they as dark and foreboding as those in her own? Could his secrets kill him? Because hers could. Her and anyone she came in contact with. She had already learned that once. She had learned the hard way...

Annie felt so alone. She knew Maura was alone, too, but Coal was here with *her*, not with Maura. He would not have come here if he didn't want to. He would not have come here if he didn't want *her*. Would he? She stared at him. He looked so peaceful.

Burro got bored and went over to lie down in front of the couch, on the other side of Coal's feet. Annie rose and with great care added two logs to the fire. Then, feeling brave, she walked over to the couch, forsaking her hard chair, and eased down next to Coal. She set her hands softly on his leg, laid her head over on his chest, and made believe that he was hers, and that there was no one else in the world who could come between them.

Oh, but there was...

CHAPTER TWENTY-EIGHT

Coal came awake still in a dream state. He felt so warm and comfortable. One of the dogs was licking his face, and he was so tired he didn't even try to push it away. Suddenly, he remembered that both Dobe and Shadow had been so carefully trained not to lick that this couldn't be either of them. He jerked his eyes open.

There was no dog close by. There was not even any licking—not per se. But Annie Price was right there, with her face near his now, and he realized she had been gently kissing his cheek.

"Hey, sleepy head."

He smiled and shook his head. "Jeez, Annie. I am so sorry. I feel like a truck ran over me."

"You've had a rough time."

"Yeah. So I woke up because I thought one of my dogs was licking my face. You wouldn't know anything about that, would you?"

She held up her hand in the manner of taking an oath, a mock serious look on her face. "Honest, Coal, I was *not* licking your face!"

He laughed. "Good. I'm afraid you'd get whisker burn."

She winced and put her fingers to her lips, dabbing at them. "Ooh, that's what that is!" She giggled. "I'm sorry. I thought about just letting you sleep there all night. But you should probably get going, huh? Your family is going to think you sleep around."

"Yes, which apparently I do."

Again, she laughed, her eyes twinkling. "Not that I wouldn't love for you to stay, of course."

He heaved a big sigh. "What time is it, anyway?"

"Nine-thirty. The movie's been going for a little while. I guess we missed the premier."

"Yeah. I would have slept through it, you were right about that."

"Yep. So you gonna be okay?"

"Sure. Nothing a night's sleep can't cure."

She gave him a big smile, dropping her eyes demurely. "So I want you to know I was a perfectly good girl. Well, mostly."

He smiled back. "I know you're a good girl, Annie. That's the problem: Good girls shouldn't hang around with widowed bad boys."

Not waiting for a response, he struggled up out of what had become a very warm nest on the couch. Burro jumped up to make sure whatever was about to happen didn't happen without him.

Coal gave Annie his hand, and she stood up too. He was unsuccessful in letting go of her hand, because she continued to hold on, her grip tightening as she felt his relax. "So there's absolutely no reason you can think of for you to stay a little longer yet... right?"

Coal smiled gently but shook his head. "Not tonight, okay?" He was saddened by the look of disappointment she tried to hide, and he raised his hand and tucked two fingers under her chin, lifting her face up. "Hey, no sad faces."

She tried to smile. "No sad faces." He was aware that she started to stand up straighter to kiss him, but he turned away hurriedly and tried to pretend he didn't notice.

He went and got his coat and shrugged into it. "So what about the dog?"

She shrugged. "I'm off work tomorrow, so I guess I'll drive around the area where I found him and knock on some doors. The paper hasn't helped."

"How long are you keeping him?"

Another shrug. "I don't know, Coal. What do you think I should do?"

"I think you would do fine with a dog."

She looked down at Burro and stroked his head, giving him a huge smile. "Yeah. I probably would. But you know, I start to get attached to something and then something always happens." She quickly looked up at Coal, and he knew what she was thinking.

"Yeah, that's the hard part." He wasn't going to fuel her fire.

"Well, I'm going to get home and try to get a full night's sleep. What are the chances?"

She giggled. "Better take the phone off the hook!" Then a light came into her eyes, and she said, "Oh! Coal, I have to tell you something before you go."

He wasn't sure he liked the look in her eyes. "Okay... Shoot."

"Well, I was feeling guilty about your family, so I called your mom's house to tell her you fell asleep on my couch—so they wouldn't worry about you. But... she didn't answer."

He turned more fully to her but didn't reply. He only waited.

"Maura did."

A sick feeling came into Coal's stomach. "Okay... And how did that go?" He could feel his heart starting to hammer.

"Well, after she got over the surprise, she thanked me and then pretty much just hung up on me."

Coal searched the woman's eyes, trying to see what she was feeling. Finally, he gave a little shake of his head. "I don't know what to say, Annie."

"You don't need to say anything. I knew because of the girls that she had been staying there with... your mom. But I didn't expect her still to be there. It took me by surprise."

"Sorry. I didn't know she'd be there either, to tell you the truth."

The feeling of nausea was settling in now, and considering what was, or was *not,* between him and Maura, he wasn't sure why.

"Coal, I have been really unfair to you, and we've never really talked about anything serious. Is the reason you don't... Oh, darn it, what am I trying to say? Is there something between you and Maura?"

Coal's swelling heart seemed to be closing off his throat. "Um, not that I know of, no."

She looked at him askance. "You can be honest with me, Coal. I'm a big girl."

"I've never talked with her about anything serious either. Is that what you want to know?"

Annie nodded. "Yeah, I guess. But she..."

"She what?" Coal said after several seconds of hard silence.

"Nothing. She just sounded pretty disappointed when she realized who I am and where you were. I think..." She stopped, and it was obvious she was having a hard time finishing her thought.

Coal rescued her. "Maura came over there because of those girls, and now she has her horses in our pasture. But now that the girls are gone, I'm sure she's just there until she can get the horses loaded back up and moved."

"Okay." Annie nodded and looked down at the top snap of his coat, reaching out absently to fondle it. "I just... I don't want to complicate your life any more than it already is."

"You aren't. Don't worry about that." The fleeting thought of leaning down to kiss her crossed his mind. But that would be crossing a new line. So far she had always been the one kissing *him.* His guts told him the whole game would change once he initiated his first kiss with her. By a miracle, he restrained himself.

"Thanks for the drink. And the nice spot to nap. It felt good."

"There's no reason to say thanks. It felt good to me, too. This house is too big for me by myself. And lonely."

"That's why you need the dog," he said, too quickly. A disappointed smile crossed her face.

"Yeah, the dog." She forced a little smile. "Okay, Coal, you get going and give your kids a big hug for me, okay?"

"I will. And you snuggle up with that big hairy mutt. You could both use a friend."

All the way home, Coal couldn't stop thinking about Maura. What was he going to say to her? It was going to be an awkward situation, no matter how he looked at it. It would probably be best if he simply said nothing at all.

But Maura had already solved the issue. When he pulled into the yard, her pickup was not there. With a heavy heart, he went in the house, feeling the wall of warmth from the Franklin stove envelope his whole body as he took off his coat.

Connie was sitting in front of the TV, in his chair. She saw him glance around.

"Hi, Son. Don't worry. She's gone."

Thursday, December 14

The sky was crystal clear, and thick frost covered all the vehicles, when Dobe messed the covers all up getting out of bed, and Coal struggled out to the smell of bacon frying. Even his room was cold, and when he got up he dragged his bedspread with him, wrapped tightly around him.

The kids were all sitting around the table already, eating pancakes. The twins greeted him and Dobe exuberantly, as did Shadow. Virgil smiled and said in his soft voice, "Hey, Dad."

Katie forced a smile and hurriedly took another bite of pancake. Giving Shadow only a quick scratch of the head as Dobe made all his rounds of the others, Coal took a deep breath and went over to Katie, crouching down close to her chair. He rubbed her shoulder, which caused her to look over quickly at him and give him a smile. There was more sadness in it than happiness.

He leaned close to her and kissed her cheek, and a mist of tears came into her eyes. It seemed extra hard for her to swallow her bite, and she reached hurriedly for a glass of milk and took a drink.

Coal looked over at Connie, who was scooping strips of bacon out of a skillet. But she was watching him, not the food. She just raised her eyebrows and gave a little shake of the head.

More determined, Coal put his mouth close to Katie's ear. "Hey, sweetheart. Can I come and get you after school and take you somewhere?"

With moist but glowing eyes, his dark-haired beauty of a daughter turned and met his gaze. She nodded, at first hesitantly, then vigorously. He realized that she wanted to speak but couldn't. That knowledge made a lump rise in his own throat. Come hell or high water, this was a date he had to keep.

He reached an arm all the way around her shoulders and gave her a tight squeeze, then dragged himself and his bedspread back to the bedroom and got dressed, tugging on his brown work boots last of all before he stood back up.

Mentally, he made a note of things he had to do today: go visit Cynthia at school—and he ached for a way to see Sissy, too, but that had been stolen from him; see what Todd Mitchell wanted to tell him; check with Rick Cheatum to see if anything had been done about a raise for Jordan Peterson; get someone to help him shuttle both the new pickup and the Ford either back here to the house or to the courthouse so one or the other would not always be cluttering Ken Parks's lot; drive by Hope Street and do a license plate check on the Mileys' car; and take Katie out. Last, but by far not least: *take Katie out.*

As for Maura and Annie, he had to put them out of his mind. Some things simply could not be handled with any grace by a mere mortal man and were better left alone.

He wanted to give Cynthia a little time to get settled in at school, so the first item on the agenda was to go drive by the Battertons' and run the Mileys' plate. As he had feared, nothing came back.

He went next to the jail to look for Todd. When he reviewed the schedule hanging on the wall, which he had made up himself but had such a hard time keeping track of, he saw that Todd wasn't coming in until two. And Jordan was already off, so the place was cold and quiet. There was half a pot of coffee keeping warm on the burner, though, and he poured himself a cup and took a tentative sip. Good old Jordan. He had learned the art of coffee making fast.

He got on the phone and did a little follow up on some traffic tickets, went down and met with the prosecutor for a while to go over pending cases—all small items, infractions and misdemeanors, and then went back to the jail. He had cranked up the radiator to fight the bitter cold outside, and its clanking, clicking and hissing was his only company in the room as he sipped down another cup of coffee, emptying the pot.

It was nine-thirty now, and school should be well under way. His next most important thing was to see Cynthia. He drove down and had her called out of class to meet him at the office, and he waited anxiously.

When she arrived down the hall, she glanced up at him but then quickly lowered her face and slowed her pace considerably. Thirty feet away, she hesitated, almost as if she were going to turn into the restroom, and then she steeled herself and came on. This was not the reception Coal had been expecting. What was wrong?

At the last second, just as she reached him, Cynthia raised her face. There was a big bruise around her right eye and cheek. A fresh, ugly bruise.

CHAPTER TWENTY-NINE

"Hey!" Coal stepped toward Cynthia, and she instantly started to cry, throwing her arms around him. He stood there patting her back for half a minute. Then finally he took her by the shoulders and eased her away from him so he could see her face. The bruise was mostly red, but turning purple in places, and he noticed that it started at a horizontal cut across her eyebrow. "What in the world happened?" he asked. He tried to pretend that his first reaction wasn't to blame the Mileys.

Cynthia gave a nervous laugh and brushed at her eye. "I'm so stupid! I had one of my drawers open, and when I dropped my socks I leaned down to pick them up and had totally forgot the drawer. It hurts!" she added.

"Yeah, I imagine so. Wow, you really whacked it good."

"I know. So how is everyone? I miss you all so much."

"We really miss you too, honey. It hasn't been the same without you. But we're all doing okay, I guess."

She smiled at a thought. "I looked out the window and saw you in your truck that night."

"I saw you open the curtains. I'm glad I was there."

"Me too." She leaned close and hugged him again. "Who was with you? I thought I saw someone else. Was it Maura?"

"You're a good guesser. It sure was. She had to work the next day, but she insisted on being there. I tried to make her stay home, but she said she would just drive her own pickup if I did."

"I love her, Coal. I'm so happy you have her."

Coal almost said, *I love her too,* but the words caught in his throat. It was just a bad habit to reply in kind. "She's sure lost without you girls. I think she would give anything to have you back."

Cynthia hugged him tighter.

"How's Sissy?" he asked into her hair.

"Fine. They make her sleep in her own bedroom."

"*What?* Does she do okay?"

A long pause.

"Cynthia?"

"Yeah, I think so. She..."

"What?"

"Oh, nothing."

Coal waited for a long time. When he realized she had clammed up, he asked, "Are you getting plenty of food?"

"Uh-huh."

"What do they feed you?"

That one caught her off-guard. "Um... Well, you know, just normal stuff."

"Like what did you eat last night?"

"Uh, potatoes."

"Mashed potatoes?"

"Yeah, mashed."

"Did you have cereal before you caught the bus this morning?"

"What? Oh, yeah. Yep, cereal."

To anyone listening, Coal's line of questioning would probably sound pretty strange. For him, it was anything but. He wanted to see if she simply agreed with every guess he made. Coal was no psychic. It was highly unlikely that he would be able to guess every meal right. So to him, if she continued to confirm every guess, it meant something else altogether... Mostly, that she probably wasn't being fed at all.

Coal eased the girl away from him again and led her a ways down the hall, away from the office secretary. He looked her directly in the eyes, and she was only able to meet his gaze for a second or two.

"Cynthia, nobody is here. Nobody can hear us. I need to be able to help you. Can you tell me how you really got that bruise?"

"What?" She stared at him, seeming suddenly confused. "I told you, I hit my drawer."

"That hard?"

"I guess so." Her eyes flickered away.

"And they aren't really feeding you much, are they?"

Cynthia seemed to be getting agitated. "Sure. We get plenty."

"You've got to trust me, honey. We can fix this. But you have to help me."

Cynthia's chin started quivering. "Everything's fine. I promise. Why don't you believe me?"

"I want to believe you, Cynthia. I really do. But I know how these things go. They're holding something over you to make you lie."

"I'm not lying." She stomped her foot. "I have to go back to class." She whirled and almost ran back down the hall, never looking back before she had turned the corner.

*   *   *

In a controlled rage, Coal went out and got in the car. He fired it up and drove to Hope, then headed west. When he got to the Battertons', he pulled up to the curb the wrong way and slammed it in park. The red Buick was in the driveway, so he knew they were home. Taking a deep breath, he blew it out slowly through pursed lips, repeated it, and then threw open his door and got out.

He sauntered up the walk to the door and knocked very deliberately. Soon, Linda Miley opened the inner door. She was startled to see him, but she instantly put a mask over her face, which was tan from caked on makeup.

He pulled open the storm door. "I'm here to check on Sissy."

"What do you mean check on her?" she said casually, putting a hand on her hip. "She's fine."

"I just need to see her."

"Who is it, Linda?" Coal heard Bud call from back in the house.

"The sheriff."

"Can I come in?" said Coal.

At that moment, Bud Miley reached the door. "I don't think you really need to."

Coal's face settled into hard lines. "I'm here to check on Sissy and make sure she's okay."

"Well, she's sleeping right now," Bud said. "She doesn't need to be disturbed."

"I'll just peek at her."

"Do you have a warrant?" asked Linda.

"I don't." Coal clenched his teeth.

"So... Maybe you'd better come back some other time," said Bud.

"Yes, when you have one," Linda added.

"I'll do that," said Coal. "No telling what else I might find when I do."

Linda laughed. "Probably not much. Go on! Get!"

Without another word, Coal turned and walked down the sidewalk. He had never felt more ready to explode. He had to get away from here before he did something that would cost him every possibility of ever having those girls again—and perhaps his job as well.

Coal drove up to the courthouse, parked, and went upstairs to see Judge Wiley Sinclair. The judge was a less-than-imposing figure, some sixty-five years old or more, with very thin but still dark hair, almost non-existent except over his ears. His face was round, as were his eyes, and his mouth was a thin line. He wore black-rimmed glasses which at the moment were down low over the tip of his blunt nose.

"Good morning, your honor."

The judge looked up from his desk and nodded, waving a hand dismissively in front of him. "You don't see any robes, do you, Sheriff? Judge will do fine."

Coal almost smiled, because apparently to Sinclair, 'Judge' was informal as it got. "Judge, then."

"So what can I do for you?"

"Judge, you know the situation with the two girls Bud and Linda Miley just took in."

"Yes, I'm well aware of it. It's pretty final at this point, Sheriff, if you came here to try and change things."

"I understand," said Coal impatiently. "But I just visited with the older one, Cynthia, at school, and she is badly bruised around one eye and has a cut. I asked her about it, and she said she hit a drawer. But I don't think she's telling me the truth."

"You don't think?"

"I have gotten to know her pretty well."

"And you have other evidence?"

"No, just my hunch."

"Well, hunches without evidence are like clouds that don't rain. They aren't good for much. I'm afraid there isn't any way I can help you."

"It isn't really about that, Judge. I went by the house and asked to see the little girl, and they wouldn't let me in."

"Really?"

"They said she was sleeping. They told me I would have to have a warrant to come in and see her."

"I'm afraid I can't just go around issuing a warrant for every little thing, Sheriff. Can't you just put surveillance on the house? See if the little girl comes out with them sometime?"

Coal stood there dumbfounded. Who did this judge think he was? The sheriff's department was him and Todd Mitchell, and two underpaid jailers. Just who was going to do this surveillance?

"That could be days, your honor."

"Judge."

"Judge!"

"Don't get sharp with me, Sheriff. I am trying to uphold the Constitution of the United States here. You have presented me with absolutely no viable reason to issue a warrant for you to go into that house."

Coal's entire existence as a sheriff here in Lemhi County was dependent upon having a good working relationship with this judge, a man whom at the moment he despised and for whom he had zero respect. He didn't know how to leave this office gracefully. He wanted nothing more than to cuff this man of the robes upside the head.

"Thank you then, *sir,*" he said, and he turned and walked out.

He went back downstairs, outside, and then down the three concrete steps into his office, sitting down at his desk with a fresh cup of coffee he sipped slowly to try and calm his nerves. This job was getting very personal to him right now. He knew he needed to back up a little. He wished in some ways that it was K.T.'s baby. K.T. had always had much more ability to stay calm than he did. Maybe he would have known just what to do in a situation like this.

Old K.T. Memory of his friend made Coal feel suddenly very sad.

On a whim, he dialed up Todd Mitchell and told him he had some free time if he still wanted to talk. At first, Todd seemed reluctant, but finally he agreed to drop whatever he was doing and come in early.

Coal was still sitting at his desk ten minutes later when Todd arrived.

"Hey, Todd. I apologize that we didn't get a better chance to talk when you asked. I've had a lot going on—as usual."

"No problem, Coal. I understand."

"What's on your mind?"

Todd looked over at the coffee pot. "Mind if I have a cup?"

"Of course not. Go ahead."

Todd poured himself a cup, then stood by the window looking up at the parking lot as he swished it around the cup, his back to Coal.

"Hey, Todd, you know how things go in this job—feast or famine, right? One minute, no calls. Next minute, the world falls apart. You know? Make hay while the sun shines, and all that. You'd better unload whatever you need to say before the next wave hits. Is it that bad? If it's your wages, I really am working on it."

Todd's brown hat tilted back as he looked up at the ceiling. Finally, he turned around to face Coal, but he could hardly meet his eyes.

"I don't really know how to say this. I guess I'll start out by saying I have a confession to make. I haven't had much else on my mind for quite a while. I really thought maybe when I helped you out with that Hague Freeman deal it would make things square for me, but it hasn't. It's still eating at me, and I've got to tell you."

Coal felt himself starting to get as nervous as his deputy seemed. "Go on."

"Well, you know how Phil Harringer got wind of K.T. givin' that petty cash to Jordan?"

Coal sat still, staring. *No...* He didn't even want to hear the rest of what Todd was going to say.

"Yes, Todd, I do. I mean, I don't know *how,* but I do know it happened."

Todd stood there looking down at him. His lips started to open twice, but in the end, nothing came forth.

"Oh, man, Todd. Please don't tell me you went to Phil Harringer. Please don't tell me that."

"I didn't!" Todd replied adamantly. "No, sir. I didn't. But... it was my fault he found out."

Coal took in a deep breath and slowly stood up, no longer willing to look at his deputy. Now he was looking down at him. "I'm not following you."

"Oh, damnit. I was playing pool with a couple of my buds—or at least I thought they were buds. I'd been drinkin', and I was mouthing off a little about K.T. I can't remember what happened that day, but he did somethin' that made me mad. Before I knew it, I was telling this friend of mine what K.T. did, giving that petty cash to Jordan without permission, and how I could have used that money too, but he didn't offer me a dime. I'm real sorry, Coal. I had no idea, but this guy's friends with Phil Harringer. Fact is they're next-door neighbors. I haven't talked to him lately, but I think he really thought he was doin' me a favor. I think he thought K.T. would be forced to help me out the way he did Jordan. I don't know if he ever thought it out enough to think about him losin' his job over it."

"Oh, man." Coal closed his eyes. "Oh, man. Todd." Coal plopped down again on his chair and leaned way back, staring up at the ceiling.

"I don't expect anything from you, Coal. Nothin'. I know I don't deserve any trust now. I've felt that for a long time. I'm even ready to put my house on the market over this so I can move to the Falls and look for other work."

"Just hold on. Hold on." Coal raised his hands, as if patting the tension back down. He sat back up straighter in his chair, laying his hands stiffly on top of the desk. After a moment, he raised them back up to his forehead, rubbing at it and at his eyes, as if trying to ease a bad headache. He sat there for a moment longer, then finally stood up and walked to the door, staring out at the cold.

"Just tell me if I'm done," said Todd to Coal's broad back. "I understand. I can't expect better."

Coal drew a big breath and turned. "You don't need me to tell you how much this job relies on trust between officers. You've got to know you can rely on each other in a bad spot. Loose lips sink ships. You got a damn good man fired, Todd, with those loose lips. I understand the drinking and all. It makes us say things we otherwise might not. But this is big. You've got to see it from my side."

"I know, Coal. Damn it, I know. I told you I've been struggling with it. I'd give anything to take it back. Do you want my badge? No hard feelings, at least on my end."

"You love this job, don't you, Todd?"

Todd nodded. "You know I do, more than any other job I could have."

"We've had our differences, but I do know that. And you've turned into a good deputy. I'm going to sound like a real hypocrite here, but I need to ask something of you."

"Anything."

"First, I want to give you one more job, a pretty big one. And then for the hypocritical part. Would you be willing to take a couple of days off so I can think this thing through? Get my head wrapped around what really happened? And maybe even let me go talk to your friend that knows Harringer?"

Todd took a moment to digest everything. "Sure, Coal. That's only fair."

"All right. You're already scheduled off the next two days, so your administrative leave will be Saturday and Sunday. At least you'll have a four-day weekend. And don't worry about the missed pay, for now. I won't let you and your family starve."

Todd tried to smile. "That'll be good. But... what's the big job?"

"I need you to take your personal vehicle down to K.T.'s old house and try to get a photograph of the man who is living there now and drives the red Riviera. He won't recognize you, so I'm hoping you can get away with it. But Todd, I'll understand too if under the circumstances you don't feel like doing it."

"No, Coal. I do. I told you I'd do whatever you needed. You've got a photograph as good as in your hand."

"All right. I'll bring my personal camera up to your house later then. The department one is a piece of garbage."

"I'll be there waiting. And Coal?"

"Yeah?"

"I hope someday you can find it in yourself to forgive me, no matter what happens."

CHAPTER THIRTY

Coal went home for long enough to get his camera and bring it back to Todd's house. Todd's wife was there, and she said hi, but she was very reserved. He guessed Todd had told her everything.

After that, he went to Ken's and ended up enlisting him to help shuttle the pickup to the courthouse parking lot, and dropped him back off in the LTD.

A quick visit to Rick Cheatum's office at the bank revealed nothing of any help as far as Jordan's requested raise, but at least he kept the bug clawing around in Rick's ear.

He went down to Saveway and bought a barbecued chicken, which he polished off in its entirety for his lunch, followed by three stalks of celery and twenty ounces of ice water—typical body-building fare. He did one hundred and fifty pull-ups on a bar that he had made so it could sit across the top of the doorway on two supports, then five sets of fifty pushups. After he had toweled off and cooled down, he got on the phone and called Jordan Peterson, asking him to come to the courthouse early.

Big Jordan showed up thirty minutes later, and as he shut the door quietly he turned to see Coal at the coffee pot. "Hey, Coal. So what's up?"

"Have a seat."

Coal waited until Jordan was sitting in front of his desk, and then he went over and sat with one cheek on the edge of the desk, so he was looking down at his jailer.

"I've been wanting to have this conversation for a while, Jordan. There's going to come a day when I can make this permanent, if you want, but you've already had one taste of being a road deputy, when we arrested Paul Monahan, and I want to invite you to do the job for a couple more days, at least. What do you think of that?"

"I'd be honored, Coal. But why? Something happen?"

"Well, let's just say Todd's going to be off at least until Monday, and I'll need someone to fill the vacancy. I think you're a good fit for the job."

Jordan paused and looked worried. "I won't be replacing him, will I?"

"Not likely, but that's still up in the air. If you can do it, tell me. Your shift will start... well, pretty much as soon as you can start it. Tomorrow at two as well. Todd wasn't really supposed to be on until Saturday and Sunday, but at worst, it'll just be a couple more days' experience under your belt and a little extra pay on your check."

"Well, I'd love to do it, you can bet on that. As long as it's not causing any trouble for Todd. I'm a single man, and he's not, so I don't need to make as much as he does to get by."

"I know all about it, buddy. It's nice of you to think about him first, but believe me, you aren't the cause of Todd's troubles."

* * *

There would have had to be a wildfire raging out of control through the streets of Salmon for Coal not to have been waiting at the front door of Salmon High, on Daisy Street, when the students began to file out that day.

Instead of sitting in his car, he was standing at the door, in uniform, as the door flew open and teenagers started streaming by. Coal recognized that he cut the kind of figure in a crowd that even high school kids took note of, so he was used to being greeted with interest by them. He smiled and said hello to each of the students who dared to hail him on their way by. It made him happy when he heard one of them turn to another after they passed and say, "That's Katie's dad!"

Number fifty or so out the door, and already scanning for a familiar face, was Katie Leigh. A huge smile burst over her when she saw him, and Coal could have cried when she ran to him and threw her arms around him, saying, "Daddy!" It had been a long time since he had had such a greeting from his girl.

Still holding her, he asked into her deep brown hair, "How's my girl today?"

"I'm good, Daddy. How are you?"

"I'm good now." He leaned back from her, and saw that her eyes were full of moisture. He chose not to risk embarrassing her by bringing it up. "Where are we going to go eat?"

Without hesitation, she asked, "Can we go to Wally's?"

He laughed. "You really want to go to Wally's?"

"Yeah."

"Okay, it's a deal. Come on."

Throughout their conversation, other students had been streaming by them. They were like a boulder in the stream, and they didn't care.

* * *

Todd Mitchell pulled up in the courthouse parking lot and scanned it quickly. Disappointed at not seeing Coal's LTD, he got out more slowly than he intended, bringing Coal's camera with him, and went down the concrete steps and into the jail. Jordan was there cleaning a service revolver.

"Hey, Jord. What's new? Are jailers going to start packing iron now?" He laughed. "Where's Coal, do you know?"

Jordan's hands had stilled, and he set the revolver and cleaning rod down and stood up, wiping his hands on a rag. "Uh... He left a while ago. I think he's taking his daughter out to eat. Hey—did he talk to you about me yet?"

Todd gave him a confused look, shrugging. "About you? No, why?"

Jordan's shoulders slumped a bit. "Man, I don't know if he expected you to come back in today."

Frowning, Todd shook the camera in front of him. "He had me get some photographs of that Miley guy that's living in the Battertons' house. Hey, what's goin' on, Jordan?" He seemed for the first time to notice that Jordan had a gunbelt and holster on.

"I'm not sure he'd want me to say anything, but... Well, he asked me to be a deputy."

"What? You're kidding me, right?"

"No, wait, man—it's just temporary."

"Hey, I gotta go. Tell Coal thanks for everything, all right? And I took the film down to Rexall's to be developed."

"No, wait! Hey, Todd!"

The door shut behind Todd just as Jordan reached it. He hesitated at the glass, looking out, but to judge by Todd's stiff and determined pace, there was no point in trying to stop him.

Todd got in his car and drove home, going in quietly and hanging his hat on a hook by the door. His wife was in the kitchen stirring Spanish rice in a pan, and it filled the house with an aroma that could not quite rid the place of the stale smell of cigarette smoke. She heard him come in and turned, pushing a hank of stringy blond hair back behind her ear.

"What's up now?"

"Nothin'."

She got a concerned look and turned the stove down a couple of notches, then came around more fully to him. "Todd?"

"Seriously, honey. Nothin'."

She walked close to him and put her arms around his neck. "You can't fool me that easy."

"Jan, I think Coal's firing me. He already put Jordan in my spot. Can you believe that? I haven't been gone half a day. I know I deserve it, but I just thought he'd at least think about it longer."

Shocked, Jan stared at him. "What are we going to do?"

"I don't know. I have no idea."

"Have you even started applying for anything in the Falls yet?"

"Well, no. I was hoping we'd still be able to stay here."

"I hate that man," she said suddenly. "He has turned our lives upside down ever since he came back here."

"Hey, Jan, don't hate him. He's turned out to be a good man."

"What? I can't believe you're saying that."

"I can't help it." He turned and walked to the kitchen window. Looking out, he absently pulled a Pall Mall out of a half-full pack and got a match out of a drawer. Lighting it up, he drew on it for a second, held the smoke, then blew it out in a long streamer that hit the window, then deflected in every direction.

"You know what I want to do?"

"What?"

"Something big. Real big."

"Wait, Todd. Nothing illegal, right?" Jan clutched his arm.

"No! No, nothin' like that. I mean something big that's good. Somethin' to be remembered for in a good way."

Jan just stared at her husband, then finally shook her head. "Wow. I don't even know what to think. That man really must have turned your head around."

Todd reached out and stroked her hair. "It all changed that night he brought food over here for you and the kids—with money I know was out of his own pocket. That's how he is, Jan. Everything for poor people. And sad people. I'm sorry I made you think he was bad. He's as good a sheriff as K.T. was. Maybe even better. But he's a hard man, too."

"I know. And that's why I thought you would hate him."

"I'm done hatin', honey. It's never got me nowhere before."

"So then what are you gonna do? What are *we* gonna do?"

"I don't know what our family's gonna do. But for me, I'm going to think of something. Something big. Something nobody could ever forget. Even if I'm forced to resign, I'm going to do something that when Coal thinks back on me he's going to respect me."

Jan Mitchell stared at her husband like a man she had just met. Finally, she said, "Come here." And she took his arms and drew him to her.

And the clock, at that very moment, began ticking for Deputy Todd Mitchell.

*   *   *

Sitting in the big corner booth in Wally's Cafe, with plates heaped with the famous Wally's fries and brown gravy, Coal gazed at his beautiful daughter. It was hard to believe this was the same little girl he had just rocked in his arms, it seemed like yesterday. He had missed so much of her childhood, watching her growing up in pictures. It made him want to cry knowing he could never get those days back.

Katie had turned quiet ever since they got in the car. She was her usual bright self when Wally and Beulah came out and made a fuss over her, and she even greeted their daughter Karen with a big smile. But after that, clear up to this very moment, it was hard to get her to talk. She just kept looking out the front window at the street, and although she didn't act angry, or even surly, she just did not respond with any long answers to all of Coal's questions, his attempts to make conversation.

At last, in desperation, he reached across the table and squeezed her arm. He would have taken a hand, but they were both under the table.

"Hey, Pumpkin. Something's been going on with you for a few days now. I don't know how to help you—or me either, for that matter—if you don't give me some kind of hint. It seems like this is hard on you, but believe me, it's hard on me, too. Sometimes I feel like I just got my little girl back and now she's slipping away again."

Katie suddenly brought her right hand up from under the table and took his, which was still in the center of the table, with a tight grip. Tears had come into her eyes, and she tried to stare at him. She tried as hard as she could. But soon, the tears were so heavy that she couldn't possibly see.

"Daddy, I think you'll hate me," she said, trying to hold back a sob. Her chin began to quiver.

"I would never hate you, sweetheart. Hey! What's wrong?" He got up and went around to her bench, scooting in beside her and putting an arm around her shoulders, squeezing tight and giving her a kiss on top of her head. "There's nothing you could say that would make me hate you or even think less of you. This is something to do with a boy, I'm guessing. Is it Lance?"

She whipped her face over, and her eyes darted back and forth between his. "No, Daddy!" A laugh almost erupted from her. "No!" The laugh dissolved into tears. "Daddy! I did something really bad."

"What did you do, sweetie? It's nothing we can't fix."

"I prayed that Cynthia and Sissy would get taken away, Daddy. I wanted to have you back, all to myself." And with those words, Katie broke down in the tears she had fought so long and hard to hold at bay.

CHAPTER THIRTY-ONE

Katie was inconsolable for so long that Coal finally had to take her back out to the car and hold her while she cried out her pain. It was just too much for her young heart to deal with, feeling like it was because of her that the girls had been taken away, when they could have, and should have, been like sisters.

But even after Coal convinced her that it wasn't her prayers that had done it, because others were praying just as hard that the girls would get to stay, the very thought that she had felt that way about them made her deplore herself.

When the tears subsided, Coal kept holding onto her and patted her back, whispering in her ear. "Don't worry, sweetie. We're going to do everything we can to get those girls back safe, okay?"

"Okay, Daddy," she replied with a sniffle after a few moments. "Daddy?"

"Yeah?"

"I don't even want to live anymore if something bad happens to Cynthia and Sissy."

*   *   *

Todd Mitchell did more thinking than socializing during supper. When the meal was finished, he stood up. "Hey, I have to go back down to Rexall's real quick, okay? I'll be back as soon as I can."

With no more explanation than that, he returned to the drug-store and told them he had to get his roll of film back. Then he drove over to the home of Clyde Stone, who had been a friend of K.T. Batterton's and was acquainted with Todd.

Clyde answered his knock, wiping his mouth with a napkin as he opened the front door. "Hello, Deputy. What can I do for you?"

"Hello, Mr. Stone. I need to ask you a huge favor. The sheriff has a suspect here in town who may have robbed a store in Mis-soula. We need to get his photo sent up there as soon as possible, and the drugstore takes a whole week to get it back. I think K.T. used to get you to do some work for him. Do you still develop film?"

"Well, yeah, I do, but I'm pretty tied up tonight."

Todd's heart fell. "It's really important. This man and his wife are trying to steal some insurance money from K.T.'s daughter. It's supposed to be her aunt and uncle, but she's never seen them be-fore. Anyway, they got custody of her, and I don't think things are going very well."

"They got Cynthia?" Clyde Stone rose up taller, and looked quickly behind him. "Ma! Can you go to that dinner by yourself? I've got something real important I need to do."

A woman walked in, her face full of concern. "I heard," she said. "Of course. You need to develop that film."

"Thank you so much," Todd said. He whipped a notepad out of his pocket and scratched his telephone number and name on it. "Please call me at this number as soon as you're done, all right? The sooner the better."

"I will. Hey, Deputy, is Cynthia going to be okay?"

"I sure hope so, sir. I hope so."

*   *   *

That evening, right before McPherson's would close for the night, the phone rang at the Savages', and Connie answered it. Coal, Katie, and the boys watched her eagerly from the dining table.

"Savages."

Long pause, while she listened and a look of loving concern came over her face.

"Of course you can, Maura. You know that. You should never even have to ask. We'll be anxiously waiting."

Connie hung up the phone and gazed at Coal as she walked back to her place at the table and rested her hands on the back of her chair. Coal was watching her, trying to appear casual. "That was Maura. She sounded like she'd been crying." *Again* thought Coal. *Or, more likely still.* "She asked if she could spend the night."

In spite of his best intentions, Coal's heart started pounding woodenly. Inside, he swore. Outside, he took a deep breath and slowly let it out as he reached for the serving fork and helped himself to another slab of roast, another fifty grams of protein. He didn't need it, but his hands needed something to do.

Katie was openly watching her father for a reaction. The boys only looked at him now and then, except for Virgil, whose feelings were always kept in an iron box.

Coal finally sighed, conscious of eyes on him but not meeting anyone's gaze. "I might better do a night shift then."

Connie tapped her fingers on the chair. "Son?"

He looked at her.

"It's cold outside, but I think Dobe and Shadow need to go for a walk, don't you? Not to mention Chewy and Dart."

"I suppose so." He couldn't hide the resignation in his voice.

"And I'm going with you. We haven't walked for a while."

Or talked, thought Coal. He wasn't silly enough not to know it wasn't about the walking, but the talking, that she was concerned.

Different from any other time since Coal brought his family back to the valley, all of them went on the walk that particular night. All three of the boys ran ahead with the dogs, and it did Coal's heart good to see Shadow running like a pup again. Katie walked ahead, but he noticed that she stayed back far enough that she might casually eavesdrop.

As Coal walked along, Connie reached over and took his arm in her hands. "Look at your girl," she said, just above a whisper. "She's turning into a real woman, Son."

He chuckled. "You mean because she's trying to listen in on our talk and get the real dirt?"

Feigning shock, Connie slapped his arm. "We aren't like that! Shame on you." Then she laughed.

"It's pretty cold out here, huh, Mom?"

"Sure is."

"Don't you think you'd better talk fast, before Jack Frost nips off our noses?"

"You think you're so smart, don't you? All right, I'll talk. Coal, I don't want you to leave tonight. The kids don't either."

He sighed. He walked, feeling the nip of frost, watching the gush of each icy blue breath that burst from his mouth. The air was clear as crystal, and the snow on the mountains and in the fields was evening-blue, with yellow stalks of grass and the awkward, bare branches of willows spearing up out of it in final defiance. Across an empty pasture, a red fox froze and stared at them, confident in the invisibility of his pose. It must have worked, because although Dobe stopped to test the air, then looked upwind and let out a little whine, he and the other dogs walked on, and the little sharp-nosed fox remained safe.

"I don't really want to leave either, Mom. I'd like to snuggle up in my bed with Dobe and just sleep a whole night through, for once. But just think how awkward this might be. Maura stumbled onto Annie kissing me at the hospital, and then she happened to be the lucky one who answered the phone when Annie called to say I was over at her house. If what you said is true, and Maura really does like me the way you think she does, then I don't know how we could comfortably sleep in the same house."

"Frankly, I'm not sure either. But Maura surely believes you'll be there with us tonight. And if she is willing to risk it, why aren't you?"

"I guess I can always change my mind later."

"Sure you can."

They walked another quarter of a mile along Lemhi Road. Gravel broke from the frozen road when their footsteps came down on it. Coal noticed that Katie had dropped back even farther. The gravel was making it hard for her to hear.

He spoke her name, and she turned, and his heart skipped a beat. Glory, how beautiful their little girl was in her sweet adolescence. Her long dark hair was as straight as a preacher in a glass house, and even in the evening light it seemed to glow. Her brown eyes, in spite of all they had seen, were full of wonder, and her mouth had a sweet, innocent almost-smile. Her cheeks glowed deep pink with the cold, giving them a perpetual blush. How had he been a part of creating something so beautiful?

He motioned her back to them and put his arm around her. "You're a grown woman now, Katie. There's no reason to keep you out of this."

"I don't have to be in on it, Daddy," she said.

"No, I want you to be. What do you think about me staying at the house if Maura comes tonight?"

"You really want to know what I think?"

"I wouldn't ask if I didn't."

"I want you to stay. I want you both there."

"Yeah?"

"Yeah."

"You know, Grandma thinks Maura likes me."

Katie laughed. "Any girl could tell you that, Dad."

"Aren't you a little young to know about that kind of stuff?"

"I'm old enough to have eyes." She giggled.

Coal felt his mother squeeze his arm harder in her hands, but she didn't say anything except by that act.

He sighed. Well, it was two against one. The only thing neither of them had addressed was that their estimations of Maura's feelings had all come before she saw Annie kissing him.

When they got back to the house, Maura's truck was parked in the yard.

She must have been watching from the window, because as they entered the yard, she opened the front door. She had her heavy coat on, and a stocking cap. And somehow, the way it framed her face, Coal thought she looked alarmingly attractive.

She came down the steps, and she and Connie greeted each other with a long, warm hug. "Aw, Maura. It's so good to have you home."

Maura gave her a big smile. Her eyes sparkled in the dusk. "It's good to be here." Coal tried not to stare at her, but he couldn't help it. And he couldn't help wondering what had come over her, to look so happy.

The twins ran over and hugged Maura, as did Katie. Virgil just waved his hand and said hi. There were too many people around for him to offer, or accept, a hug.

"Virgil, will you make sure Chewy and Dart get plenty of food?" asked Connie.

"Sure, Grandma." He called the heelers to him and trotted across the yard.

"Come on, everyone. Let's go get some chocolate."

"I'll be in in just a minute, Connie," said Maura, looking over at her. Then her eyes returned to Coal's, where they had settled before Connie spoke. They stood looking at each other for twenty seconds or so, as the kids and the dogs went past with Connie, into the warm house.

Coal couldn't pull his gaze away from Maura. He had forgotten how pretty she was. But at the moment, his stare was perhaps more the morbid fascination of a man waiting for a bomb to go off.

"Can we talk?"

Coal stared. He had thought a knee to the groin more likely than those calm-sounding words.

"Sure."

"You've already been up to Lemhi Road. We could walk down to the highway," she suggested.

Coal was half frozen, but he wouldn't admit it to Maura, not when it must have taken all her strength to ask him to talk. "Sure, let's go." The dogs had already gone inside. It would be peaceful to walk alone, although he also loved to watch them frolic.

At least it would be peaceful if the person walking beside him weren't Maura PlentyWounds.

The last glow in the West faded from the sky as they walked out of the yard and down the road, with one foot of space between them.

Coal waited a long time for Maura to speak, but the silence went on, and all the sound they made was their steps crackling the gravel.

"I had no right to treat you bad, Coal."

Like a big rock thrown suddenly into a still pond, the words dropped right there between them. Coal looked over at her, but she wouldn't return his glance. He thought of several things to say, and none of them sounded right. He was going to say he was sorry, but then he didn't know what for. He was going to say she *did* have a right, but he knew she didn't. And yet the last thing he intended to do was come right out and agree with her.

He finally found a safe place to ford this dangerous river, and he took it on the instant it appeared. "We've both been under a lot of stress lately. How do people figure out their feelings when they're being hit by something from every direction every time they turn around?"

From the corner of her eye, he saw her nodding. "I know you're right there. Totally. You can't trust your own heart when you're under fire."

"I've enjoyed being friends with you, Maura," said Coal suddenly. "I hope you know that."

"Yeah. Me too. And we'll keep being friends. I just had to get my head screwed back on right. I guess that's really what I wanted to tell you."

Maura stared straight ahead, and she could feel tears in her eyes that, thanks to the darkness, Coal would never see. She had sworn never to love a man again, and she had fought that feeling with Coal from the very start, and lost. She had fallen for him, and she had even thought he might feel the same way for her. She loved Coal Savage, but it was a love that would never be returned, and a love she would never admit to anyone.

She could never trust her feelings again. Ever.

Coal walked on, feeling the pressing cold around him. It felt like specks of ice were darting in and hitting against his skin, then dancing away.

He felt Maura's closeness. He didn't remember for sure if he had ever wanted to kiss her. But he wanted to now. He wanted to pull her into his arms and kiss her with all the passion she could endure. Yet somehow he knew it was too late.

He had lost her, and that was plain. Anything she had felt for him was gone, and he doubted it could ever return.

CHAPTER THIRTY-TWO

Friday, December 15

Cynthia showed up to school with bruises again. This time Coal only knew because he checked with her first teacher of the morning, right after class change. He caught Judge Sinclair shortly before he went into a court hearing and told him about it, and his *honor* once again told Coal he could not issue him a warrant. Cynthia had presented the perfectly good excuse that she was carrying a tray of food to Bud Miley, her new guardian, and didn't realize that Sissy was lying on the floor watching television. She tripped over her and hit her face on the arm of the couch, and that explained why she had a big bruise on her cheek. It was a perfectly good explanation, in the judge's eyes, and he said nothing could be gained by going into the house to snoop.

"How long until a bruise a day is too much to believe?" Coal asked. It was all he could do not to make an overtly sarcastic comment.

The judge simply told him they were going to have to wait and see. And then he dismissed him, like royalty booting a serf.

Coal departed, and his ire continued to grow—magma rising in the tube of a volcano.

An hour or so later, back down in the sheriff's office, he was thumbing through paperwork when the door to the outside opened, and Todd Mitchell walked in.

"Hi, Coal."

"Hi, Todd. What's up?" Coal put a smile on his face that, after leaving Judge Sinclair's office, he really didn't feel.

"I got your photo. Easy as pie."

"You did! Great. Let me see it, and we'll take it down and get it developed."

"Already done," replied Todd with a smile. "Took it to Rexall's yesterday afternoon. They said it'll take a week to come back."

"Oh, man." Coal could not hide his feelings this time.

"Something wrong?"

"Ah, it's okay. I just would've taken it somewhere else, either down to the newspaper office or to some guy Jim used to use here in town, some friend of his who could get a photo done in a few hours."

"Sorry about that. I didn't know."

"That's all right. You can't know about everything. Thanks for doing that, anyway. That takes a big load off my mind."

"All right. Well, I've got a big day planned, so I'll be seeing you."

Coal almost called after Todd as he turned to take the door handle, but then he thought better of it. He had, after all, told him his administrative leave began on Saturday, and this was only Friday. He still hadn't really had time to think over the seriousness of what Todd had done, and he really didn't want to make any snap decisions. Besides, it would do Todd some good to think about his carelessness for a while.

That afternoon on the way home from the office, Coal saw Annie Price's Buick in the parking lot. So he had to drive around the block to make the hospital parking lot be on his way home—*somebody* had to patrol the place for suspicious-looking characters.

He parked and went inside, finding Annie drinking a Coke in the break room.

"Oh, man! You're going to kill yourself."

Annie whirled around, almost spilling her drink. "You scared me! Okay, so you caught me. Now you've found out I'm not perfect. What about it?" Laughing, she stood up and gave him a big hug.

"So I've got some news," she announced.

"Oh, yeah? What's that?"

"Someone took Burro."

"You're kidding! The owner?"

"No. Nobody ever called. I wonder if it wasn't someone passing through."

Coal felt strangely disappointed. He knew how it felt to lose an animal. "Who took him then?"

"I had him out in front of Saveway, and a man just happened to be walking by. He said it looked like a nice dog, and I told him it was free for the asking. He said he likes to hunt, and he took him, just like that."

"What if the owner calls you now?"

"Well, he doesn't have a phone for me to call him, but I gave him my number and asked him to call me in a few days, just to make sure no one had tried to claim him."

Coal gave her a sad smile. "It won't be the same without old Burro around. Well, I hope they at least give him a real name."

She giggled. "Oh, stop it. Burro was original!"

"It sure was. Can't argue that point."

"So our movie's still down at the Roxy," Annie said.

Coal thought of Connie and the kids. The house was free of Maura, who had gone to pick up her boys and bring them home for the weekend. But he hadn't spent any time with his mom and children, at least no quality time, for quite a while, it seemed.

"I need to stay home with the kids tonight."

Annie sighed and smiled. "It's okay. I kind of thought you might say that, and I was just testing you anyway. I have to work until midnight."

"All right then. You tease."

She laughed. "I just wanted to know what you'd say. So how about tomorrow? Want to go for a drive? We could take the kids and your mom too."

This time, it was Cynthia and Sissy Coal thought of. While they were being held captive—which was exactly what was going on, as far as he was concerned—he just did not feel good about being very far away. He told Annie his thoughts.

"I don't blame you. Okay. There will be other weekends."

Annie hugged him goodbye, but before she turned away he saw an uncharacteristic sadness in her face. He almost walked back to her and told her he had changed his mind. But his family had to come first—and Cynthia and Sissy, to him, were family.

Saturday, December 16

The Mileys slept in on Saturday morning. Sissy had left her room, which Linda Miley had only screwed shut the one night, and lay on the floor in the hall in front of Cynthia's room, her blanket draped over her. She squeezed to her body the scroungy Teddy bear that Cynthia treasured so much but Linda would not let her sleep with any longer. Sissy was now the bear's guardian.

When Linda Miley got up to use the bathroom, she didn't see the little girl, through hung-over eyes, and she tripped and almost fell. Furious, she whirled around and reached down to grab the terrified girl by the arm and jerk her to her feet. She began spanking her as hard as she could, and Sissy started crying.

Hearing the commotion, Cynthia got up and started pounding on the door furiously. From the other side of the door, she yelled, "Leave her alone! Leave her alone!"

The voice set Linda Miley off so bad that she threw Sissy down and marched into the kitchen, grabbing the hammer and coming

back down the hall. She practically tore the nail—Bud had managed to find her one, since she insisted on keeping Cynthia con-
fined to her room every night—right out of the door frame, taking
part of the frame with it.

By now, there was a frantic, angry barking coming from the
Mileys' bedroom, but Linda Miley was oblivious to it. Slamming
open the bedroom door, she sought out and found Cynthia, now
cowering on her bed, her knees drawn up to her chest. With the
hammer in hand, Linda strode toward her, raising it over her head.

Just as Linda was about to swing with the hammer, Cynthia
threw herself forward and against her, knocking the woman back
and sending the hammer flying. Linda caught her balance, and her
bleary eyes, now full of ferocity, focused in on Cynthia. Whirling
around, she sought out something to use as a weapon.

At that moment, the barking dog that had been down the hall
streaked into the room, raising a commotion. It was a beautiful
golden retriever.

Behind the dog came Bud Miley, his eyes jumping this way
and that. He immediately saw his wife pick up a lamp and almost
run for Cynthia, to club her over the head.

"Hey!" he roared as loud as he could. Linda hesitated just long
enough for Bud to get his hung-over body to her and grab her
around the waist, pulling her back. "Stop it! Judas, Linda! Settle
down! You're gonna kill her. Damn it, stop it!" Savagely, he threw
her to the side, and as she came back around, raising the lamp to
strike him, he growled her name and raised his fist as if to punch
her in the face.

"Calm down! You've lost it, woman. You put one more bruise
on that girl and we won't be able to sell her to a slave market."

CHAPTER THIRTY-THREE

Bud Miley ordered Linda to nail the girls back into a bedroom, this time in *one* bedroom, and then he told her he was going to go get something that would fix their problem for good.

"But I swear, woman, if you lay a hand on either one of them before I get back, I'm gonna beat you. I'm startin' to think I married one sick woman."

Linda's last act of defiance was to give her husband her middle finger as he left. And then she turned to the girls and pointed down the hall. "Get. Both of you. Into Cynthia's room. And if I hear one more noise I'm gonna burn this house down—with you in it."

Neither of the girls dared to pick up Buddy as they passed him in the hall, but Linda stooped down and grabbed him, and then, as the girls passed into Cynthia's room, she flung it at Cynthia like a missile. Grabbing the door knob, she slammed it as loud as she could, then nailed it shut and went to sit down in front of the television with a six pack of Olympia beer and a pack of cigarettes.

Half an hour later, Bud came back into the now smoky room carrying a brown paper bag, with the retriever trotting beside him. They had given the dog the trite name of Rufus.

Bud threw the bag on the table, and it made a metallic clinking noise. "Now get those girls out here."

"What are you doing?"

"What am I doing? What I should have done the first day. You know, that check is going to be here probably in the next four days. And then we can be done with this crap. We'll take those girls and head to Mexico, and after we cross the border I'm just going to open the door and throw them out on the side of the road, and we're gonna keep on driving all the way to Acapulco and live the high life until we die."

"But... what are you doing now?"

"You'll see! Judas! Just get the girls."

With a pouting face, Linda went to Cynthia's room and yanked out the nail for what would be the last time. She glared at the girls and motioned to them with a wide sweep. "Come on, let's go."

Fearfully, the girls hurried to file past Linda, and just for spite she shoved Cynthia into the door frame. Cynthia didn't dare look back at her. Cynthia had never before known any people who were insane, but it had become very obvious to her in a short time that Linda Miley was one. Cynthia had no idea what she was capable of, but she had seen terrible things in the movies and on TV before her parents realized what was on and shooed her out of the room. Cynthia had become terrified of every move Linda made now, aunt or no aunt. She feared for her own life and for Sissy's.

"You girls go down in the basement," Bud ordered as they came within sight of him.

Cynthia stared at him. She froze in place. Somehow, she sensed this might be her last act, and that going down in that basement meant she would never come back up the stairs alive. "Please, sir, we'll be good if you just lock us in my room together. We won't cause you any more trouble."

"Just get going." Bud was smart enough to know his wife's anger could not be controlled forever. Leaving the girls upstairs where she was likely to come into contact frequently with them was not an option.

Seeing the anger in Bud's eyes, Cynthia reached down and took Sissy's hand, and she led her toward the basement door. Her eyes had filled with tears of terror.

When they started down the basement stairs, Cynthia could hear Bud's steps behind her. She half-expected him to shove her down the stairs, and she held tight to the wooden railing, praying that she could protect Sissy from harm if they fell.

They reached the bottom without incident, and Bud pointed at the water heater. "Now go stand over there."

He followed the girls to the water heater just as Linda, curious, came down the stairs and stood there with her arms folded, still glaring at them.

From the paper bag, Bud drew out a long length of chain, and then a padlock, from which he tore a tag. He wrapped one end of the chain around Cynthia's waist, then padlocked it into place. He gave it a good yank to make sure it wouldn't come free. Then he pulled a second padlock from the bag and locked the other end of the chain around the water heater.

The girls just stared at him, and finally he chuckled, as he was giving the end of the chain around the water heater a tug. "Looks good. You two ain't going anywhere now."

Cynthia's eyes dropped involuntarily to Sissy, who was still loose.

"Oh, don't you worry about her," Bud said. "She's not going to leave unless you do. Are you, sugar?" He knelt down and grabbed the girl's arm, pulling her in so their faces were only inches apart. "If you try to leave here without Cynthia, you know what I'm going to do? I'm going to take a knife and I'm going to put it in your hand, and then, really slowly, so she'll feel lots of pain, I'm going to make you cut off your sister's head. You got that? *So stay down here!*"

He turned to climb the stairs again, shooing Linda up in front of him. When they got to the top, he walked over to the cupboard and grabbed a bag of Wonder Bread, a knife, and a jar of peanut butter. He turned and shoved them into Linda's wiggly belly. "Now take that down to them, and then some blankets and pillows.

And you'd better not lay one damn hand on them, you hear me? I've had enough crap from you for one day."

Linda stared at him, but they had been together long enough for her to know when to keep her mouth shut, and she did as she was told. When she was done, she came back upstairs and flopped onto the couch, coaxing Rufus up onto it beside her. She settled into mindlessly watching the television, gently stroking the retriever's head like a lover.

At two o'clock that afternoon, Bud Miley set down his wallet, which he had been thumbing through. It wasn't much thicker than a piece of paper now. "Get up, Linda."

"Why?"

"We're going to Mud Lake."

"Mud Lake! Why in the world do we want to go there?"

"Because we're running out of money, fatty. And they have a store there. That's why."

Linda stared at him. "I told you I don't want to do that anymore. We could get caught. Can't we wait a couple more days?"

"No, we can't. You've drunk about all my beer, smoked all my cigarettes, and I think we have two bucks left, not counting whatever's in the ash tray in the car."

"You said the check's coming soon. Can't we wait?"

"No, I said! It'll be here. But in the meantime I'll have me some beer and some wine coolers. Just get up. I can't believe how lazy you are."

So Linda got up. And they went out to rob a store. Rufus went with them—an unwitting future accomplice to a crime.

*   *   *

Coal took the boys out shooting that afternoon. Due to the cold, the boys didn't last long, even Virgil, and all of them ended up in the Ford while Coal was still out finishing off a whole covey of pop and beer cans he'd picked up off the side of the road.

The .357 magnum had an incredibly satisfying kick that struck back at the heel of his hand at the same time as it leaped up into the air. Ever since childhood, Coal had loved the feel of a pistol kicking in his hand. It was especially therapeutic on those days when his anger and hatred for something would otherwise have consumed him. He fired thirty-six rounds through the revolver, then two magazines through his father's Winchester, before calling it a day and climbing back in with the boys to warm up.

On a whim, he drove by the Battertons' house, and the Buick wasn't in the drive. "Stay put, boys," he ordered. He got out and went up to the door, knocking three times. He was hoping that maybe Linda was home alone, although so far he had had no more luck with her than he would have expected to have with her husband. There was no response. At that point, in a straight line, he was only fifteen feet from Cynthia Batterton and little Sissy Miley.

Disappointed, he turned and walked back down the sidewalk. He felt a strange pang as he walked away. It was as if something were calling him back.

Coal drove back home to find that Connie had a huge feast waiting for him and the boys, more food than any ten men could eat. But they did their best to try.

Monday, December 17

When Coal woke up Monday morning, it was spitting snow. He got dressed quietly, in the dawn, then went outside to help Connie feed the horses, since Maura, who usually liked to do that with his mom, had gone back to her own place for the weekend with her boys.

Coal had gotten a call the day before that the grocery store over in Mud Lake had been robbed, but they had no suspects. By the time the call came in, and he drove by the Batterton place on a whim, the Riviera was parked there, but that meant nothing. They only needed two hours to get from Mud Lake to Salmon.

Coal chided himself. He really had nothing to go on with these people. What if they really did just want to have a family? What if they had never broken a law in their lives, even a speed limit, much less robbed a store? What if the accidents Cynthia had described had really happened to her, just the way she said? Sometimes he wondered if he was just jealous and feeling bad that he didn't have the girls anymore. But his gut instincts told him there was much more than met the eye with the Mileys. They didn't even feign friendliness, at least not for very long. Then again, perhaps that was a good thing. At least he didn't have to worry that they were putting on a show.

Connie and Coal came back in stomping the snow off their shoes. She made breakfast while he went downstairs and did his forty-five minute workout and showered, and then he came back upstairs, and the family sat to the table. This was the children's last week of school before Christmas break. It was tearing his heart apart that Cynthia and Sissy weren't there, that they were most likely scared and lonely and feeling like they had been deserted.

After breakfast, Coal put on his hat and gunbelt and drove the children in to school. He told them it was his early Christmas present to them.

Each time he stopped, first at the kindergarten, then the high school, he got out and gave all of his kids a big, long hug. He had learned too much about how fast lives can be snuffed out.

He went up to the jail and had coffee with Jordan before sending him and Victor Yancey, the night jailer, home for the day. Then he sat there in silence. He got up and checked the jail, just to make sure there were no prisoners, and then he went over to Jim and Betty Lockwood's place, where he shared everything that had been going on in the department—including the report of the robbery over in Mud Lake, in Jefferson County.

Old Jim smiled knowingly at Coal as he took his first sip of Betty's coffee. "Huh? Huh?"

Coal raised his eyebrows and looked up, the steam rolling past his face. Realizing what Jim was trying to say, he looked down at the steaming black liquid. "Oh, yeah. You're right: It's the best coffee in town, for sure. I never questioned that, buddy. My compliments, Betty." He raised his mug to the silver-haired Mrs., in a mock toast.

"Thank you, Coal. You just come on over any time you want a cup. But don't pay any attention to that old man. What would a sour puss like that know anyway?"

Coal laughed. "Well, good coffee, for one."

They chatted for a time, and then Coal looked over his now-empty cup at Jim. "Hey, I need to ask you a favor. I don't remember for sure, but it seems like you've said you and Judge Sinclair had a pretty good working relationship."

"I think so. Better than most."

"Well, I don't. He seems to think *I'm* the criminal."

"How so?"

"Oh, this deal with those Mileys. Cynthia keeps coming in to school all beat up, and he won't let me have a warrant to go check on Sissy. That girl could be dead for all we know. You don't suppose you'd have enough sway with him to get him to change his mind, do you?"

Jim reached up and scratched the white whiskers on his scarred chin. Then he rubbed a hand over his balding head. Last of all, he looked over at Betty. "Mama, you're probably pretty tired of me hanging around here, aren't you?"

"Just go on, Jim. You won't be any use here now, not after hearing that."

Jim grinned, then looked back over at Coal. "Son, let's go over to the high school. I want to see if I can get a peek at Cynthia for myself—and maybe a hug as well."

Coal smiled with relief. "Thanks, Jim."

They drove to the high school and went in to the office. The secretary paged Cynthia, and they waited. At last, a figure appeared down the hall, from around the corner Cynthia usually came. It was the girl's teacher, Mr. Briggs.

The English teacher came on up to the sheriff and his friend. "Sheriff, I came to tell you that Cynthia didn't come in today."

CHAPTER THIRTY-FOUR

Coal did not even bother to go into the judge's office this time. He did not think he could remain civil if Sinclair gave him the same pathetic answer a third time.

Jim was in the judge's office for twenty-five minutes before he came back out. He had a half-smile on his face. "All right, buddy, we don't have a warrant, but maybe this will make you happy. He's going to make a phone call to the Mileys and order them to bring the girls to his office. If they aren't there, he'll send you down there with a writ demanding their appearance before him at the earliest possible time."

"What does he have against issuing me a warrant to go search their house, Jim?"

"There've been judges here who issued warrants at the drop of a hat, son. A lot of 'em never should have been issued. He's just trying to be safe."

"It's not very safe for Sissy."

Jim grunted. "Come on, don't be stubborn. It's all going to work out the same in the end."

Coal finally relented, because he had no choice. It was within the hour that the Mileys showed up, with Bud carrying Sissy, and Linda holding Cynthia's hand. One look at Sissy was all it would take anyone to read the terror in her eyes. She started to cry the moment she laid eyes on Coal and had to bite her lower lip to keep from it.

Linda Miley looked over and made direct eye contact with Coal, raising her chin in defiance. Bud kept a smirk on his face all the way past and even had the audacity to give Coal a wave.

Holding himself back, Coal watched the four of them march past him and into the judge's quarters. He turned to Jim, and the older man gave his leg a couple of hard pats. But he didn't say a word. By the set of his jaw, he was unable to.

Finally, Coal found his voice, a full twenty seconds after the judge's door had closed. "Nothing to say?"

Jim looked over, and he could not hide the fire in his eyes. "You were right, buddy. Maybe now that the judge can see them it will make all the difference. There should have been a warrant."

"But Sinclair didn't trust my judgment enough to issue one."

Jim just nodded, a sour look on his face. "No, I guess not. You were totally in the right, son. I can see what made you so mad after seeing those bruises. To say nothing of the looks on those girls' faces."

"Jim, I've got to go downstairs. I don't think I can be here when they come back out." Saying this, Coal stood up, and Jim with him. Jim raised a gnarled hand that had seen its share of fist fights and put it on Coal's shoulder.

"I'll try to stay here for you. I'll come get you when they leave."

"If you want to come with me, feel welcome," said Coal. "I'll see them leave the parking lot."

"Naw, I'd better be here when the judge calls for me, I reckon."

"All right. Thanks, Jim." With that, Coal walked away. The fire that was inside him made it feel like he had just downed a tumbler of bad whisky.

*   *   *

Twenty minutes later, Coal watched the Mileys walk across the parking lot to where their Buick was parked. It was hard to see the girls' faces, so he tried to concentrate his attention on Bud and Linda Miley. If he could have stared daggers through them, they would have been lying out there now in a pool of blood. Instead, they drove away. At the last moment, Linda looked down below parking lot level at the window in Coal's door, and it registered on her that it was his face looking at her. She just smiled—a cold, calculating smile, trying to hide someone with a heart as black as tar.

Coal went outside after they had gone and took the stairs two at a time up to the judge's quarters. The door was shut, but he could hear voices inside. Jim's, raised in anger, was immediately recognizable.

Coal took a deep breath and tapped on the obscure glass in the door. He could see dim shadows moving about, and then one came close, and the door opened. Jim was standing there, his hand still on the door. He opened it the rest of the way and looked over questioningly at the judge.

"Please come in, Sheriff," the judge said, with more humility than Coal had heard in his voice yet.

Coal walked in, and Jim shut the door.

"I apologize to you, Sheriff. I think perhaps we need to start over again. I can see after visiting with the Mileys today why you were so concerned."

Coal tried to speak, but nothing polite was forthcoming. Finally, he just nodded, hesitantly. It seemed that silence was his best tool, if he and Judge Sinclair were to have a fresh start.

"Tell me again Cynthia's story about her first bruise, would you please?"

Coal recited Cynthia's accounting of how she had had her drawer open and had dropped her socks, and when she reached for them she hit her face on the drawer, cutting her eyebrow.

The judge nodded, and his jaw began visibly to harden. "All right. I was told that she was walking down the hall, and Sissy didn't see her and opened the door in front of her."

"That's *more* than a discrepancy," said Jim, his ire mounting.

"How do you suppose she could forget her own story so fast?" asked the judge. "I agree with Sheriff Lockwood. That is a major difference."

Something suddenly struck Coal. "I don't think she forgot."

"How's that?"

"I don't think Cynthia forgot. Remember, her dad was the sheriff for years, and Jim's deputy before that. She grew up listening to stories about law enforcement. I think she purposely made up a new story, to get our attention. She knew the Mileys weren't at the school to hear her tell me that first lie, so they wouldn't know if they didn't match."

The judge's face paled, and he looked over at Jim. The older man nodded. "Coal's right, Judge. Cynthia wouldn't have forgotten a detailed story like that on accident. She was giving us a clue."

Taking a deep breath, the judge gave a long glance to Jim, then turned his attention to Coal. At last, he sighed. "Well, we have to do something. I can see that without a doubt. But I'm not sure what."

"Issue me a warrant, sir," said Coal quietly. "Please. Let me go down there and take them by surprise. We've got to at least see that they've got the means to care for them in that house."

"I am hanging my entire career on the line," the judge replied. "But I'm going to do it. I want to have officers in that house right when they least expect it. I don't for a moment believe that a girl who has never seemed accident-prone before suddenly comes up with so many bruises like those on her own."

Coal just nodded. He had a lot of anger bottled up inside. Anger not only with the Mileys, but with the judge for not listening to him sooner. But now was not the time to mention it. In all honesty, there would never be such a time.

*   *   *

Todd Mitchell had been in the courthouse parking lot when the Mileys arrived. He had written a lumber mill worker a speeding ticket half a month ago, and he had run into the man later out in front of Walt's IGA. The man had been friendly, and they had carried on quite a conversation. By the time it ended, he had decided to dismiss the man's ticket. The man's wife was having medical issues, he was barely making enough to pay the doctor bills—something Todd could well understand—and he had enough on his plate to worry about already. So Todd had just come downstairs from talking to the city attorney and gotten into his car when the Mileys pulled in in their Riviera.

Todd saw them get out, and he was about to start his engine when he recognized Cynthia Batterton. At first, he was startled just to see her, because it had been so long. Then, he saw the bruises. There were two of them, but they were bad enough that they seemed to take up half of her face.

Todd stared at her as she passed, but Cynthia didn't look over at him. She was staring straight ahead, holding onto the hand of a short, obese woman in her forties. So this was the infamous Linda Miley. His eyes quickly went to the man, who was carrying a very frightened looking little girl with a peaceful look on his face that tried to portray him as the most loving father in the world.

They had gone into the courthouse and headed upstairs before Todd realized he was clenching his teeth so hard they were in danger of cracking. He had known Cynthia Batterton for years. She would often come down to the jail with her mom, bringing cookies that one or the other of them, or both, had made for their father and the other officers and jailers. She was a sweet girl, one of the nicest, most polite young ladies he had ever met. Everyone loved her within minutes of meeting her. In his case, it had happened the moment he first saw her smile. In all the years Todd had known this girl, he had never known her to be prone to accidents. Now she had lived with the Mileys for only a few days, and her beautiful, innocent face was already covered in bruises.

Todd suddenly found his hand on his revolver. His fingers tensed. He was covered in goose flesh. He wanted to follow the Mileys into the courthouse and gun them down.

A memory flashed back to Todd from his childhood. He had been a happy boy, spending his time outdoors, playing "cops and robbers" with his brothers and their neighborhood friends. Life had been good. But a bad wreck down on the river had taken the life of their father when Todd was twelve, and everything about his life had changed.

Todd's mother had met a man at the bar, not even three months after the death of their father. He had seemed cordial enough, in the beginning, but even as a twelve-year-old Todd had sensed something more in the man—something he was hiding from the world.

Todd had one sister, Lynn. He adored her. She was older than he was by several years. Probably pretty close to the age Cynthia was now. She had gone out at an early age and gotten a job at a local cafe, serving tables, and she would sometimes give her mother part of her checks, just to make things easier for her. Like Cynthia, everyone had loved Lynn.

And then the abuse began. For some reason, his stepfather had never touched any of the boys. All of his abuse was directed at Lynn. She could often be found sporting bruises like those on Cynthia's face now, and the stories she had to tell people to cover her terror and shame made Todd cringe even now. It took him years to realize that the beatings of his sister stemmed from a lot more than just his stepfather's anger. As was often the case, he had been abusing her sexually, too, but in that day and age it was something people didn't talk about, especially the victims, and Lynn had never told a soul until they were caught in the act by his poor little brother.

All these years later, Lynn resided in the state mental hospital in Blackfoot. The sexual abuse and the endless beatings had finally taken not only her virtue, but her mind.

And Todd Mitchell was left with a deep-seated hatred for any human being who would harm a helpless child, especially one with whom he had been trusted.

Todd saw Coal Savage come down from the upper floors of the courthouse and step outside, then go down into the jail. He watched him, seeing in Coal's face something that resembled the same hatred and ferocity he was feeling himself. Maybe he and the sheriff had something more in common than just a badge.

For a long time, Todd sat in his car, knowing he was too furious to drive. But at last, he had to get out of the parking lot. He had to make his departure before the Mileys came back down. He was in fear for what he would do if he saw them again. And both Cynthia and Sissy had already seen enough without having to watch two people be gunned down in front of them.

Turning the ignition, Todd heard the horses come to life, and he took in a lung-filling breath. He looked back down at his revolver. He was going to bring down Bud and Linda Miley. He promised himself this. If anything happened, and if it looked like they might get away with what they had done, those two people were going to vanish. And no one would ever find their remains.

He had at last found a real way he could pay Coal back for all he had done for him. He was going to dispose of two people that he and Coal both must hate as much as the devil himself.

CHAPTER THIRTY-FIVE

The Mileys arrived back at the Batterton residence, and they could hear Rufus barking inside the house the moment they opened their doors.

Bud turned around in his seat and looked at the girls, who recoiled in fright. They were crammed together in one corner of the back seat.

"You girls did real good back at the courthouse. I'm proud of you both. Now remember, there are neighbors around here that watch everything we do, okay? So we have to act totally happy, even just getting out of this car and walking to the house. Just like I told you before, if you're really good and look real happy to all the neighbors, I won't have to cut up Rufus in little tiny pieces and feed him to you. Does that sound fair?" He had a calm smile plastered on his face as he spoke.

Huge tears were already rolling down Sissy's face. That was something that started just on the trigger of Bud or Linda starting to speak to her. Cynthia gave a firm nod and said, "We'll look happy. Won't we, Sissy?"

Too scared to understand what her response should be, Sissy, her eyes big and round, looked up at her guardian. Cynthia was nodding at her. Sissy took the cue and started nodding, looking back at Bud while she continued to do so.

"And you know what else happens if either one of you does anything wrong, right? If one of you leaves the house, or if one of you makes Linda mad, she's going to get her little knife and start cutting you into little pieces. And you don't want that, do you?"

Cynthia squeezed Sissy tighter against her. "I promise we'll do everything you say." She squeezed her eyes shut, trying to fight back the tears.

"All right. I just want to make sure we understand each other."

Now, looking for all the world like two responsible, loving parents, the Mileys got out, and Bud reached his hands down to Sissy. Fighting to hold back tears, she allowed him to pick her up, squeezing her eyes shut and shivering all over. Bud raised her face up by his mouth.

"Now, Sissy, you aren't looking very happy. Remember what will happen to Cynthia and Rufus if you don't look happy."

Sissy froze. She was too young to understand what he wanted out of her exactly, and not strong enough to have done it if she did understand.

On the other side of the car, however, Cynthia got out like a demure young lady and allowed Linda to take her hand. She even affected a smile, and Linda smiled back, her smile carrying all the sweetness of honey and maple syrup, while her eyes had the look of a rattlesnake's.

As a family, they walked to the house and went in to greet the dog. The moment they got inside, Bud went over and drew the front drapes, hiding the sofa from view, and deposited Sissy roughly. He turned to Cynthia and jabbed a finger at the spot beside her. "Sit down!"

Cynthia instantly dropped into her place.

Bud turned to Linda. "Linda, you get in their rooms and start cleaning up. As fast as you can. I'll get the kitchen—after I put away the chain and padlocks downstairs."

"Why? What's happening?"

"Are you kidding me? You don't think that judge is going to issue a warrant and send someone over here now to check out the house? Don't be so gullible. Come on! Get busy!"

*   *   *

Fifteen minutes later, Coal's tires screeched as he pulled up in front of the Batterton house and slammed on the brakes. Behind him came Jordan Peterson, then special deputy Jim Lockwood and police officer Bob Wilson.

The four of them disembarked from their cars, and while Bob hurried around back with a shotgun, the others converged near the front door. Coal hammered on the door with his fist, standing off to one side.

"Sheriff's department! Open up!"

Within moments, the door swung open. Standing there was Linda Miley, that sickeningly sweet smile glued to her face. "Why, hello, Sheriff. What a surprise."

Coal slapped a piece of white paper out between them. "This is a warrant to search the premises."

"What? Search for what?" Linda asked, acting shocked.

"Just move out of the way. Where's your husband?"

At that moment, Bud stepped from the hallway. "What's going on?"

"We're searching your residence—*with* a warrant."

"Why? Have we done something wrong?"

"That's what we're here to find out. Where are the girls?"

"In Cynthia's room," said Linda with an innocent, almost hurt look on her face, then glanced at Bud. "I think they're coloring."

Coal nodded. "Jordan? Watch them. You two, sit down on the couch and stay out of our way."

When the couple complied, and Jordan Peterson stood menacingly over them, looking somehow much meaner than Coal had ever seen him before, Coal and Jim called Bob Wilson in, and the three of them started down the hall.

Coal tried the first door and instantly saw that the room was empty. On he went to the next one, opening it carefully. There, to his surprise, were Cynthia and Sissy, lying on the floor over a coloring book, and both coloring furiously.

"Hi, Cynthia. Hi, Sissy," said Coal. His demeanor was hesitant. He had no idea what kind of reaction he was going to get.

Cynthia instantly looked past Coal. Seeing only Jim, she jumped up and ran to Coal, throwing her arms around him and squeezing with such strength Coal actually thought he was going to have to pry her away. He looked past her at Sissy, who was still seated on the floor, staring. Her eyes were red.

"Say hi to Jim for a second, sweetie," Coal whispered to Cynthia, and she obeyed, greeting her father's former boss with the kind of love a child might show to her grandfather.

Coal came a little closer to Sissy, then knelt down. "Hi, Sissy." The little girl, seemingly terrified, just stared at him. Suddenly, her face broke up into what seemed to be a grimace of pain mixed with relief. She scrambled up off the floor and ran to Coal, throwing her arms around his neck. Now she was crying openly.

As he held her, Coal felt no need to fight tears. What he felt in his heart was ferocity, not sadness—the urge to make someone pay. This little girl had come so far since that day when he first saw her in Roger Miley's pickup. How long was it going to take now to get her back to where she had been?

As they embraced each other, Coal looked down at the coloring book and crayons that cluttered the floor. It seemed obvious to Coal that the page had just opened and two somebodies had simply started throwing color on the paper, trying to get as much color down as they could in a short time.

Coal sucked in a deep breath, then another. He had to get control of his temper. Everything could depend on how this search turned out. He could not afford to go off half-cocked.

Standing up with Sissy in his arms, he went out of the room, walked down the hall, and started to open the last door. A noise startled him inside, and he jumped back and slammed the door, before realizing it was a dog.

"Is this dog friendly?" Coal yelled down the hall.

"Well, you tell me," Bud Miley replied.

Coal took another deep breath. "No. You tell me."

"Yeah, I think so. Want me to come and give him a kiss for you first?"

Coal looked back at Cynthia, who was standing with Jim, and tried to look at Sissy, but she was clinging to him too tightly. "Hey, Sissy, do you like this dog?"

The girl hesitated a moment, then nodded vigorously. He knew it was doubtful that she would speak, so the nod would have to be enough.

Easing open the door, he looked down at the sleek, long-haired animal that was pawing at the door. For a moment, he just stared. And the dog stared back. But suddenly the animal started shaking all over, wagging its tail as if a long-lost friend had returned to claim it.

"Hey! Burro!" The dog seemed to be laughing, with his tongue lolling out and his big white teeth glimmering. He tried to jump up to get closer to Coal's face, but he didn't need to, because Coal crouched down, holding Sissy in his left arm and trying to keep her out of the line of fire. The dog instantly started licking all over his face.

"Hey, buddy! Cut that out!" He started rubbing and scratching the dog vigorously with his free hand. "Well, I'll be danged, old boy. How've you been?"

"You two married?" Coal heard Jim say, behind him.

Coal looked back and chuckled. He wanted to see Cynthia laughing too, but although she had a tentative smile on her face, there was no laugh forthcoming. "Funny. No, Jim, I know this dog.

I'm serious! Annie Price picked him up out on the highway the other night and couldn't find his owner, so she started looking for a home for him. She told me she found one—now I guess I know where."

"His name is Rufus."

Someone might as well have fired a shotgun in the hall. Coal was that startled. He looked at the little burden in his arm, who now had leaned away from him and was reaching out one hand to the dog. Burro—or Rufus—turned the attention of his licks to Sissy now, and a tiny giggle actually escaped her before she caught herself, and quickly looked over her shoulder, as if afraid she would be caught.

"Rufus, huh?" said Coal. "Well, his real name is Burro—but you'd better call him Rufus while you're here." He reached over and lovingly scrubbed Sissy's hair around with his fingers, looking hopefully at her eyes. "You like this guy, huh?"

Sissy had already caught herself talking once. This time she just looked at him and nodded, and then just for a moment, as their eyes locked on each other, he thought she was going to start crying again. She pulled herself back against him with both arms around his neck and buried her face.

Coal stood up, gently pushing the dog away from him. He turned with Jim and started back down the hall, but Jim stopped partway, at the door to Cynthia's room. He was looking at something along the doorframe and gently touching it with his finger. It was a ragged hole, and there was a piece of the frame missing. There were three holes, in fact, right close together, the first one where the wood was broken away worse than the other two.

"Hey, what are these holes in the doorframe here?" Jim spoke to the couple around the corner.

"What holes?"

"Bring them in here, Jordan," Jim said evenly.

When the couple's faces appeared, Jim jabbed a finger. "These holes."

"Search me," replied Bud. "We just moved here, remember?"

Jim stared the man down, looked back at the holes for a thoughtful moment, and then said, "All right, get back." Jordan and the Mileys moved back into the front room, giving Jim, Coal, and the girls room to get closer to the other bedroom door. There were two similar marks in the doorframe there, and two corresponding marks in the door. Going back to the first door, he saw the same sign there.

Jim turned to Cynthia. "Hey, did your folks ever used to keep these doors nailed shut for any reason?"

Cynthia froze. She stared at the holes, her mouth open, her eyes fixed. Finally, with a face shot with fear, she looked at Jim and slowly shook her head. "No, I don't think so."

Jim raised his head in contemplation. He leaned closer to the holes and picked at something. It was little splinters of wood around the holes—obviously nail or screw holes—and they came off with only the slightest pressure.

Jim turned and looked at Coal meaningfully. The holes were new. Coal crooked a finger at Cynthia. She came to his beckoning. He leaned close, looking into her eyes. "Hey, Cynthia," he whispered. "You do want to come home with us, right?"

Cynthia's head whipped toward the front room. The Mileys were still standing there, staring. Hurriedly, she looked back at Coal, shaking her head vigorously. Coal looked down the hall. "Get them on the couch, would you, Jordan?" He didn't mean for his voice to be so gruff.

"Sure thing, boss."

When the couple was out of sight, Coal turned back to Cynthia, who now was staring at his belt buckle, and again he whispered. "Cynthia, do you want to come back home?"

The girl's eyes had welled up with tears. She stood as still as a stone, and then suddenly she began to shake her head. It became a very adamant motion after five seconds.

Coal reached down and hooked a finger under her chin, trying to raise her face up so she would look into his eyes, but the girl jerked her head away.

At last, still holding onto Sissy, Coal leaned close and with his other arm gave Cynthia a long, warm hug. Then he turned to Jim. "All right, let's finish this. Basement next."

His eyes were on Cynthia when he said that, and her face jerked upward. She looked at Coal, and then her eyes shot to Sissy, and Coal caught the faintest shake of her head, almost imperceptible.

"And we'll take the girls," he added.

The four of them trooped down the rickety stairs into the unfinished basement whose ugly gray concrete walls reeked of must. It was mostly empty except for some old, mostly broken down chairs, a furnace enclosed in its own room, and a water heater that squatted almost in the center of the wall, with a floor drain nearby.

They looked all around the room, and nothing seemed out of place or strange. They happened to stop at the water heater before going back upstairs, just because it was in the most central part of the room.

Jim suddenly jabbed a thumb in Coal's lower back, and when he winced and looked back at him, the older man was motioning with his eyes toward the girls. Coal looked over at Cynthia, and she was staring Sissy down. Sissy stared back, as if trying to decipher some message Cynthia was trying to relay.

Cynthia seemed to realize they were watching her, and she dropped her eyes. But Sissy kept staring at her, obviously upset that she hadn't been able to understand whatever clue she had been giving her.

"Have you been down here before?" asked Coal.

At the exact same time that Cynthia started shaking her head, Sissy was nodding. But her nod changed abruptly to a sideways shake, and she hurriedly looked over at Coal, for all the world as if she thought he was going to strike her.

Coal looked straight into Sissy's eyes. "Sissy, have you ever been down here before?"

The little girl froze, staring at Coal. Her eyes shot over toward Cynthia, who was staring at her in near terror. Finally, Sissy seemed to gather up the clues that were being fed her, and she slowly turned her eyes back to Coal and gave three big shakes of her head.

"Jim," said Coal, "why don't you hang down here for a bit while I take the girls back upstairs?" He indicated the water heater with his eyes, since it was that water heater that seemed to draw the eyes of the girls the most.

Then he took Sissy back upstairs, and Cynthia followed.

They waited in the front room in silence for a minute or so until finally Linda Miley, who seemed to have foot-in-mouth disease, said, "What do you people think you're going to find here?"

"Who knows?" asked Coal.

"Well, I want a cigarette."

"You can smoke after we leave."

Linda glared at him. "When do the cops around here ever find time to do their jobs, when they're always out harassing innocent people?"

Coal glared at the woman, knowing he should not speak. But some things could not be helped.

"Other than these two girls, sugar, it's been quite a while since I saw any innocent people. And especially since I came into this house."

"Ohhh-kay." Jim's voice right behind Coal startled him. "I guess it's time for us to go."

Coal's heart was dying. He didn't want to look at Sissy, but he had to. "Hey, honey, I'm going to take you back to your room again, okay? So you can color?"

In obvious terror, the girl stared at him, then looked over at Cynthia as her eyes began to well up with tears. Burro stood beside Coal's leg, whacking it over and over again with his tail, and gazing up at Cynthia.

Coal steeled himself. "All right, girls. Come on." He started back down the hall, and the whole time Sissy was staring over his shoulder at Cynthia, who followed. Coal took them into Cynthia's room, trying to conceal his terrible fury. He hugged Sissy when he set her down, and to his joy she hugged him back. He ruffled her hair and whispered, "We'll come and bring you home soon. Okay?" His last words caught in his throat, but just for a moment.

"I promise."

CHAPTER THIRTY-SIX

The three men drove back up to the courthouse and met inside the sheriff's office. Coal walked out of habit to the coffee pot, picking up his mug, then slamming it back down when he realized the pot was empty and cold.

Jordan had gone and sat down on the desk, while Jim stood behind Coal with his hands thrust into the pockets of his Levi's. Coal finally turned back around, once he thought he had control of himself.

"I'm going to get those girls out of there, Jim. No matter how I have to do it."

"Don't do anything rash, son."

"Rash? Jim, have you thought about those holes in the door frames? That isn't something K.T. or Jennifer would have done. Those pukes are nailing my girls inside their rooms. I'll bet you a thousand dollars."

For a moment, Jim chewed on the ends of his mustache. "That's a bet I wouldn't take."

"So what? I'm supposed to just let that keep happening?"

"No. But we can't do anything just yet. Our time will come, Coal. You've just got to keep a level head."

"So what about the basement?"

Jim stared at him. "Yeah? What about it?"

"That water heater. There's something going on down there."

Jim sighed and nodded. "I agree with you. But I just can't figure out what it could be."

"Neither can I. But I can tell you one thing: Those girls are scared to death of that thing."

*   *   *

Todd Mitchell was slumped back on his dirty sofa watching television and eating a bag of Clover Club potato chips. He intended to eat the entire thing—every last crumb. He didn't care what was on the screen. Right now, he was watching mindlessly, thinking about Coal, and K.T., and Cynthia, Sissy, and the Mileys.

He had been sitting there stewing ever since coming back from the courthouse that morning, and now it was noon. He had calmed down a little since first starting to plan out a way to kill the Mileys. That was just a gut reaction, and once he had returned to his wife, and thought about his children, he knew he could not endanger them by trying to murder the Mileys and hide their bodies—even though in some ways it seemed much more like justice than murder. But the plain truth was he could not endanger his family, no matter what. They had no way to make a living without him. No-where to go. Nothing they could do. He would rot in hell if he went to prison for murder and left them here alone.

So what to do? His hope had been that the photograph he had gotten back Thursday night from Clyde Stone, then sent on up to the police in Missoula on Friday would cement Bud Miley as their store robber. He had sent his personal home phone number to the police chief there in hopes that they would call him with the iden-tification, rather than the sheriff's office, and then he could just take a chance and go over to the Battertons', arrest the Mileys, and in some slight way look like a hero in the eyes of Coal Savage. But that prospect seemed pretty bleak right now. Four days had passed since Coal had told him he was giving him two days off, and he hadn't so much as called to tell him his status. And the Missoula police hadn't called yet. So here he sat, in limbo.

And then, as if his thoughts had willed it, the phone rang.

Jan picked it up. "Hello? Yes, it is... Umm... Yes, he is. Hold on, please."

Todd heard the receiver click down on the kitchen counter top, and then his wife came in and looked down at him. "Todd, that's the sheriff."

Todd took a deep breath, then finally nodded and struggled up out of the broken down couch. He went meekly and picked up the phone. "Hello?"

Hi, Todd. Do you think you could come down to the office in about an hour?

A long pause. "Uh, sure."

All right. I'm really sorry I haven't called sooner, but I've been dealing with some pretty bad family issues. Anyway, I've had some time to think things through, and I guess it's time we met and try to button this thing up, all right?

His heart falling, Todd took a deep breath. *Button this thing up?* Coal could not have made it sound more final than that. His job here was finished.

"Okay, Coal. Thanks for calling. I'll try to be there in an hour."

He hung up and turned to find his wife staring at him hopefully. "I think I'm done, Jan. He said he wants to 'button things up'. I don't know what else that could mean. I'm not going to be a deputy anymore."

"I'm sorry, honey, but I hate that man."

He took her slender frame in his arms and held her. "I don't. He's turned out to be the best boss I've ever worked for. I just wish I hadn't let him down."

*   *   *

At the Savage residence, Connie had taken it upon herself finally to start sorting through all of the papers and memorabilia they had brought from the Batterton house before the Mileys took it over.

She found herself smiling at old photos that hadn't been put in books yet, photos memorializing tender moments between K.T., Jennifer, and Cynthia. She smiled at old school assignments of Cynthia's that had been saved, at an old corsage in a box that could only be from the Battertons' wedding. Cynthia would treasure these things. Connie set them aside carefully in a pile of their own.

It was just things like old bills and receipts that she put in a pile that would probably go to the burn barrel, things that would never matter to anyone.

She picked up a manila envelope filled with love letters between K.T. and Jennifer, setting those without reading them in the pile of keepers. Then she picked up another manila envelope, a little worn around the edges, probably just from being pushed around in a drawer. It was addressed to "K.T. and/or Jennifer Batterton," with their home address on it. And it appeared never to have been opened.

Connie sat for a moment, turning the envelope from front to back to study it. There was something important looking about this envelope. Or perhaps it was just a gut feeling. She stared at it for several more seconds. Somehow, it seemed wrong to open it, but she had taken this task upon herself, and it there could be no stone unturned. At last, overcoming her guilt, she carefully opened the envelope.

Inside, there was a tri-folded piece of thin legal paper, almost translucent, and another envelope, a legal envelope, this one fairly new, and crisply white.

On the bottom front of the envelope was written in bold print that could not be missed one single word: WILL.

Connie stared at it for a second. She had been rummaging through these papers now for an hour, perhaps two. It seemed like words and letters were starting to run together, and her tired eyes were beginning to ache. So it took a moment longer than it might have otherwise for that one word to register. Will. *Will?*

She froze. This envelope, like the big one, was sealed, and it, also like the big one, had been addressed to the Battertons. Instinctively, Connie knew this envelope was sealed for a reason. This was something that must be opened in front of witnesses. What did she do? Contact Coal? That was the first thing of course.

The folded piece of paper drew her attention. She could see right through it that there was typing on it, and it was not sealed, so her curious eyes could not resist. Picking it up, she unfolded it, and the very first word she found, in red lettering at a slant on top of the page, said, COPY. Just below that, in type that had obviously been done with carbon paper, it read, "Last will and testament, K.T. Batterton."

With her heart in her throat, Connie read through the will. As she would have expected, every single thing K.T. owned was left to his wife and Cynthia. What she did not expect was the last lines, and she had to read them over several times for them to register over the top of her disbelief.

The will stated, in no uncertain terms, that in the event that both K.T. and Jennifer should pass away, their daughter, Cynthia Louise Batterton, was to go to the home of Connie Savage, until such time as she turned eighteen years of age.

At just that moment, the dogs began barking excitedly, and after a light knock the door opened. Maura stuck her head inside and saw Connie sitting there at the kitchen table. Connie's mouth was still open, and the papers had fallen from her limp fingers.

* * *

It was half an hour before Coal was to meet with Todd Mitchell, and Jordan Peterson had just come in, when the phone rang. Coal picked it up and answered.

Coal? The voice seemed almost afraid.

"Hi, Mom. What's up?"

Coal, I'm here at the house with Maura. Nothing more. But her voice seemed strained and abnormal.

"Mom, is something wrong?"

I've found something you have to see, Son. Right away. Don't leave the office.

"For hell's sake. You're scaring me. What is it?"

She didn't even bother to scold him for his language. *I found an envelope that says it's K.T.'s will, Coal. And you've got to forgive me for this, but I read it.*

A chill went up Coal's spine. "What does it say, Mom?"

It just doesn't seem like it could be real, but... it says if anything happens to K.T. and Jennifer that Cynthia is to go to me for her care until she turns eighteen.

Coal sat trying to digest her words for a moment. "Wait. Did you say to *you?* It mentions you by name?"

I swear it. Connie sounded as out of breath as Coal suddenly felt.

"I'm coming home to get it! We've got to get that into the judge right away. Those girls are in danger there."

No, Son, wait! I have to be here for when the boys get out of kindergarten, but Maura is here, and she's going to leave now and bring this down to you at the jail. Don't leave!

*   *   *

By the time Maura came squealing her tires into the courthouse parking lot and screeched into a spot, throwing open her door, Coal was up the concrete stairs and standing by her truck. He had forgotten all about his meeting with Todd Mitchell.

Neither of them said a word, but their eyes met with incredible intensity, and the woman's filled with tears of anticipation. Maura held out the envelope in a trembling hand, still not speaking, and Coal took it the same way. He turned it over once, then opened it and looked at the sealed envelope. He unfolded the single page, scanning it quickly until he saw his mother's name, where he stopped. After reading the words over carefully three times, he looked up at Maura.

"We've got to get this up to the judge."

Together, they raced up the courthouse stairs, and Judge Sinclair's secretary, Wilma Frank, met him outside his office, sitting at her pine desk.

"I need to see the judge," said Coal, his breath coming hard.

"I'm afraid he's in a conference right now."

"This is too important to wait, Mrs. Frank."

"I'm sorry. It's going to have to. He gave me specific— Wait, Sheriff. You can't go in there!"

Coal had already started past her, and he shoved open the judge's door and walked in, Maura fast behind him.

Sinclair looked up from where he was sitting with another man whose back was to the door. "Hey! What's the meaning of this?"

"I'm sorry, sir, but this can't wait." Coal lunged right up to the judge's desk and shoved the envelope across it. "Just read the bottom of the paper inside there, and then I'll be gone."

Judge Sinclair's face got suddenly very red. "Sheriff, I have had just about all I'm going to take of your attitude. This man is every bit as important as you are, and you *will* wait until we're finished. For heaven's sake, it won't be more than five minutes."

With anger surging through his veins, Coal reached across the desk and snatched the envelope up. "Thanks." He strove to make the word quiet, but its sarcasm was not easy to hide.

Coal shoved his way out of the office with Maura following him, and they walked right past Wilma Frank's office and out into the hall. He headed for the stairs, but Maura caught his arm.

"Wait! Coal! Aren't we going to wait for him?"

"Not me, sister. I'm going over to Keith Perkins. He's the lawyer I've been working with, and I think he can tell me anything the judge could have."

"Then I'm coming."

"All right, but you had better bring your own truck. I might not be in any position to bring you back here when I'm done with what I'm going to do."

And so the two of them drove out of the parking lot together, headed downtown to see attorney Keith Perkins.

*　　*　　*

When Todd Mitchell pulled into the courthouse parking lot, he was as calm as he could be. He had had to sit in his car for five minutes at his house, breathing deeply, before daring trust himself even to drive down the street.

He didn't notice that neither the LTD nor Coal's new pickup were in the lot.

As he stepped into the office, Jordan looked up at him from picking his keys up off the desk. "Hey, Todd!"

"Hey."

"What's up?"

"I'm supposed to meet with Coal."

"Oh, wow. He didn't say a word."

"Where is he?"

Jordan quickly went over what had happened and told him Coal had gone downtown to talk to his lawyer. "I'd stay and visit with you myself, but I just got a call someone had a wreck down the river, so I've gotta get."

"Oh, yeah, you'd better."

"See ya!" said Jordan as he scrambled out the door.

Todd watched Jordan race up the stairs to the parking lot and run to his car. He had a painful moment as he wished he could have been accompanying the younger man. He was going to miss this job.

But no sooner had Jordan's car left the lot than a thought hit Todd, and he looked over at the phone. If Coal was down at his lawyer's, looking over some will, then... That meant one of two things: Either it had turned out that Bud Miley couldn't be identified by the store clerk in Missoula, or they hadn't called back yet.

With his heart instantly in his throat, Todd went to the desk and sat down, he pulled a list of phone numbers out of the top left drawer of the desk and ran his finger down it until he found what he was looking for: the Missoula police department.

Trying to calm himself, he spun the dial of the phone and waited.

Missoula police. How may I direct your call? It was a pleasant female voice on the other end of the line, but Todd hardly noticed.

"Detectives, please."

One moment.

Todd turned and stared out the window at the parking lot. *Hurry, lady. Hurry!* He was not going to be able to excuse being on the phone if Coal returned to try and catch him for their meeting. He was going to have to disconnect. He also had some big explaining to do, because Coal thought the roll of film still would not be back for several days. He had no idea Clyde Stone had developed it and that Todd had sent Miley's photo off to Missoula Friday morning.

Detective Riggins, came back a gruff voice on the other line.

"Yeah, this is Todd Mitchell, with the Lemhi County sheriff in Idaho. Do you know who's—"

Hey! the voice came back. *I was just meaning to call you, Deputy. So I just got back from the Circle K that was robbed, right? The clerk said this is dead-sure the guy who robbed him. You got a lead on him?*

"Yeah! He's here!" Before the detective could say another word, Todd hung up the phone. He turned and stared at the rifle rack against the wall, at the chain through the trigger guards, at the padlock on one end holding them all in safely.

With a trembling hand, he reached for the middle drawer of the desk and slid it open. His fingers were shaking so badly he almost could not pick up the key to the padlock that would unlock those rifles and shotguns.

But only almost.

CHAPTER THIRTY-SEVEN

Bud Miley drove to the post office, where he had rented out box number 348. Sitting in his Riviera, he sipped on a bottle of beer and stared at the front of the building. He had been in this place too many times. He was starting to hate it. But he had to go. Every day. Sometimes three or four times a day—just in case.

He took a big breath and looked around at the light traffic in the street and on the sidewalks. The weather had warmed up considerably from a few days before, and it was now almost up to freezing, at least in the high twenties. That had gotten people out and about, but there were few people in this town who knew him or anything about him, so he did not have to face the scrutiny and malice that he did from those few who did know him, like Coal Savage and his family.

After a few more minutes' study of the street, he patted Rufus, who sat on the seat beside him, and told him to stay, then got out. He walked to the post office with his heart in his throat—or so it seemed. Taking the door handle, he swung it open and once more walked into this place whose smell he was beginning to hate. He just wanted to see an envelope in his box—just one, the only one that would ever be there under his name. Then he and Linda, along with Cynthia, would be gone from this town, and he would never have to smell the guts of this building again. As for Sissy, he didn't care to bring her along. She was his oldest brother's mistake, and the mistake of his just older brother, Roger, for keeping her and not putting her up for adoption when he had the chance. She meant nothing to him, and he had only taken her in because he thought it would look suspicious if he and Linda adopted only the niece who was in line for an inheritance and not the other. His original intention had been to take her and drop her off in Mexico with Cynthia, but he had changed his mind. She could just stay in the Batterton house until they found her. Then he would not have to have her on his conscience.

Bud smirked at himself as he neared his post office box, in a wall full of others that looked identical to it, and realized his hand was shaking as his fingers grasped the key down in his pocket. He took another calming breath, then stuck the key into its slot and turned it. One more breath, and he opened the box.

Just for a moment, the envelope sitting there seemed like an apparition. No matter how badly he had wanted it here, no matter how strongly he had willed it to come, he really had never expected it so soon. He had expected New York Life to hang onto it with everything they had until the last bitter minute. But there sat an envelope with a plastic window in the front of it, where letters and numbers were typed, in bold black. And in the place of the return address was the printed name, NEW YORK LIFE.

Trembling, he picked up the envelope and turned it around, looking at it closely to convince himself it was real. His pessimistic side took over, and he started to think that perhaps it was only a letter letting him know that the check was going to be on its way in a few days. It could not really have been this easy... could it?

Very slowly, he used his car key to slice open the envelope, withdrew a piece of paper from it, and stared at it until it became real. It was a check, written out to Cynthia L. Batterton, in the amount of two hundred thousand dollars... and zero cents. For a moment, Bud felt like he couldn't breathe. He blinked at the check, then looked up and scanned the area all around him. No one was close. There was no one to take this money from him. Who in this day and age would buy an insurance policy for two hundred thousand dollars! He had thought this before, many times, and now he thought it again. Only a fool. And Bud Miley was the man lucky enough to clean up after that fool.

He left the post office feeling numb and drove to the liquor store, where he bought a fifth of Jim Beam and drank part of it in the car, not caring who saw.

When his hands quit shaking, he started up the engine again and drove to the bank, where he deposited the entire check in an account under Cynthia's name. In several days, they would transfer the money to some other account, in some other town, give them notice, and then come back and withdraw the full amount when the bank advised them that it was there and waiting. He did not trust banks, and if he had thought he could cash that check the same day he would have.

After this, he drove back to the house. A nice plan was forming in his mind of how he and Linda would spend the next few days.

Bud Miley pulled up in front of the house and got out. He went in, and when Linda called to him he did not reply. He found her in the bathroom, in pants and a bra, doing her makeup, with too many rolls of cottage cheese-filled skin rolling up and over her waistband. She looked at him in the mirror. "Thanks a lot for answering me, butthead."

He grinned wickedly. "You're welcome." Throwing his arms around her middle, he gave her a big hug.

"How was I supposed to know someone else wasn't coming in the house?"

"Oh, yeah, like anybody else would want to come in here and attack you. It's not like you're Marilyn Monroe or something."

Indignantly, she tried to squirm out of his grasp, but he held tightly to her.

"You're a jerk," she said finally. There was real hurt in her eyes.

"Oh, come on. You know I'm just kiddin' around."

She turned her eyes back to the mirror, trying to apply another quarter pound of eye makeup in one swath. "I look as good as Marilyn, don't I?"

"Seventy pounds ago!" Bud laughed. He had a smug look to his red-skinned face that Linda sometimes hated. "Anyway, I've been trying to get you to make your hair blond like hers forever. When are you going to do that?"

Linda pouted. "Even if I'm blond I'm not going to look like Marilyn."

"That's okay, honey. You're what I've got."

"Wow. That's endearing."

In a huff, Bud dropped his arms from her. "Well, I've got a big surprise for you that might make me damned endearing."

She whirled around. "What? Did the check come?"

"Maybe."

"Serious?"

"Maybe."

"So... we're rich?"

He grinned, but the expression didn't do his smug red face any favors. It just made the wrinkles around his eyes look older and more tired. "Get some things packed up. We're going out of town for the night and get a hotel up in Montana somewhere to celebrate."

Her look of elation turned to one of dread. "But what about those girls?"

"What about 'em?" The day before he had made Linda stand down by the water heater and call to him while he went and stood outside. Her voice could barely be heard, and that was only because he knew what to listen for and when. "We'll chain them both to that water heater together, leave some food down there for them, and then we're leaving. By the time we come back, that check will be ready to cash. I'm going to go to a bank wherever we stop and tell them to have the cash on hand as soon as they can. Then when it's ready we'll pack up Cynthia and leave. We'll cash the check out, then drive down to Acapulco."

"What about the little girl?"

"I think we'll just chain her in the basement and leave her."

"We could just throw her in the river," replied Linda.

Bud laughed. "Dang, you're a bloodthirsty wench! No we couldn't. If we get that money and just turn those girls loose, that's one thing. They're not going to come down to Mexico looking for us just because we stole a measly two hundred grand. But if one of them girls dies because of us, that's a whole different story. You've got to learn to use your head."

Linda grunted. "Let me finish my makeup."

"Please do," said Bud, and then he went to the bedroom and stuffed a few spare clothes into a sack. He took the sack out to the car and threw it in the trunk, then started back to the house.

*   *   *

Todd Mitchell's heart was pounding hard, like a solemn drum. Across his lap lay the barrel of a twelve-gauge pump action shotgun, and he stared at the front of the Batterton house. There was no red car. He felt sick. Where could they be? This had to happen fast. He had to have the Mileys back, sitting in jail, and the girls both rescued and waiting before Coal even knew the positive ID had come back on the robber. He had to have this whole case buttoned up tight so that no matter what happened between him and Coal he could walk out of that office with his head held high. And the chances were pretty good that if he apprehended the robbers and saved the little girls Coal and so many other people loved, Coal would feel obligated to let him keep his job, if for no other reason.

Either way, his conscience would be clear. He wasn't going to have to kill these people. Instead, they were going away to the big house, for a long, long time, and those two girls were going to live with Coal and his mother. And Todd would be a hero.

All of a sudden, he saw motion in his rearview mirror. The red Riviera was coming down the street at a good clip, and it pulled up to the curb. In a moment, chubby Bud Miley got out and went into the house. He was gone for perhaps five minutes before he came out with a big brown paper bag, which he put in the trunk. Even as he was slamming the trunk, Todd took a big breath, grabbed his shotgun, and stepped out. He was directly behind Bud Miley, completely out of his line of vision, and he strode as fast as he could to catch up.

Just as Miley was about to hit the first concrete step, Todd called out his name. "Miley! Hold it right there!"

Miley froze. Instinctively, his hands came out to the sides. Todd caught up to him and jabbed him in the small of his back with the shotgun barrel harder than he probably should have.

For emphasis, he racked the shotgun.

"So hey, Jack. We've got some business. I'm Deputy Todd Mitchell, and you, my friend, are under arrest."

"Arrest! What for?" Miley spoke to his front door.

"Robbery. In Missoula, Montana. And anything else I can find on you. Where's your wife?"

For a moment, Miley was speechless. His body had gone taut, and now it slacked. With great satisfaction, Todd saw all of the energy drain out of him.

"She's in the house," Miley replied when Todd rammed him in the back again with the bore of the shotgun. "Man, that hurt! Be careful what you're doing with that thing. What if it goes off?"

"Right. If we could all only be so lucky."

"There's girls in here," said Miley suddenly. "They could get hurt."

"Not if you do exactly what I say, they won't. By the way, they found a will in all the stuff Sheriff Savage pulled out of the Batterton house before you took it over. Want to know what it says?"

Miley was silent.

"Well, I'll tell you. K.T. Batterton's last will and testament says that Cynthia goes to Connie Savage—the sheriff's mother. Isn't that ironic? Even if you hadn't done that robbery, you weren't going to keep those girls."

Watching the back of Miley, it seemed like his head melted down even farther into his shoulders. Todd did not remember ever seeing a man look more defeated without even seeing his face.

"Get in the house," he growled. It had suddenly struck him that anyone in the neighboring houses might see him with his shotgun and call the police before he could follow through and finish his plan. After all, he wasn't in uniform and had driven his personal vehicle here.

Bud Miley plodded up the steps into the house. He opened the door and went in with Todd right behind him. Todd quickly scanned the room, and back into the kitchen.

"Where is she?"

"How the hell should I know?"

"Call her."

"Linda? Where you at?"

No reply.

"She was in the bathroom a minute ago," Miley admitted. "And she was pretty mad at me. I'm sure she's just not talking."

"Then move down that way."

They started down the hall, past the two bedroom doors with nail holes in their trim. At the bathroom, Bud stopped. "Right here."

"Ma'am, it's the police. You're under arrest, and I have a twelve-gauge shotgun on your husband's back. Come out, real slow."

After a moment, Todd started to get nervous. "Push the door open. Slow."

Miley complied, and when it was all the way open, they both moved closer and looked in. There was no place to hide, and the room was empty.

"No more lying!" Todd growled, immediately certain that the woman wasn't even home. "Where in the hell is she?"

"Right here!" came a woman's harsh voice from behind Todd.

And then something caved in the back of his head.

CHAPTER THIRTY-EIGHT

Bud Miley was jarred forward when Todd Mitchell's limp body fell against him, and it slammed him face-first against the corner of the doorframe. He could instantly tell his eyebrow had been cut down the middle, and a searing pain went all through his face.

He stood there groaning, leaning against the doorframe for support, until finally he could overcome his pain and turn. Linda was standing there with a ball bat in her hands, staring down at Todd's limp form, where he lay in a pool of blood.

"Judas priest, Linda. You killed him!"

"He was going to kill us," she stammered weakly.

"Come on! We've gotta go—*now!* I'll get the gun. You get the girls. I'm gonna get the can of gas, and we'll set this whole place on fire so there's no evidence."

"Let's just leave the girls in here and burn it down!" replied Linda, turning to run for the front door.

In an almost blind panic, without even bothering to reply, Miley ran down the hall to their bedroom and flung the door open, grabbing his revolver off the dresser by the bed.

In the front room, he heard his wife's terrified voice, and his heart fell through the floor. "Bud, the cops are here!"

*   *   *

Coal and Maura walked out of Keith Perkins's office. Coal was still numb, but he felt elated. The door had only just clicked shut behind them when he whirled around and took the woman up in a huge bear hug. She was already crying.

"Oh, Coal. I can't believe it." After that, she lost her ability to speak.

He pulled away from her and wiped away her tears. "I'm going over there right now. Call the police. And then stay away from that place until I come for you. Maybe go over to McPherson's and wait. I'll bring the girls."

"You're going alone?"

"You bet. Those idiots have no idea what's coming. Talk about shooting fish in a barrel."

A scared look came into her eyes. "Coal, just be careful."

"I will. Just call the cops and get them on their way."

With that, he ran out and got in his car. Trying to stay calm, he drove over to Hope Street, and there like a big red flag was the Buick, parked out front. As he was parking, he happened to glance over and see something that took him aback: Todd Mitchell's car!

For a moment, he just sat there, trying to let this new discovery register on his mind. There was no doubt it was Todd's car. It had a dent right in the middle of the trunk, in line with the key hole. Coal sat trying to figure out any reason why Todd's car would be here, but he just couldn't wait. Todd could have come to the neighborhood to visit someone at any other house.

Stepping out of the car, he scanned the street, then the Batterton house. The one thing that gave him pause was the front door. The storm door was shut, but the inner door stood open wide. It was a little warmer than it had been for days, but it was still not even quite up to freezing. Who would leave their door open when it was thirty degrees or less?

With bells ringing in his head, Coal drew his revolver. Carefully watching the front windows and door, he went to the house. Instead of going up the steps, he went to the side of them, then leaned far forward and peeked in through the glass of the storm door. All seemed still inside.

Steeling himself, Coal eased open the door, scanning the room while he let his eyes adjust to the shadows. He leaped up on the landing. Then he slipped in through the door, gun up and ready. No movement in the kitchen. He peeled his ears, listening for any sound. Still nothing.

He tiptoed across the front room to the hallway and made the corner. Suddenly, he stopped. There, in the middle of the hallway, was a body. Still no sound anywhere, but the Riviera was out front; they *had* to be here, somewhere! Heart pounding furiously and wishing for once that he had waited for backup, he started down the hall. He jolted to a stop when he recognized the man in the hall—Todd Mitchell, in street clothes. A large pool of blood had leaked out the back of his head and soaked into the carpet beneath, looking like a black halo.

Coal felt sick at the sight of his deputy. Where were the girls? And where were the Mileys?

Suddenly, he heard the squealing of tires out on the street. He whirled and ran to the front door, in time to see the Riviera flying down the street at fifty or sixty miles an hour. He saw a head move in the back seat. They had the girls!

With a curse, he charged the front door and was outside, running for his car. He had only just reached it when a wave of nausea washed over his body. Both of the tires on the driver's side were flat against the ground.

Almost panicked, Coal whirled around, looking for the arrival of any police car. At that moment, a newer blue Chrysler pulled up and into the driveway of a little cottage two doors down. Coal ran toward the car and caught an older woman struggling to get out.

"Sorry, ma'am! Sheriff Savage. I have to have your car. There's just been two young girls kidnapped, and they flattened my tires."

She stared at him, in confusion, then terror. Her hand shaking, she dropped the keys on the driveway. Before he could reach down and grab them, Coal heard a vehicle's engine rev, and it careened down the street from the same direction in which the Mileys had just disappeared.

Out of reflex, Coal looked over. It was Maura's International!

Apologizing to the old woman for scaring her, Coal ran out into the street. Maura slammed on her brakes and skidded to a stop. Her eyes were filled with fear and shock as Coal threw open her door. "Get over!"

"What happened?"

"They killed Todd and took the girls. Move!"

Fire leaped into her eyes. "I'm driving. Get in the other side!"

There was no time to argue, although Coal's anger went instantly up ten-fold. Right now, he could only think about those helpless little girls.

He ran around and jumped in the passenger seat. "Go! Go!"

As they drove at breakneck speed down the street, Maura told Coal the Riviera had come screeching around the corner of Daisy onto Main Street, nearly colliding with her. They turned west on Main and accelerated to a high rate of speed toward the Bar.

Maura made the corner off Hope onto Daisy with masterful skill, impressing Coal even in his state of high tension. She did the same with the left turn onto Main, with only a slight pause to scan both ways for oncoming traffic.

The left turn was made between a car coming each direction, and both of them swerved to a stop, but neither had to leave rubber on the road—not like Maura did now, shifting gears like a professional race car driver.

They took the Salmon River bridge at fifty miles an hour, and Coal ordered her to go right onto Ninety-three.

As she made the curve, she asked, "How can you be sure?"

"I can't!"

But he trusted to his guts, and his guts told him that with a murder now behind them they were going to head out of Salmon with all the speed they could muster and try to lose themselves in Montana, or maybe even down the river, at least until they could steal a car or something and ditch the red flag they were driving.

As Maura drove, foot to the floor, Coal looked over at her and growled, "I thought I told you I'd come for you. You don't listen very good."

She took her eyes off the road for just a second. They were full of incredulity. "Are you kidding me? You really are an ass!" she snapped back at him. "If I had done what you said you'd be stuck back there right now."

"No I wouldn't. I was about to commander an old woman's Chrysler. And it would have been faster than this boat."

As she continued to stare straight ahead at the road, her hands gripping the wheel as if she were trying to choke it to death, Maura's eyes misted over with tears of fury. "Those are my girls, too. You can go to hell."

Gripping onto the handle on the door, Coal glared daggers through the side of the woman's face. Finally, the truth hit him, and he took a deep breath. "I'm sorry. That was a stupid thing for me to say. I'm glad you came."

Pursing her lips and refusing to answer him, Maura pushed the pickup without care what happened to her. Coal had been in high-speed chases before, but this one scared even him, as fast as she thundered through Carmen. When she started having to make a curve, here and there, there were times when the pickup seemed as if it were up on the tires of only one side, and one of those times he was sure they were going to roll.

"Slow down!"

"Shut up! It's my truck."

"Yeah, and both of our lives."

She hadn't had a moment to answer him when suddenly, up ahead, Coal spotted a red car in the distance as they were rounding another frightening curve. The other car was going way too fast to just be another traveler on the road. "That's them! Floor it!"

"It is!" Maura screamed back. "I can't go any faster! And you're the one who just said to slow down."

Again, Coal had reason to pause. This time, a flicker of humor almost overcame him. Maura was right: He needed just to shut up.

He caught himself actually leaning forward, as if by doing so he could get closer to the Riviera. It suddenly hit him that he had no radio, and absolutely no way of calling for help. And he had no idea how he was even going to stop the other car if they managed to catch up to them. With the girls in there, he certainly couldn't shoot at them, no matter how close he and Maura got, and he realized that they didn't even dare push them very hard, for fear that the Mileys would lose control and wreck.

They were stuck. A sick feeling came over Coal when he realized that the whole chase was going to come down to one question: Who would run out of gas first? And if it was the Mileys, then a possible hostage situation, if Miley had a gun. Whatever scenario Coal could imagine, it didn't look good. He glanced at the bouncing fuel gage of the Travelette, which seemed to hover around a quarter of a tank, and his heart began to fall.

Neither Coal nor Maura spoke another word. They lived in this moment with only the sound of the motor revving in the straightaways, the wheels squealing around tight corners, the occasional grinding of gears between third and fourth. This big old International pickup was meant for a lot of things, and suited to a lot of purposes—but none of these was high speed pursuit. The only thing in their favor, it seemed, was that the Mileys' car had not been kept up. So in spite of its great big motor and powerful V-8 engine, it just did not seem able to get out as far ahead of them as Coal had feared it would. In fact, there were times when the Travelette actually seemed to be closing the gap, sometimes so close that they could see Cynthia moving around in the back seat, although with the glare from the overcast sky, it was hard to make out any detail.

There was a tight, blind curve coming up, a curve where Coal had seen a lot of cars leave the road over the years, because not only was it sharp, but it was also shaded there from the sun, and ice tended to build up on the road and remain. The road wasn't icy today, but even dry road corners get treacherous at high speed.

Staring at the back of the Riviera, Coal went into a panic. Miley didn't know this road. He hadn't even applied the brakes.

"Slow down! Slow down!" he yelled at Maura.

He saw the Riviera go into a fish tail. The driver tried to correct, but that only sent it back the other way. Half a second more, and they saw a logging truck appear around the corner, aimed for a head-on collision.

At the last possible second, Miley jerked the wheel, and the Riviera dove off the right side of the road into scattered snow, grass, and rocks. It swerved back onto the highway, tipping up so that most of its weight was on only the right tires, then veered all the way across the highway again, right across the path of an oncoming Dodge pickup. Once again, the Riviera left the road, this time on the oncoming side. There was a wide stretch of gravel, dirt, and grass there before the bank of the river and one of the deepest places in that entire stretch of the Salmon. But even as wide as it was, at this speed it was not enough.

The Riviera was headed right for the edge of the river bank, which at this wide bend Coal knew was ten or fifteen feet higher than the river. There were cottonwoods growing there that if they struck them would stop the car from going into the river, but at fifty miles an hour, they were also certain to kill all of the passengers in the Riviera.

As Maura slammed on the brakes and went into a skid, the oncoming Dodge pickup, now almost out of control itself, barely missed their left rear bumper, running off into the gravel on the other side of the road. The front of the Travelette whipped hard to the left, bringing them around to where they had a perfect view of the out-of-control Riviera as the pickup skidded sideways on the slick pavement.

With mouths open, Coal and Maura saw Miley's car strike a boulder at the edge of the river bank and just miss the line of cottonwoods as it sailed out into thin air.

CHAPTER THIRTY-NINE

Another pickup flew past, behind a second semi-truck and trailer hauling logs, and both of them skidded to a halt just beyond Maura's pickup. Heading for the left road edge, Maura had slammed her foot down all the way on the brakes, and she and Coal flew forward. She struck the steering wheel, and Coal hit the dash with his chest as the pickup veered off the pavement.

It jerked them around, bouncing over rocks, before coming to a stop amid a spray of gravel and uprooted grass.

Coal launched his door open, grabbing his Smith and Wesson out of the holster on his hip and charging for the edge where the Buick had gone over. He could see it, roof still upright, twenty feet out in the icy river. It had just barely cleared most of a broken, blocky sheet of ice that stretched out, translucent gray, from the bank to about twelve feet into the stream. Only its tail end had struck, and broken through, that sheet of ice. The rear end of the car was up in the air, with the entire engine and hood submerged.

But it was obvious when the front bumper struck river bottom, for then the rear started sinking as well.

Coal stared, horrified. His girls were in there! He was tingling all over, aware of no one else who might be around him, as he dropped to his butt on the rocks and started jerking the boots off his feet. He could hear a voice screaming, as if from a distance. He almost thought he heard his name.

Then his boots were off, and his holster, and snatching up a fist-sized rock from the bank, he scrambled down the steep, frozen slope to the river's edge. Without thinking, he stepped forward onto the ice, then dived into the icy waters of the Salmon River.

Coal had been in the Salmon in winter before. He had done it on a dare, as a teenager—long before any amount of brain tissue had actually grown in. But it was long ago, and he had forgotten just how cold it was.

When he hit the water, his breathing stopped on the instant. He tried to swim. It felt like he was swimming through shards of broken glass. He could see the top of the car, now barely even with the river, and then all of a sudden gone from sight beneath the dark water. Even though the river here was very slow, try as he might to swim out to the car, he couldn't. He had no strength. His strokes were useless. His saturated clothing was dragging him beneath, downriver. He realized he had already lost the rock with which he had intended to break out a window in the car. He was going to die. He was helpless—a block of ice like the slushy little barges that were rolling past him in the deep green waters of the River of No Return.

In a last-ditch effort to save the only person he had a chance of rescuing from this river—himself—he turned toward shore. Almost immediately, he ran up against a large gray boulder that humped up out of the water like a breaching whale. He caught a rough edge of it and tried desperately to find other holds, anything to help him climb out. There was nothing. No way to get out of the water that would soon be his grave.

He turned back the other way, against the mighty force of the river shoving him up against the boulder, and saw something out in the water. Not ice, but something swimming! He looked closer, and suddenly he recognized the head of a dog, it was paddling furiously toward shore, but making little more progress than he was.

Burro!

The dog was ten feet away, and it was going to pass the boulder by several feet. Coal turned with a feeling of absolute loss and looked back toward shore, which lay at least ten feet away over a sheet of ice with an edge like a knife.

He had lost his girls. He was even about to lose his own life, if help wasn't here within minutes. Maybe at least he could cling to something friendly with his last dying breaths.

With complete abandon, he flung himself out into the current again, clutching to the dog by the skin of its neck. He turned and started trying to paddle for the boulder again, but it was upstream of him, and with his clothes on, and the current dragging him mercilessly away, there was no way to reach it. He turned, still holding onto the dog, and they both fought for the only thing in-between them and the icy depths of the river—another sheet of ice.

They made the ice, and Coal grabbed onto an edge of it. With every ounce of strength he had left, he leaped upward and forward, landing on the ice with his abdomen, strengthened and hardened from hundreds of hours of torture in the gym.

Somehow hanging onto the dog even though he could no longer feel his fingers, he rolled over onto the ice, and the dog came with him. Neither could move. They were both spent, and frozen through. They lay on the sheet of ice that miraculously held them, and waited for the mighty Salmon to suck away their lives.

Coal couldn't even think about Cynthia and Sissy anymore, or the Mileys. All his faculties seemed to have shut down, all but the bare basics that were trying to keep him breathing and his heart beating.

He became aware of voices—many voices. He thought he heard Jim Lockwood's voice, and perhaps that of Jordan Peterson. Someone was calling out instructions to someone else, in a calm voice. Coal floated above it all, dying. Maybe already dead. A block of hairy ice lay next to him, its golden head on his arm.

And the River of No Return rolled Coal Savage and Burro away.

*   *   *

Jim Lockwood had a rope tied with a bowline around his waist. He had used it to support himself as he plunged down the frozen dirt to the edge of the river's shore. Now he took another rope that was tossed down to him with two loops tied in the end of it and put one loop around each foot, tightening them above the uppers of his boots. Jordan Peterson stood on the bank up above him, and there had been no question who was going out on the ice. Jordan's two hundred forty pounds was too much of a risk. Jim weighed one eighty, and he had lived a long, full life. He turned and looked into the eyes of big Jordan, seeming to forget the three or four other men who clustered around him, big, bearded men in heavy coats.

"Hold onto me, son."

"If you go down, we both go," said the deputy. "If you tied those knots right, you're coming back out of this river."

With a nod of finality, Jim turned and got on his knees at the icy edge of the river. From there, he went to his belly and began to slither out, cringing at every whip-crack of the thin ice. Even dry, the cold from the ice was still biting through his clothing, but it didn't matter. His buddy was out there. His friend. Nothing else he had ever done mattered right now. He had to reach Coal Savage.

Jim crawled and crawled, praying, his teeth gritted against the cold, fighting the grip of panic that clutched for him. His outstretched fingers reached for Coal. It kept seeming like he was right there, and then it turned out that he was still so far away.

The old man inched out farther. He felt a hundred years old now, not sixty-five. He paused, and his forehead went down on his arm. "Please, God," he spoke aloud. "You've got to get me out there."

He started moving again. The ice seemed to be sagging beneath him now, ready to split right down the middle, to fold up on him like a taco. He spread his arms farther to the sides, trying to even out his weight, to stabilize the ice.

When he dared to pause and look again, Coal was there, not two feet away.

He lifted his right arm off the ice slowly, watching to see if it would buckle. When it crackled, he hurriedly put it back down and slid it sideways to Coal's arm. Finally, he had his frozen sleeve, and he shook it, watching for movement. "Coal!" He tried to yell, but his voice felt powerless. "Coal, you with me?"

Coal's head came up a little, but no sound came from him. "Buddy, I'm going to drag you back to shore. Let go of the dog!"

Coal's head sagged back down. Jim wasn't certain, but it looked like Coal's arm closed tighter about the shaggy form beside him. It certainly did not let go.

"Coal, damnit! I said let go of the dog!"

Jim saw Coal's head moving. With what seemed like the last of his friend's strength, he was shaking his head, and he clutched the dog to himself closer, like a desperate lover. Jim closed his eyes with dread and lowered his nearly bald head until his forehead touched the ice. He took a deep breath, then turned his head gingerly. "I've got him, Jordan. Haul us out now!"

He could feel the loops of the rope tighten around his feet, and then he started to slide backwards on the ice. The rope was choked up as tight as it would go around his feet. The pain was excruciating, and Jim Lockwood didn't care. All he cared about was his grip, and his now numb fingertips biting into the frozen sleeve of Coal's coat. He had never needed a strong grip more than he did now, and yet there were moments that it seemed his fingers were pulling free.

Jim closed his eyes again and dropped his head once more on the ice, and he started praying fervently, more fervently, perhaps, than he had ever prayed in his life. He felt himself continue to slide backward on the ice.

After what seemed like minutes, his feet struck something solid, and then there were hands grasping his boots, dragging him up backwards onto the bank, where some of the men had come down to be closer to the water. But even then, he did not relinquish his grip on his friend.

And when he looked, Coal still had a hold of the dog, its coat now made up of white icicles.

While other hands scrambled to loosen the ropes around Jim's feet and retie loops, both under his arms and under Coal's, Jim just stood there shaking. He felt numb all over. He didn't want to let go of Coal's sleeve, but someone pried his fingers away and guided him back up the almost sheer bank of dirt to the solid ground above.

Hands were all over Jim now, raising him to his feet, untying ropes from him. In a happy daze, he saw men hoisting Coal, whose arms were still locked around the dog, up the steep embankment. He watched as they finally pulled Coal up over the edge, and one man picked up the dog and took off at a trot toward the road.

Jordan came and guided Jim away from the embankment. Jim saw vehicles everywhere, and blue and red lights flashing. Traffic in both directions had come to a stop, and lines of five or ten cars were built up either way.

Five men dragged Coal up into the cab of the logging truck, and Maura climbed up with him, demanding blankets from anyone who had them. She and some man she had never seen worked frantically to get all of Coal's stiff, icy clothing off and to get blankets over him. She cranked up the heater as high as it would go, then lay down on top of him while the other man tried to dry off the dog, who was starting to move around lethargically, with another blanket.

*   *   *

Coal opened his eyes. Every part of his body ached. He realized the feeling of being crushed was because someone was lying on top of him, and then he realized that at least his nose still worked, because he recognized the smell of Maura's hair.

"You sure take advantage of a guy, don't you?" Coal said, knowing his voice must sound like he was trying to come back from the dead.

Maura snapped up, looking down at him. "Hey! Hi, buddy." Suddenly, an indignant look came over her face. "Wait! Take advantage! Ha! I wouldn't take advantage of you if you were awake, much less sleeping!"

He tried to grin. He felt like dying instead. He continued to lie there, with no intention of ever getting up again.

Finally, he raised his hand and patted Maura's back. "I couldn't save them, Maura. I... I tried to get out to the car, but I couldn't."

"What?"

"I lost the girls."

"Hey! Relax, buddy. You didn't lose anybody."

"What?"

"Coal, they didn't have the girls."

He stared at her silently, his foggy brain trying to decipher her words, to make sure they meant what they sounded like.

"What are you talking about? We could see Cynthia in the back."

"Oh, come on. How do you think that girl's going to feel if you admit you can't even tell the difference between her and a dog?"

As if on cue, a big, wet tongue dragged a couple of times across Coal's face, and he sputtered, "Hey!" He looked over to see the retriever, sitting there looking for all the world like he was laughing at him.

"For a second, I thought that was you licking my face!" he told Maura.

She grinned down at him. "If I ever lick your face, I hope it does more for you than a dog." She instantly blushed, and Coal knew he would have too, but icicles can't blush.

"So... The girls really weren't in there? It was just Burro?"

"Yes, it was. I promise. The girls are both safe, Coal. They were chained to the water heater in the basement when Bob Wilson found them. Just ask Jim and Jordan. They got the call on the radio when they were coming after us."

"No kidding." Coal lay his head back down on the seat. As the blood vessels in his nearly frozen scalp began to dilate, he started feeling light-headed, as if he were going to pass out. "You don't say." And then the warmth of the cab conquered him, and he was asleep. When Maura got up, he had no idea.

A full hour later, Coal woke to a grinding noise, and he lay still. He looked over, and the dog was asleep on the floor by his side. His eyes came to focus on a pile of fresh clothing that was folded on the dash, and he recognized a steel blue shirt he often wore and a pair of tan Dickies.

Sitting up, he looked outside to see a huge tow truck parked as close as possible to the edge of the embankment about where the Mileys' car had gone over. The inside of the truck cab was powerfully hot now, and there was only a little bit of tingling left in his fingers and toes. But it was so stifling that he struggled to breathe.

He sat up and turned down the heat, then pulled on dry socks from the pile of clothing—wonderfully dry socks. He squirmed into long john underwear and the Dickies trousers. Last, he shrugged into the shirt, and realized he had been sleeping on a rolled up coat for a pillow—his lined Wrangler jacket.

For a moment, feeling too exhausted to rise, he watched the work going on outside the window and patted Burro's head. Finally, he tugged on his boots and laced them up, then got gingerly down out of the truck. The dog, seeming completely normal now, jumped down behind him, and Coal walked out toward the tow truck and the crowd of people standing around it. There was evidently something wrong with the towing operation.

Suddenly, from a car he hadn't seen—a teal blue Chrysler with bold white top—people began to stream. There were eight of them in all, begging the question of how they had all fit in the one car: Connie, Maura, Katie, Virgil, Wyatt, Morgan, Cynthia, and Sissy.

Like a human wave, they swept toward him. The boys and Katie fell all over him, nearly weighing his still-weak frame to the ground. When they stepped away, it was at Connie's insistence.

And there stood Cynthia and Sissy, with Maura behind them, holding onto them for dear life.

Coal went to a knee, and Sissy ran into his arms, while Cynthia knelt beside him and cried.

There were going to be a lot of things to work out now, Coal knew. The will was legal, and Cynthia now belonged with Connie Savage and her family. No one else had spoken for Sissy, and now that the red Buick and its owners lay at the bottom of the River of No Return, it was obvious that there were only two choices for her as well—Connie, or Maura PlentyWounds.

Maura came over to Coal when the girls finally let go. It seemed like five minutes, but it might have been more. Without a word, she softly leaned into his body as he got to his feet and enclosed him in her arms. "Know something, Coal?" she said into his ear.

"What?"

"Tomorrow is Sissy's birthday."

He smiled, though his face was buried in her hair and she couldn't see him. "Then we're taking the day off work."

"Yes, and the damn phone off the hook," she added, and didn't even laugh.

Again, Coal smiled, and the corner of his mouth touched her warm neck. It stirred him down deep, and he wondered if the feeling did anything to her. He wanted to kiss her, but he guessed that chance had passed.

So he just held her, his good friend Maura, and nearby, the water gurgled as it charged by, and big, broken chunks twirled and churned in eddies along the edges of the blue-green ice, and the lonely song of the River of No Return played its age-old tune.

THE END

Look next for ***BOOK 3: LOCKDOWN FOR LOCKWOOD***

Author's note

In writing *River of Death,* I began delving even more into the lives of real people who at one time or another have populated the town of Salmon, Idaho. Florin Beller was the actual owner of McPherson's clothing store in that time period, and only recently passed away before the publication of the first book in this series. His son Steve was a huge help in rebuilding the history of that store and also the town itself.

Karen Lugo, the daughter of the real Wally and Beulah Richardson, owners of Wally's café, was a huge help in bringing that iconic establishment back to life on these pages, and I enjoyed the chance to introduce her as a character as well.

To those who would wish for another action-packed crime novel, I apologize, as I know for them I delved too deeply into the world of emotions in this book. But the *Savage Law* series has, from the outset, been geared toward the reader who likes deep character development and real human feelings, and that kind of emotion will drive future books throughout the series. I hope there is a balance in these books for everyone, for there is so much possibility in these characters to show themselves as nearly real people that I feel it would do them—and myself—a vast injustice, to write this simply as a murder mystery series, rather than a character play that is riddled with crime drama as well.

In this book of the series, I introduced my close friends, attorney Keith Perkins, and veterinarian Scott Darger, from Queen Creek, Arizona. Scott and Keith are, in real life, two of the good guys, and two of the best friends a guy could ever hope for. Thank you to Scott and Keith, for being examples to us all of what men, friends, and human beings should be like, and thank you to every other good sport within these pages who allowed him or herself to be a part of the fun.

I also had the pleasure of including my friend, fan, and wonderful supporter, Nancy Pearson, of Tetonia, as the counselor of the same name in the book.

Thanks also goes to my wonderful "cast of characters" on the cover: the beautiful Ashley Bullock as Maura PlentyWounds, Isabelle Capson as little Clarissa "Sissy" Miley, Natalie Hansen-Jonas as Cynthia Batterton, and, of course, the one ugly duckling in the crowd—me—as Sheriff Coal Savage.

About the Author

Kirby Frank Jonas was born in 1965 in Bozeman, Montana. His earliest memories are of living seven miles outside of town in a wide crack in the mountains known as Bear Canyon. At that time it was a remote and lonely place, but a place where a boy with an imagination could grow and nurture his mind, body and soul.

From Montana, the Jonas family moved almost as far across the country as they could go, to Broad Run, Virginia, to a place that, although not as deep in the timbered mountains as Bear Canyon was every bit as remote—Roland Farm. Once again, young Jonas spent his time mostly alone, or with his older brother, if he was not in school. Jonas learned to hike with his mother, fish with his father, and to dodge an unruly horse.

Jonas moved to Shelley, Idaho, in 1971, and from that time forth, with the exception of a few sojourns elsewhere, he became an Idahoan. Jonas attended all twelve years of school in Shelley, graduating in 1983. In the sixth grade, he penned his first novel, *The Tumbleweed,* and in high school he wrote his second, *The Vigilante*. It was also during this time that he first became acquainted with Salmon, Idaho, staying toward the end of the road at the Golden Boulder Orchard and taking his first steps to manhood.

Jonas has lived in six cities in France, in Mesa, Arizona, and explored the United States extensively. He has fought fires for the Bureau of Land Management in five western states and carried a gun on his hip in three different jobs.

In 1987, Jonas met his wife-to-be, Debbie Chatterton, and in 1989 took her to the altar. Over some rough and rocky roads they have traveled, and across some raging rivers that have at times threatened to draw them under, but they survived, and with four beautiful children to show for it: Cheyenne, Jacob, Clay and Matthew.

Jonas has been employed as a Wells Fargo armored guard, a wildland firefighter, a security guard for California Plant Protection and Inter-Con, and police officer. He is now retired after almost twenty-four years of proud employment as a municipal firefighter for the city of Pocatello, Idaho, and works full-time job as an armed security officer guarding the federal courthouse under contract with the security company Paragon.

Books by Kirby Jonas

Season of the Vigilante, Book One: The Bloody Season
Season of the Vigilante, Book Two: Season's End
The Dansing Star
Death of an Eagle
Legend of the Tumbleweed
Lady Winchester
The Devil's Blood (combination of the *Season of the Vigilante* novels)
The Secret of Two Hawks
Knight of the Ribbons
Drygulch to Destiny
Samuel's Angel
The Night of My Hanging (and other Short Stories)

The Badlands series
Yaqui Gold (co-author Clint Walker)
Canyon of the Haunted Shadows (currently only on Kindle)

Legends West series
Disciples of the Wind (co-author Jamie Jonas)
Reapers of the Wind (co-author Jamie Jonas)

Lehi's Dream series
Nephi Was My Friend
The Faith of a Man
A Land Called Bountiful
Shores of Promise (forthcoming)

Books on audio tape

The Dansing Star, narrated by James Drury, *"The Virginian"*
Death of an Eagle, narrated by James Drury
Legend of the Tumbleweed, narrated by James Drury
Lady Winchester, narrated by James Drury
Yaqui Gold, narrated by Gene Engene
The Secret of Two Hawks, narrated by Kevin Foley
Knight of the Ribbons, narrated by Rusty Nelson
Drygulch to Destiny, narrated by Kirby Jonas

To order autographed books, go to www.kirbyjonas.com or write to:

Howling Wolf Publishing
1611 City Creek Road
Pocatello ID 83204

Or send email to: kirby@kirbyjonas.com

www.ingramcontent.com/pod-product-compliance
Lightning Source LLC
Chambersburg PA
CBHW030344020726
47493CB00003B/684